# Deviant Desire

## The Clearwater Mysteries

Book one

## Proofread by Ann Attwood
## Cover Design by Andjela K

Printed by CreateSpace, an Amazon.com company.

ISBN- 9781798895108

Available from Amazon.com, CreateSpace.com, and other retail outlets.
Available on Kindle and other devices.

*Also by Jackson Marsh*

Other People's Dreams
In School and Out
The Blake Inheritance
The Stoker Connection
Curious Moonlight

The Mentor of Wildhill Farm
The Mentor of Barrenmoor Ridge
The Mentor of Lonemarsh House
The Mentor of Lostwood Hall

The Clearwater Mysteries
Deviant Desire
Twisted Tracks (June 2019)

www.jacksonmarsh.com

www.facebook.com/jacksonmarshauthor

# Deviant Desire

## Jackson Marsh

# *One*

Silas Hawkins was searching for coins in an East End gutter when a man four miles distant and ten years older sealed his fate. Silas had no idea that the discussion taking place concerned him, or that it was even happening. He wouldn't know the details for some time, but even if he had heard the conversation, he wouldn't have believed it. It wouldn't have concerned him if he had, because Silas wasn't the kind of youth to shy from a challenge, not even one that might threaten his life.

Every night on the grimy, gaslit streets was dangerous, and every unlit customer a potential killer, but the threat of starvation gnawed harder than the fear of violence. In these times, hunger was a keener motivator than sense. It drove need, need drove experience, and in the four years since he had turned his first trick, experience had prepared him for the dangers of life.

Or so he thought as he flicked over rotting cabbage leaves and dung-covered straw. Crouched on his haunches, he shuffled along the edge of the roughly cobbled street, probing beneath tilted carts where the barrow boys sang as they loaded their *unsolds*, pausing in their lusty renditions now and then to talk of lasses and whores. Silas listened. Their songs were soothing despite the rough words. They spoke of secrets Silas had never known and never would know. Mysteries that he was happy to leave unsolved. The boys sang of women and love, and Silas had no interest in the former and no need of the latter.

He watched while he warmed his fingers beneath his armpits. The grocer-boys wore tilted caps which they constantly adjusted to cover their ears against the biting wind. Strands of long locks flowed from beneath, and they religiously brushed their brown aprons and inspected them for blemishes. The butchers' lads, who had started the day pristine white and flawless, were now drenched in the day's crimson business. Their smiles broke their expressions of bloodied exhaustion, and they passed jokes along with their crates, bantered carcasses between them and kept their humour alive. It was the only way of making it through each day. They celebrated the fundamental fact that they were earning money.

Yet, as happy as they were, the barrow-lads knew they were one day's pay away from having to be like Silas. All except the wealthy were, but would these boys be as prepared as him to walk the cobbles after dark in the hope of income? Could they shadow themselves in doorways until the click of leather soles on stone alerted them to an opportunity? Could they be confident enough to submit themselves to an anonymous man in the most intimate way possible? Not every young man could put aside his masculine dignity for the price of a bread roll. On the outside, they had what was needed. Some still had their youthful looks, smooth faces and innocent eyes. Others offered brooding masculinity and the allure of danger. They were individuals with one sellable thing in common.

Youth.

Silas released his hands and flexed his fingers before wrapping his coat tighter around his slight frame. He stood to relieve the cramp in his legs and kicked over rotting fruit, his watery eyes alert for the dull glint of copper, even better, silver. There was neither in this street. The restaurateurs and the wealthy sent their servants early and paid by account. The clerks and bookkeepers were far too cautious with their purses to open them, and everyone else? Well, they were in the same worn, sole-flapping shoes as Silas.

He crossed the street to face the sombre window of the funeral parlour, ignoring the bullying chants of the barrow-boys and ducking the thrown detritus. The purple curtains hung in reverent silence, safe from the bawdy voices, creaking axles, and disrespectful horses shitting in the street. The inside of the shop was soaked with velvet sympathy beneath a lopsided, tear-dripping chandelier, but nothing could disguise the stark reality of what was on sale. The cream void of the coffins offered a plush eternity, but the headstones merely promised finality. Nameless now, they would soon become the most personal and wept-upon of reminders.

Silas was not contemplating the inside of the shop. He was

considering his reflection as dusk submitted to night, and the dull, yellow glow of gaslight flickered on his face.

Like the grocer-boys, he wore a cap, but his was peaked and tugged to the back. His Irish-black hair flopped in a fringe above his forehead and trailed to his collar behind. It had an aversion to his ears and circled them as if their prominence wasn't enough embarrassment. He had a generous smile when he had the opportunity to use it, and a large mouth that was beneficial in his line of work. He didn't think he was handsome, but men — married, queer and noncommittal alike — found something attractive as they swerved towards him through the blue fug of a public bar. Those who sought him in the anonymity of darkness had no care for his looks.

He wanted to open his coat, to see his body and remind himself that he still had what he needed to survive, but the October wind bit colder, and hunger ate at his stomach. Nightfall was on him, and with it came his three fundamental needs. To find a bed, a copper for a gin, and food to sustain his strength. Fingering the last two coins in his pocket gave him a choice; to spend them on gin, or to secure a place on the rope in a dosshouse, a four-penny coffin as they were known. Those, like Silas, who could not afford a bed, could at least rent bench space, lean on the rope and doze as best they could, while waiting for turn-out at dawn. It was marginally better than a tenement hallway or the butcher's sty, but it came with risks. The ever-present threat of attack, robbery or worse didn't concern Silas, he worried that he would waste his money. Four-penny coffins were two a penny in the East End, but they had to be rented before eight in the evening, and if he spent his coins on sleeping space, he would have none for the gin. Without at least a penny, he wouldn't be allowed to work The Ten Bells, the safest place to meet paying customers. On a cold night such as this, few men would seek him in the streets until after closing, by which time he would have lost his place at the rope. It was a cruel trap, but Silas was accustomed to cruelty.

He had deliberated at this window so often that some good had come of his indecision. That good appeared beside him bringing the smell of apples and the reflection of a tall man of similar age.

'Privet, Banyak,' he said in his native tongue.

'Evening, Fecks.' Silas acknowledged his mate's reflection with a nod towards a marble angel.

Fecker, like Silas, was nineteen and had picked up a street-name known only to his close mates. Silas had given it to him not long after they met. Andrej, his real name, knew that it was Irish slang for fucker, but he took pride in that. Unlike Silas, he wasn't queer, and only rented when he was desperate. His cock was usually enough to secure him an income. There were plenty of men who were happy to pay for the youth's substantial endowment particularly as it was attached to a six-foot-two blond lad built like a docker.

'You alright, mate?' Fecker asked, nudging Silas and nearly knocking him over.

Silas had been distracted by the way Fecker's reflection matched the body of the sculptured angel, and looking at him, was surprised to see that his friend, in real life, had no wings.

'Still breathing. You?'

'Da. Caught punter at Limedock. Not looking, just happened. Nearly lifted, but gave police slip.' Fecker was able to speak reasonable English when it suited him.

'Good for you.'

'Safer in daylight.'

'Not if you get collared.'

'How you know, Banyak?'

Silas was known for his ability to evade the law. He'd dodged a lifting on many occasions and had slipped from custody so often that the beat bobbies tended not to bother with him. His knack of slithering through their fingers had become such an embarrassment that they turned a blind eye to him; it was easier than explaining to their seniors that they had lost him again.

'You ate?' Fecker regarded him with a mixture of concern and suspicion, knowing that Silas would say yes even if he hadn't.

'This morning.'

The tall lad reached into the pocket of his greatcoat, stolen from a seaman in Limedock last winter, and pulled out an apple.

'I'm alright, Fecks,' Silas refused.

'Fuck off.'

Fecker pressed it into his chest forcing acceptance, and Silas took it with pride-dented gratitude.

'Owe you one.'

'You walking?'

They left the reflected gloom of the undertaker's candle-glow with Silas eating, Fecker turning up his collar, and the butcher-boys drifting away to warm homes, their songs fading into the clatter of hooves. At the corner, they passed a grocer's boy loitering hopefully, his dewy eyes on Silas' unwashed, soft features, one of his light eyebrows raised. His hopeful questioning was noticed, but went unanswered. The youth, probably only sixteen, was attractive in looks, but unattractive in pocket. He was after something unconditional, and that was of no interest to Silas. One day he might find himself stationed enough to do what he did for free, but not tonight and not with this boy. If there was ever to be sex without payment, it would be with someone older and experienced. Someone who could accept Silas' past without question or judgement.

The grocer boy's face fell to sadness as it did each time this encounter took place, and Silas felt rotten. Like him, this lad knew what he was and what he wanted, and Silas wanted the same; legality. Until that time came — and it never would — he and all others like him were forced to play a perilous game of winks and gestures in the hope of finding companionship while under the constant scrutiny of the world's invincible ignorance. At least Silas had a semi-legitimate cover in his profession. Everyone assumed that boys who earned their living from sex would, if they lived long enough, father a family. They were only doing what they had to do to make enough money to start that family and, abhorrent though it was to decent society, it was mostly accepted by his fellow underclass.

'Worried about Banyak,' Fecker said, leading Silas into an alley.

'Eejit.'

The narrow passage was barely lit, but what weak light there was glinted on the brick path where the mist had settled. They passed barred windows and recessed doorways where any number of threats might lurk, and Silas tensed instinctively. A heavy arm landed on his shoulder as Fecker tucked him under his armpit.

'You hear what happened?' he asked, taking Silas' apple to bite. 'Greychurch again.' He passed back the apple, chewing.

'I've been hearing, Fecks,' Silas replied. 'But I ain't got to worrying. No point.'

Fecker huffed a laugh of disbelief. 'Da, sure. Another done. Worse than rest.'

Silas preferred not to think on the matter.

'Slit open.' Fecker didn't mind. 'Strangling first. Quick, else he make scream, right?'

'I'm not in the mood, mate.'

'Da, but…' Fecker was not to be dissuaded and went on to tell the rumoured details of the latest ripping. Neither of them knew the boy well, but that was no cause for celebration. From hunger or greed, from madness or necessity, in this part of the city, death came as regularly as the wicksman extinguished the streetlamps. What made the recent killings of concern to the street boys was that each victim was one of their own and each had suffered unimaginable horror that had, so Fecker reported, increased in 'de-gravity' each time.

'The word is depravity,' Silas corrected, trying to cover his anguish with humour. 'You daft dope.'

At the end of the alley, and just as Fecker started relating more gory details, Silas interrupted him by asking if he had a room that night. Fecker hadn't, but promised to find Silas at their usual rope if he got lucky, by which he meant if he found a man who was willing to pay for a pair of nineteen-year-olds together, or if he made enough to rent a lock-room, in which case they would share that too. They had done both on many occasions.

No sooner had their arrangements been made than Fecker threw himself back into his story with unsavoury gusto. There had been four boys ripped now, and the killer's circle was tightening. The slayings were random in location, but consistent in victim, and the backtalk was that brothel boys weren't safe, let alone the innocent street-rats. Even the messengers and guardsmen who worked the respectable parts of the city might be targeted.

Silas thanked Fecker for the apple, returned the promise to find him should he get lucky with lodgings, and the two parted company in Saddle Square.

Silas shivered as he watched Fecker leave. Despite the cold, Fecks walked with his coat open and the tails swishing behind him like an opera cloak. With his stature and his purposeful stride, he gave the appearance of a soldier on a mission. An unlikely one considering he was heading directly for a gin palace to start an evening's work fucking married men for money, but Fecks approached his evening routine with stoic determination, and apparently undaunted by the fact that renters were being murdered a few streets away. Fecker had no regard for his own safety. He was unconcerned by the presence of danger, but his security didn't come from his size or his proven ability to defend himself. He simply wasn't worried about dying.

Silas understood why.

There was no point. It was going to happen, and life wasn't going to get any better in the meantime. He was destined to live like this for as long as he was able to keep himself alive and whether that was for a year, or just a few more hours, it made no difference. All he had was a will to survive, the hope that one day something would change for the better, and — he sighed sadly — a best friend he could fall in love with, if only love meant anything.

This, of course, was before he learned of the conversation being had at that very moment four miles distant.

# *Two*

Logs crackled in the iron grate, sending sparks heavenwards and waves of warmth across a sea of Turkish rugs. The fire-glow washed up on the slippered feet of the recently elevated Viscount Clearwater, a man in his late twenties seemingly drowning in the depths of a sumptuous wingback armchair. His hands were draped over the armrests where his fingers undulated like kelp in a current as he pondered what to say next.

'I understand your reticence, Tripp,' he said at length.

'I don't doubt it, My Lord.'

The servant's reply was politely insulting, as was the man himself.

'There are reasons why I cannot explain my request.' Archer tried to control his annoyance, but it spiked through his words. 'None of which have anything to do with doubting your discretion. You have been with us so long, Tripp, I imagine you are listed on the inventory. Your loyalty to my father was without question, and I am in no place to demand the same. I will seek to earn it as we adjust to each other, but, for now, I must ask you to accept your station and thus my order, and see it done.'

His seaweed fingers stiffened to drumsticks and beat out a steady rhythm on the damask.

'I understand, Sir.'

'I take it you don't approve?'

'Approval is a privilege denied to me.'

'That's an interesting word, Tripp. You have never been denied anything.'

'Except a life outside Clearwater House... Sir.'

The full stop was palpable, as was the butler's disapproval of what Archer had asked. It didn't help that the man refused to sit and talk, but instead remained statuesque facing his master, his hands at his sides and his sagging eyes locked on the curtained window.

Archer gripped the armrest and pushed himself to his feet. His open smoking jacket fell apart, revealing his unbuttoned shirt which, in turn, exposed his chest and muscled stomach. Not even the flash of flesh disturbed Tripp's expression of withered boredom. He stood as he always did, aloof and with the face of a disinterested bloodhound.

'As the head of my staff, I expect you to speak nothing of this request outside of the house, nor within the household.' Archer tied the beaded belt of his jacket and took a step towards the sideboard.

The bloodhound smelt action in the form of a task that needed to be performed, in this case, the pouring of a glass of wine, and one of Tripp's gangly arms swung towards the decanter.

'Don't be ridiculous, man,' Archer chided. 'I'm more than capable of pouring myself a drink.' A wicked smile twitched on his stubbled face, knowing that such a break in protocol would send shockwaves through the butler. He was certain Tripp stiffened, but it might have been a trick of the gaslight, because surely no-one could stiffen further. Either way, Archer had won a point. Just because the young upstart had come to the throne, didn't give the ancient retainer the right to be superior. He was at the beck and call of the viscount no matter who held the title.

It must have been unnerving for Tripp to witness The Viscount Clearwater pouring his own wine (and so early in the evening), and no doubt he despaired at the modern times he was living through, but to give him his dues, he controlled himself and continued to study the intricate pattern of the drapes.

Having helped himself to a generous measure of claret, Archer slipped back into his chair and, because he could do what he wanted, kicked off his slippers and tucked his feet under himself on the seat.

Tripp stifled a gasp which Archer ignored. 'I will ask you one last time, Tripp,' he said making himself comfortable. 'Will you carry out my request?'

Tripp's head descended from its elevated position in the manner of a curtain coming down on a very sad final act, and the bones in his neck clicked into place. His gaze landed hard on the viscount, and his permanent frown wrinkled into words. 'As you wish, My Lord.'

'Tonight?'

The butler's head tipped gracefully to one side in deliberation.

'Or would you rather I sent Thomas?'

The tortoise retracted its withered head and retreated into the shell of contained outrage. 'I hardly think that is appropriate, My Lord.' Tripp swallowed, disturbing the ruffles of loose skin that was his neck. 'The man is barely old enough to know of such people.'

'How kind you are,' Archer said with sarcasm. 'He is but two years my junior, well towards thirty, and undoubtedly more worldly wise than you or I. Thinking on it, perhaps Thomas is a better choice for this responsibility.'

He knew for a fact that Thomas had received lessons in subjects that would make Tripp baulk and wouldn't flinch at the task the new viscount had awarded the butler. He could easily have asked Thomas and not suffered such a song and dance, but it was time he asserted his authority over the man who would be king of what was now Archer's realm. Setting Tripp such a demeaning task, although not the most pleasant way to educate the man, was a good start and made several points at once.

'It is, of course, your decision to make, My Lord.' Tripp was once again upright and unwaveringly dull. 'I shall not refuse. I was not, it is true, expecting such a request, and my failure to comprehend your instructions with immediacy is a fault I shall address. If I may suggest, Sir, perhaps you would be kind enough...'

'Oh, get on with it, Tripp. Yes or no?'

Archer wanted to find humour in Tripp's dilemma, as he sought humour in any difficult circumstance, but the man was trying his patience harder than the brick wall Archer was subconsciously banging his head against.

'If we may be clear...?'

'Yes, yes, Tripp, have it your way.'

Archer untangled his legs and marched to the desk taking his wine with him. He collected a drawing and brought it back to the fireplace where Tripp stood guard. He waved it at the man's tailored dress shirt until the butler took it in the manner of an indignant boy being handed back unsatisfactory schoolwork.

'Him,' Archer emphasised. 'He must look like him.' He returned to the sideboard to refill his glass. 'Or as near as damn it as you can.

I appreciate that the lighting may not be in your favour, and you may have a lengthy search, but anything you can do will be greatly appreciated.'

'And you require this to be brought here?' Any 'My Lord' that there should have been was swamped by disbelief. 'To Clearwater House?'

'I do, and please don't use the word *this*. It's a him.'

'If only I could be so sure.'

'Was that meant to be humorous, Tripp?'

'I merely intended—'

'To insult the man depicted in my sketch, I know.' Archer was riled by his servant's moral judgement. He was forced to look up into Tripp's eyes as they were level with the top of his head, but he was not about to let the man's height intimidate him. 'The point is, Tripp, you and I know nothing of men like this, or what they must endure.'

'My concern is for you, Sir, and the reputation of the family.'

'Which is why I trust you with this task. Surely you can see that's flattery, man?'

'Indeed...'

'And yet you want me to send Thomas? A young footman of, according to you, innocence, and a man who, although I know to work diligently and well, in whom you have no trust. Make up your mind and spit out your objections. I shan't take offence.'

'Thank you, Sir, but if I could only know your reasoning, I am sure I would stand more at ease with your demand.'

Archer sat, crossing his legs and pointed his glass to the hearth. 'More wood. It's cold enough to castrate a brass monkey.' Tripp leapt into action. 'And there's no need to...'

It was too late; he had rung the bell-pull.

'Thank you.' Archer conceded.

Sometimes it was best just to let Tripp do what he had always done. Sometimes it was more entertaining to throw him out of his comfortable regime and have him step into the unordinary, just as Archer was asking him to do this evening. Or trying to ask him to do, at least. Tripp had still not agreed to his assignment.

The butler placed the drawing on a side table as though it was a work of art and not a quick charcoal sketch an amateur artist had scribbled after lunch. 'If I may be permitted?'

Archer knew that was Tripp's way of apologising in advance for the impertinence of what he was about to say, and he nodded, taking a deep breath to prepare himself for the monologue to come.

'I fully understand your instructions,' the butler said and turned a raised eyebrow expectantly to the double doors. 'You have instructed with the utmost clarity. You may rely on my discretion and not only for the reasons I have indicated. If I am permitted to be as frank as I dare, I wish no harm or scandal to befall this house, but fear both shall arrive with the delivery of a man such as this… A man such as the one depicted in your most accomplished drawing.'

'Forget the flattery, I am not my father.'

'A statement as true as it is apt. Indeed, you are not your father, and this is why I feel I have an obligation to protect you. An obligation to my late master and to my present one.' He bowed his head deferentially and turned fully to the doors in answer to a knock he expected twenty seconds ago.

'Hold!' Archer called, and clicking his fingers to attract Tripp's attention, invited him to finish what he was saying.

'You have asked me to do a most unusual thing,' Tripp said, and Archer hoped that the urgency of the waiting maid might hurry the butler to his conclusion. 'A task which I would endeavour to see as a worthy challenge were it not so unworthy of the house.'

'I beg your pardon?' It was Archer's turn to let outrage show.

'I apologise, Your Lordship. I am unusually ineloquent this evening. My concerns are that, firstly, I may fetch someone who will bring shame to the house, secondly, who may cause distress… A theft, perhaps? We must consider that such a…'

Another knock brought another barked 'Hold!' from Archer, followed, to Tripp, by, 'I won't hold you responsible.'

'Have you considered the condition of such a person?' Tripp asked. 'And I mean its health, what disease it might bring, its behaviour, language…'

'His, Tripp. His!' Archer bellowed, his tether finally snapping. 'Yes, I have considered all of those things and more. What you have not considered is that people such as you and I should not have to ponder such things in the first place.' He put down his glass with

18

such force that claret spilt onto the inlaid table. 'Who are we to judge those who suffer? Those in need, those who are forced to do what...' He thrust an angry finger to the sketch. 'What *this* must endure nightly. We will never know such horrors unless we seek them out, and only then can we question them and effect change. Yes, I know you will say it is not our responsibility.' Archer rose and stalked to the doors. 'My father would have agreed with you and yet he still blustered off into the East End each night to save half a crown by buying a Cheap Lane whore. A woman, a girl more like, he could leave in the gutter where he found her and feel no remorse, because he left her a ha'penny tip.'

He stopped halfway across the room, his face darkened by anger. Tripp's eyes remained on the spilt wine as he waited for an opportunity to deal with the blemish.

'We have to do something for those wretches,' Archer continued.

'There are the new charities, perhaps?'

'Charities?' Archer derided. 'Like my father's? What was that intended for? Let me see...' He reached the doors and grabbed both handles. 'Ah yes. A mission to educate the working-class poor. Bah! A way to write off taxes and be seen to be philanthropic while actually being a cover for his after-dark forays into the East End.'

A horrified gasp from the butler caused Archer to leave the door and turn to him.

'My charity begins here at Clearwater, Tripp,' he said, doing his best to quell his temper. 'I am in the process of creating something charitable and lasting, but first, I must know what I am dealing with.'

'Ah.'

'Oh, go on, say it.'

'It is precisely who you intend to help that causes me the utmost consternation.'

'A whore is a whore, Tripp.'

The butler blanched and finally unglued his eyes from the spilt wine.

'But these are boys.'

'Men. And your point is?'

'You want me to procure one.'

'Yes. But not for the reason you think.'

'If you would allow me the pleasure of knowing why, I am sure the task will sit more lightly about—'

'You know what, Tripp? Forget it.'

Archer swung back to the doors and threw them open to reveal not a maid, but the footman waiting vacantly outside. He stood erect and silent, the auburn of his trimmed hair matching the colour of his waistcoat.

'Good, Thomas,' Archer said, beckoning him in as he strode to the side table. 'Tripp rang for you to build the fire, a task which is beneath the both of us, apparently. Would you mind?'

Thomas bowed his head and sailed across the Turkish rug until he found port at the hearth where he crouched on nimble legs and removed the guard.

'You see, Tripp?' Archer spread his arms wide. 'Not a word of dissent, no concern, no wrestling with a moral conscience. A man who gets on with the job.'

'With respect, Sir, building the hearth is not the same as procuring a...'

Finally, Tripp wavered, and Archer won some ground.

'Thomas,' he said before the butler could fuss further.

The young footman was on his feet in one graceful swish of his cotton tailcoat. 'Your Lordship?'

'What would you say if I asked you to do something for me?'

'I should be delighted, My Lord.'

'Of course.' Archer picked up the sketch and thrust it towards the footman. 'Be a decent chap and pop into the East End would you? I want you to find me a street-rat who looks something like this. Like *him*,' he corrected. 'I am looking for a youth with particular features, you understand, thus it may take you a while to locate such a chap.'

Thomas regarded the drawing with a furrowed brow, but it was one brought on by concentration not, as Tripp's had been, alarm.

'Very good, Sir.' Thomas said.

'Before you go, Thomas,' Archer continued, 'I understand that this is rather out of the ordinary. If you would rather go with a companion, I would suggest one of your more robust acquaintances, either from Lady Marshall's household who, for reasons allegedly known only to her Ladyship, are all former stevedores, or one of

20

your more trustworthy friends from the Crown and Anchor. I shan't chastise you if you are late returning, or if indeed, you are unsuccessful. You may take all night if you must. You shall have a letter from me with proof of my credentials, I shall tell you what to offer the man should you find one suitable, and you may go in your civilian clothes, but take the carriage. Can you do this?'

'Of course, Sir.'

Thomas, mildly confused and trying desperately not to show it, flicked his eyes to Tripp. There was no encouragement there.

'And there we have it, Tripp. Tripp!'

Tripp was edging surreptitiously towards the wine spill, one hand mining a deep pocket for a handkerchief.

Archer caught him in the act. 'You see? No questions.'

'And his discretion?'

'I trust Thomas.'

Having checked that Tripp was still obsessed with the spillage, Archer winked at Thomas. The footman blushed the colour of his hair, darkening his freckled cheeks. The late viscount never winked. He hardly even looked at servants.

Archer had known Thomas since he was a hall boy. He had come to the house through a connection with Lady Marshall's country cousin and was the first boy on whom Archer had a crush. He still did, though he fought gallantly to drown it beneath the weight of his title.

Thomas returned to the fire, and Archer allowed Tripp to mop up the spit of wine that threatened his reputation.

Crouched, the tails of Thomas' frockcoat parted theatrically to reveal the lower half of his back and the waistband of his jet-black trousers. They stretched over his backside which divided into two agreeable curves. Above them, his back widened at the shoulders where his hairline was separated from his coat by a streak of pale flesh. The line of his hair perfectly matched the cut of his collar, a detail which Tripp no doubt inspected daily.

'I have decided,' Archer said when both jobs were done. 'Tripp, if you have such an aversion to my suggestion, then I will not hold it against you if you decline. It's wrong of me to order you, because this is not part of your duties. The same for you, Thomas. I imagine my late father never asked any of the staff to drive into the East

End with the intention of bringing home a street-rat, and I also imagine that my reign over Clearwater House will be immeasurably different. Hideous for Tripp, but perhaps less shocking to someone young and more progressive such as Thomas. I cannot ask the maids. Mrs Baker would die of shock, and you are the only two men I trust. Perhaps you should go together.'

'The honour should go first to Mr Tripp,' Thomas said. He spoke with clarity despite a mild lisp.

'Don't speak to His Lordship out of turn,' Tripp admonished.

Archer felt bad for Thomas and wanted to reassure him that he didn't mind, but to say so would be to embarrass the man further. Just because they were of similar age didn't mean he could treat him as anything other than a servant, not in front of the butler.

'My apologies, My Lord.' Thomas was still blushing.

'No, no,' Archer waved it away. 'This is a most unusual request, but it can so easily be dealt with if we don't question what Tripp considers my bizarre behaviour.'

'Unconventional is perhaps kinder,' Tripp suggested.

'And you, Thomas? What do you make of it?'

Thomas glanced at the butler for permission before speaking. 'Intriguing is the word I would use, Sir.'

'Then I am correct.' Archer leapt triumphantly to his feet causing confusion. The cord of his jacket unwound with the action, and once again he revealed his muscular body. Tripp's unwavering stare held the curtains to attention, but the unveiling had not gone unnoticed by Thomas. In a flash, his eyes had travelled from His Lordship's navel to the dark hair between his pectorals and swung sideways in an arc to land safely on the fireplace.

'I am correct to ask you both to go, because you both display the qualities needed. Scepticism on the part of Tripp, and enthusiasm on the part of Thomas. I know neither will speak of this, nor question my motives, and that taken as read, I shall award you both an extra half day with full pay.'

Thomas' eyes brightened.

'As long as you promise not to spend it at the Crown and Anchor.'

Thomas' eyes dulled.

'That was what I call a joke, Thomas.' Archer finished his drink. 'You may do what you want with your money. So, are we settled?

Good,' he continued before either could reply. 'Now then, Tripp, I have some work to attend to in the study before I dress for dinner. Afterwards, I suggest the three of us convene to discuss details, though I think there are none. Can you drive the carriage, Thomas?'

'Me?' Thomas gasped with boyish excitement. 'Yes, certainly.'

'Or would the trap be more appropriate?'

'The trap is without livery and more anonymous,' Thomas said, and immediately glanced at Tripp for a rebuke.

'Then it's the trap, Tripp.' Archer chortled at the assonance.

That, for Archer, was the end of the matter and he dismissed his men with thanks.

Alone in the room, he sighed deeply. The mantle clock ticked away the seconds as it had ticked away his father's entire life and that of his grandfather. The burning logs crackled and spat against their demise, and the gas lamps hissed gently in the warm comfort of the drawing room.

He had been liberated on the death of his father. Grief had arrived with the shock of Archer's unexpected elevation but had not been a lengthy visitor. It was a title he wasn't born to inherit; it should have gone to his older brother, but now Archer was Viscount Clearwater, and with his first confrontation with Tripp under his beaded belt, he could begin to enjoy his position. He had wealth, two fine houses, staff to command and plenty of philanthropic interests to indulge, but he had to live up to the expectations that came with his title.

Balancing the life he desired against the one expected of him would not be easy, and inviting a street-rat into his home could very easily cause a scandal. Tripp was right to be concerned. He had, however, no choice. People were dying in squalor and slums, and he was in a position to do something about it. It was his moral duty, no matter how immoral others might think his motives.

Assuming, of course, his intentions were moral in the first place.

# Three

Leaving Fecks was never an easy thing to do, and that evening Silas watched his friend until he had crossed Saddle Square. He waited for Fecks to turn and wave, knowing that he wouldn't, but even the sight of the man's back gave him strength. He wasn't alone in this hell he'd chosen to inhabit.

Not chosen, he reminded himself, no-one would choose to live this life. There had been no work in Westerpool where his mother had birthed him nearly twenty years ago. She had come looking for respite from her famine-struck township, crossing the troubled grey sea with Silas heavy in her belly using money made from the streets of her home town to pay for her passage in steerage. She had arrived expecting the hospitality of a distant cousin who, family rumour said, had found work making straw bonnets for wealthy ladies in the thriving north-west port. The promised hospitality had not been what she was expecting. One room between twelve, seven of them infants, one tap shared between three similar families, a gutter for the bucket-slops and glassless windows. Silas was sloshed out onto a wooden floor, delivered by a grandmother who kept her only eye more on the gin bottle than her duties, and had escaped death in the first weeks of his life purely by chance.

He went on to survive worse while four of his seven cousins died before he was old enough to remember them, and his mam bore twins to an unknown man. He was existing, which was more than his mother was, but he had his sisters to care for, and their well-being was the only reason he was now standing in the October drizzle watching Fecks turn into Leather Lane on his way to The Ten Bells. Silas would join him there later and wait outside. That was the best he could hope for, needing his two coins to pay for his place on the bench.

Fecks had gone, and Silas left the square. He took the passage, heading east and emerged from its dripping gloom into the wider City Street where the last of the market traders were wheeling their barrows back to their yards. Carthorses plodded methodically, dragging drays, while boys as young as six worked together to carry woolsacks into shops. Women crouched in the gutter taking whatever pickings had been left, and Silas knew he would find no more coins here. Always optimistic, he kept his gaze on the cobbles as he crossed the road in case something caught his eye. Despite the apple Fecks had given him, his stomach growled, and pain jabbed. He scoured a pile of broken crates to no avail, but a few paces further, he found an orange behind a bundle of rags someone had kicked up against the crumbling brick of a disused mission hall. The fruit had been trodden on, and the skin was split, but the insides revealed themselves as edible, and with his fingers sticky from the juice his mouth salivated for, he lifted a piece to his lips.

'That's mine.' The bundle of rags moved, and a bare, pale hand appeared.

Silas looked down into the large round eyes of a small girl, her grubby face apologising. She was younger than his sisters, but her situation was identical. He handed her the orange as he knelt.

'I was just opening it for you, Ellie,' he said, a smile covering his disappointment as she grabbed it. 'Be more careful, yeah?'

She nodded fearful thanks and retreated beneath her blanket.

He walked on. The rope-house was situated a little way from City Street at the far end of Tanner's Yard, and as soon as he turned into the dead end, the smell hit him. He stepped over the sewer channel in the centre of the street without looking at it. If there was money in it, it could stay there. There would be a queue for the tap at this time of day as returning factory workers washed up after their twelve hours at the machines, and Silas had no time to hang around to wash his hands.

The church clock struck six as he mounted the steps and entered the rope-house. Already bustling with sweat-soaked navvies, the lobby was alive with foreign tongues and foul language. A chain of small children weaved through his feet as he burrowed into the throng of rustling skirts and damp jackets, seeking Molly, the proprietor.

He found her at her table towards the back of the entrance hall, guarding the doorless entrance to the rope-room. Her grey hair was down, suggesting she had not had a good day. When she had found success in a transaction, which was mainly being paid the rent owed by her tenants on the higher floors, she wore it up and pinned neatly beneath a straw hat, or had it plaited and arranged with a lilac flower behind one ear. Today, it half curtained her furrowed face and covered one of her cloudy eyes. The other kept a vigilant watch on those entering and leaving the room, but when she saw Silas, she swept the grey curtain away and revealed not only two dulling eyes doing their best to twinkle, but a smile as crooked and cheeky as his own.

'Here's me lad,' she announced as she wavered to her feet.

Once she was as stable as a gin-soaked proprietress could be at six in the evening, she opened both arms to him, and Silas was obliged to accept the over-enthusiastic greeting. Her jacket was tacky and smelt of fish, her breath of alcohol, and her skin was cold as they touched cheeks.

'And here's my only lady,' Silas replied, standing back and letting her go. His words, said loudly enough for those close by to hear, were intended to curry the favour he needed to secure a space. 'How d'you get to looking so beautiful with all your hardships, Molly?' he beamed, and for good measure gave her a flirtatious wink. 'You got that something special about you.'

'And you've got the stinking charm of the Irish,' she shot back. 'Which don't pay the rent on an arse space. You got money?'

As usual with Molly, it was a case of a drunken hello, a quick tease, and then straight to business.

'How much are you wanting for a place on the rope?' he asked, looking into the room where half the bench space was already taken.

'Tuppence,' she answered, as if he was ignorant to ask.

'But, how much for me?' He sidled up to her, placing one hand on her shrivelled backside and wished he hadn't. It was wet.

'Tuppence,' she repeated, unimpressed. 'And a farthing for the grope.'

He let her go and patted the greasy hair of a passing child in an attempt to dry his hand while his other fished for his coins.

'You can have the grope for free, Molly,' he winked back,

26

confusing her. 'And I'll give you many more if you give me two for one in case me man, Fecker, needs to hang his head. A grope for a rope?'

'Fuck off. You want it or not?' She sat, any vestige of amiability gone while the deal was in progress.

'Then here's your tuppence.' He handed it over. He wouldn't eat, he wouldn't know the relative comfort of the public bar, but at least he would have somewhere to sleep. 'If Fecks shows, I can sleep in his lap.'

'I'll have no doubling on my ropes,' Molly complained as she scrawled in her ledger. 'You arse-dippers can do what you want out there, but this here's a respectable establishment.'

A man vomited on the flagstones three feet away. Molly ignored it.

'In on time,' she ordered as she always did. 'Else you'll find the door locked and your money gone.' By locked, she meant guarded as there were no doors.

Silas sat side-saddle on the table glancing at her ledger and wondering how anyone could read it.

'Now don't you find it ironic, Moll?' he said, engaging the rich Irish accent he had learned from his mam.

'I might if I knew what it meant,' she replied and bit both coins before dropping them into the bottomless pocket of her apron.

'Ironic that you call me a molly 'cos of me work, like it were some word only the devil should know, and yet that's your name. But what's even funnier is how you say you'll lock the door come two a the morning, but this dosshouse ain't seen a door for longer than I've been using it.'

'Get off me desk.'

'Give us a kiss there, Molly.' He leant in closer, holding his breath.
'Fuck off.'

'It'll be the only offer you get,' he warned, playfully. 'One kiss from the charmed lips of your Irish lover boy.'

She threw back her head and cackled, the crack of her mouth revealing two uneven rows of wooden teeth. 'I know where your lips 'ave been,' she slurred. 'And they've been places I don't want to think about. Now get off me desk and slap this on your place.' She took a numbered tag from the desk's only drawer and threw it on the table. 'I saved it for you, and it's the best I can do for me favourite blue-eyed charmer.'

'And it's a mighty fine gesture.'

Silas snatched the wooden tag before anyone else could steal it. She had given him number one, the bench space furthest from the doorway and the draughts. It was also the safest as he would have plenty of time to see thieves clambering over the sleepers to reach him.

Others were aggressively calling for Molly's attention now, and Silas had no desire to make himself unpopular by holding up the queue. He slipped from the table and left her to her business, which in this case involved speaking very loudly to a Polish man who understood no English while fighting off an insistent child trying to rob her apron.

He secured his place by tying the tag to the rope in the furthest corner and sat a while on the bench to rest his legs and plan his evening. He wouldn't stay here long, there was no need to guard his place. Despite the desperation of those who used it, the rope-room had an honour code. If anyone took his place or stole his tag, they would find no respite here again, nor at any of the other houses Molly's extended family ran, which was most in the City Road area. Stealing from a sleeper's pockets, however, was not in the code, but his place was secured until two in the morning should he need it.

He hoped he wouldn't. He had used the rope twice the previous week when neither he nor Fecks had earned enough to rent a bed, and on both occasions had wondered why he bothered. He would have had more sleep lying down in the main road for all the snoring and farting, the sleep talking and sounds of sex that accompanied the numbing of his arse on the wooden bench. Leaning with the rope beneath his arms so he could hang his head cut off the circulation and pained his chest, and there was always the possibility of picking up lice from the stranger crammed in beside him. So far, he had avoided that, but in his line of work, lice were the least of his worries. There were far more dangerous things than crabs in the dark alleyways and unlit courts of the East End, and as far as he knew, he had escaped syphilis and the coughing sickness that had seen off his mother.

If Silas had a reputation among the street-rats, it was for being

28

clean, and the hour he spent waiting for two minutes' use of the communal tap would pay off later if he caught a trick. He dropped his trousers with his back to the queue and washed his dick to the jeers of men in line. He always cleaned his dick first. The cold water shrivelled it and tightened his balls until they were nothing better than two Christmas walnuts and he believed that they needed as much time to warm and recover as he could give them. The jeers became shouts of outrage as he washed his arse under cover of his coat, but he ignored them with ease. Such taunting was part of his daily routine. By the time he was done, he felt marginally cleaner, slightly refreshed, but just as famished.

'Two sausages, a chunk of bread and an apple,' he mumbled to himself as he tied his belt and moved away from the muddy ground. That was all he had eaten in the last three days. 'At least the orange smelt good.'

The church clock struck seven-thirty as he wandered back across City Road. There was no point in hurrying. There would be no activity in the yards and backstreets until later in the evening. He was not like Fecks, he had rarely risked daylight trade for fear of being seen, arrested and thrown in a workhouse. Sure, there he would be fed gruel and be given reasonably fresh water, but he would be forced to conform, to weave baskets and to pray. It was worse than being in prison. At least there he could trade his body for favours, but more people died in the cells than died in the workhouse, although only just, and the one thing he valued above all else was his freedom.

Night trading it was, and tonight his hunger once again led the hunt. He walked to the river and along where the boats landed their catch, hoping to find fish heads to boil, or better, a whole mackerel discarded by accident. He found no such luck, only more like him doing the same, and sat a while on a bench outside a warehouse to wonder how his sisters were doing in the care of their cousin.

His legs were the coldest part. Unprotected by his waist-length coat between the top of his boots and his thighs, the worn-thin wool of his trousers was no defence against the damp chill. At least there was no wind, which when blowing from any point of the compass, cut through the material as easily as a bushelman's blade through straw.

It was his left leg that first alerted him to the presence of trade. A hand landed on his knee, jerking him from his reverie, and he silently berated himself for being caught off guard. The touch, brief but understood, came from a large man who caused the bench to groan as he sat.

'Share a light for my tobacco?' the man asked, withdrawing his hand.

His voice was heavily accented, but Silas couldn't place it. Overseas for sure, but the origin of the potential customer was important to know. The Poles liked to fuck hard, the Germans had bigger dicks and could hurt, while the French preferred to be sucked.

'Where you from, mate?' Silas asked, risking a quick glance at the man as he searched his pockets for a match he knew he didn't possess. All he could see of his potential meal ticket was a full white beard, dark eyes and thinning, white hair. His bulk was shrouded by a heavy overcoat forming him into a black boulder.

'Ireland,' the man replied.

Silas knew that was a lie. 'More like Russia,' he ventured.

'Da,' the man confirmed.

Silas was now forearmed. The Russians didn't care what they did as long as long as the boy was young, but they were known for trying to run without paying.

'I ain't got a match,' Silas said and, as if to prove it, stuck a finger in his top pocket.

'You have anything else I can suck?' The Russian wasn't exactly subtle.

Silas' finger brushed against something hard in the pocket which he had thought was empty and he drew it out by his fingertips.

A sixpence?

'Hey,' the Russian insisted. 'Boy?'

Where had he found sixpence? It was enough for a bed, a drink in the Bells and food on top with enough left over for the morning. He had no recollection of finding such riches.

The Russian grumbled something in his native language and prepared to leave.

Silas snapped back to the present. He might have struck lucky in his pocket, but there was no point turning down work.

'Yes, mate,' he said. 'I've got something you'll want if you've got...'
A thought struck him, and he changed his price. 'A shilling.'

Whatever it was the Russian hulk said, it sounded like a swear word, and it preceded, 'Go fuck yourself.'

'I'm fifteen,' Silas lied. 'You have to pay more for fifteen.'

The man was interested. 'Three pennies.'

'Eight.'

'Six.'

The deal was done, and without another word, Silas left the bench and walked ahead of the man until they came to a gate in the warehouse wall. This wasn't his usual turf, and he had no idea what to expect on the other side, but was relieved to find the lock easy to pick and the yard beyond a maze of sheds and recesses. He chose one near the gate for ease of escape should things turn violent, and backed into it, balling his fists.

The hulk panted in after him, one of his flabby hands reaching eagerly for Silas' belt while the other busied itself in the shadows of his own trousers.

'Six,' Silas repeated and gripped the man's wrist to prevent him from grabbing his cock until he had been paid.

'After.'

'Six.' His grip tightened, and he raised his other hand ready to strike.

More Russian swearwords were followed by the press of a cold coin against Silas' fingers, and he released his hold.

'But tell me you are fourteen.'

Silas was as young as the disgusting creature wanted him to be. He now had a shilling to his name.

'That's right,' he said, grimacing at the man's perverted fantasy.

The heavy body pressed against him as the Russian tried to kiss and dropped a bulky arm onto his shoulder.

Silas turned his head away. 'No.' The only man he would allow to kiss him was Fecks, and that had never happened.

Fecks!

Fecks had swung his arm around his shoulder and held him close for mutual support. As they walked, he must have secretly slipped the sixpence into Silas' pocket. The act of generosity warmed his heart, and thoughts of his friend stirred his cock. Just as well as the creature now grappling with it as though it was an eel, did nothing but turn him off.

He imagined a day that would never come. Fecker standing beside a warm bed, naked, gleaming clean and smiling. He turned back the eiderdown to revel in the sight of Silas, his slim, near-hairless body on show with a tuft of black crowning his youthful erection. Fecks straddling him and lowering his swelling shaft gently, so their cocks touched as he bent willingly until their lips met…

He was hard, the Russian was chewing on his dick like it was a bone and thumping inside his own trousers. Silas cursed himself. He had let his guard down again. He should have insisted the man kept his free hand where he could feel it so he would have warning if the trick reached for a knife. He was vulnerable enough with his dick in a stranger's mouth, but he had been lucky. This man had no teeth, and the hand he wasn't beating his own dick with was wrapped around Silas' length. He relaxed, thought of Fecks, and came in the man's throat within a minute.

The Russian's enthusiasm increased as he swallowed and jerked, grunting through his mouthful as he spasmed to a halt. Silas hurriedly withdrew his cock and was buttoned up and belt-tied before he reached the gate, leaving the man to find his own way back to anonymity. He slipped down to the shore and, under cover of the bridge, washed himself in the incoming tide. A barge chugged past, lanterns casting dancing beams of yellow on the ironwork and lighting Silas' naked crotch, but no-one shouted or complained. The bargemen did the same after a day's work, even though the river water was barely cleaner than the gutter.

Washed, Silas continued on his way, following the shore to the Cheap Lane steps where he returned to the black and grey throng of humanity busying itself with its own desperation. He fitted right in and made for The Ten Bells.

It was the same route and routine as always, but tonight he was different. He was rich in money and richer in companionship, because Fecks had, without fuss or word, given him food, shelter and hope. Above all, he gifted the warmth of friendship, and it was that which carried him on air into the pipe-fogged sweat of the gin palace.

Silas had journeyed from gloom to happiness in half an hour, and his life was back on track. It was just as well that he could afford a couple of hours to celebrate his good fortune, because his life was about to become far more complicated.

# *Four*

Thomas drove a trap on his father's farm when he was able to visit, but the viscount's was more stylish, quieter and didn't smell of dung. It was pulled by one horse, a fact for which Thomas was grateful as he had not led a team for several years. It handled well, and he drove quickly at Mr Tripp's insistence. The butler could not bring himself to ride in the back like a gentleman and so sat up-front with Thomas, a blanket over his knees and a scowl on his face, terrified he would be recognised. Thomas shared the blanket against Mr Tripp's wishes but on Viscount Clearwater's insistence. His Lordship had raised Tripp's eyebrows to new and dizzying heights when he offered Thomas the use of his tailored overcoat and leather gloves. Thomas had accepted them after the required amount of protestation and found, as he was of a similar build to His Lordship, that they fitted him.

They set off from Clearwater House through the back gates with Tripp mumbling about how this modern approach to etiquette would bring the house into ill repute, and Thomas ignoring him as he wallowed in the joy of being allowed to drive.

'Slower, boy,' Tripp scolded as they took a corner.

'You said you wanted to go fast.'

'We are now safely distant from the neighbourhood, so, a more dignified speed, if you will.'

They were entering an area of the city Thomas had only visited on foot. He knew the way to the river where the grand houses around Clearwater fell away, taking their autumn-leafed avenues with them and gave way to the workmen's cottages of the middle-class. Trotting through these, the two easily passed for a father and son making their way home from a day's cabbing, and it wasn't until they were taking the embankment road eastwards that Thomas' nervousness manifested itself.

'Where do you think we should start, Mr Tripp?' he asked, passing Prince's Bridge where the road narrowed.

'How should I know?' Tripp replied. His words were muffled through his upturned collar, but his annoyance rang out with clarity. 'I can safely say I have never visited this part of the city.'

'Never, Sir?'

'What do you take me for, boy?'

'Not meaning to cast nasturtiums, Mr Tripp,' Thomas said, trying to lighten the mood. 'Just looking for advice.'

'My first piece of advice would be that you invest in a dictionary,' Tripp huffed. 'Aspersions. You were casting aspersions by suggesting I am a man who might know his way around the sewer which is the black void ahead.'

'Thank you for that, Mr Tripp,' he said. Humour was wasted on the man. 'Everything you say has value.'

Tripp growled and pulled the blanket up to his nose either for fear of the smell or of being seen. Thomas was enjoying the rhythm of the horse and the swaying of the trap too much to worry about the cold that numbed his ears, and awkward though it was to be pressed close to his senior, he was grateful for his body heat.

'His Lordship suggested Greychurch,' Thomas said. The very word sent shudders through him. He had travelled through it on his way home when Clearwater House closed for the season, and he was not required at the viscount's country house, but always in daylight.

'Have you read about what goes on there?' Tripp sounded more concerned than outraged.

'I have, Mr Tripp. His Lordship lets me read his newspapers when he is done with them.'

'What?' That was definitely outrage.

'I'm sure he would offer them to you first if you had a mind to ask him.'

'You asked His Lordship for his newspapers?' Tripp's head was fully revealed by blanket and collar as he sat bolt upright and turned to Thomas in horror.

'His new Lordship,' Thomas clarified. 'I would never have asked the late Lord Clearwater.'

'You shouldn't have been impertinent to ask the current one,'

Tripp admonished. 'We will discuss this in my pantry on our return,' he added, retreating under cover.

Thomas rolled his eyes to a passing church and said no more on the subject. He had left home at eight to go into service uneducated beyond farm work, but had taught himself to read and write a little during his precious free time. His determination had seen him progress rapidly from hall boy to second-footman, and from there to first. He had his heart set on a butlership, but had a long way to go, as Tripp had once again reminded him.

He consoled himself with his responsibility. Their destination was up to him, and he had read of the places the street-rats worked. As well as the shady backstreets and endless cramped courts around the slums which the newspaper called "the sodomites' walkways", the street-rats also gathered at what some still called molly houses, boy-brothels in plain speak. These would offer the safest access to men such as the one their master had sketched. Thomas had it folded in his inside pocket, but the image stayed in his memory.

That he should so clearly remember the features of a nameless young man after only a few viewings was something of a concern for the footman. His Lordship had drawn a good-looking face, and when they met after dinner to finalise details of the expedition and listen again to Tripp's misgivings, Thomas had taken the time to study it. There were two reasons for this. Firstly, he didn't want to produce it in public for fear of being thought an undercover policeman looking for a villain and therefore risk a beating. Secondly, he had been unable to stop looking at it. The youth, for he was without question younger than Thomas and looked more like a boy than a man, was to be in his late teens. His Lordship had been insistent that they find someone no older than Thomas, but not below the age of eighteen. He was to be honest of looks, and if they could discern it, of character. The face in the drawing was open, and there was a pleading look about it, which appeared to be a natural feature rather than a put-on one. The portrait's hair was dark, his mouth soft and the slight smile drawn as impishly crooked. It was a likeness of a youth Thomas considered handsome, with an air of innocence that hid his true age and experience. All these facets caught his imagination, but the eyes of the drawing were the most compelling feature. The charcoal was more intense

36

in the pupils than anywhere else, giving the youth a stare which pierced the viewer, captivating him and refusing to let go.

The subject was as unnerving as he was attractive, and it was that attraction which unnerved Thomas. He didn't fear the imagined street-rat, and although he steered the trap with deepening trepidation as they entered Greychurch, he didn't fear the task nor failing it. He wasn't even concerned at His Lordship's request, or his motivation.

What most concerned him was that he found the youth attractive and the sketch left within him a curiosity which he had never previously experienced.

'God, this is a cesspit.' Tripp was upright again and clutching the blanket tighter.

They clattered under a railway bridge, and the road became a lane with barely enough room for two carriages to pass. There were no pavements, and an oily river channelled down the centre, pooling where the undulations of the brick prevented its passing. Human waste and dead vegetables formed dams, leaving a viscous trickle of everything else unwanted to pass by for the horse to splash through.

They had left the river and turned north, entering Greychurch from the west.

Thomas mapped their route in his head so that he could remember his way out, and brought to mind the description of the alehouse he sought. The newspaper had described it as, "A place of outwardly respectable appearance, but inwardly, it seethes with the depravity of a Bacchanalian orgy to which only sodomites and their catamites have been invited." He remembered the sentence, because he had needed to look up sodomite and catamite in Mrs Baker's dictionary. Had she known what he was learning from her gift, she would have taken her own life in remorse. Thomas even knew the page numbers for the words, he had read them so many times, their meanings and what they suggested setting his curiosity to boil.

'Is that it?'

Tripp's gruff voice focused his thoughts, and he realised how far they had come while his mind had been drifting. Had it not been disloyal — though incredibly exciting — to think it, Thomas might have supposed that the horse knew its own way to The Ten Bells having made this journey with His Lordship on many occasions.

There was no mistaking their destination, they could smell the smoke and alcohol fumes. Warm light glowed through arched glass etched with patterns that disguised the shifting silhouettes on the other side. A hurdy-gurdy was being cranked in the street where prostitutes stood with one stockinged leg on the wall, their ruffled dresses falling between their legs like the ruched curtains of the Clearwater dining room, but cheap, mud-stained and more regularly lifted.

Tripp poked his head from hiding and scanned the street like a turtle coming up for air.

'I am not sure if I should be reassured or panicked, but thank heavens,' he said. 'A Peeler.'

'Two,' Thomas rightly pointed out. 'But young people call them bobbies now.'

Tripp sneered.

'Perhaps you should let me do the talking,' Thomas suggested.

'I'm not talking to a policeman,' Tripp objected. 'I am just glad to know they are within calling distance.'

'I meant inside the pub.'

'Inside the…?'

Thomas waited for Tripp to explode in volcanic indignation, but the butler restrained himself. 'Dear God,' he said. 'I didn't imagine I would have to go inside.'

'You can wait out here with the trap if you like,' the footman said, enjoying the novelty of talking to Tripp as an equal.

'Yes, good idea. I'll do that. Be quick.'

'But then those ladies might think you're looking for game and approach, and under the watchful eye of two bobbies.'

Tripp was suddenly no equal. He was a trembling mass of cowardice while Thomas, now that he was here, approached the task as an opportunity. This wasn't exactly his turf, but it definitely wasn't Tripp's, and of course, he could be sure it wasn't His Lordship's. Therefore, of the three of them thus far involved in this eccentric caper, Thomas was the clear leader.

If he could carry out his master's wishes successfully while displaying an ability to lead, he would stand a better chance of gaining the promotion he longed for.

'I hate to say it, Mr Tripp,' he said, knotting the reins and putting aside the blanket. 'But you're coming with me.'

Silas was having a profitable time, but was unable to share the good news with Fecks. He had not seen his friend all evening and wanted to repay his earlier kindness by renting a bed for the night. The Russian pervert had brought him luck with his early business and Silas now had three shillings in his pocket and three glasses of gin in his belly along with a fair wedge of cheese, two bread rolls and a hunk of ham. It was gone midnight and nearing closing time, but the Bells never threw anyone out until the police came knocking, and Silas no longer needed the bench space he had booked and paid for. In fact, he had given it away to a girl he knew and met behind the pub two tricks ago. The transaction was done as they individually masturbated two sailors and although the seamen objected to their matter of fact conversation during the act, when it was done, each of the four people involved went away satisfied.

He had even been in the unique position of refusing the suggestions of an effeminate man wearing a lace collar, the first time he could remember turning down a trick. What had been even more unusual about the night was that he hadn't had to drop his trousers. Everything had been one-way and quick. One of the men had even been attractive, and when he invited Silas to dine with him, Silas was tempted. He refused. Experience had taught him that trade in the open, no matter how dark and unsavoury, was safer than visiting a man's lodgings where privacy might allow for more intimacy, but where it also hampered escape and calls for assistance should they be needed.

Not that the streets were any safer at that time. The talk among the whores and molly boys was of little other than the recent killings, the fourth at the knife of a murderer the papers were calling the East End Ripper. There were worse terrors than a quick death waiting for Silas and his colleagues on the streets. Venereal disease, gang rapes and starvation were some, but surprisingly, murders were few and far between. Either that, or there were so many the papers didn't bother reporting them. Not until "The Ripper" was born in a Sunday edition of the Central Star. The name and the savagery of the killings caught imaginations and the retelling of events by those who had not actually witnessed them increased fear as gossip spread.

The girls had agreed among themselves to work in pairs, and some of the boys had done the same. The tougher lads, the stevedores by day and cross-dressing angels by night, made a show of not being afraid as if that made them any safer, but Silas still noticed them leaving in groups or pairs when only one had a punter.

It was while watching two such men leave, singing badly and holding each other for support after several too many ales, that Silas noticed the unlikely pair entering the public bar. He might have passed them off for lost tourists had he not seen them stop the two drunk street-rats to purposefully study their faces. They could have passed for disguised bobbies but for their uneasiness. As they made their way to the bar under the unwanted gaze of renters and whores, the older man turned his collar to hide his face. It was a move so obvious it brought a cackle of, 'I won't tell yer missus, Mister,' from Lady Quickpurse, named after his ability to get a man off within thirty seconds by the things he did to his balls.

The younger man was of more interest to Silas, and it was he who approached the bar in a practised manner, leant across it and ordered drinks. While the older man remained still, hoping no-one had noticed him, the younger rested his back on the counter and, with the attitude of an experienced drinker, ambled his eyes around the room. He spent longer looking at the men than the women, and because he made a long, slow arc, Silas was awarded plenty of time to study his features.

He lounged not five feet away and stood out from everyone else because of his sobriety. His hair was the colour of a polished copper coin though most of it was confined to a peaked cap not dissimilar to the one Silas wore. His face was pale and his nose slightly freckled while either side, two thoughtful eyes moved gracefully from one boy to the next. Silas could not see their colour as they were shaded by dark brows beneath a smooth forehead, but the man's lips were full and pink.

In any other life, Silas would have taken him to bed without payment, but in his current existence, he could only see the man as business. Even so, as the redhead's eyes finally came to rest on Silas, a pang of longing shot through him and he repaid the stare with an involuntary smile.

It was returned immediately, and Silas' heart leapt. Surely he couldn't have been so lucky as to earn a feast, a bed and still have enough good fortune left over to catch such as attractive trick? He had rested long enough, and if this punter was as well off as his clothes suggested, he might pay enough for Silas to rent lodgings for a week.

He offered his most alluring wink, but his excitement turned to suspicion when the man conferred with his companion. Perhaps, after all, they were police. When the older one regarded Silas, whispered in the other's ear and nodded, a more terrifying thought entered Silas' fast-beating heart. What if the one was the Ripper and the other an accomplice? Was a man as handsome as the one now approaching him worth that risk?

He would decide after hearing what he had to say.

With that in mind, Silas maintained his smile as best he could and slid along the bench seat to offer a place, aware of the behaviour of the older man now hiding behind a glass of ginger beer.

'Do you mind?' The stranger asked, holding his bottle towards the vacated seat.

'Whatever you want, Sir,' Silas replied. 'I am at your disposal.' That phrase usually had the punters licking their lips, but this one was different. He coughed to clear his throat, said his thanks and slipped into the seat.

'What's your name?' he asked, a standard opening line.

'Whatever you want it to be.' It received a standard reply.

'I want it to be your name.'

'Fair enough. Billy,' Silas said. Again, standard. 'Some call me Hawk, 'cos I got fingers that grip like claws and never let go 'til the job's done if you get me.'

'Oh.' The man sounded surprised. 'I assumed it would be on account of your large nose.'

'I haven't got a large nose,' Silas protested. It was true, he hadn't. If anything, it was small and snubbed.

'I was quipping. Perhaps it has something to do with your yellow eyes?'

'My eyes are blue, Sir, as you can see.' Silas had encountered all kinds of punters, sober and drunk alike, probably as many mad as sane, but none had begun an encounter like this.

'Indeed they are,' the man said, staring into them as if he couldn't believe what he saw. 'The blue of lapis lazuli.'

'Wherever that is.' Silas laughed, noting as he did so, that the stranger's own irises were the greenest he'd seen.

The man gave him a sympathetic smile before glancing around the bar. When he was satisfied that they were not being overheard, he said, 'This is not what I usually do, so forgive me, but are you…?' He faltered. 'That is to say, would you be willing to…?' He took a sharp breath, opened his mouth, thought better of it and sighed before trying again and failing to ask his question. He sipped his beer while he thought of another way of putting it.

The punter was so obviously new to this it was embarrassing for both, and Silas thought it best to come to the point. 'Do you want to fuck me?'

The man spat beer across the table. He held his hand over his mouth while he sought a handkerchief to wipe it on, his jade eyes flicking to the bar where his companion looked on in horror.

It was strange, but amusing, and the man's reaction stirred sympathy in Silas' heart.

'Didn't mean to shock you, Sir,' he said. 'Keep easy. There's nothing to worry about with young Billy.'

He squeezed the man's thigh to reassure him.

If his suggestion of a fuck had caused concern, his touch caused outright panic, and the man shot to his feet. His companion's nostrils flared as he glared from the bar and, strangely, the look calmed the potential punter.

'Sorry about that too, Sir,' Silas said. 'Just tell me what you came over here for.'

It took the other man a moment to respond, but he sat, put his bottle on the table and half turned to face Silas.

'Billy,' he said. 'I am going to be honest with you. I am not here looking for…' Another glance at the older man, and he shifted his posture, putting his back to the bar. 'I'm not looking for sex.'

'That's a shame.'

'Sorry… What?'

'What are you after, mate? 'Cos you've landed yourself right in the wrong place to make friends.'

'And yet that is exactly what I hope to do, but not for me, you understand.'

'Ah, I get it. For your dad?' Silas nodded to the companion.

The youth's large lips turned in on themselves as he growled in his throat, but the action released the tension in his face so that a grin as matey as any Silas had seen broke through.

'Oh, mate,' he said. 'If he were me fader, I'd a left 'ome way afore the eight year I did.'

It was Silas' turn to be surprised. What accent was that? And where had it come from? He asked the same, and as the man explained, Silas warmed to him further.

'I come from a village south a the city,' the redhead began. 'I affect a voice fur me work 'cos I be in the employ of… a gentleman. Being in such a place as this, I reckon it be best if I be meself, and this is meself. Thomas Payne, son of a dairy farmer not the old wrinkle what's shitting 'imself behind me like a parson in an 'ore 'ouse.'

Silas laughed but hurriedly covered it. Whoever this young man was, he didn't want to betray him to the disapproving onlooker.

'It be a bit of a story,' Thomas said. 'But I be 'ere on me master's behalf. I be a footman, see? When I ain't playing messenger and, a-be 'onest wi' ye, it be such a relief a-be able a-speak as meself I'd 'appily take an ale more wi' ye just fur the pleasure a-getting a-know your good self, but we ain't got time fur that. That being said, I be wanting a-take a clicker a your time a-be asking…'

'Er, yeah, hang on there, mate,' Silas interrupted. 'I think I like you, so I'm happy just to talk while I finish my drink, but if you're going to tell me what it is you want, you're going to have to do it in some language I understand, right?'

'I do apologise.' The tone of an educated young man from the city was back, and the footman returned. 'Terribly sorry, Billy, but this whole adventure has churned me up in such an unexpected manner.'

'And there's no need to be posh, neither,' Silas said. 'Just get on with it.'

Another swig of beer, another check-in with the now confused older man, and Thomas was settled enough to make sense.

'I can't tell you who,' he said, 'but my master has asked us to come here in the hope we may find a boy... Excuse me, I can see you are more mature than a boy, and your age is one thing I must ask you momentarily, but it is the language of my master.'

Silas hurried him along by waving his nearly-finished gin in his face.

'Quite. Billy…'

'Hold your horses there again, Mister,' Silas said. 'Me name's not Billy.'

'Oh?' Thomas was taken aback. 'My instructions were to find an honest street-rat.'

'Well then, mate, you've been lucky enough to find the only one this side of the river. My name's Silas, and I'm pushing twenty. Yeah, I'm a street-rat, and no, you ain't putting me in a carriage and taking me back to your master. I don't do home visits, not since I got caught by an angry wife who threw knives more accurately than she threw insults. If you want me to go back to your master's place, it ain't going to be happening.'

Thomas was crestfallen. 'But you look so much like the picture,' he moaned. 'I thought I'd done well.'

'Picture?'

'Oh dear.' Thomas sighed and pulled out a sheet of paper. He opened it beneath the level of the table for a reason known only to him and showed it to Silas.

'Jesus, Mary and Joseph!' Silas swore. 'That could be me.'

'Indeed it could, and that means you are exactly what His Lordship wants.'

'Oh, His Lordship now is it?'

Thomas clutched Silas' arm in anguish. 'Please don't tell Tripp I said that.'

'Tripp?'

'Bugger, I've done it again.'

Silas couldn't help but laugh, not at Thomas but with him and they laughed together.

'You're okay, mate,' Silas said. 'I'll have forgotten all about you come morning. Sorry I can't help.'

'Oh, but you must.'

'No, I don't.'

'My master is… He wants you.'

'He don't know me,' Silas pointed out. 'Unless he's had me before. Did he draw that?'

'Aye. I mean, yes, he did.'

'I'm pretty sure I've never been with a lord,' Silas thought aloud. 'Then again, on a dark night, a dick's a dick, and an arse is an arse, and unless you get a good look at their hands, a punter could be a docker or a judge. All the same, I don't go to houses.'

'It's not for sex.'

'Then I definitely don't travel.' Silas downed the rest of his gin. 'Sorry Tommy, you're a nice bloke, pretty sexy too, but you're wasting your time with me. I've got a mate to meet.' He began to rise, but Thomas was still holding his arm. It felt so natural that Silas hadn't noticed.

'Please,' Thomas pleaded. 'He only wants to help you.'

'Heard it before.'

'He wants to talk to you, that's all.'

'Heard that too. Talk leads to other stuff and when you say no... Sorry, mate. I'm off.'

Thomas stood, placing one knee on the bench so he could face Silas in the gap between the table. His grip tightened.

'I'm not so dissimilar to you,' he said, and Silas gave him an up and down with a sneer. 'I know, it's my master's coat, and I have a safe job in a comfortable house, but there for the grace of God go I.'

'If you want to talk about God, you're definitely pissing on the wrong lamppost.'

'I don't, and neither does Lord...' Another growl. 'He only wants to talk to you about your life, so he can understand your troubles. He has a mind to help people like you and the money to match. You would do well out of it and, once again, he has not sent me here to procure you for sex.'

Silas considered the offer a full two minutes while Thomas waited hopefully, and the second man fidgeted with his collar. The renters were giving him more unwanted attention than he could cope with, and Silas thought, out of basic human compassion, that he should agree to Thomas if only to release the older man from his torment.

Thomas was sexy, but that was not a reason to go home with a stranger. He might not have been telling the truth. For all Silas knew, this could be how the Ripper operated. He was safer on the streets he knew, where those as unfortunate as himself would look out for him.

As if reading his mind, Thomas produced a paper and showed Silas a crest with a name embossed in gold. Silas read what he could. Thomas' finger covered the address leaving only the borough visible. It was one Silas had never dreamed of visiting, four miles away and at least two social classes above.

'Still say no,' he said, adjusting his cap. 'Nice to have met you, Tommy.'

'Please. He'll beat me if I return empty-handed.'

'Then definitely no,' Silas replied. 'And if I were you, I'd find another job.'

'I made that up,' Thomas admitted. 'Sorry. He's a good man, but if I do this job right, he will see I am better than a footman and can be trusted. Not only that, I like him. He's not like his father, who did beat his staff until my master intervened. And he wants to help boys like you. If that's not enough, he is willing to pay you for your time and, knowing him, will feed you and probably buy you new clothes. I'm not lying. Why should I? Has anyone else ever asked such a thing of you?'

No, was the answer, but Silas kept it to himself. The more he looked on Thomas' desperation, the more his copper hair and soft lips appealed. Perhaps a night in a warm house might be a fitting end to what had turned out to be a good day. That was if he could trust Thomas.

There was one way to find out.

'Let me grope your dick,' he said, inching closer.

'Let you… Pardon?'

'Grope your cock.' Silas ran his tongue over each word. 'If you're telling me the truth, if I'm in no danger and you're sincere, prove it.'

'How will letting you… Oh, never mind.' Thomas looked over his shoulder. His companion was tapping his pocket watch. He turned back to Silas. 'Here?'

'Yeah, no-one'll notice nor care.'

'Right here?'

'Yes. Open your coat. I'll do the rest.'

'And that will convince you I am genuine?' It was as if Thomas couldn't believe it. Nor, to a certain extent did Silas, but it would be interesting.

'It will,' he said, now standing so close to Thomas he could smell his nervous sweat.

'Very well.' Thomas swallowed and looked away as if about to be examined by a doctor.

Encouraged at the speed at which the sexy redhead had given in, Silas reached out his hand and expertly weaved it between the buttons of the coat at crotch level. He found Thomas' groin and ran his palm across it before carefully squeezing what he found.

'Fuck me, you've got a big one,' he whispered.

'Thank you.' Thomas replied in a polite but husky voice.

It wasn't just big, it grew firmer at his touch.

Thomas brushed away the hand and looked Silas in the eye. 'So, now will you come with me?'

Silas gave him the cheekiest of grins. 'I'll think about it,' he said. 'Meet me outside tomorrow night at six, and I'll let you know.'

He resisted the temptation to grope Thomas again and, with his own cock stiffening, he left the footman confused and, hopefully, wanting more. He gave the other man a nod on his way past and had to stop himself saying 'Good night, Tripp,' because it might have caused Thomas trouble. He'd enjoyed teasing the man so much he was sorely tempted to agree and go with him right there and then if he promised to let him do more than grope that fine cock of his. Instead, he controlled himself and left the bawdy chatter of the Bells. He'd had enough entertainment for one night and, if he was going to spend the next evening in the company of a lord, he wanted a good night's sleep.

He set off into the night wondering where Fecks might be found, keen to share his news as well as his earnings.

# *Five*

Silas had arrived in the city four years previously, a fish out of water, and quickly learned how to live on the streets. He realised after a month that the few saved coins he possessed were not going to last him long, work was not going to be easy to find, and starvation was not a way of life. He had been sure of only two things. Since his mother had died, he was solely responsible for the welfare of his younger, twin sisters until they were married. He left them behind in the care of the cousin, but she needed to feed them, and Silas had promised, with his usual confidence, that he would find a way of sending money.

The reality, of course, was different. Had it not been for a fortuitous encounter with a tall Ukrainian on a November night, he would undoubtedly have died in his sixteenth year.

He had met Andrej in Cutpurse Lane in broad daylight. Needing to relieve himself, he slipped from the bustle of East Street and approached what he thought was a vacant, well-hidden niche between two windowless buildings. He was looking back to ensure no-one was watching, and didn't see that the space was in use. He had his fly unbuttoned and was fishing for his dick as he stepped in and turned.

Confusion struck him as unexpectedly as it did the boy looking back at him. Tall, with a long mane of blond hair and blue eyes wide in surprise, the lad was facing him and let loose a string of incomprehensible words that could only have been foul. Silas was desperate to piss and already had his cock in his hand, but he would have fled had there not been a third man in the tight space.

He was on his knees, his back to Silas and his face buried in the other boy's groin. The realisation of what was taking place coursed through Silas' veins in an instant and horror and excitement collided. The blond was stunning, the other man was sucking his cock and Silas' first thought was to wonder if he would be allowed a go. That ridiculous notion was forgotten when he saw that, unknown to the lad, the man was drawing from his pocket a flick-knife, presumably to rob him or worse.

'Fuck off,' the blond said in a richly accented voice. 'My place.'

Silas had no choice, but to do what he did, and he let go a stream of steaming piss that splashed the kneeling man causing him to break away and stagger back, complaining loudly. Silas crunched his boot over the knife, trapping a couple of the man's fingers and forcing him to let it go, heard him swear, and continued to piss at him while he scurried away. That left him with his dick in the wind staring at the tall blond and marvelling at the size of his cock left dripping and on show.

'Why you fuck that up?' the blond shouted, seemingly unbothered by his condition.

Silas kicked the knife as he shook the last drops from his dick. The blond saw it, and his shoulders slumped.

'I get no luck,' he complained, shrugging as if falling prey to knife attack while getting his cock sucked was a regular occurrence. He looked from the blade to Silas, and his attitude changed. 'Spasibo. Thanks.'

'Sorry I disturbed you,' Silas replied, attending to his fly, but unable to take his eyes off the length of meat still standing proudly above the boy's massive balls beneath a crown of corn-coloured hair.

'You want?' the youth asked.

'Fuck me, yes.' Silas had hankered for male love and attention since he could remember, but this was the first time he had seen another boy's dick so close and in such a condition.

'Two shillings, I fuck.'

'Pardon?'

'I need money. Five shillings you fuck.'

'Hang on…'

'I spend in your mouth, one shilling, your hand, six pennies, you spend in me I cut your throat.'

Silas' head buzzed as he tried to take in the information, and then realisation dawned.

'I ain't got money,' he said. 'Sorry, mate, only came here for a piss.

Are you going to put that away?'

'Why you not want?' The youth was hurt.

'Oh, I want, mate,' Silas said. 'But I ain't got money.'

'You get money.'

'Yeah, that would be good. I'll come back tomorrow.' He buttoned his coat while gawping at the cock. Like his, it was hooded, unlike his, it was at least eight inches in length and curved slightly to the right.

'Yours. Let me see.'

'Get away with you, man,' Silas objected.

'You get much if you use this….' The blond pointed to his temple. 'And that.' He pointed to Silas' crotch. 'And these.' He held up his fists. 'But mostly that and this.' His dick and his head.

'Look, mate,' Silas babbled, preparing to leave. 'I don't mind telling you that thing of yours is mighty impressive and attached to a body like that with the face of a holy angel… Well, I'd best shut up and go.' He didn't know this youth, and he'd never felt compelled to admit his attraction to other men, but the blue eyes had recovered from their shock and were now inquisitive. Not only that, Silas was sure they were also friendly. The boy was attractive, but still a stranger.

'Why you go?'

'I need to look for a job.'

'You work like me. What you name?'

So began an unlikely friendship which, for Silas started as infatuation and, for Andrej, an instant like of the dark-haired Banyak. He did eventually pull up his trousers, and when he threw a powerful arm around Silas' shoulders and half-dragged him to a nearby pub to spend two shillings he had earned the previous night, the pair quickly fell into an easy friendship. Andrej was grateful for Silas' timely intervention and explained that he had been working the streets since he was fourteen — a fact which, at the time, shocked Silas, but which he came to accept as common. Within a week, the pair were as close as lovers but without the sex. Andrej, it turned out, was only interested in women but never did anything about it, preferring, he said, to keep himself clean for work. Sex with men was acceptable only when accompanied by the exchange of money, and despite Silas declaring his love for him on many a drunken night, was only able to handle his prize dick on the rare occasion the two were hired together. Even then, it was only to do as the punter asked and whatever delicious acts he could perform on or with Andrej were just that, acts, at least on Andrej's part.

After a time, as Silas learnt to be as streetwise as his same-aged mentor, he came to appreciate that their friendship was more important than sex, and the drunken declarations of love, though still regularly made, were platonic. He liked Andrej more when the Ukrainian explained that a Banyak was a cooking pot, and he used the word for Silas because a banyak was compact and cute. In turn, Silas referred to him as Fecks because he was 'A right sexy fecker,' which, when translated from Silas' Irish accent, Andrej found flattering. They had been looking out for each other ever since, with Banyak helping Fecks with his English and Fecks teaching him the way of the streets.

As Silas roamed the labyrinth of alleyways between the Bells and Molly's rope-house, he missed his only friend and wondered where he might be.

His encounter with the redhead had left him out of sorts, and the streets had a different feel to them that night. The cold snap was present in his painful fingers and toes, the lamplight shaded by drizzle and the doorways littered with the forgotten dreams of the inebriated hopeless, but there was something unfamiliar, and he couldn't decide what. Those he passed, of all classes and nationalities, whispered as if not wanting to be heard. The lights of the opium dens and molly houses, the brothels and even the blue lamp of the police station at City Street, were dulled. It was if the East End was biding its time, waiting to hear the news of another slashed victim, another grisly murder, another desperate boy tricked and slit, left in disembowelled indignity in a yard or a square's unlit corner.

Following the third gruesome murder nine days ago, there had been talk of civil unrest, and two days ago when word spread of a fourth messy killing, Silas sensed an increase in the unease among the homeless and housed alike. The misty night simmered with discontent which might easily boil over into riot. He'd heard a rumour that a carriage had been seen in the area of the murders and that the killer within was of royal blood. Others said that he was a mad artist driven to carnage by taking arsenic, while many believed that the man had medical training, and because the victims were street-wary, able-bodied young men, was probably in the military.

His flesh crept beneath his undershirt, although it may have been the scratching of mites, and Silas kept his wits about him as much as his celebratory gins would allow. Thomas was working on behalf of a nobleman, he'd admitted it, and going by the borough, must have travelled to Greychurch in a carriage. Was the uneasy older man with him the Ripper? He hadn't looked the part, but then neither had the Russian by the river, the sailor or the apprentice he'd sucked off behind the Bells who, he suddenly realised, he knew to be one of the butcher boys from Cheap Street market.

Any of his punters could be the Ripper, and if he wanted to live, he had to accept that fact. He did, but it would be so much easier if he had Fecks by his side.

He avoided a trap as he crossed City Street, giving it a glance to see if the sexy redhead was driving. He wasn't, but the sight did make him wonder about the strange offer. A... What was he? A viscount. A viscount sent his footman to bring home a lad who resembled his drawing. That was strange enough, stranger was the likeness the sketch bore to Silas. That was coincidence, there were any number of nineteen-year-olds with black hair and large eyes who would have done, and they would all skip at the chance to be entertained by someone who put 'Lord' in front of his name. Why was Silas worried? Thomas seemed amiable enough and genuine. Silas had read him in the time it took to sip a toothful of gin. Mid-twenties, well-built and affable, but as nervous as a choirboy in a room of cardinals.

That Thomas had been out of place was obvious, but what came as a surprise was his instant erection and the spark that Silas experienced when he first saw the man approach.

His worn boot slipped on the curb, and he stumbled. Cursing himself for dropping his guard, he checked his sole to find he had trodden in orange peel. He was about to kick it towards the bundle of rags who had undoubtedly thrown it there when he saw the girl's hand was exposed from her blanket. With her fingers open and her palm skywards, Ellie could have been begging were it not for the pallor of her skin and Silas' bitter experience. Her palm was not just skyward, it was heavenward, and if she was begging for anything, it was forgiveness.

He covered her as best he could and left her to whoever came picking first, the police or body-snatchers.

Entering the yard, he was relieved to see Fecks hanging around the rope-house door, swaying slightly and holding the wall for support. Better still was that Molly's attic room light was still burning. She had not yet let the room, and not only was there a bed, but there was also a washing jug, and, if Fecks had a spare copper, they could burn a log for warmth. As Fecks hugged him, sneezed, giggled and sneezed again, Silas was as warm as he needed to be.

Archer realised he had not sat at the kitchen table since his thirteenth birthday. That was the last time his father had permitted him to mix with the servants, and even then, he was only allowed below stairs to talk with Mrs Baker about how she kept the household accounts, and to Mr Tripp to learn the cost of brass polish and bad behaviour. These 'lessons' were the only unorthodox thing his father had treated him to, but he insisted that the visits stop when Archer left prep school and joined the training ship at Dartmouth. His fondest memories were of sitting at the well-worn table in the servants' hall watching Cook make her overly sweet desserts. Always accompanied by his nanny, he was not often able to engage the intriguing hall boy in conversation, but when Nanny and Cook fell to discussing the servants, they would send him to help the redhead. Among his finest memories was the time when, alone between the flour sacks and potatoes in the second pantry, allegedly looking for oatmeal, the boys had revealed to each other the contents of their breeches. He had no recollection of how that came about, but the image of Thomas' long, pink cock stayed with him until he found more tangible playthings at naval college.

He smiled at the memory and glanced towards the kitchen, wondering how much longer he would have to wait for Tripp's return. It was past one o'clock, but he had told them to take their time. While he waited, he attended to his plans for his charity, and reread letters from Marks, his solicitor in Shagpile Street, a name he always found amusing. Archer's intentions for the charity were deemed philanthropic enough, but Marks, like many of the would-be trustees, was on edge about those Archer wanted to help.

The copy of his first letter to Marks made his philosophy clear; no-one else was assisting these male wretches, and something had to be done. Parliament admitted their existence and tried to legislate against them as if laws could control one man's urge to bugger another. At least the opposition called for social change which was, without question in Archer's mind, the root cause.

Marks' reply tactfully pointed out that although the assistance of women in a similar position was acceptable, because they were the weaker sex, to assist sodomites was to sail unchartered and potentially turbulent water. (He had written sodomites in Latin as if too ashamed to pen the letters which, together, spelt a word for what Marks himself probably was.)

Archer countered with a bluff, declaring his intention to engage another solicitor which, Marks admitted was His Lordship's prerogative, but would not be in his best interests. The matter was settled when Archer's neighbour and godmother, the unorthodox but powerful Lady Marshall, was delighted to become the charity's chairman and made the fact known in the newspapers. In the same public letter, she congratulated Marks for his forward-thinking views and courage, and spoke highly of his firm, thereby assuring him excellent business and herself, his indignant loyalty.

The charity was now at the stage where work could begin. Archer had the finance, the trustees and an inner desire to help young men, particularly (but carefully) those who like him were *masculorum concubitores*, in Marks' prissy translation. If he was to be truthful, he wanted to help young homosexual men live as un-discriminated a life as those who slept with women, but to admit that publicly risked all manner of troubles. Until society evolved, he would wrap his true calling in the respectable cloak of charitable work for the destitute, which was satisfying enough. Insisting that his cause was solely boy-whores raised eyebrows among his peers, but mainly out of fear that they might, somehow, be unmasked, and if Archer's suspicion was correct, rightly so.

Turning the letters and papers in his ribbon-bound portfolio, his mind switched to the more pressing and personal matter of the

54

Ripper victims and his interest in them.

The first murder of such a boy had convinced him that his charity could help. The second, and the authorities' lackadaisical attitude towards it had angered him, but the third had caused him to think about the situation in a different light.

He had seen a pattern as, presumably, had the police — and still done nothing about it — and the pattern intrigued him as much as the plight of the boys angered him. Managing to separate his feelings from the evidence, he studied what he could find and came to a disturbing conclusion. How he acted on what he deduced was another matter, and he was no detective. Neither was Inspector Adelaide, the man put in charge of the investigation who, according to the papers, had no clues and very little inclination to do anything about the murders, despite their headline-grabbing cruelty. It wasn't Archer's place to intervene, but he couldn't sit back and watch without doing something. Whatever he was to do, however, had to be done carefully. If the name of Clearwater became involved, even through assistance to the investigation, the feathers of the upper classes would be ruffled, Archer's life and motives scrutinised, and public attention would shift from the boys who were dying to the lord who had a suspicious interest in them.

Archer had to find a way to prove his theory, investigate without drawing attention and, if correct, expose the killer in such a way that the police would catch him without realising Archer had played a part. With a fourth slaying so recent and prominent and with the Ripper showing no signs of stopping, every boy on the street was in danger, and time for some was running out.

Now was the time to act and act he would, no matter how unconventional his approach.

He was reviewing his evidence with a cold heart but a fevered brain when the back door opened. Thomas admitted Tripp and a rush of cold air as stony as the butler's face when he saw the viscount drinking whisky at the servants' table.

'My Lord!' Tripp exclaimed as though Archer had been discovered at the wrong end of his own cutlass. 'What has happened?'

'Happened, Tripp?' Archer replied, hurriedly tidying away his papers. 'Nothing's happened, except half a bottle of malt.'

'Let me accompany you to the correct side of the baize, My lord.

You will be more comfortable.'

'I am comforted enough by your safe return, Tripp, although…' He watched Thomas close the door. 'I would be happier had you not returned empty-handed.'

'Ah.' Tripp bowed his head in his obsequious, annoying way. 'Therein lies a tale best told by a footman,' he said. 'And, if I may, in the morning.'

'I've not waited up half the night to be sent to bed, Tripp,' Archer scolded. 'If Thomas has the story, you can retire, and I shall learn from him. If you're up for it, Thomas?'

'I am, My Lord.'

'Then, it's best if I stay with you, Sir, for fear that the tale might trouble you.'

Archer laughed and made no apology for it. 'Dear old Tripp,' he said. 'I am not an ancient duchess given to fainting at the drop of a social indiscretion. I have served in the navy and been to the Indies. If the atrocities I witnessed there were not enough to harden my constitution, I have also served my time in the British public-school system. Go to bed. I will need you fresh in the morning as I am giving Lady Marshall an early lunch.'

Clearly unhappy, Tripp engaged an unaffected air, bid goodnight to His Lordship and unnecessarily reminded Thomas that he, too, had duties in the morning. Archer and Thomas remained silent until the butler's precise footsteps had faded on the backstairs and the only sound was the hissing of the gaslight.

'I feel like I've just been told off by Nanny,' Archer whispered. 'Do you think he was really saying, "You two boys don't be late to bed and no talking after lights out?" Silly old duffer.'

Thomas shuffled his feet uncomfortably and coughed.

Archer had embarrassed him with his overfamiliarity, and that angered him. Not because he had broken archaic rules of etiquette, but because he had to be so carefully aware of their existence. He wanted, no *needed*, a companion with whom he could be himself, and that need manifested itself in the way he wanted to treat Thomas, the only person inside the house close to his age.

'I'm sorry, Thomas,' Archer said, rising. 'That was rude of me. Please, sit.'

'Sit, Sir?'

'Yes, as in…' He wanted to tell him to park his pert arse, but he waved towards a chair instead. He brought another glass from the sideboard, and Thomas waited until Archer had sat before he followed suit, sitting opposite still wearing his master's coat.

'Suits you,' Archer said, pouring a second glass of whisky and nodding to the garment.

'Oh! Very sorry, My Lord.' Thomas leapt to his feet and set about removing it.

'No, no, leave it,' Archer ordered. 'At least wait until you warm up. Here, drink this and tell me what happened. You weren't successful, I take it?'

Thomas stared at the drink unsure what to do, and Archer thought it time to clear the air.

'Listen, Thomas,' he said, leaning into the table and lowering his voice. 'I know this is not what you are used to. This is to go no further, and certainly not to go to your head, but honestly? I am screaming out to have someone normal to speak to.'

Thomas' head shot up.

'Even when I'm chatting with Her Ladyship next door, I have to play the part my title demands, and I am not ungrateful for it, just fed up with having to live it all the time. Thus, as I am master in my own house, I have decided we are permitted to talk like we did when we were little, as friends. Only when I see fit, you understand. I'm sorry if this makes you uncomfortable, but try not to let it. If anything, I mean to flatter you in appreciation of your dedication. Just, don't tell the others. Mrs Baker will lecture me, and Tripp will expire. You can't be my public friend, Thomas, it's not allowed, but can we pretend when we're alone?'

Thomas had paled and his brow furrowed.

'When I say alone, I don't mean alone anywhere specific,' Archer tried to clarify, sensing that Thomas thought he was insinuating, and suddenly remembered a second time he and Thomas had been over familiar in their youth. 'Just when and where I need some normality.'

'I am flattered, Sir,' Thomas said with an uneasy smile. 'But if I may?'

'You can say what you want, Thomas. In these moments we are not viscount and footman, and nothing you can say will give me any cause for grievance at all. So, please, go on.'

'Very good, Sir. I was going to say that, surely, for yourself, normal is above stairs in the company of educated men. Not the likes of us. Still flattered though I am by your ardour.'

'I think the word is candour, Thomas.' Archer felt his cheeks redden. 'But you speak of educated?' He emphasised the last word with derision. 'The most highly educated men of my acquaintance are idiots when it comes to the needs of those less fortunate. That's not the kind of normal I crave. I want this. Just two old friends in conversation about all and everything with no distinction between us. Will you agree to my second eccentric request of the day?'

'Forgive me, Sir, but it doesn't seem right. Apart from anything else, I am not educated.'

'Oh, come on, man,' Archer challenged. 'Page two-hundred and twenty-one of Mrs Baker's dictionary?'

'My Lord?'

'I know you have been educating yourself and the housekeeper has been helping.'

Thomas had evidently remembered what particular word was on the page of that book, and was aflame with embarrassment. The word in question was "catamite". Mrs Baker had confided to Archer not long ago that Thomas' interest in the English language appeared to have stalled on certain words and their definitions. Archer told her not to fuss, it was quite normal, and she had been happy that the subject was not discussed further.

Archer smiled knowingly. 'I too studied Mrs Baker's dictionary, Thomas, and whether you do so out of a need to understand yourself, or just for morbid curiosity, it shows me that you want to better yourself, and it takes an educated man to accept that he needs bettering.'

Thomas was now confused.

'We'll leave that subject there,' Archer said. 'And once again, my apologies if I shock you, but you had best get used to that as the mission we are on will bring many more uncomfortable moments, of that I am sure.'

'Mission, Sir?'

'All will become clear in time. For now, are you happy to accept and sit here with me as yourself?'

Thomas blinked his long, blond lashes and considered the whisky, a treat usually only reserved for New Year's Eve. 'As you wish, Sir.'

'Then raise your glass to mine, Thomas, and forget for five minutes that you are my footman.'

They clinked their glasses, and Thomas copied his master in taking a sip.

'Thank you,' Archer said. 'We are just two men talking about your expedition to pick up a rent boy.'

For the second time that evening, Thomas spat alcohol across a table, and for the first time since he was thirteen, Archer laughed in the kitchen and found himself talking with Thomas on the same level.

'So, old friend,' he said, relishing the use of the word and Thomas' still-glowing cheeks. 'Tell me what happened.'

# *Six*

Weak sunlight struggled through a crusty window, and for Silas, the morning brought rare comfort. He was woken by unfamiliarity in the form of a dry mattress and warm blanket. Along with them came a more familiar feel, that of Fecks, spooned in from behind with a leg and an arm holding him close. Fecks' breathing was light and through his mouth, where he made an inward sucking sound followed by a soft moan. His breath smelt of stale alcohol which mixed with the smell of damp beneath the eaves.

This was about as good as waking up could be for Silas, and he lay peacefully in Fecks' friendship enjoying it, but expecting Molly to appear through the curtain at any moment and throw them out. He lay innocently stroking his friend's arm until a clock struck the hour, and, realising they had slept until eleven, wondered why Molly had not already evicted them.

'Fecks,' he whispered, pushing back against the man to wake him. 'Oi, Fecker, we've got to get up.'

Fecker mumbled something in his native tongue, but even before he opened his eyes, sensed that he needed to be moving. He rolled onto his back, releasing Silas who got up to use the piss pot.

When he came back to the bed, Fecks was sitting on the edge rubbing his face with his mighty hands, his mightier erection peaking at the front of his long johns. Silas had long learned that Fecks was not talkative in the mornings, and they dressed in silence. As usual, food was the first thing on their minds as they descended the creaking, narrow stairs to the ground floor.

'What time d'you call this?' Molly complained when she saw them. A couple of drunks were seeking a place to sleep after finishing their night shift at the meat market, and she was fending them off.

'You should've kicked us out,' Silas answered, searching the table where she sometimes kept cachous to freshen her breath.

'Nah.' Molly said. 'I did look in on yer, but you was sleeping like them babes in the wood, and I couldn't bring meself to chuck ya.' She kicked the drunks into the yard.

'You've got a heart of gold there, Molly,' Silas laughed.

'But teeth are wooden,' Fecks mumbled as they passed her.

'What's he saying?'

'Wishing you a good day is all.'

Silas poked his head into the rope-room just in case there was anyone about who owed him a favour, a copper, or something to eat, but there was nothing in there except empty benches and the familiar smell of the unwashed.

'My arse.' Molly booted one of the drunks trying to re-enter and hurried Fecks outside. 'Not renting tags 'til later,' she told Silas.

'That's alright, Mol. I won't be needing one tonight.'

It wasn't until they had used the last of Silas' money to buy a loaf of bread and some milk, and were devouring it in the relative warmth of the baker's doorway that Fecker was awake enough to ask, 'Why you don't need rope?'

Silas had expected the question and had used the time to weigh his concerns against his intrigue, and the dangers against the benefits of accepting Thomas' proposition. He repeated to Fecks what he had told him the previous night, but which Fecker had forgotten, because he'd been inebriated, and his friend listened intently to the story. Silas had said he would give Thomas a decision that night, and he intended to keep that promise out of decency.

'You say what?' Fecks asked, passing the milk bottle. 'You go?'

'Yeah, I think I am,' Silas admitted. 'I want to know what it's about, the bloke I spoke to seemed legitimate. I didn't get a bad feeling, you know?'

Fecker shrugged. 'If you want go, we go. I don't mind.'

'We? Sorry, mate, it was only me he wanted.'

'No. This is not so.'

'It is so, you bloody Russian arse. You weren't there.'

'I make never-mind. I am from Ukraine.'

'*The* Ukraine,' Silas corrected. 'If that's what it's called now. Either way, you're still Russian.'

'Nyet,' Fecks insisted, using the crust of the loaf to clean between his teeth before eating it. 'You not go alone.'

'They only want a man who looks like their drawing. You don't.'

'Why do I care?'

'This toff will. They won't let you in the carriage.'

'You don't go in carriage. Not safe.'

'Wish I'd not told you now,' Silas mumbled. 'I'd just got used to the idea I was going to do it, now you're putting me off.'

'Good.'

'Not good. I ain't going to have another busy day like yesterday, they only come along once in a blue moon, and if I got the choice between hanging off Molly's rope or being entertained in a gentleman's house, I know what I should choose.'

'You don't go to houses.'

'Yeah, I did say that, but I've changed my mind.'

'I drink.' Fecks took the milk bottle, noted the level, drank exactly half and passed it back. 'For you.'

'Thanks. Anyway, what are you doing today?'

'No work. I go to baths. I wash. I come with you tonight.'

'No, Fecks, you fecking fecker, I told you...'

'And I tell you this. You go alone, you get yourself dead. I go with you, or you don't go.'

'You're not my lord and master, mate.' Although he found Fecker's concern touching, he was only his best friend and not his mam. Silas could protect himself, he was savvy and hadn't just fallen off the potato cart.

'Nyet, I am not master,' Fecks agreed. 'But you are only friend and no use dead. Four boys, Banyak. More maybe.' He shook his head and looked sideways at Silas from beneath his shaggy fringe, drawing a finger across his throat. 'You make them take me with you.'

'I'll share the money when I get back.'

'This I know. But I worry for you.'

'Don't.'

Silas' insistence that he go alone got the better of Fecker, and he stood, angry. 'You don't care,' he accused bitterly. 'You don't care what happen to you.'

'I'll be fine. I got the luck a the Irish.'

'Which you isn't, and is not point. You disappear, what happens to me? You don't care. "Oh, Andrej," you say. "You are only friend. I love you." But is only when you drink, or when you want fucked. I love you too much to fuck you. You are not trade.'

He sat heavily, and sulking, snatched the loaf from Silas' hands.

Silas had heard this before, and it always confused him. He'd never understood how Fecks could appear so outwardly manly and yet talk without embarrassment about love, particularly of another man. Theirs wasn't sensual love, he reminded himself, no matter how much he wanted it to be.

As they ate in silence, a paper seller trod the opposite pavement, calling his sensational headline. 'Fourth victim of the Ripper,' he shouted. 'Carnage terrifies East End.'

'This is old news,' Fecks grumbled, and he was correct.

'And miswritten,' Silas noted. 'Carnage doesn't spread terror. The act of creating it does.'

'You too clever to be rent,' Fecks decided. 'But you go alone, you be tomorrow's news.'

'There's nothing I can do about it, Fecks.'

'You take me, and I let you suck big cock from Ukraine.'

'Ha!' Silas laughed. 'I've done that before.' He had, but only during paid-for sessions, and each time Fecker's reluctance had been so apparent Silas felt terrible about it.

'This time I let you suck,' Fecks said, 'because I prove you are my friend.'

'You turning queer on me there, Fecks?'

'I not queer. I'm from…'

'Yeah, I know.' Silas sighed. 'Fecks, mate, you know that If I still had one, I'd sell my mam so you and I could live clean and quiet in fresh air away from this shit. Who knows? Maybe tonight could be the start of me making a fortune. Loads of boys go to the houses of gentlemen. There's that one over Cleaver Street the messenger boys rent at. Molly's family's got that one down Limedock, and what about Jimmy-the-Nob? Got a house and a wife now, afforded by his visits to toffs in their own homes. No-one's been found dead at any Lord Snotalot's house that I've heard of.'

'No. They die in prison when policeman catch them and toffs go free.'

Whatever excuse Silas could think of as a reason to go, Fecks would find a reason why he shouldn't and a good one too. It was reassuring to be cared for in this way, but Fecker's well-placed concern caged Silas' optimism, and he didn't want to end up resenting his friend, because he was trying to protect him. This was why he shied away from what most people called love, it was far too complicated. He loved Fecks for sure, but as the Ukrainian constantly pointed out, it was friend-love only. Love and sex were two different things, and although Silas could perform sex at the pop of a buttoned fly, when it came to sharing feelings and emotions with another, his guts churned.

The only way to settle this was to make Fecks an offer.

'I tell you what, mate,' he said as he watched the paper seller amble away, fighting off urchins who tried to tamper with his money tin. 'You be with me at six, and I'll ask them, but I can tell you they'll say no.'

Fecks considered this, staring at Silas and chewing. He nodded, swallowed and pulled Silas to him, keeping him tightly locked beneath his arm.

'This we do,' he decreed. 'But, if I get the bad feeling, you stay.'

'We'll see.'

The embrace tightened. 'Nyet. I see first. If okay feeling, I go with you. If okay feeling, but only you...' He waggled his head and scowled. 'Maybe. But bad feeling, no going by no-one.'

'And I still get to suck your cock?'

'Who knows,' Fecks said. 'Maybe I let you sit on it.'

'Now you're just teasing.'

Fecks laughed and kissed Silas' hair before pushing him away. The matter was settled.


Which was more that could be said for Viscount Clearwater as he paced the drawing room waiting for Lady Marshall to react.

'I hope that was not too graphic a description for you, Dolly,' he prompted, turning at the window to retrace his steps. 'But you did insist on honesty.'

Lady Marshall, a grand galleon of fashion, rose from her chair, a billowing cloud of maroon velvet pinched at the middle but voluminous in the bustle. She was a rakish woman who hid her slight frame behind lashings of material that rustled obediently around her, only settling when she did, and even then taking its time to deflate. Her Ladyship wore a mix of the decade's styles having recently thrown off the shackles of her grandmother's time, the crinoline skirt, to replace it with a French bustle and corset that would have guillotined anyone else's waist. She was a patron of the arts and numbered many painters and writers in her wardrobe of glamorous accessories. She supported the struggling and the oppressed, but, ironically, drew the line at actors.

She faced Archer across the room, her expression halting him in his tracks.

'You're bringing one here, Archie?' she asked. 'To Clearwater?'

'I can hardly go there.'

She took a pace towards him in a fashion reminiscent of his nanny bearing the slipper, her narrow eyes marvelling at his stupidity.

'I understand,' she said. 'But here?'

'I will be quite safe, Dolly,' he assured her. 'I have fought for my country.'

'I know that,' she replied, taking another step, one slender arm snaking into a fold of her dress. 'My husband pinned enough medals on you to attest to that.' She withdrew from somewhere secret and satin a pair of mechanical lorgnette and pressed a button to release the lenses. She held them to her face and scrutinised the viscount, drawing near until she had found her focus. He waited patiently, trying not to smirk. She did this often, and it was for show. It was her way of reminding him that whereas he had inherited his title, hers had been awarded to her in her own right, a most unusual honour.

After taking a deep breath that swelled her bosom and ambitiously tested her stays, she let it out with an unladylike guffaw.

'You're going to send Tripp to an early grave,' she said, clicking the lorgnette closed. 'I wish you had invited me to be present when you informed him.'

'It was mildly amusing.'

'You sound like a bad review of a good tragedy,' she said before spinning on her heels and throwing herself dramatically at the mercy of the settee. 'Oh, Archie! What am I to do with you?'

'It will all be above board and perfectly respectable,' he promised.

'The young man, should he acquiesce, will be brought to the tradesman's door, and I will meet him below stairs. Tripp will be nearby, and I shall have Thomas with me. I shall interview the youth as privately as possible for his sake, and when I have learnt all he can tell me, I will see to it that he is given a decent consideration for his time. I'll instruct Mrs Baker to feed him too if he wishes. He shall be gone from the house after a few hours, and I can assure you, no-one else in the street will see him come and go. Even if they do, there is nothing flouncy or effeminate about this young man, so Thomas tells me. He could easily pass for a sweep, Thomas says, or any apprentice come to be interviewed…'

'You're boring me now,' Her Ladyship declared. 'Except for your enthusiastic repetition of Thomas as if he was your lover.'

'I cannot help the imaginings of your fancy, Your Ladyship,' Archer teased. 'You know how I am, but I know how I must be. Now then!' He clapped his hands to change the subject. 'Now that you know my plan and my intention, and have come to realise there is nothing you can do about either, shall I offer you a sherry?'

'Heaven's no. Filthy. Do you have Absinth?' She grinned hopefully from where she reclined. 'I rather fell in love with it in Paris when travelling with my niece. Sadly, it didn't agree with her, but her spell at the infirmary gave me time away from disapproval to nurture a taste.'

Archer crossed the room to the fireplace. 'Perhaps in the dining room. I can ask Thom… the footman to see if any can be found.'

'Don't trouble Thomas,' Her Ladyship said. 'I am sure he is troubled enough by your intentions.'

'I have no intentions towards Thomas,' Archer exclaimed in mock outrage. 'Except to train him to take over from Tripp if the fossil ever retires.'

The sprawling swathe of fabric shimmered with laughter. 'We are wicked,' she said, enjoying the naughtiness. 'There's nowhere else in this city I can be so frolicsome and listen to such talk, but your mother would berate me for not pulling you up on the way you speak about your servants behind their backs.'

'Only Tripp,' Archer said, as if it excused him.

He tugged the bell-pull and noted the time. 'Luncheon will be served in five minutes.'

'Oh, then I shall wait.' Her Ladyship pulled herself upright. 'The eon of time between now and alcohol will enhance the flavour of your champagne. We really must talk about what we are to do with your endowment,' she said. 'Were you thinking of a home for these unfortunate boys? Or a hospital? It must be something lasting, we know that cash donations will only be squandered, and it must be well run. Have you spoken with Quill?'

Archer waited for her questions to fall into line in his head before constructing a reply.

'I shan't address the precise nature of what our trust will afford,' he said, 'until I have interviewed at least one boy with experience. That way I can learn first-hand what is needed, what they think would be best for them. As for Benji Quill, yes, I have had an informal chat with him, and he is prepared to assist with his medical expertise should it be required. I was mooting the idea of a clinic. Somewhere the boys can go for treatment and learn about nutrition, perhaps hygiene, health and… so on.'

'My word, must we now call you Saint Archie?' Her Ladyship joked. 'But very sensible. I am happy you know what you are doing, apart perhaps, from this evening's promised escapade, should your chosen sewer rat know what acquiesce means.'

'Now it's me who should be telling you off, Dolly. If we are to help these unfortunates, we should start by not referring to them as rats.'

'I think rats are quite lovable,' she said.

'Until they bite you, or pass on the plague.'

'That's a good word,' Her Ladyship decreed. 'It is a plague. Not the boys themselves, the squalor that confines them. It is against that we must rage, but not to the detriment of the good name of your family or your title. Once again, dear boy, be cautious.' She took his hands in hers in a motherly fashion. She was old enough to be his parent, but they behaved with each other like siblings despite Lady Marshall being thirty years older. 'I know that you have a predilection for men,' she said, as if it was the most natural thing in the world. 'And that bothers me not one bit. But, I have seen your heart given away and returned damaged on at least one previous occasion that I fear it will soon cease to function.'

He knew what she was referring to, and the tragedy of that time burned in his mind like acid as his stomach lurched.

'I was young then, Dolly.'

'You still are, but you are not as young as you think. Your father's death landed responsibility upon you, and although you are now master of your own fortune, you must address the unpalatable fact that you are required to sire an heir.'

Archer had heard this before. 'You are not here to discuss that,' he said, squeezing her fingers and letting them go. 'We are here to talk business.'

'I only reiterate what I have iterated before,' she insisted. 'You have a big heart set on a noble cause, but you are a man, and we all know how men are. Don't let your base instincts cloud your judgement. If you are serious about your mission, you will apply your favours to every young man who works the streets and alleyways, and not only the one who matches the drawing of your ideal.'

She knew him too well, and he regretted showing her the sketch. It sounded not only foolish but also perverse to specify who he wanted to meet according to appearance when he had publicly set out to help all street boys. On the other hand, he had the wherewithal to make up his own rules.

'The trouble with youth,' Lady Marshall said, 'is that it wastes itself on itself.'

Whatever lecture she was about to give was made to wait. Thomas arrived to answer the bell-pull and announce lunch.

Archer took her Ladyship's gloved arm, and they fell in behind Thomas who led them silently across the hall to the dining room.

'I have to say, however,' Lady Marshall whispered when the footman was out of earshot. 'I can see why you should want to elevate Thomas. If I had a penis, it would no doubt elevate in his presence.'

'Now you really are being naughty,' Archer replied, and unable to hold back, laughed his way to the head of the table.

# Seven

Silas spent the afternoon at the public baths where religious fanatics offered cold showers and crusts of bread in return for a lecture on the sins of the flesh. The mention of flesh increased Silas' resolve to find some, and Fecks complained that if they were going to talk about temptation and gin, they should at least give out some free samples so he could see what the fuss was about.

They kept their positive spirits alive by bathing in their clothes, as time and clean water were limited, and stayed to sing a hymn with their hosts, mouthing rude words as they scoured the congregation for potential tricks. They found none and left the baths slightly cleaner, less hungry, but still as spiritually unfulfilled.

Later in the day, the drizzle stopped, and the temperature warmed, bringing with it a fog that thickened across the East End as if trying to hide its depravity. It failed. Debauchery simply moved inside the brothels and molly houses where only those with money could attend. This left the likes of Silas and Fecker outside in the murky dusk at the mercy of the unseen Ripper and his knife.

The alley seemed darker as they cut through to Cheap Street, and the lanes were unnaturally subdued. The eerie quiet wasn't out of respect for the lame and the dying. The wealthy passed by hurriedly in pairs. The barrow boys carted their unsolds efficiently, but without song, and there were fewer beggars to be seen. Shopkeepers boarded their window against the talk of unrest. In Saddle Square, where until recently Silas would have found the recesses and hidden doorways safe places for business, he now saw gaping voids. Where they had offered frolic and florin, tonight they promised a free ticket to the morgue's marble slab.

'There's something in the air,' he said as they walked through Greychurch to The Ten Bells. 'It's like the lull before the storm.'

Fecker's opinion was expressed in a grunt and a shrug.

It was noisier at the pub. They arrived as the Christ's Church clock struck six, and saw the smart, half-hooded trap on the far side of the street, its lanterns glowing fiercely against the gathering gloom. Two figures sat huddled in the driver's seat; the older man shrunk into his cloak and the younger fighting off the attentions of whores.

'This is them?' Fecker asked, holding Silas back.

'That's them,' Silas replied, moisture dripping from the end of his nose. 'Talk about standing out like a spare prick at a tart's wedding.'

'I do talking.'

'Well, you could, mate,' Silas laughed. 'But we'd be here all night.'

'Is good. Is safer.'

'Oh, come on you old grandma, stop fussing.'

Silas crossed over with a mixture of trepidation and excitement. His ideal would be for him and Fecks to ride in the trap, be delivered to a grand house in the west, given dinner, warmth and money while discovering what this charade was about, and then being allowed to spend the night in a proper bed with the redhead waiting on them in more ways than one. He suspected that all Fecks was interested in was the food, money and the possibility of a good fight if things turned ugly.

As they approached the carriage, the older man, Tripp, peeked out at them and, oddly, his wizened face alleviated any fears Silas had that he was being led into danger. Tripp was clearly not ecstatic to be there and scowled disapprovingly at Fecks, but he was every inch a man's man and had about him an air of watchful experience.

The sight of Thomas stepping expertly down from the trap stirred the more accustomed quiver of sexual tension, but Silas reminded himself he was not being invited for work. He was attending a gentleman who only wanted to talk. It didn't matter either way. The chance to travel in such a carriage was a break in his routine and one that only twenty-four hours ago he would never have dreamt possible.

'Who's this?' Thomas asked as the tails of his Inverness coat slithered down the steps behind him.

'My best mate, Andrej,' Silas replied, using Feck's real name as it seemed more appropriate. 'He wants to come with me.'

Thomas' head snapped back to Silas. 'You are to come alone.'

'I come, or Banyak don't,' Feck grunted.

'I'm sorry?' Thomas looked at Silas for a translation.

'He wants to come with me,' he repeated. 'For protection.'

'Against what?'

'How we know your trap is not trap?' Fecks said, stepping closer to Thomas and threatening him back a pace.

'The trap is… What?' Thomas glanced up to Tripp who shook his head vehemently. 'This is no trap,' Thomas continued and opened the door.

'Oh, that's plush.' A woman in poorly applied lip colour said as she nosed inside.

'Madam, please remove yourself,' Tripp barked from above. 'All of you. We are not interested in you.'

'Get 'im!' the working girl cackled, appealing to her comrades for support. 'Come over 'ere from up west in their fancy carriage. An arse is an arse, you bloody shitten-prick.' She aimed that at a horrified Tripp.

'Oi, Ruby, you dryshite,' Silas shouted in his strongest Irish accent. 'Get a your fecking gin and keep your snout out-a me business.'

'Ain't no toff going a find much to sport with on you, you scut,' the girl spat back. 'Don't see the point of a cock on a lickarse pup as yerself.'

'Ah, go feck yourself you culchie luder, you don't even know a gent when he sits a your face.'

'Feckin' want some a this you piss-head ponce?'

Fecker grabbed her by the scruff of the neck and threw her away from Silas, who turned to Thomas, smiling pleasantly.

'You have my apologies, Tommy,' he said as if nothing had happened. 'I shan't address your master in such a fashion. Now, are we taking my mate here? Or are we leaving you and Tripp to the mercy of these…' He rounded on the woman now being held at arms-length by a grimacing Fecks. 'Diseased-addled pot-boilers?'

'I think we should leave,' Tripp squeaked from the safety of the driving bench. 'Thomas? At once.'

'Not without my mate,' Silas insisted.

'His Lordship was adamant…'

'Oh, now it's His Lordship!' The Irish girl, having been dropped in an ungainly heap by Fecks, was scrambling to her feet, her inebriated condition numbing her body, but fuelling her tongue. 'Fecking waste of space, sitting in their fine 'ouses while we go dying in the shit.'

A gang of street boys, attracted to the diversion being caused by several angry whores, brought beer bottles, and punters heading for The Ten Bells took an interest.

The sense of simmering tension that Silas had breathed in Greychurch during the day was fast approaching boiling, and from the corner of his eye, he saw two bobbies approaching cautiously, batons at the ready.

'We need to go, Tommy,' he warned. 'This is going to get ugly very fast. Let Andrej come, he can always wait outside.'

'Yes, you're right,' Thomas said, relieved that a decision had been made. 'You there, Russian lad, get in.'

'What are you doing, Payne?' Tripp yapped, his fear causing him to forget himself and use Thomas' surname, thereby elevating him to an almost equal status.

'Saving our arses by the looks of it,' Thomas whispered to Silas as he ushered Fecker into the trap.

'And what a fine arse I bet yours is.' Silas winked, and couldn't help but relish the blanched look of confusion on the footman's face.

The carriage rocked under Fecker's weight as he clambered aboard. The crowd pressed closer, making their anger plain in threats and complaints that the rich used their streets as a playground, but, 'Do sod all about the Ripper.' Someone grabbed at Thomas' coat as he mounted the step, yanking him to the ground.

The gang of youths closed in on him. One smashed a bottle on the carriage wheel, inspiring the rest.

'Slash the bastard.'

'Cut that pretty face into a doily,' a woman encouraged.

'I'll fuck his arse with it,' the youth sneered, gripping the bottle tighter. 'See how he likes it.'

Thomas screamed as a sea of angry faces rained hate. He tried to stand, but a filthy boot pinned him to the stones.

'Get your fucking bootshoes off a me master's coat,' he shouted, but it only made the boys laugh louder.

Silas was half out of the carriage and kicking away the closest of the mob when the trap rocked. Fecker clambered into the front seat, grabbed the whip from Tripp's hand and standing high over the crowd, flailed it, cracking it across the face of the boy wielding the broken bottle. The lad screamed, dropped his weapon and lurched away, blood spurting from his cheek.

Silas leapt from the step, aiming his foot at the man standing on Thomas. He sent him flying, grabbed Thomas' lapels, and hauled him to his feet. Another crack of the whip snapped over their heads, and he bundled the trembling man into the back and shouted, 'Go!'

The horse reared and whinnied, its front legs blasting away those caught in its path. Panicked, it lurched forward, throwing Silas and Thomas to the floor. Fecker cracked the whip above its head, and the animal shuddered into a canter nearly overturning the carriage as it took the corner.

Silas had landed uncomfortably on Thomas who was struggling to right himself.

'There ain't room… Hang on.' Silas contained Thomas' flapping arms and pinned them over his head.

At being held, Thomas' panic dissolved, and he realised where he was. He looked at Silas pressing down on him, and it took a moment to understand what position they were in.

'Release me,' he ordered, but his voice cracked, and he squeaked like a mouse.

Silas sniggered.

'This is not funny.'

'You've got to laugh, man.'

He shifted his legs, only a little, but enough to snuggle his crotch directly over Thomas'. Even through the overcoat and their trousers, his cock reacted.

Thomas must have felt it, or imagined it, either way, he apparently dreaded it. He began fighting back.

'If His Lordship's carriage is damaged…' he complained, but stopped when he discovered the only way to push against Silas was with his hips, and that was what the street boy wanted. 'I was only meant to bring you.'

'Well, now we can have a cosy foursome, can't we?' Silas grinned.

'You're disgusting. Get off me.'

Thomas rolled onto his front when Silas released his wrists, but found the position worse. Somehow Silas had slipped between his legs and would have been buggering him were it not for his master's coat. Silas sniggered in his ear, but pushed himself to his knees, and with a little more jostling, they separated and sat.

'This is most irregular!' Tripp bellowed from the front.

He twisted in his seat, holding his hat against the wind and backed by fast-moving streams of mist coming and going beneath the streetlamps.

'Boy, tell this foreigner to slow the horse.'

Silas was impressed with Tripp's forcefulness and, panting from the recent excitement, shouted up to Fecker.

'Oi, Fecks! Slower, mate.'

Fecker whooped with exhilaration and whipped the horse into a faster frenzy.

'He's still learning English,' Silas apologised through his cheeky grin. Fecker had been brought up with horses and when he fled his homeland, had ridden all the way.

Tripp crossed himself and turned to face front where, unless he was flapping at Fecker to slow down, he maintained a firm grip of the front rail for the next few miles.

This left Silas alone in the back, semi-covered by the carriage hood, and pressed close to the handsome footman. Thomas had his hands splayed over his lap like a portcullis protecting the crown jewels and stared ahead at Tripp's back. With each sway of a corner, or jolt of a hoof-scraping stop, Silas found an opportunity to press against Thomas, or reach out and grab his knee for support. On each occasion, Thomas pushed him away, returning his hands to his lap and tightening his coat.

Silas had had enough fun and thought it was time to stop teasing the man. The trap slowed as they passed through the cleaner, better-lit streets of the west and the steady rhythm of a gentle trot lulled its passengers. Fecker soon tired of the monotony and handed the reins to Tripp who accepted them graciously. Now in charge, he straightened his back and scrutinised the road ahead. He was only ruffled when Fecker hung his legs over the handrail and slouched in the seat, but soon found it a game to pull the horse to a halt without warning, thus sending the tall blond slipping from the bench and into the well, his legs upright.

The further they travelled, the more Silas' apprehension returned. The trouble at the Bells, which he thought of as an every-day nothing, and the speed at which Fecks had made their escape had been enjoyable, because it diverted his mind from the possibilities ahead. He was either on his way to good earnings, or he was being led to the slaughterhouse.

The fog thickened, dulling the sound of the horse's hooves and Tripp's voice when he announced they were nearly at their destination and should address their appearance. Silas watched the grand house as they passed. Wide steps led up to a porched entrance of grey stone where a brass knocker clung to sturdy doors. Beyond them lay warmth and comfort, wealth and safety, and Silas wondered if he would find any of those things tonight.

Archer, meanwhile, had caused much discussion below stairs, firstly by appearing in the servants' hall, and secondly by informing Mrs Baker that the maids, the cook and the housekeeper herself were to take the evening off. Mrs Baker, as always, was dressed in black, her grey hair pulled savagely back from her powdered face. Despite being caught off guard with her feet up before the kitchen fire, the housekeeper was impeccably calm about the order.

'No-one is in trouble, Mrs Baker,' Archer said standing in the doorway, marvelling at the amount of work being undertaken by the servants in order to make his dinner. 'And I don't mean to upset your routine, Cook, but if you can find your way home, or to your rooms, ladies, or to anywhere, by six, I would greatly appreciate it.'

'Certainly, My Lord,' Mrs Baker agreed, immediately turning her attention to a contingency plan. 'Are you dining out? If so, Cook can easily hold tonight's preparations over for tomorrow.'

Cook was not happy at this decision, and her angular face said so. Open-mouthed, she brushed a wooden spoon over the table, a battleground of pastry, vegetables and a skinned rabbit.

'That's kind, Mrs Baker,' Archer said. 'And once again, apologies, Mrs Flintwich.' He avoided the cook's eye. He had always been wary of her. She was his mother's appointment from years ago when his father had said it was unwise to hire a thin cook because they obviously never tasted what they made.

'On your stomach be it, Sir,' the cook drawled in her northern accent, and set about organising Lucy to clear the kitchen.

Archer took Mrs Baker aside and explained there would likely be disruption to the house routine that evening. Glad of some free time, the housekeeper eventually retired to her rooms at the front of the basement, reminding him that she would be available if required. He had time for Mrs Baker, she was rarely flustered, always professional and yet had something maternal about her. She was a far cry from Tripp, but their chalk and cheese characters worked efficiently, and that was what mattered.

Archer was in his study turning the pages in his portfolio when he heard a carriage in the street. Parting the drapes, he saw his trap swirling fog at its wheels as it turned into the side alley that led to the mews. It was a fleeting glimpse and seen through a misty haze, but he was sure Tripp was at the reins and that the man beside him was not Thomas.

His pulse quickened as he fiddled with his clothes. There had been two shapes in the back. One of them was Thomas and the other wearing the same kind of peaked cap. This had to be a street boy, perhaps even two brought here and agreeable to his interview. Even if these boys did not resemble his drawing, as long as they had experience of life in the East End, he would derive benefit from the visit.

As the Honourable Archer Riddington, he had faced naval skirmishes, dignitaries and tribesmen from the Indies. He had led strategy debates at Greenwich, run cannon drill at Dartmouth and stood before Admirals in defence of his crewmen. His experience of meeting lords, politicians and royalty dated back to his days in the nursery, and on all of these occasions, he had not been as nervous as he was now. He drained his wine glass and tidied his waistcoat. The fire was burning, and the table lamps created patches of warm light that glinted on the gold lettering of many books. The desk was angled to face the double doors, and he had at first, thought that he should be behind it when his boy was brought to him; it would remind the lad of his station. Later, he remembered how he had felt when called to the headmaster's study at prep school, and changed his mind. He wanted this boy to trust him and to subject him to that kind of belittling introduction was not likely to win his favour.

'All in good time,' he said checking his collar in the mirror. 'Patience captures all.'

He passed through the drawing room to the hall and stood on his side of the green baize door. It, like the hall's panelling, was oak. The baize was on the servants' side. Once again, he was crossing a line but this time, in more ways than one. He imagined Lady Marshall egging him on while his father growled threats and warnings from heaven above, or more likely, hell below.

He glanced to a dark and sombre portrait on the stairs. 'I have no choice, Father,' he said. 'If lives are to be saved, lives are to be changed.'

With that, he swung open the door and stepped over the threshold.

# Eight

Thomas stabled the horse with the un-asked for assistance of the cumbersome Ukrainian, while Silas was made to wait in the carriage. When Tripp was satisfied that the animal was well bedded, he addressed Silas with a click of his fingers and ordered him out. Gravel crunched beneath his feet as he followed the others to a door set in the back of a house that towered over his head. Craning his neck, the brickwork faded into darkness before it reached the roof.

'Pay attention.' Tripp gathered them in the porch. 'I will inform His Lordship that you are here.' He spoke to Silas. 'You will both wash your face and hands in the scullery and ensure your shoes are clean. Thomas will escort you to the servants' hall where you will await His Lordship.' He turned to Fecker. 'You will remain outside.'

'Nyet,' said Fecker. 'I stay with Banyak.'

'Are you insinuating against His Lordship?' Tripp blustered. 'How dare you insult a man of honour.'

'Oi, keep you skiddies on, Tripp,' Silas said, wading in. 'Me mate is worried about me safety, that's all.'

'And you only speak when you're spoken to,' Thomas ordered.

'Oh, sorry I saved you from a beating, Ginger,' Silas sneered like a child. 'No, don't mention it.'

'I go with Banyak, or we feck off.'

'And we shall have none of that kind of language from either of you,' Tripp insisted. 'Very well. The foreigner can wait in the kitchen, and Thomas can explain his presence. Now, check your shoes, all of you.'

Silas liked to learn, and his mother encouraged him to take what lessons he could, going without new shoes, so she could pay for them. Scraping his own worn boots reminded him of her, and he wondered what she would make of all this.

'Get your hand off the wall,' Thomas barked and knocked the arm Silas had been using for balance.

It hurt, but he said nothing. It was entertaining to watch Thomas' behaviour. Inquisitive at first but after finding himself body to body with the renter in the trap, angry. Was he annoyed with Silas for holding him down, or with himself for enjoying it? Either way, Silas thought Thomas needed shaking up, and he looked for an opportunity to get his own back for his mistreatment.

Passing inspection by Tripp, they were led into a short passage of closed doors, past a hatstand and into a cavern. At least, that's what it felt like. The ceiling was arched and high, and the walls tiled. The far wall was taken up by a recess that housed a fireplace and ovens, a row of barred windows lined the top of another and beneath these stood huge dressers displaying pans that glinted the colour of Thomas' hair. It was all set around a massive table with a central avenue of jars lined regimentally from one end to the other. It was hard not to swear in awe, and it suddenly occurred to Silas that he was warm. It was the first time in weeks.

He was made to wash his hands in a sink and do what he could to tidy his face and hair while Thomas stood over him and Fecks waited for his turn. It took Silas a full five minutes to scrape the crud from beneath his fingernails. Luckily for him, the kitchen smelt of pie and herbs, and it masked the smell of his clothes. He was grateful that he'd not been made to take his shoes off.

Thomas gave Fecks instructions to wash and wait at the table before he beckoned Silas to follow him through to another room.

'You pissed off with me, Tommy?' Silas asked, when they were alone in the servants' hall.

'Do not speak until you are…'

'Yeah, I heard you.'

Silas helped himself to a chair at another long, worn table, but Thomas told him to stay standing facing a passageway and a staircase.

'I thought we got along fine last night,' Silas said, doing as he was told, but choosing to stand directly beside Thomas and close.

'Be quiet.' Thomas took a step forward and away.

'Your dick was happy to say hello.'

'I said, be quiet.' It was more of a hiss than a sentence.

'Why you being mean to me, Tommy?' Silas inched closer.

'Please, shut up.' Thomas took another step.

Silas caught up. 'At this rate we'll be in the front garden by the time you tell me what's pissing you off. Is it 'cos you fancy me?'

'Be quiet.'

'Or is it 'cos you find my kind… What was the word? Disgusting.'

'Shut up,' Thomas insisted. 'Now kindly…' He was interrupted by a sensation completely new to him and gasped. 'Get your hand off my backside.'

'Want it on your cock instead?'

Silas slid his hand towards the front of Thomas' trousers, but the footman turned on him, grabbed him by the throat and held him against the sideboard, rattling crockery.

'What are you playing at?' Thomas whispered through gritted teeth.

Unconcerned by the hold Thomas had, Silas grinned. A swift kneeing and the man would be in agony, but instead of raising his leg, he raised his hand and cupped Thomas' crotch.

The footman's green eyes bored into him, and their anger intensified.

'Why are you doing this?' Thomas pleaded. His cock was hardening, his cheeks flaming, and his grip tightened.

'What do you want?' Silas croaked.

He searched Thomas' face, but found no answer. He didn't want to hurt the man, he just wanted to know where he stood, but there was only one way out. Silas pulled Thomas to him by his cock and pressed their mouths together with a clash of teeth.

'Oh.' Fecker appeared in the doorway. 'I hear noise, but it is only you fucking.'

Thomas immediately released Silas and pushed himself away. He straightened his hair and wrestled with the front of his trousers.

'You safe, Banyak?'

'Go on with you, I'm fine,' Silas said, gasping for air as he stared hard at Thomas.

'I wait in here.' Fecks returned to the kitchen and Thomas returned to being a footman.

'You are His Lordship's guest,' he said with great restraint. 'You will not behave like that again.'

'Thought you'd like it, Tommy.'

'And stop calling me that, you guttersnipe.'

Whatever Silas had been trying to achieve, he forgot about it when footsteps overhead suggested Fecks had intervened just in time. Sexually charged though he was, Silas stood behind Thomas and left him alone. It was only fair.

Whoever was coming was taking their time, and the footsteps stopped at the top of the stairs where a muffled discussion took place. It gave Silas time to clear his thoughts, but it was in vain. He couldn't move them on from Thomas, what had just happened and how it left him trembling. Where had the need to kiss him come from? He thought that he had picked up from Thomas a possibility of something new, perhaps something physical that was outside his normal boundary of sex for money. Thomas had potential for... for what?

Silas was confused. Maybe he wanted more than sex, but he had Fecks for companionship, he didn't need anything else. Thomas was someone new, an unknown quantity and gave an impression of being amenable to Silas' advances, but what did that all mean? What was this incomprehensible longing gnawing his insides? It wasn't just physical attraction to other men, it went deeper and was far more disturbing. The conundrum occupied him until the mumbling upstairs stopped, and Thomas stood to attention. The click of the footman's heels broke Silas' thoughts.

He looked up into the eyes of the most striking man he had ever seen and, at that moment, knew his life would never be the same.

The viscount was the same height as Thomas, an inch or two taller than Silas, but he seemed larger. His clothes were a surprise. Silas had expected shining gold and silver, but he wore plain, white breeches, buttoned over at the front, with silk slippers on his feet. A cream waistcoat began at his middle and spread to broad shoulders, parting to reveal a shirt with no collar whose sleeves barely constrained the muscles beneath. The man's costume might have given him the appearance of a soldier, had he not been in the process of adding to the uniform a long, black smoking jacket on which was embroidered gold dragons. He left it casually open at the front, rubbed his hands together and held one out.

'Viscount Clearwater,' he said.

Although he had taken in the man's body in a heartbeat, the face deserved a more studied approach. The soft chin, prominent cheekbones and shadowing of stubble showing a white scar on his jawbone were captivating enough, but it was the eyes that Silas could not let go. They were brown, compassionate and glistened in the gaslight.

Thomas, who Silas had instantly forgotten, clicked his fingers and Silas pulled himself together. He had let his guard down again, but this time felt no remorse. Somehow he knew he was to be well treated.

He thrust forward his hand but was not close enough to reach the viscount's.

'You may step forward,' Thomas whispered.

Silas did, and his hand was grasped before he had a chance to put his foot down.

'It's so good of you to come,' the viscount enthused, pumping Silas' arm. 'I've sent Mr Tripp to his rooms for the evening, Thomas,' he went on without pause. 'It wasn't easy, but it means you are in charge. Good Lord! Did you have an accident?'

His hand was finally released, but Silas wasn't sure who the man was talking to. He remembered Thomas' command and kept his mouth shut. He had thought that he would meet an old duffer, effeminately dressed and easy to manipulate, but his assumption had been wrong. The viscount wasn't much older than Thomas, was just as fit, and had left Silas' legs trembling. His presence had sucked Silas' confidence, leaving him too empty to speak.

'A skirmish, My Lord,' Thomas replied. 'I apologise if my appearance is a little off, and I shall pay for any repairs necessary to your coat.'

'Last of my worries.' The viscount dismissed the offer and, to Silas' surprise, took Thomas by the shoulder and led him to a chair. 'Sit there,' he said. 'And tell me where Mrs Baker keeps whatever she uses on scrapes.'

'It's nothing, Sir,' Thomas insisted as he was gently pushed into a chair. 'I shall attend to it.'

'Easy, Thomas,' was the viscount's reply. 'It's one of *those* times.'

Silas didn't know what that meant, but the words unnerved the footman who smiled weakly, swallowed and pointed to the dresser.

His Lordship fiddled in several drawers while Thomas related the story of the unrest and the journey, and Silas waited, irked that the footman had made no mention of Fecks in their escape.

The viscount returned to Thomas and handed him a bottle and a cloth.

'Are you injured?' he asked, and Silas realised he was being spoken to.

'No, Sir.'

'If you're sure, good, but let me have another look at you.'

Being examined was strangely stimulating, and Silas wondered if slaves sold at market had felt the same. A weird combination of apprehension and excitement. He was sure they wouldn't have experienced the same growing interest in their would-be master as he did.

'It's remarkable, Thomas,' the viscount said. 'So similar to my drawing.'

'I thought so, Sir. Oh...' Thomas stopped administering to himself and stood. 'I must inform you that we were forced to bring another street... another young man with us. He is waiting in the kitchen.'

'I was going to ask,' the viscount said, heading that way. 'I saw the trap come by. Hello?' he called, and a second later Fecks appeared, filling the doorway.

His greatcoat reached the floor a long distance from his shoulders which were covered by hair left uncut for a year. Silas was concerned that the viscount would feel threatened by Feck's bulk as most people were, but if he was, he showed no signs of it. Quite the opposite. He shook Feck's hand as if they had known each other for years and showed him into the room. Seating Fecker, he indicated that Silas should take the opposite chair.

'Tell me your names,' the viscount beamed, clasping his hands on the table when they were seated.

His affability left no excuse for falsehood, and Silas gave his real name, something he never did at a first meeting.

'And you?'

'People call me Fecker.'

'Why is that?' His Lordship enquired.

'I feck hard with big cock.'

Thomas coughed angrily, to which Fecks gave one of his noncommittal shrugs, but the smile the viscount had applied to his lips remained. His dark eyelashes flickered, and he narrowed his stare towards Silas.

'His name is Andrej,' Silas said as if it explained anything.

'Thank you. And you are of Irish descent.' His Lordship sat back, folded his arms and thought. 'I can hear it, but you have a second-hand accent.' He held up a finger as Silas opened his mouth to give him the story. 'I would hazard that one or both of your parents were Irish, but you were brought up… Tell me your name again?'

'Silas Hawkins.'

'You were brought up in the north-west. Westerpool, I should say, or nearby. What are you? Twenty-three? Four?'

'You are right about the accent, Sir, but I'm twenty in two weeks.'

'I am sorry,' His Lordship said. 'Perhaps it is your hair that makes you appear older. I understand it must be difficult to find good barbering in your…'

Silas would have forgiven him for saying poverty, because it was true. The viscount was as unused to entertaining a street boy as Silas was out of place in his house, even the kitchen.

'It's alright, Sir,' he said. 'You're right. We don't have money for food half the time, let alone barbers. Now, if you don't mind me getting down to it, we'd both be happy to know what we're doing here, only me mate there thinks it's for sex, but Tommy says you only want to talk.'

The viscount was unphased by Silas' directness, in fact, he appeared reassured by it. He paused Silas with his finger again and addressed Fecks.

'You're from the Ukraine area of Russia. Am I correct?'

Fecker beamed with delight. 'Da!'

'South, perhaps, and I am looking at your stature rather than your accent. Let me guess at Odessa, or nearby.'

Fecks was amazed for a second, but fell suddenly serious, if not a little scared. 'How you know this? You gypsy?'

'Come on, Fecks,' Silas said. 'You can talk better English than that. Show some respect to the gentleman.'

Thomas looked at him in surprise and, Silas thought with a little admiration.

84

'Sorry, Lord,' Fecks said, lowering his head in shame. 'I am not education like you.'

'Let's get over this divide right now,' the viscount sighed. 'Andrej, I can tell where you are from, only because I have been fortunate enough to travel there, to the Black Sea mainly, and I know they build fine figures of men. Your language skills, considering your position, are to be applauded, and thank you for taking the trouble to converse with me in my own tongue. Silas, you are more of a mystery, and I imagine you feel intimidated. The reason for this is simple. Thomas, or more likely, Tripp, has told you to ask no questions and yet has told you none of my intentions.'

He spoke fluently, and his tone was reassuring. Within a sentence Silas found himself admiring the man. The unusual attraction he had for Thomas — the need for something more than just a grapple of his dick — shifted to the viscount and intensified. The man commanded the room just by being in it and filled it with his good nature. He was handsome for sure and would have been a prize for any street boy, but the moment Silas thought of him as a potential trick, he knew the viscount was above that and, more worryingly, he knew that he didn't want to see the man as just another shilling in his pocket.

He had no more time to ponder what that meant because His Lordship continued.

'The lack of information concerning your visit is not the fault of my staff, but is mine alone,' he said. 'They are doing their duty, they have done it well, and I shall explain in time. Firstly, however, I am not one for distinctions when below stairs unless necessary, as Thomas may attest. It makes him uncomfortable to know this, but I hope he will adapt.' The last part was added with a smile at the footman, who while remaining po-faced, nodded. 'Which is my way of saying that I am aware you two live a wretched life whereas we don't. We couldn't be further apart, and you must both excuse me if I speak disrespectfully, or out of turn, or in ways that embarrass you. If I do, it is purely because this is a new experience for me, and I have no understanding of your lives. And that is the reason I asked you here.'

He had finished what he wanted to say and rose from his seat.

'What that all mean?' Fecker asked.

'He can't help being a snob,' Silas clarified.

'Do you mind!' Thomas was outraged, but the viscount was laughing. 'My Lord?'

'Disarm yourself, Thomas,' he said. 'The man is quite correct and much more succinct.' He turned at the dresser, holding a bottle of wine. 'If I may offer you gentlemen a drink, I will explain my purpose while we take it. What say you?'

In the dumfounded pause that followed, Fecker's stomach rumbled, mimicking the sound of a passing carriage, but he showed no awkwardness.

'And after,' the viscount said, a smile breaking on his face. 'We shall eat.'

# Nine

Archer fell into a state of ecstatic confusion the moment he saw the street boy waiting in the servant's hall. His attire was what he had expected. Boots without laces and the sole of one flapping at the toe when he moved his feet. Trousers threadbare at the knees and a roughly-made, woollen coat long in the arms. Beneath this, he wore a black scarf tucked in at the lapels. The costume gave him bulk and a stocky appearance, but the jutting cheekbones and the scrawniness of his neck indicated that this man had no fat on him.

'Viscount Clearwater.' He offered his hand, wanting to demonstrate from the outset that he was amiably disposed to his guest, but the hand was ignored. The man appeared lost in some thought, no doubt bewildered by his surroundings. The hiatus in the formality should have been impolite, but instead, Archer was amused, and the pause allowed him a moment to study the face.

The likeness to his sketch was remarkable. The dark hair, voluminous and to his shoulders, was understandably not well cared for and parted on one side. It was tucked behind a pair of elfish ears, virtually pointed and at right angles to his face. His eyes were blue, where Archer had imagined green, but the mouth had just the right amount of upturn to match the drawing. His posture and his countenance warned he was no fool, but the overall impression was of vulnerability. He was, in a word, perfect.

'You may step forward,' Thomas whispered.

Archer's hand was shaken by a smaller, rougher one than his own but with a strength that returned his enthusiasm. His body made an unexpected connection between the skin of the man's palm and the front of Archer's breeches. The rush of adrenaline caused him to grip more firmly, and he swallowed, aware that his knees had weakened.

He reminded himself of the etiquette expected and greeted his guest before explaining to Thomas the absence of Tripp. The normality of talking to a servant was reassuring in an otherwise extraordinary situation, and he was grateful for the footman's presence.

Archer intended this meeting to be informal, but that didn't stop him being polite. After he had seen to Thomas' scrape and heard the outrageous story of the incident in Greychurch, and even after the shock of the six-foot Russian, to whom he took an instant liking, Archer treated them as if they were above-stairs guests. He was well-bred, a fact of which he reminded himself each time his eyes lingered too long on Silas, captivated by the man's positive energy.

By the time he had seated them and offered wine, he had an insane desire to take his guests upstairs, have them washed and clothed and, afterwards, treat them as he would any other visitor of his own status. A ridiculous notion for the security aspect alone.

As soon as he saw the street boy, he longed to be allowed to know Silas more intimately, both cerebrally and physically. Silas was his perfect match and, perversely, to know him physically would have been easy and almost acceptable. Plenty of men in society were homosexual, one only had to ask their wives, and to engage the services of a male prostitute, although illegal, was less of a sin than a gentleman being seen to generally associate with someone of a lower class as if that person was his equal.

Class, social standing, education, finance, location, there were so many reasons the two were expected not to mix, but the division came down to one uncontrollable fact true of all humanity; the randomness of birth. Were it not for the chance of a myriad of ancestral couplings, Archer could have been standing in Silas' boots. Why, then, was it so wrong for the viscount to want to help the man?

That was a debate for another day. Tonight, he must concentrate on the outward purpose of this unusual meeting, his charity. By doing so, he might be able to ignore his churning emotions and stirring breeches when he looked upon Silas' alluring features. He must see the man as a professional, there to be interviewed.

With that in mind, he set the wine before them and poured.

'I'd rather not, My Lord,' his footman said.

'Oh, come on, Thomas. You're not in your livery,' Archer cajoled. He was hoping for a smile and to see Thomas relax, but the footman was in a complex mood. 'Are you in shock from your earlier trouble? If so, a drink will help.'

'No, Sir.'

Thomas shifted in his seat, his arms folded tightly against his chest, his eyes darting to Silas beneath furrowed brows. Archer assumed it was because he didn't approve of the street boy's presence.

'Thomas,' he said. 'I insist. Consider it an order that you take a drink with our guests, and that you remember our conversation of last night. We are not viscount and footman right now. We are hosts, entertaining two gentlemen who can be of use to me. No matter our circumstances, Thomas, I hope we remain men of manners.'

He had employed a tone borrowed from the captain of his training ship. "The man had a way of charming one while metaphorically kicking one in the scrotum," Benji Quill had remarked of him only last week, and it was an accurate description. It was also a device which worked on Thomas, and although he continued to glance untrustingly at Silas, he did accept his drink and, along with the street boy, sipped politely when Archer did.

'Za zdorovja!' The tall blond, however, downed his in one and slammed down the glass.

Archer produced a notebook and a pencil from his waistcoat and arranged them on the table.

'Gentlemen,' he began. 'My reason for inviting you here is quite simple and above board. Let me get to the point. I am in the process of creating a trust, a charitable body to help a particular section of society. To the alarm of many, but the approval of enough, I have chosen...' He faltered.

In meetings and letters, he had referred to those he wanted to assist as street-rats, which was a far kinder term than others in use by his peers, but one he had, only today, spoken against. He had been thinking he would be meeting a street boy, but Silas looked older than his nineteen years, and the Ukrainian was far from a boy. Male prostitutes was too clinical a term, and mollies too "gutter".

'I'm terribly sorry,' he said. 'How do you refer to yourselves?'

Fecker didn't understand the question, but Silas was astute. 'Billy and Fecks,' he said.

Was that quick-wittedness or insolence?

'I meant, what is the title of your profession?'

'Ah, I see.' Silas grinned. 'Fecker's a labourer when there's work, but I'm a renter all day and night.'

Again, Archer found the man's directness refreshing. The only other person he knew to be so forthright was Lady Marshall, and he had always found her a welcome antidote to the dullest of social occasions.

'So you call yourselves renters, do you?' he asked. 'When working the streets?'

'No,' Silas replied. 'I call myself Billy, least until I get to trust a man, then I let him know my real name.'

'And what does it take you to trust a man?'

'At least a two-shilling wank and a reciprocated sucking.'

Archer had been taking notes, but his pencil refused to write after 'Two-shilling', and he thought it best not to jot every word.

'Reciprocated?' he queried with as much calm as he could muster. The image of Silas sucking his cock flashed before his eyes. 'Did you mean something else?'

'I've has some schooling,' Silas said and winked.

It was not insolence, Archer decided, simply the way the man was.

'I don't mean to patronise,' he said. 'As I explained, your life is not something I understand. To rectify that, as I must if I am to assist you and other… renters, I need you to tell me of your experiences.'

Thomas sucked in air which, as Archer shot him a look, became a stifled yawn followed by an apology.

'In as much detail as possible,' Archer emphasised. 'Despite Thomas' veiled protestations.'

'I'll be as honest as you want me to be, Sir,' Silas said. 'But first I'd like to know what you got planned for us.'

'Planned?'

'Yeah. As in, are we just going to chatter, then you put us back on the street with this glass of grape as payment? Or is our visit to be a regular thing? 'Cos it's going to take me a fair few hours to give

90

you all the details of last month on the street, let alone four years.'

'Four years? Since you were sixteen?'

'Been longer for Fecks, but different circumstances. He wanted to make money on top of his job 'cos they don't pay labourers much, especially when they're fourteen like he was.'

'You mean he does it for fun?' Archer was wide-eyed.

'No. I do it for fun,' Silas clarified. 'Sort of. Fecks does it 'cos he can. He's got sought-after… equipment and he doesn't care where he puts it. Though he'd prefer a woman's… front than a man's arse, he's not bothered if there's money in it. Me? I'm one-way only. Man-to-man at work or at leisure.'

The terminology reminded Archer of his early days at prep school, but the admission of homosexuality was alien.

'And you make this publicly known?' he asked, shocked but intrigued.

'If anyone asks. Don't you?'

'That's enough!' Thomas shot to his feet. 'How dare you accuse His Lordship of being a…'

'Oh, do sit down, Tripp,' Archer moaned. 'I mean Thomas, sorry. Just sit.'

Thomas sat, visibly trembling, and Archer thought it best not to answer the renter's question. He might appear trustworthy, but during his years on the streets he would have learned many tricks, and deception was probably the first.

'Let's talk about those experiences,' he said, pouring Thomas more wine. 'What can you tell me of your life as a young working man? Start with where you operate.'

Silas told his story with generous detail which at times, turned Archer's stomach. This was when he described his living conditions and the sanitary arrangements of those around him. He was keen to point out that he was not a vagrant and had only slept beneath bridges and arches on the rarest of occasions. These were times when he had not 'pulled a trick' or 'found an interesting gentleman,' and Archer gained the impression that the man worked methodically. He took opportunity when it came his way, but otherwise he was the kind of person Mrs Baker could have tutored in bookkeeping. It wasn't always possible, but Silas tried to ensure he had his rent money first, anything from a few coppers for a night on the rope

— which sounded monstrous — or a shilling or more for a decent shared room. His next income was saved for sustenance, and anything after that was for luxuries such as an hour at the baths, or a drink in a public house. He also made it clear that whatever he made was shared with Fecker.

'You make an hour at the bathhouse and a drink in a pub sound pleasant enough,' Archer said. 'I imagine, however, it is the opposite.'

'Not always,' Silas admitted. He sipped his wine in a civil manner whereas Fecker was tapping his fingers on his empty glass and keeping his eyes fixed on the bottle. 'It's like everything else, Sir. When it's busy the water gets dirty really quick and stinks, but then you get to see a lot more cock and there's more chance of pulling a trick. When it's quiet, it's the only place I feel clean, but I spend more on the wash than I make out of the other bathers, if you get what I mean. As for the pub, it's the same thing. The likes of me, Sir, we don't go to The Ten Bells or the Lamb and Compass to make hoity conversation or mates like some do. We go to look for trade, scrounge a drink and learn the backtalk, the gossip. It's a good way of finding out where the bobbies are plodding, or what brothel's been raided, who's out for your blood and who's paying for arse, get me?'

The conversation continued in this honest, rough fashion and Archer found himself adjusting to the language to the point of acceptance. By the time Silas had told him about the places he had sex, he was almost nonchalant about the details, a fact that surprised and delighted the viscount.

After an hour, when Fecker's growling stomach became too much of a distraction, Archer waited for Silas to finish a tale, and rose from his chair.

'I think we should rest there,' he said. 'For a while. I would very much like to talk about my plans, so that you may give me your opinion on them, but first, I believe Cook left us some supper, er, Thomas?'

'Indeed, Sir.' Thomas scrambled to his feet.

'Slowly, man,' Archer laughed. 'Just tell me where it is, and I'll bring it.'

'I am sorry, Sir.' Thomas blanched. 'But I will not have His Lordship waiting on me in the servants' hall.'

'Will not, Thomas?' Archer affected a stern expression, but underneath he was touched by the footman's loyalty.

'Yes, Sir. Will not.' Thomas stood his ground. 'Unless you order me to do so, in which case, of course, I shall oblige. I only inform you of my view because you have invited me to be honest.'

'And because you want to?' Archer probed. ' I assume you don't often get the chance to voice your opinions down here.'

'I do not, Sir, and that is how it should be.'

'But do you not find it refreshing?'

Thomas wavered for a moment before summoning his nerve. 'I do, Sir, and I thank you for the opportunity, unusual though it is.'

'And do you not also find it liberating?' Archer persisted. He could tell from the footman's expression that he did. 'Then come and talk with me in the pantry while we dig for whatever buried treasure has been left for us there.'

'Perhaps the… guests would feel more comfortable eating in the kitchen,' Thomas suggested.

'You mean you don't trust them to be left alone in here? Thomas, you sound more like Tripp as the minutes pass.' Archer turned to Silas and Fecker. 'Thomas is actually quite right,' he apologised. 'Please don't take it as a sign of mistrust on our part, it's the way things have to be done.'

Silas' chair scraped on the tiles as he stood. 'Your Lordship,' he said. 'You've already shown us more trust on first meeting than any other man, and we are not in a position to refuse.'

He spoke so eloquently, Archer imagined he had been in service himself. He asked the question, but received a negative reply to which Silas added, 'I'm just a good mimic, Sir. In speaking as well as behaving. It helps, see?'

'Helps?'

Silas explained. 'Say if I'm meeting a proper gent, I put on manners like whores put on rouge.' He slipped into an East End accent. 'Unless a gent's after a dirty gutter-oik to treat 'im rough the way 'e likes it, Mister.' He switched to an innocent, pathetic voice, batted his eyes and said, 'Or unless Sir decides I am a lazy pupil who deserves the headmaster's cane.' Before Archer could react, he was a cheeky Irishman. 'Excepting when I be straight off the boat and in need of a fatherly hand in your fair city, there.' Returning to the voice Archer was accustomed to, he completed his performance with, 'But most of the time, I'm a lad who's out for your loose change, and I'll be anything you want, seeing as that's the only way I get to eat. So, Sir, no, I've not been in service, but I admire men like Thomas who are.' The statement caused Thomas to appear the most shocked he had all evening. 'But I wouldn't want to live in his shoes, not unless I was employed by a kind gentleman such as yourself.'

'Thank you for your entertainment and flattery,' Archer said, impressed. 'Now, let us eat, and over supper, perhaps you can tell me what you think a charitable organisation might offer. Something that is sorely needed, but specifically for men like you. After that, I want you to tell me everything you know about certain locations in which I have a particular interest.'

'What's he say?' Fecker followed as the small party moved through into the kitchen.

'Wants to know the best brothels,' Silas translated, and Archer laughed aloud.

Supper consisted of a sumptuous pork pie and potatoes kept warm in the range, tomatoes, bread, cheese and an overwhelming pear tart to follow. Archer couldn't help but see the dessert as a subliminal message from his housekeeper that read, "This is what we could have been eating, but instead we have a cold tray in our rooms. Yours, with a hint of arsenic, Mrs Baker." He smiled at the thought, and at the sight of Thomas heating hot chocolate in a pan, his jacket off and his sleeves rolled.

The viscount's guests told him what they thought of his charitable idea as they devoured the meal in the manner of starving vultures. 'Very good of you, Sir. I'd need to think,' and 'Do you mean I can suggest anything?' had been Silas' first questions jabbered between mouthfuls of pie and swigs of beer. He had followed with, 'A lot of the boys ain't clean like me, don't know about washing after a shafting,' at which point Thomas had dropped his fork. The more his appetite was satisfied, the slower and more considered Silas' answers became until he rounded off by telling Archer that something medical for men would, in his opinion, be of most use.

It was a mature and enlightened idea, and Archer said so,

regretting it instantly for the way it showed he was still judging Silas. The man was nearly twenty. At that age Archer was a lieutenant on the Britannia and expected to make life or death decisions, why should he not expect the same amount of maturity from Silas? The man knew more hardships than Archer, he'd probably seen more danger. He had no right to judge him and resolved not to thereafter.

'The problem might be,' he said, having considered Silas' suggestion, 'how do we ensure it is used solely for renting boys? I mean,' he corrected himself. 'For boys who rent?'

'Which is why I said for men,' Silas grinned back, completely engaged in the conversation. 'There's places for women already, and there's places for both, though you're better off not going in a Russian social if you're not a Jew or a Jewish one if you're Irish. And no-one goes near the church missions excepting pissed up whores and them as should be in the bedlam. But I'm talking about two things.' He conducted his thoughts with his fork. 'One, a place where any man who ain't working can see a quack. Maybe it cost a penny, we can all scrounge that. I don't know how much a doc charges, of course, but that'd be where your money comes in. Ditto for number two. It ain't only a place for men to get treated, it's a place for them to learn. Now, I know you'll say that what if they don't want to, or they'll be too busy working, or that's what these schools are for and all that, but this is the clever bit. What you'll find is that most renters won't be bothered and won't use it. They're not ill, why d'they need to know about their health? They're alive, so there's no point. That's how they'll see it, get me?' He speared a slice of pear. 'So, what you'd get would be us renters looking for somewhere to go to keep dry, sleep, eat, have a night off, I don't know, but while we're there, someone tells us...' He was running out of steam. 'You know, helpful stuff.' He popped the pear slice in his mouth and smiled broadly as he chewed.

'You thought of all of that while you were eating a pork pie?' Thomas asked.

It was hard to tell if he said it with a sneer of doubt or amazement, but then Thomas was an enigma.

By way of reply, Silas carefully probed Thomas about his work and Archer was happy to let them talk, half listening while he reread his notes. He had been aware of the tension between the two as soon as he walked into the servants' hall, but it was lessening now, perhaps only because of the wine, food and warmth, but it was good to see. As they chatted quietly about a footman's role in the house, Archer thought it polite to engage the Ukrainian in conversation and put his book aside. The man seemed to understand English well enough, but was apparently not much good at speaking it.

That is until Archer bade him 'Good morning, young man. What a fine day,' in Russian, and Fecker upended his chair, springing defensively to his feet.

'Why the fuck do you tell me that, man? After I've had dinner with you and…?' Fecker realised he had given the game away. He was as fluent in English as anyone else around the table. He shrank back to his seat and sulked.

'Another master of disguise, eh?' Archer mused aloud. Rather than being outraged at the deception, he understood its purpose and couldn't help but admire Fecker more for keeping up the pretence. To survive on the streets, he decided, took a shrewdness few men possessed.

'Do you know what you just said, mate?' Fecker asked. He may have been fluent in English, but he was not so slick with his manners.

'I thought I had wished you a good morning and commented on the weather.'

'Oh, you said good morning… sort of,' Fecker explained. 'But then you wished a slow death. And you called me a girl.'

'My good man!' Archer exclaimed. 'I had no idea. I was taught the greeting by a Ukrainian man in Odessa. I humbly apologise.'

'Not Ukrainian.' Fecker wagged a finger. 'None of my people deceive like that. They were from Georgia.'

'You are all Russians to me.'

'Best leave it there, Your Lordship,' Silas intervened. 'It's a touchy subject.'

Archer was inclined to take his advice for fear of losing Fecker's trust. 'Once more my apologies,' he said, offering a hand. 'I don't mean to offend, but I am concerned. I made the same greeting to the Russian Ambassador last week.' He pulled a face. 'I had best send an explanation.'

Fecker laughed. 'Nyet, good for you,' he said before taking the hand, shaking it and folding his arms.

Diplomacy completed, Archer instructed Thomas to bring another bottle of claret from the hall which went some-way to cementing Ukrainian-British relations, and, when all four were once again seated, he prepared himself to move on to the third subject on his agenda.

'Gentlemen,' he said, adopting a sombre tone for the first time that evening. 'I would like you to tell me about four specific locations in your area if you would. Contrary to Mr Hawkins' earlier assessment, my interest has nothing to do with molly houses.'

'Oh?' Silas sat up, interested.

'No. I have no concern for them. I want you to tell me everything you know about the locations of the four Ripper murders that have so far taken place.'

'Why are you interested?' Fecker unfolded his arms and clenched his fists as if ready to pounce. 'And why do you say, so far?'

Archer wondered if he could trust Silas and his man with what he knew.

'Patience always wins,' he said and decided he would, for now, only tell them what they needed to know.

# Ten

The man was quick to be humble, fussed over his guests and allowed them the freedom to speak as themselves. Was that his nature, or was it an act? Silas hoped it was his nature. The more he looked at the viscount and the more he heard him speak, the more he was in tune with his ideas and believed him to be genuine. The more time he spent in the viscount's company, the more he admired him, and it wasn't only his good works that attracted Silas. There was also his physique, his face, the way his breeches bunched at the front when he sat and unashamedly outlined what lay beneath when he stood. He was sexier than the fascinating footman with attitude. Everything about him made its home under Silas' skin leaving him wanting more.

Of what?

They were never going to be friends despite the way the man treated him. They were probably never to meet again, and there was no way they could be social equals. That only left sex. If His Lordship wanted it, Silas was happy to give it, and for a man offering warmth and food, companionship and kindness, he would give it willingly, even for free.

Everything about the viscount suggested charm and perfection, and Silas' concerns quickly faded once he realised the man was keen to cross their social barriers and treat him as an equal as far as he could. Even Fecker had shed his distrust.

That was, until the viscount mentioned the Ripper.

Fecker tensed, and for a split second, Silas wondered if everything that had gone before had been a cover for a darker purpose; entrapment.

Why would someone in His Lordship's position be interested in the killing of street boys? If it was morbid fascination, he could read the newspapers. If he knew something about them, he could tell the police. How else could he be involved, and why would he want to be?

The moment of doubt passed with a silently exchanged agreement between Silas and Fecker. Viscount Clearwater was no threat. How could a man who treated street-rats as if they were gentlemen be anything but genuine?

'Have you both had enough to eat?' the viscount asked picking crumbs from the empty tart tray with his fingertips.

If Silas ate anything else, he would be sick and said so, but Thomas was asked to bring another loaf for Fecker who ate half and put the rest in his pocket for later. The viscount, of course, didn't object and instead, told him to also take the remaining cheese.

It was things like that Silas found so... He was unable to think of the word. It fell between attractive and perfection, and all he could come up with was lovable, but Silas would not allow himself to think of that subject, and concentrated on the man's business rather than his effect.

'What can we tell you that you've not already heard about?' Silas asked.

He was sweating beneath his jacket and wondered if he could take it off. The viscount had discarded his own, leaving it hanging from the chair, and was now in the process of unbuttoning his waistcoat. Although his shirt was filthy, Silas followed suit and took off his jacket enjoying the rare sensation of being warm without it.

'Firstly,' His Lordship said. 'Tell me a little about each murder.' He turned to a page in his book and read an address. 'Starting with the first at Harrington Street. What do you know of it?'

Silas told him what he could, that it was an ordinary row of bland, brick buildings, a dead-end behind a tenement block and mainly known as a place where female prostitutes took their clients.

'And did you know the unfortunate Edward Sellinge?' the viscount asked, checking the name.

Silas admitted he hadn't, and Fecker shook his head.

The viscount seemed disappointed. 'So, it was an ordinary street, but not one you would expect a renter to take a man?'

'As ordinary as any street in Limedock,' Silas said. 'The main road leads down to the wharves, but you could pass it without seeing it. It's a narrow opening that goes nowhere, used as the back way into the lodging houses, but most people use the front. That right, Fecks?'

Fecker agreed. 'Da. I only saw it after the boy was killed. Went to look, like many people. Not been back. Not our patch.'

'What made you take an interest in this murder?' His Lordship asked. 'I was under the impression that, horrific though it is to admit, death is commonplace in the East End.'

'And you'd be right, Sir,' Silas said. 'But it was what the Ripper did to the boy that got people heated up.' He hoped that His Lordship would not ask him to give details of the mutilations and was thankful when he already knew them.

'And the second?' he asked, turning another page. 'Simon's Yard. Martin Tucker was the lad's name.'

'Didn't know Martin well, Sir,' Silas told him. 'He was new, down from Westerpool like me and only off the boat a month. Someone told me he came straight to the city to find work, same as all of us, saw there was none and did what he had to do.'

'And you knew him?'

'In passing.'

'Did he know Edward Sellinge?'

'No idea, Sir. I doubt it. Not been in the East End long enough. Simon's Yard is about a mile from Harrington Street, and the only similar thing is that it's also a no-through. Draymen use it for their horses in the day, no-one uses it at night 'cos there's no lights.'

'When you say no-one, you mean no-one other than renters?'

'Nyet,' Fecker said. 'I don't think so. There's no lights, but there's windows of a whorehouse.'

'So it's not that private?'

'It's a brothel, Fecks,' Silas said. 'So the windows is mostly closed and curtains drawn. It's as private as anywhere, Sir, but 'cos it's right by the knocking shop, the lads tend to stay away. Again, not our territory, see? Of course, that lad, being new, might not have known that.'

The viscount was scribbling in his book. 'So, these first two murders committed… one month apart had, as far as you know, no connection other than the way the boys were butchered.'

'None of them do, My Lord,' Thomas said. 'The newspapers have said so.'

'The role of newspapers is to sell newspapers,' the viscount said. 'They can't be relied on for actual news, not from those who know what they are talking about.' He smiled at Silas. 'I would rather trust someone who understands the area than a hack with a brief to sell copy.'

Silas had a rough idea what he was getting at, and the man had managed to convey his meaning in a compliment which, along with the smile, quickened Silas' pulse.

'But your point is pertinent, Thomas,' His Lordship continued. 'As we will see from site number three. Two weeks later and we find a third horrific crime, worse than the others but with the same hallmark, and the body found in the rather mistitled Lucky Row. The victim, an even less fortunate youth by the name of Michael.'

'Micky-Nick.' Silas had known this boy and liked him. The mention of his name, which he knew was coming, brought sadness. 'Yeah, I knew Micky,' he sighed. 'Nice lad, only just seventeen. Experienced too. Micky and I used to drink at the Lamb and Compass and nick from Cheap Street market where we had a scam going. Only for a few weeks, Sir, I don't steal unless I have to. It was a bad time for us, 'cos the talk was still of Martin's murder, the butchery fresh in the mind if you like. Punters were wary.'

'Da,' Fecker agreed. 'I got work at the docks, so Banyak and I was alright. He only scammed with Micky-Nick to help him.'

'But it's interesting that you knew him. Oh, I'm not questioning you, Silas,' the viscount calmed Silas' confusion. 'I understand how a man might have to steal to live, and I am not judging you. But you actually knew this renter?'

'Well enough to like him.'

'I imagine you fall to liking people quite easily,' His Lordship said in a way that suggested Silas was required to answer.

'I usually make up my mind about someone within the first minute. Doesn't take me long to get the measure of a man,' he said and looked at Thomas. The footman, who had been watching him, suddenly found his cup of chocolate more interesting.

'And the boy's injuries, as reported by the papers, were accurate as far as you know?'

Silas didn't even want to think about what the killer did to his victims, but it was the reason he was here. 'Yes, Sir. Micky's throat was cut one side to the other, deep enough to show bone, and he'd been sliced from his throat to his dick.'

'And his insides messed up,' Fecker added, seemingly unaffected by the detail. 'He had things missing.'

Thomas groaned.

'I'm sorry, Thomas,' Archer said. 'If you'd rather not hear this?'

'My place is with you, Sir.' Thomas sounded even more like the old butler. 'I was brought up on a farm. I've known slaughter, although of a different kind.'

The viscount returned to his notes, satisfied that Thomas had the mettle to cope with the discussion.

'And the most recent murder,' he said opening a fourth page. 'Alexander Chiltern, aged eighteen by all accounts, no permanent address, known to be a heavy drinker, from an Irish immigrant family, found in Britannia Street in a worse condition than the others.'

'Can you be in a worse position than dead?' Silas asked. It was not meant to be an insult, but it came out that way.

'Quite,' His Lordship said. 'Was he a friend?'

'Of sorts,' Silas admitted. 'But by accident. People thought we looked similar and some got us mixed up.'

'Very the same,' Fecker slurred, tipsy.

'You looked similar?' The viscount sought clarification intently.

'We all look the same from behind in a back alley,' Silas said.

The viscount was briefly disturbed by his honesty. He grimaced and asked, 'What is Britannia Street?'

'A street like many others,' Silas explained. 'Narrow. Leads to Tanner's Yard from Merry Lane. Often used it for business on account of the alcoves between buildings. It's the sort of alley I'd expect a renter to use if he was working.'

'Expect to? Why? Because it's dark and out of the way?'

'Opposite, Sir. Because there are people about if you get in trouble, and there's a maze of even narrower runners… that's lanes, leading off it so you can get lost quick.'

'But no-one saw or heard anything? The same as in the other cases.'

'No-one *said* they heard or saw nothing,' Fecker pointed out. 'Don't mean that people don't know things.'

'But you don't know any more about any of these killings than you have told me?'

'No, Sir,' Silas said, mildly affronted. 'If we did, we'd say.'

'I believe him, Sir,' Thomas added. 'This young man is nothing if not direct.'

He flashed Silas a white-toothed smile, false and childish, which immediately twisted into a scowl. Whatever he was trying to convey it sailed over Silas' head to splat against the tiles.

'Cheers.' Silas replied as if he had been paid a compliment. 'Having said that, Sir. I expect we do know more, it's just that we try not to think about it. If you ask more questions, other stuff might come to mind, but I don't want you to think we're holding information back on purpose.'

'I don't. You are most helpful and, I believe as Thomas does, honest.'

'Then can I ask you something, Sir?'

'Certainly.'

'What's your interest? Are you something to do with the law?'

The viscount laughed. 'Heaven forbid,' he said and shared out the last of the wine. 'No, Silas, I have nothing to do with the law except I live within it as all men should. Perhaps we can recap.' He returned to his notes. 'Let's go back to Harrington Street...'

It was obvious from the change of subject that the viscount didn't want to talk about why he was interested. There was something the viscount wasn't telling them, but His Lordship's curiosity was a puzzle Silas didn't need to worry about. As he kept telling himself with sadness, he wouldn't see the man again after this visit, so there was no point wondering about the aristocrat's fascination. Silas was part of a wider picture, the state of the East End, and that was His Lordship's concern. He had, through the evening, asked more about the living conditions and the plight of the poor than he had so far asked about the Ripper.

The viscount ran through the known details of the murders once more, but they sparked no more memories for Silas. At one point, Fecker added some gory details that had not been released to the newspapers, facts that he had learned from eyewitnesses, and the viscount was amazed to hear that these had not been given to the police. He was outraged when Silas explained why.

'They don't talk to us,' he said. 'And we don't talk to them. No trust in either direction, so we ain't going to help uniforms what do no favours.'

'Well, that's a matter for the government, the Commissioner and another day.' The viscount closed his book. 'I fear I have kept you gentlemen from your business too long. What time is it, Thomas?'

'Approaching eleven, Sir,' Thomas said. He began gathering plates.

'I'll do that.'

'You most certainly will not.'

Silas laughed at the way he spoke. 'That told you,' he said, sharing a joke with his host.

The viscount was mildly taken aback and might have been annoyed, it was hard to tell as the moment was so fleeting. He did raise a smile, however, and it was followed by a wink that suggested he and Silas were co-conspirators in a plot against the footman. The wink was a surprise, but a greater shock came from what His Lordship said next.

'Where are we going to house you for the night?' He stood and buttoned his waistcoat considering Silas and Fecker in turn, while Thomas froze, plates in hand.

'House us?' Surely the man wasn't going to let them stay?

Thomas had the same thought, but where Silas was amazed at the prospect and wouldn't have put it past the man to offer them a room, Thomas was horrified and probably for the same reason.

'I shall drive them to the edge of Greychurch,' he said. 'That would be best for all concerned, Sir.'

The viscount sighed and rolled his eyes at Silas. This time, the familiarity was awkward. The aristocrat was poking fun at his footman, and Silas thought that was rude.

'Thomas,' he said. 'I do wish you'd get a grasp of things. I am not my late father, and you are not my butler. Please, try not to think like Tripp. Yes, the man is excellent in his capacity and has been good to us both. I mean no disrespect, but we here are all younger men than they. The world outside these walls needs to change, and it is my belief we should play a part in changing it.'

'But, My Lord…'

'I am not inciting anarchy,' the viscount interrupted with good humour. 'I am not suggesting that I invite you to my club, but I am hoping that, as I have repeatedly said, we could co-exist on less formal terms at times. That being said…'

He paced the table with his hands behind his back, and Silas was able to feast his eyes on the man's fine figure, particularly where his breeches buttoned. He looked at Thomas, also standing to attention, whose casual trousers gave little away of the bulk Silas knew to be inside. Fecker caught him looking and knew what he was imagining.

'That being said,' the viscount continued, standing behind Silas. 'We must behave like gentlemen, and I am not sending our guests back to the streets after they have been so generous with their insight.'

The viscount gripped Silas' shoulders, jolting him.

'These young men are staying here tonight.'

A kaleidoscope of images tumbled through Silas' mind. A grand staircase, a curtained bed, roaring fire, a bath, His Lordship inviting him into it, naked, his life changing…

'They can sleep in the mews.'

The vision shattered. A mews was better than nothing, and the man's hands were still on his shoulders. The touch, even through his coarse shirt, meant everything. He was prepared to touch Silas with no sexual intent. He treated them as guests.

'They could bed down with the horses, Sir.'

Whereas Thomas didn't.

'Certainly not. But the coachman's quarters are unoccupied.'

If not guests of equal status, then at least the level of servants. But would an aristocrat rest his hands a servant for so long?

'You've blanched somewhat, Thomas,' the viscount said, amused. 'Don't. You're not a snob. Of course they can use the coach house, it is equipped.'

'Would that be wise, Sir?'

The Viscount's hands, from being on the crest of Silas' shoulders, slid to hold them at the sides as if he meant to lift the street boy from his chair.

'If you're worried about what Tripp will say, don't be. Mrs Flintwich is the first to arrive in the morning, I will leave her a note, so she is not taken by surprise.' He leant to Silas, cheek to cheek and his grip tightened. 'You two sleep as long as you want. And be sure to use the bathtub if you would like.' He patted Silas' arms and finally let him go. 'You can't drive through this fog again, Thomas, you wouldn't be safe, and neither would they. No, this is what will happen.'

He continued his pacing as he spoke until he stood behind Fecker, looking directly at Silas.

'I shall put Mrs Flintwich's kitchen to rights while you show the gentlemen to their quarters and ensure they have a fire to warm water with, and plenty of bedding. That done, I will leave you to lock up, because I can see that our security is your main concern.' He did the same to Fecker as he had done to Silas, taking his shoulders and holding them while he spoke. 'When Silas and Andrej wake, they can knock at the tradesmen's door for breakfast before being sent on their way. I shall tell the staff the truth, not that it's their business. These men have been of assistance, and the peasouper is too thick for them to leave. You and Tripp will not elaborate, of course.'

He released Fecker and completed his circle to stand opposite Thomas. He looked at the footman challengingly, but spoke to the street-rats.

'You will accept this for your troubles, I hope,' he said, fingering coins onto the table. 'And I shall add a shilling, so you can take a cab in the morning. Is it a shilling to the East End, Thomas?'

'How would I know?' Thomas exclaimed, momentarily forgetting his position. He added a subservient, 'Sir.'

'I had better give you five, then every eventuality is covered.'

Silas couldn't believe it. 'Five shillings?' It was enough to keep him and Fecker in decent board and lodgings for a fortnight.

'Don't be ridiculous, Silas,' His Lordship chided. 'Five pounds.'

'Pounds?' Thomas was aghast.

'Yes.'

'My Lord, in a situation like this, Tripp would give the boys sixpence, perhaps, and they would be grateful. But five pounds?'

For the first time, Silas saw the viscount angry. Whatever odd relationship he had with Thomas it didn't allow for the servant to criticise.

The shock of being given five pounds hadn't even begun to sink

106

in when the viscount stunned Silas further in reaction to having his decision questioned.

'Five pounds,' he insisted, containing his anger within the gravity of his voice. 'Each.'

Thomas was silenced, and Fecker, his mouth open wide showing his uneven teeth, was too amazed to swear even in Russian.

'Don't worry, Thomas,' the viscount continued. 'I have the same in my pocket for you as I have for these two.'

He meant money, but of course, Silas couldn't help thinking of something else. Something he craved as much as the notes being drawn from the man's trousers.

'I will give you coins,' he explained, 'because I assume a note would arouse suspicion.'

Silas nodded his reply in astonished silence. A note would also be impossible to change, assuming he wasn't robbed of it the moment he stepped inside Greychurch.

'Then we are settled.' The viscount collected the glasses. 'Thank you for your time, gentlemen,' he said. 'Thomas will show you to your room. There's only the one bed, I'm afraid, but I can't let you sleep inside the house. It's not that I don't trust you. I hate to say it, but even allowing you to stay above the stables would be thought inconsiderate by many. Those who don't know you as I now do would accuse me of placing my staff and house in danger. It's ridiculous, but that's how it is. I am sorry, but the coach house is quiet enough.'

He indicated to Thomas that the evening was over and handed a collection of coins to Fecker who counted them into various pockets. With the enthusiasm of a man being led to the gallows, Thomas bowed and rolled down his sleeves.

Silas rose to put on his jacket.

'A quick word with you alone, before you retire,' the viscount stopped him, approaching with a similar collection of coins.

An older man coming towards him with money and wanting a "quick word" was something Silas faced most nights. He would need a wash first, but he was happy to let the viscount suck his dick in the kitchen, or, better, take him bent over the table. There was no end to what he would do and how much time he would give for five pounds.

'Silas,' the viscount said once Thomas had led Fecker from the room. 'I am worried about you, and I am certain you are the man I need to be worried about. Here, take this.'

Confused, Silas accepted the money and, like Fecker, hid it in secret places about his clothing.

'That was for tonight, but if you could, I would very much appreciate it if you would save enough for a return cab and come again tomorrow.'

There was to be no sex tonight. It made sense. The man had not been expecting Fecker.

'You don't need to ask twice, Sir. Anything you desire.' Silas replied, falling into his street urchin character. The viscount obviously had a thing for them.

'Good, but I think, from your tone, you have grabbed at the wrong end of the riding crop, as it were.'

Kinky sex? Not impossible, not for another five pounds.

'I want you to return tomorrow. Bring Andrej if you like. Come at five, because I have to go to the House in the morning and am seeing an old chum in the afternoon. Tripp will be expecting you — back door, sorry — and will have something for you to do before he brings you to me.'

This was getting weirder by the second, but Silas was fascinated. The viscount was an inch away, within touching distance.

'I don't mean to be clandestine, but that's all you need to know for now. Oh, and keep the evening free.'

As if Silas had a social diary to consider.

'As you want, Sir,' he stammered. 'Can I ask why?'

'Yes, of course.' The man held his shoulders again, and Silas swallowed, his throat dry. 'I want to show you something in my study.'

Riding crops, the study, an aristocrat and a street-rat? It was worthy of The Penny Magazine, but to take all evening and to involve Fecker?

'Shame I have to wait until tomorrow,' Silas winked flirtatiously. 'My arse could do with a proper thrashing.'

It would have worked on any other punter except Lord Clearwater. 'Don't be disgusting, man,' he said, his face reddening. 'I don't mean to have sex with you. I mean to save your life.'

# *Eleven*

Sleep, that unavoidable slice of death, did not come easily to
the men staying at Clearwater House. As the fog thickened
and hung, deadening voices and hooves outside, the lights
within the house faded to darkness one by one.

Thomas locked the basement doors and bolted them, inspected
the kitchen, ensured the windows were secure and closed the
shutters. Climbing the stairs and passing through the baize door,
he set about the nightly routine, his duties this evening augmented
by the absence of the butler and maids.

The footman, ill at ease without his livery, ensured the front
doors were locked and bolted and tidied the arrangement on
the circular hall table. He progressed through each room of the
ground floor closing shutters, drawing curtains, extinguishing oil
lamps, turning down the gas and guarding the dying fires. In the
drawing room, he tidied the cushions on the settees, straightened
a picture, put a footstool in its proper place and folded his master's
smoking jacket which, as was his custom, His Lordship had left
thrown over the back of an armchair. He looked into the library,
although it had not been used, and closed its double doors silently
before approaching the study where he knocked, uncertain as to
His Lordship's whereabouts. There was no reply.

The viscount was particular about this room above all others
and only permitted entrance in his presence unless it was to close
the house or clean the grate. The curtains were drawn, and the fire
had died, but even so, Thomas inspected the guard. He touched
none of the books that had been left scattered on tables and the
desk, seemingly in random order, but open at marked pages.
A copy of Black's travel guide for the north-west counties was
open at Westerpool, and beside it, a train timetable for the City
connections and a copy of the latest Baedeker for Holland and

Belgium, closed. A large map of the city covered the reading table beneath the window, and Thomas gave it a passing glance as he dimmed the chamber lamp before blowing out the flame, noting that four streets in the East End had been ringed in red. Seeing it brought back uncomfortable memories of the evening and he moved on to turn out the banker's lamp at the desk and replace the tantalus on the sideboard.

With the downstairs of the house secured, he climbed the main stairs, his footfall silent on the carpet until he came to the first floor where he approached the viscount's rooms. Light spilt from beneath the bedroom door, and Thomas wondered if he should knock. He had not been called for, and it was usually Mr Tripp's job to attend Lord Clearwater before the staff turned in, but the viscount had not exactly been playing by the rules recently.

He was lifting his knuckle to rap gently when the light beneath the door faded, and he knew he was not required. He continued along the corridor to the end. With no guests in the house and the Dowager Viscountess Clearwater away in the country, there were no other rooms to inspect. He collected a candle and let himself through the servants' door to the back stairs where he continued to his garret room above.

There were no signs of life under the eaves. Mr Tripp's door was firmly closed, and no sound came from within. The butler might have taken himself out for the evening, or he may have been asleep for hours, it was not Thomas' business, but he crept past, avoiding the boards that squeaked. The maids had their rooms beyond the dividing door, where only Mrs Baker and female members of staff were allowed, leaving Thomas alone beneath the roof to ponder on what had happened.

He stripped to his waist and washed at his nightstand, not wanting to wake Tripp by lighting the water heater in the bathroom. The water was cold, the hour was late, and Thomas' back ached from where he had been pulled from the carriage, but despite the physical trials of the night, it was a mental one that occupied him. He rested on the nightstand and spoke to himself in the mirror.

'What's going on wi' ye, Tom?' he whispered, speaking freely in the accent of his youth. He found it comforting. It grounded him and reminded him how far he had come in life. 'Look at where you

110

be compared to those wretches,' he said. 'Why ain't you trusting them, not even wi' a night a the stables?'

His reflection remained blank-faced until he found an answer.

'Truth be, Tom, you want a-trust a lot a things, right?'

He did. He wanted to emulate His Lordship and show compassion to those less fortunate. How could he not? But for the grace of God, he could have been one of them, although he had the fortune to be born elsewhere and to parents who wanted him to better himself beyond the mucking out of cow sheds and the herding of cattle. He supported his master in his endeavours and wanted to be utterly loyal to the man, but His Lordship had recently made it difficult.

''E only wants a-treat you well,' his reflection reasoned. 'Play 'is game and you'll be the next Mr Tripp.'

'Aye, I be playing along best I can,' he said. 'But 'e be wanting something more from me and I ain't sure I want a-give it.'

He studied his face, trying to see what others saw in him. He was just a country lad, barely educated, ginger and pale. Why was His Lordship apparently so attracted? Why had the street boy showed him so much attention? Why did anyone?

Was the viscount really after someone of his own age to talk to, as he had said? Did he want Thomas to be his escape from the constraints of his privileged life in pockets of time when they were alone?

Could Thomas be his servant one minute and his friend the next?

'That ain't my job,' he said, and towelled his face. 'We got nothing in common.'

He hung the towel neatly on its rail.

'Not strictly true,' his reflection challenged, and he knew it was right. 'When you going a-make up your mind?'

He answered himself with a questioning expression lit by the flickering candle. 'About the way His Lordship wants a-be wi' me, or about the other thing?'

'The other thing ain't something you got control over.'

He left the mirror and, alone with only his thoughts for company, he pulled back the counterpane and removed the rest of his clothes. He stood naked in his room lit by the candle. His pastel skin contained a healthy body. Farm work from an early age had moulded his muscles, the miles he walked daily within the house kept him trim despite Mrs Flintwich's attempts to fatten him, and the mind beneath his well-cut, auburn hair was sharpened with learning. What else could he offer, but a healthy body, commitment to his role, and loyalty?

'You just answered yourself,' he said as he put on his nightshirt and brought the candle to the bed. 'But it can't happen.'

Did he want it to? Even if it was possible, was that what Thomas was? Was that what the viscount was?

'You shouldn't be thinking that.'

No, he shouldn't, but he couldn't keep the thought from his mind and, trembling, he slipped into bed and pulled up the covers.

'There's stuff you been wanting a-do fur years,' he said, rolling over to face the candle. He watched the flame flicker in his breath. 'There's men not a hundred feet away who would do it wi' ye willingly if you'd only be honest wi' yourself.'

He sounded like his father telling him to stride out into the world and strive to be the best he could be, but he answered as his mother.

'Sleep on it,' he said and, wishing he had someone other than himself to talk to, he blew out the candle.

Archer sensed Thomas outside his door and turned down his reading lamp. A day ago, he might have called the footman in to at least bid him goodnight. It would have given him the chance to be alone with the man, something which always stirred his imagination. He would have asked Thomas to straighten the pelmet above the bed so that he reached up, drawing his livery trousers tightly at the front. Or he might have asked him to poke the fire, allowing him the opportunity of seeing the man from behind as he bent to the grate. He might have tried any number of tricks that Thomas was aware of and played along with in silent subservience, but, tonight, something had changed.

It wasn't that he didn't find Thomas attractive, he had since they were teenagers. It wasn't that he didn't know him well enough to trust him with his deepest secret; the man's loyalty was unquestionable, but even Thomas' loyalty might not stand the rigours of what Archer wanted. They had grown up together, but on either side of a baize barrier, a simple device that kept Archer from knowing someone who would have otherwise become a friend.

The man was on the other side of the bedroom door now, and all Archer need to do was call for him, invite him in and tell him what he needed. Thomas would do it, Archer had no doubt that he wanted to. He knew Thomas was the same as himself even if Thomas didn't, and he also knew that should he make any advance, he would not only embarrass the man, but would also destroy the friendship he was striving to nurture.

Wouldn't it be perfect, though? To call Thomas into the room, have him close the door, greet him with an embrace that led quickly to passionate kissing. To feel Thomas' bold cock in his hand and his mouth, know the taste of his lips, every inch of his smooth chest. Have Thomas lay him down, undress him with his fingers always so precise and delicate in their duties. To have Thomas administer to the rage between his legs, soft lips polishing his shaft and drawing him in deep. Thomas beneath him. Entering him as he gripped the sheets and moaned his pleasure while Archer drove his desire until he spent himself deep within the man. Connected, bound, desired, fairly giving Thomas the same pleasure in return.

How perfect would it be to fall asleep in another mans' arms knowing that when dawn came and the curtains were drawn on the cold, misty light of day, they could stay there, a fire burning in the grate and in their hearts?

It would be too perfect. It was as far beyond Archer's reach as it was beyond Thomas' loyalty. Besides, as much as he felt for Thomas, and their roles in life aside, someone else had appeared in Archer's life and brought with him an unexpected longing.

Thomas had moved on now, Archer heard the soft thud of the servants' door as it closed, and he was alone on his floor, in his bed with his cock demanding attention and his frustration demanding release.

To calm himself, he mulled over the information he had been given that evening, and the thoughts and images of Silas' life poured cold reality on his ardour. At least, they would have done had Silas not replaced Thomas so readily in Archer's imaginings.

'Ridiculous,' he said, trying to make himself comfortable in the excess of pillows and down.

Silas was too young, the wrong class, a working street boy here for the money, and he had no other interest in Archer but that.

He countered himself. The age was not a barrier. Silas was nearly twenty, not that what Archer desired would have been any less illegal with a man his own age, another man with a title, or simply with another man. The class barrier was immaterial, save for when the two might be seen together in public. The work was something Silas would be glad to give up in return for a life at Clearwater with Archer. But as what? A stable lad? The hall boy? Tripp said he needed one, the housekeeper insisted they could manage. He needed only one footman in the city house, and there were no other roles he could legitimately offer. And then there was the Ukrainian bodyguard.

Silas might appear street-clever and independent, but he was vulnerable. Beneath his unkempt hair and dirt-clogged clothes, his bravado and mimicry, he was a lost young man surviving day to day on chance. They all were, so why was Silas different?

It was something to do with the charge that had connected them when they shook hands. Archer felt it again when he touched the man's shoulders. He had not felt it with Andrej, proving to himself that there was something extraordinary about Silas. If only he hadn't thrown himself into his working-boy character and said those things about the riding crop and the study. Archer had no interest in that, but had lied when he said he wasn't interested in the man for sex. He was, but within the bounds of love.

Love?

His thoughts were not helping, and sleep was evasive. The mention of love, however, did go some way to settling his mind.

Thomas was strapping and sparked erotic thoughts, but these were superficial. Archer's attraction to Silas was more profound. If only he could discover if the man felt the same way… If only he could confide in Thomas…

He growled and turned, a headache beginning to trouble him, and reminded himself of his purpose. Not his charity. That would take care of itself in time, but the other, more desperate matter.

He lay awake running through dates and times, street names and facts until no more carriages passed the house, no more muffled footsteps disturbed the street, and the fire died in the grate. If he was wrong, he would be exposed as a laughing stock and his family name ridiculed. If he was right, he could save the lives of many men doomed to the streets of Greychurch.

Whatever the outcome, there was little time left to achieve it, but tonight, he had at least found the man he needed. In more ways than one.

The leafy borough surrounding Clearwater slept soundly and in comfort, blanketed by the dense fog. Streetlamps glowed through it like misty fireflies in the damp air, and nothing beneath them stirred. It settled across the city, a grey mass that swamped the river from the iron bridges in the west to the wharf cranes in the east where it anaesthetised the mournful groan of the dockland's foghorn.

In Greychurch, the homeless slept where they could, while dogs snuffled about them for scraps and lifted their legs on the inebriated. The lights of wharves and whorehouses, pubs and rope-rooms burned weakly behind grimy windows, and wet streets echoed with the footsteps of those seeking the fleeting warmth of a penny-whore of either sex.

Among the darkened recesses of Cutpurse Lane, where it tunnelled unlit beneath the Cheap Street depot, a darker form than the night around it waited and watched. Men had passed, unaware of its presence. Men lurching from the hazy comradeship of The Ten Bells to the stinking anonymity of the dosshouse. Men on the hunt for women or boys, their heads down, eyes alert and coins jangling shuffled past in silent guilt, lust giving their lives a purpose. The boys they sought prowled carefully, watching over their shoulders to find security in one of their own kind following.

He smelt them as they passed. The perfumes of the women, the oils of the businessmen's hair, the sweat of the dockers, but these were not the scents he sought. These were not the aromas of the whore-boys he was down on. Their flesh stank with the hellish stench of greed. Greed for other men, but not for him. Longing for companionship, but not with him. These others, these meaningless shapes of whore-boy bodies, had no time for him. They were the same as the one who had spurned him. They were as uncaring as the boy who once refused his attentions and snubbed his affection. They were as deserving of his knife as anyone, but they played their part in his work. A carefully planned and timed undertaking that would, with patience, rid him of the putrefying bile in his gut. He had taken great pains to see to it. As many pains as the whore-boys had suffered, fooled by their protector, the night. The shadow that hid them could also take them. He had, and he would again.

But not tonight.

The time and place had to be right and the sequence made obvious to the man who had stolen his love and replaced it with pain.

He would come. After all, death always favoured the weak.

# Twelve

The sound of an unfamiliar church bell and the sedate clop of well-trained horses on level streets drew Silas from the numbing depths of sleep. He was naked in a bed that didn't smell of someone else's piss, in a room that had a door, glass in the windows, and his head rested on the chest of a man he loved.

He had never woken this way before. Apart from being with Fecker who pushed him off and continued to snore, the experience was as new as it was welcome. He lay on his back, his hands behind his head and looked at the beamed ceiling.

'Even that's clean,' he said, running his palms over the cotton sheets until he connected with Fecker's firm thigh.

He rolled onto his side and dug his chin into Fecker's collarbone as he hugged him. His friend's hair still smelled of soap. Untangled, unmatted, it covered his face as Fecker lazily lifted his head.

'What?' he grunted. His head fell back into place, and the bed trembled on silent springs.

'We gotta get up, mate.' Silas nudged him with his hips, enjoying the press of his morning stiffness against Fecker's buttock.

'Why?' His mate sighed when Silas squeezed him, adding 'Fuck off,' when Silas rubbed suggestively against him.

'I don't know what time it is.'

'Who cares, Banyak?'

'We can't outstay our welcome.'

'Wait 'til they chuck us out.'

Silas shook him. 'Fecks, come on, man. He said we could have something to eat.'

'We got money. We buy what we want.'

Silas dug his fingers beneath Fecker's armpits and tickled him, but it only made him growl.

'You asked for it.'

He mounted his friend in one deft movement, pushing his knees between Fecker's legs and his stiff prick against the crack of his arse. Knowing it wasn't going to be a lengthy visit, he wrapped his arms beneath and clung on as Fecker pushed back and bucked angrily.

'You know you want me, you queer Russian,' Silas teased.

Fecker, being stronger by half, had no trouble pushing himself up on his hands and tipping Silas off. As soon as he hit the mattress, Fecker was over him. He caught Silas' hands and trapped them in his, straddled him and shuffled his way up so that his cock banged against Silas' chin.

'You know you want to, you queer Paddy,' he said, grinning playfully against Silas' protestations.

Silas pretended to bite his cock, but Fecker wouldn't let him anywhere near. He did, though, dump his heavy balls on Silas' chin before leaping nimbly from the bed and declaring his need to piss.

Silas heard him laugh as he half-filled a chamber pot in the next room from where he called, 'Hey, Banyak! Look at us. Yesterday not a pot to piss in. Today a whole bloody room.'

'Could get used to this, Fecks,' Silas replied.

He dragged himself from the playground of the bed and, as he stood, the misty morning beyond the window brought back reality. A more immediate reminder was the smell and feel of his street clothes hanging damp before the ashes of the fire.

Thomas had shown them the rooms speaking only to point out the necessities. After His Lordship's parting words, Silas' mind was too preoccupied to badger the footman for fun as they crossed the yard, but once he saw the accommodation, his only thoughts were for a warm bath. They had taken it in turns as the tub was barely big enough for Silas alone, and had rinsed their clothes in the water afterwards. His long johns were damp when he drew them on, but they were most mornings, and the only thing different about dressing that day was that they smelt more of soap than they did of stale sweat.

No, he thought as he buttoned his trousers, it's not the only thing. Everything was different about today. He was not dressing beside a tap in a shit-soaked yard, was one thing, the offer of a waiting free meal was another, and that was without the five pounds, the unsettling intrigue of the viscount's parting words and everything he had asked of Silas last evening. It all played through his mind while he waited for Fecker to dress, and although he thought about everything carefully, there remained a nag at the back of his head; something he hadn't yet placed.

He realised what it was as they left the coach house and crossed the yard to the back door.

He was also different. It wasn't the clean skin or the way Fecks had trimmed his hair with his pocket knife, and it wasn't even the fact that his boots were tied by string he had found in the stables. Apart from the scent of lavender, he was essentially the same on the outside as was yesterday. On the inside, however, he was changed.

As he approached the door, his enthusiasm for the day waned beneath trepidation. Being brought to the house had been exciting, particularly as it came with the benefit of a half-decent scrap outside the Bells. Excitement had given way to caution which in turn led to intrigue. Once the viscount had made it clear that Silas was there because of his knowledge of Greychurch, it had become almost businesslike, and Silas glowed in the respect he was given.

Now, however, nervousness took control. It wasn't because he was afraid of the strangers he might meet on the other side of the door, nor was it because he didn't know how to behave or what to say. He would make that up as he went along.

What concerned him was that he might see the viscount. He didn't fear him or his authority, he wanted to be with the man again and although he had been called back to the house that evening and would come willingly, the distance of time between now and then was too great.

He wanted to see the man again now and was picturing him when the door opened. He turned his attention to someone he expected to be Thomas. It wasn't. It was a young girl no older than himself. Her chestnut hair was parted in the middle and arranged neatly beneath a white halo of lace, and her slim body was shaped by a long apron over a black dress. Everything about her was impeccable, including her manners.

'We were expecting you, Sirs,' she said with a politely inviting smile and the suggestion of a curtsy.

Fecker nudged him out of the way to get a better look, but Silas was so surprised at being called Sir, he hardly noticed.

'Are you included?' Fecker asked looking the girl up and down as though she was on offer.

'Fecks, for God's sake...' Regaining his composure, Silas stepped in front of his friend who was salivating like a terrier over a trapped rat and nodded to the girl. 'Morning, Miss,' he said, pulling his cap from his head. 'His Lordship did say we could get something to eat.'

Her smile developed into a laugh. 'Well, you could of course, if we hadn't done with the breakfast three hours ago.'

'Done what with it?' Fecker asked.

'Ignore him,' Silas said. 'What time is it?'

'Near on twelve,' the maid replied.

'Feck me. I ain't slept so long since that time I...'

'Yes, alright, Fecks,' Silas interrupted before his mate could get too graphic. 'As I say, Miss, best to ignore him.'

'Bit difficult,' she said, giving Fecker a lingering once-over and apparently liking what she saw. 'His Lordship said to feed two men who have been of use, so I am sure he wouldn't object to me bringing you something from the pantry. I'll see what Mrs Baker has to say. Wait here.'

With that, she closed the door on them, returning some minutes later with a tray and a stern woman dressed entirely in shimmering black. She regarded Silas as if she had just stepped in him, but drew back when Fecker rose from where he had been sitting, picking his nails on the bottom step.

'You are to eat this, leave the tray, and go,' the woman said. She turned and bustled her way inside telling Lucy to 'Leave the workmen to their lunch.'

Workman was a lot better than other titles she could have used, and Silas was grateful to whoever she was for her politeness, even though it had come through clenched teeth. He took the tray from Lucy, but it took longer to separate Fecker from her gaze. Her name, barked from the depth of the kitchen, finally made her move, and he and Fecker returned to the relative warmth of the coach house to eat.

Having completed his business at the Lords, Archer took a cab across town to The Grapevine in the fashionable area of Five Dials. The maître d' welcomed him like a long-lost nephew and clicked his fingers enough times to have His Lordship divested of his overcoat, hat and gloves. Suitably flanked by a man more supercilious than Tripp and a waiter less attractive than Thomas, he bade polite but discrete hellos to several acquaintances on his way to a private banquette. Here, he was welcomed by a gentleman suffering premature baldness who stood, shook his hand and waited for Archer to sit before he did the same. A flurry of linen and servitude later, and they were left alone.

'Archie.'

'Benji.'

'I had the wine opened.'

'How's the soul?'

'It's always good here, Archie.'

'I meant your soul.'

'Ah. Then I repeat my answer. Why d'you ask?'

'I am here for business.'

Dr Benjamin Quill was a man renowned for his ability to drink two bottles of wine at lunch and still be able to remove a man's appendix in the afternoon without fatality. Nevertheless, Archer had served with him on the Britannia where he learned that Quill spoke coherently before lunch and rubbish after it, and as he needed him sober, he leapt directly to his purpose.

'I need you to do two things for me, Benji,' he said reaching for the wine bottle chilling in the ice bucket.

'I am at Your Lordship's service,' Quill said.

The sudden formality between the two friends alerted Archie to the waiter who had appeared from nowhere and reached the bottle first.

'Thank you, Doctor,' Archie replied and waited until the waiter had poured a suspicion of wine into a bucket of a glass. As soon as the man had backed and swished away, Archer helped himself to a decent measure and continued. 'I had a fascinating chat with a couple of young men last night,' he said, launching straight in. 'About the conditions in the East End.'

'You didn't go there did you?' Quill's eyes, usually half-closed and dozing, sprang wide with alarm.

'No. They came to me.'

'Good Lord.'

'A long story and irrelevant, except for its purpose.'

Archer told him of his discussion with Silas and Fecker, referring to them as, 'Two extraordinarily diverse but helpful fellows,' rather than by name, and explained his reason for inviting them to the house. He didn't mention the similarity of Silas to the drawing, nor the attraction he felt towards the young man. Quill knew of Archer's predilection for the male sex, as well as Archer remembered his, but their silently shared secret remained undiscussed between them as it did everyone else. Except for Lady Marshall, of course, but Quill didn't know that, and it was best for all concerned that things remained that way.

Apart from liking Quill for his forthrightness, generous heart and discretion, Archer admired his medical skills. The scar he wore on his chin was only one reminder of a time when Quill saved his life, because, at the same time as stitching that minor wound, he had also stitched a far greater one on his side. 'Just tucked back a few entrails and remembered how Mother did her embroidery,' Quill had joked at the time.

When the obsequious waiters fussed at the table, they discussed the weather and the trivia of life, but when alone, they spoke passionately about Archer's charitable trust and how it could be used to forward the idea of a "Facility for the Health of Destitute Men" as suggested by one of the 'helpful fellows'. Quill was behind the idea from the start and rattled off a long list of suggestions and ideas in such detail that Archer's mind drifted.

That it should drift to the men he wanted to help was understandable — it was what the lunch was about. That it sailed so frequently to Silas and how Archer might spend more time with him was more difficult to fathom until Quill said, 'Get them in and let them get on with it. That's what I fancy.'

He was referring to possible staffing arrangements at the 'facility', but Archer realised his friend had hit upon the right words. He had, in effect, diagnosed Archer's problem without knowing he was suffering.

Put bluntly, Archer had taken a fancy to Silas. This, he knew. What he didn't know was what he could do about it, not until Quill advised him so succinctly

'You mean, Benji,' he said. 'That once there is a building, and it is prepared, we should appoint a superintendent and let the staff take it from there?'

'As soon as it's acquired, I should think,' Benji said. 'As long as we appoint the correct man to trust. I can think of several directly, all medical men with enthusiasm for the poor, if you take my meaning, and any one of them I would confidently leave alone to hire and fire.'

Archer couldn't help but hear his words as an analogy between the charitable building-to-be and Clearwater House. He had the building, his home, and he had a man to run it, Tripp. What he wanted was someone to administer to his needs, Silas. All he had to do was put the man in there and see what happened.

It was exciting, but there were problems. Tripp didn't need any more staff, even if Silas was amenable, he would be a kept man. An invisible mistress to be called from the servants' quarters during the night's darkest hours. That wasn't right. If he wanted Silas, a stranger at best, a criminal some would say, living with him as the friend and lover he wanted Thomas to be, there had to be another way to do it. As for the staff, they, in Quill's wise words, could 'get on with it.'

'I'm sorry?' Quill cut short whatever he was saying, and Archer realised he had spoken aloud.

'Get on with it,' he repeated. 'Talking about the charity. We should do as you say. Get in the man we want and run with it. See what happens.'

'There will be something of an outcry, of course,' Quill said, considering the matter almost as deeply as he was considering another bottle of wine.

'A huge outcry.' Archer imagined Mrs Baker storming from the house, closely followed by Tripp on a stretcher.

'People will ask why we are not helping the women.'

'It's not about divisions in gender,' Archer said. 'There are many places that attempt to care for the women. Why, every mission and workhouse cater for both, and there's Markland, a man at St Mary's who runs a clinic only for... a dry spell come next Thursday.'

At the click of Quill's fingers, the waiter had sprung like a rabbit from a hat, and the weather was dissected to the last isobar while the two men sat through the ritual opening of a bottle.

'It's my money, Benji,' Archer continued when the coast was clear. 'Her Ladyship agrees with me. It is perhaps an unsavoury cause, but a necessary one and we are, after all, in the business of charity.'

'Her Ladyship?' Quill asked warily. He and Lady Marshall only liked each other when they had an audience.

'Both Her Ladyships,' Archer said. 'Mother and Lady Marshall.'

'How is your mother?'

'Not having to sell her body on the street,' Archer snapped. 'Let's return to the subject.'

'I think we've covered it, haven't we?' Quill pouted, abashed and put in his place. He poked his fish. 'The trustees will meet in a few weeks, we'll all sign off on it and we'll appoint someone to find a building and take it from there.'

'Perfect,' Archer enthused. 'But as for a suitable building, I have been making enquiries.'

'Oh yes?' Quill had discovered hidden treasures beneath his sole; three green beans that were of great interest.

Archer took out his notebook and referred to it. 'That decided, this is the second thing you can do for me,' he said. 'Tell me, Benji, what do these names mean to you? Edward Sellinge, Martin Tucker, Michael, and Alexander Chiltern.'

'Michael Chiltern?' the doctor asked, distracted by his find.

'There was a comma, Quill. Pay attention.' He reread the names, but Quill shook his head.

'Who are they? Possible superintendents?'

His coldness towards the victims was unusual and unattractive, but then so was the man himself, and Archer forgave him. Not everyone in the city was aware of the boys' names. Why should a busy doctor in the west of the city know the names of a colleague's corpses in the east?

Quill's ignorance was shared by many, but hearing it so close brought home the true horrors these young men had suffered and continued to suffer even after death. Doing what they could to drag themselves through a squalid existence, each gave away their only two possessions; their innocence and their life. They had been strangled and cut about in the most horrific of ways and left wide open for all to see. Their names, their likenesses and now even a

124

photograph had been shown in the newspapers, their ignominious ends were the sensation of the middle-class breakfast table. They would be buried without care, their bodies dumped un-coffined into pits, there to lie forgotten. They deserved respect.

Archer took a deep breath to regain his composure. If he was to win the battle ahead, he needed to separate emotion from fact.

'Now how about these,' he asked when Quill's beans had been eaten, and the doctor was more attentive. 'Do these places mean anything to you? Harrington Street, Simon's Yard, Lucky Row and Britannia Street.'

Quill twirled his knife as he thought. 'That last one rings a bell,' he said. 'Something to do with a murder...' His head snapped up. 'You're not thinking of renting a building in those places, are you?' he gasped. 'I understand it must be in Greychurch, but Clearwater, that would be too morbid.'

Archie placated him. 'I am not,' he said. 'Those are where the Ripper claimed his four victims.'

'Ah yes,' Quill considered. 'Then you're right. Definitely addresses to avoid.'

'You're not taking my point, Benji.'

'Do you have one? What's the matter with your lamb?'

'I am not hungry. Quill, stop fussing over your lunch and listen.'

'Go on.' Quill pointed his fork to Archer's plate before setting about a potato.

'I'll read them again,' Archer said. 'In part. Harrington, Simon, Lucky, Britannia.'

The potato was halfway to Quill's mouth when he dropped the fork. It clattered against his plate before bouncing off his lap in a complicated celebration of freedom. Quill's hand and expression, however, were frozen.

'I know,' Archer said. 'I thought the same when I noticed.'

'Damn odd coincidence,' Quill dismissed it. 'Who'd a thought it?'

'Indeed,' Archer said. Quill's reaction was all he needed. 'I thought it would interest you.'

'Wait a moment.' The doctor was aghast. 'You're not thinking...?'

'I wasn't at first. As you say, coincidence. But now, after the fourth one... Can it be?'

'Where is he?' Quill enquired. 'Not heard news for a long time.'

'Holland.'

'Hell. I bet both Her Ladyships are glad of that.'

'I think we all are,' Archer said.

Quill studied him for the time it took him to down a glass of wine. 'You can't possibly think…' he said, but apparently too shocked by where Archer's suggestion led him, shuddered. 'You, Sir,' he said, 'have too much time on your hands and too much imagination. Ridiculous,' he mumbled. 'And, if I may say, rather sick. On the subject of which, we must be aware of this new Mycobacterium tuberculosis when the facility is opened.' He launched into his pet subject, contagious diseases, preferring the details of the charity's medical needs over Archer's suspicions.

With his friend happily babbling into the second bottle, and glad of his scepticism, Archer turned his mind to his concerns.

He had reached a decision about Silas, and he had nearly completed a transaction with himself on what he should do about Thomas. Quill had confirmed his suspicion on his other matter, and it was that which occupied him as the doctor enthused about ailments.

He drank no more wine, he was heady enough with the thought of what lay ahead. As the doctor prattled and the bottle emptied, Archer drew his plan. By the time the lunch was over, and they were solemnly led to their coats, he knew what he must do.

What disturbed him was how it was to be done.

# Thirteen

For the second time that day, Silas stood at the back door of Clearwater House waiting for the bell to be answered. He could think of only two reasons why the viscount had asked him to return; he either wanted to talk further about the East End and how he intended to help, or he wanted to expand on his parting words of last night.

*'I don't mean to have sex with you. I mean to save your life.'*

Silas had gone to the coach house carrying a mixed bag of emotions. He was disappointed because the viscount had been outraged at his flirting and adamant in his refusal, and confused, because he thought that was the true purpose of last night's visit. It was reassuring that the viscount wanted to save him from the streets. When he saw where he was to be staying, amazement overcame him, quickly followed by a new sensation, that of knowing he would be able to sleep safely. He hoped that this return visit would bring clarity and the chance of another night in a warm bed.

He shook the thoughts from his head when the door opened and the maid appeared as fresh and sprightly as before.

'Punctual,' she said. 'Mr Tripp will appreciate that.'

Fecker blundered to the top step. 'Afternoon, Miss,' he beamed. 'Been looking forward to seeing you.'

'No need to be so direct, Fecks,' Silas said, noticing how Lucy's eyes lit up at the sight of the long-haired blond.

She was pleased to see him, she even blushed, but she remembered her station. 'You are to come into the servants' hall,' she said, standing back to allow them across the threshold.

'Very kind, Miss,' Silas smiled. 'Thank you.' Even though he was entering the grand house through a tradesman's entrance, he noticed a change in himself. It was as if the building itself demanded manners, and he was expected to behave as if he had some. Almost like entering a church where voices were hushed, and people carried themselves with respect.

He knew the way along the passage, past the coat rack and into the high-ceilinged kitchen where the table was now strewn with vegetables, bowls and pans at one end, and flour and baking equipment at the other. A narrow woman stood at the range with her back to them, and another maid peeled potatoes at the far end of the table. She glanced up, giggled and returned to her work. The room was clammy as they passed through. Something bubbled in a large copper pot on the stove, steam escaping from under its clattering lid, and condensation hung in the air.

As he passed into the servant's hall, he expected to see Thomas glaring it him, but it was worse. At the head of the table, which was waiting to be cleared of its tea plates and cups, stood Mr Tripp, his hands behind his back. The folds of his chin rested on a winged collar half-covering a white bow tie. His tailcoat was open to reveal a starched, white dress shirt with a ridiculously small amount of waistcoat across his stomach, his trousers were grey striped, but the rest of him was black, including his mood it seemed.

'Stand there,' he barked, halting Silas and Fecker in their tracks. 'Thank you, Lucy.'

The maid curtsied and left them. Fecker watched her go, grinning.

'I will thank you to keep your eyes off the maids,' Tripp said.

'No need to thank me,' Silas said. 'He can have them. Evening Mr Tripp.'

Tripp closed his eyes, a silent prayer for strength, perhaps, and took a deep breath that swelled his chest. He was not fat, but there was no way the tailcoat would do up, even if he sucked in his stomach. Silas wondered at the point of the buttons.

'I have instructions to take you to His Lordship,' Tripp announced as if imparting grave news. 'Before I do that, I have instructions.' He fixed his distrust on Silas, too intimated by Fecker to look him in the eye. 'You are not to go anywhere unaccompanied. You speak only when spoken to. You stand when His Lordship, or anyone other than a servant enters a room, and, below stairs, when I enter. You only sit when invited. Keep your language clean, and your hands to yourself. Should anyone ask your purpose here at any time following this evening, you are assisting His Lordship in his charitable work, and you say as little as possible. Do not swear in his presence and on no account sit on the furniture.'

'Lot to remember,' Fecker mumbled, earning a hard stare from the butler.

'And remember them you shall.' Tripp spun on his heels. 'Follow me.'

He led them from the hall and into the passage leading to the stairs. Silas' heart skipped a beat as he imagined they were being taken up and he would see the inside of the viscount's house. It was not to be. Tripp passed the staircase and took them through a door beneath, continuing along another passage, darker and colder, until they entered a room with a stone floor, a long, blackened table in the centre and shelves lining the walls. An arched and barred window let in the last of the afternoon light and Silas felt the chill of the room in his fingertips as his breath clouded.

'Let me see you,' Tripp said, pointing to the precise places he wanted them to stand.

Once again Silas imagined he was being sold into slavery, this time by an undertaker. Tripp examined them from a distance, his eyes picking over every detail of their clothing.

'Do you have another overcoat?' he asked of Fecker who laughed.

Another elbow from Silas and he fell silent. 'Unfortunately not, Mr Tripp,' Silas said. 'This is all we own. What you see is what you get.'

Tripp nodded thoughtfully and, Silas thought, perhaps even sympathetically. Any outward sign of emotion was dismissed in a blink.

'Your shoes?'

They examined the soles of their feet, and they passed inspection, as did their hands.

'You are remarkably clean,' the butler said with surprise.

It was on the tip of his tongue to offer to be as dirty as he wanted, but Silas held it back. Sexual innuendo was a habit that had become a way of life, and he fought hard to play a different role. If he could keep his mouth shut and his ears open, he might discover the purpose of this song and dance.

'All the same,' Tripp said. 'Clean your shoes and wash your hands.

Then, you will wait until I collect you.'

With that, he marched from the room and closed the door.

'What's this about?' Fecker asked, hitching himself onto the table.

'No idea, mate. Just wants us to look like city toffs and a bit miffed that we don't.'

'Not cleaning my hands again,' Fecker complained. 'No point spitting on my boots.'

'Yeah, alright, Fecks. Don't get grumpy. Just keep the man happy.'

Silas rinsed his hands and dried them on a towel which he then realised was grimy with shoe polish. He washed them again and let them dry in the frigid air.

Tripp returned after five minutes just as Fecker was sniffing a tin of beeswax.

'Touch nothing!' the butler roared from the doorway causing Fecker to drop the tin. He kicked it under the table to hide the evidence. 'Follow me. Silently.'

Tripp turned and led them back through the passage to the stairs and up. Silas' pulse quickened with every step. He had been brought up in cramped rooms in broken down tenements with shared taps on landings for washing and hardly any sanitation. This house had a room just for people to clean their boots, and he couldn't imagine what lay on the other side of the large door they now approached.

Trip gave them one last examination before leading them into the house.

The first thing that struck Silas was that it was no warmer above stairs than it had been below. The expanse of tiled floor, the high ceiling and the open staircase had something to do with it. There was a fireplace in the entrance hall they entered, but it was unlit. After a few paces, they were told to wait beside a huge round table set with nothing but an oversized bunch of flowers. Above it, dead centre hung a glittering brass and candle chandelier, unlit, whose chain could well have held back a river tug. It vanished into a ceiling painted with clouds and cherubs, where half-men half-beast creatures attended to topless ladies.

Looking at the ceiling made Silas dizzy, and he steadied himself by gawping at the carpeted stone staircase which swept towards the back of the house before dividing and doubling back. Fecker, of course, had discovered the semi-clad figures on the ceiling.

'Don't think much of their tits,' he complained.

Luckily, Tripp was at a distance, facing a pair of doors as if he had been told to stand in the corner for being naughty. His confident knock covered the word 'tits,' but he did let out an urgent, 'Shush,' before knocking a second time and entering. Silas was impressed by the way he opened the doors and stepped between them at the same time, letting them go but not allowing them to fall back against the walls.

'Your visitors, My Lord,' he said, and Silas was sure he heard an echo.

There was a moment when nothing happened, and then Tripp walked further into the room leaving them alone. Silas pulled at Feck's coat sleeve. He was still craning his neck at the ceiling. They had time to gawp at each other wide-eyed before Tripp returned.

'This way,' he said, and waited for them to fall in line before returning to the room.

If the hall had been an introduction to the viscount's way of life, it had not been a subtle one, yet it was nothing compared to the room they entered. Silas could see why the butler had insisted they check their boots. The carpet almost came up to his ankles, and he wondered if he had time to squat and touch it. Sadly not; Tripp was setting a fair pace.

He had a moment to glance at a roaring fire, several fancy chairs and settees, a few tables and a mass of glass that glittered or glowed depending on whether it was hanging or standing. Tripp halted before another pair of open doors.

'Your names?' he whispered.

'Mister Silas Hawkins,' Silas said, thinking the Mister was called for given his circumstance. 'And Fecker... Sorry, Andrej...' He leant into Fecker and whispered, 'What's your last name?'

'I am Andrej Borysko Yakiv Kolisnychenko,' Fecker said, squaring his shoulders proudly.

Tripp blanched, but recovered his composure to announce, 'Hawkins and his man,' before backing away apace.

A man crossed the room in front of them, his head in a book. He didn't look at them as he passed, he was intent on whatever he was reading, and Silas was unable to see his face. The man wore a crisp white shirt with sleeves neatly rolled to the elbows, smart woollen trousers with braces hanging behind, and what Silas thought were riding boots.

'You may step in,' Tripp instructed, and they did as they were told.

The hall had been impressive, but cold, the next room plush and padded, but this was a room for work. Not the kind of work Silas was used to, but work of the mind, a place to read and write among rich colours, dim lighting and a flickering fire. The rugs were deep red and green, as were the curtains that swagged across the window. The chairs were a mismatch of styles and materials. A leather one faced a desk, a pair of large armchairs faced the fire, and every surface was cluttered with curios.

Tripp asked if there would be anything else, and a familiar voice replied, 'That will be all. I will ring if I need you.'

As the doors were closed behind him, Silas felt unexpectedly at home, and when the man with the book finally put it down and turned, Silas realised why. The viscount grinned at him and opened his arms wide.

'What do you think?' he said, turning a circle to show off his clothes. 'Will I do?'

Silas couldn't find the words. He was dressed like a shopkeeper who spent his income on barbers and grooming.

'Oh, wait,' His Lordship enthused, dashing across to an armchair and throwing on a dark grey jacket. It was not dissimilar to the waist-length one Silas wore, except it looked like it still had the price tag on it. He modelled it for his guests in the centre of the room looking very pleased with himself.

'What do you think?' he beamed.

'You want me to be honest, Sir?' Silas asked unable to hide his confusion.

'Naturally.'

'What are you?'

His Lordship's expression melted and, as his boyish enthusiasm drained from his face, it uncovered a look of anger which quickly passed and was replaced by disappointment.

'You can't tell?' he asked adjusting his jacket as if doing so would help.

'Nyet.' Was all Fecker had to say on the matter. He was more interested in a display of cut-glass decanters on a silver salver, each one filled with wine-red promises.

'It's smart,' Silas said. 'But… Why?'

'Oh dear,' the viscount murmured. 'I think I've got it wrong. Smart?'

His gaze wandered over Silas, appraising him, and Silas read the look as displeasure.

'I'm sorry,' he said, keen to stay on the right side of his host. 'But you wanted the truth. Oh, I just wanted to say thank you for letting us stay last night. It was a luxury for the both of us, and we are very grateful, Sir. You look very fine, if I may say. Ready for the theatre, are you?' It seemed polite enough and Silas could imagine any guest at Clearwater House saying the same thing.

The viscount burst into laughter and threw off the jacket. 'I'll have to think again,' he said. 'Come in and sit down.'

Much to Fecker's delight, the viscount strode to the decanters and began pouring drinks, something of which he was fond, Silas thought. He had never seen the man very far from a glass of something.

'He said not sit on furniture, didn't he?' Fecker said, hovering uncertainly at a chair by the fireplace.

'Go ahead, Andrej,' the viscount encouraged. 'When the Tripp's away, us lads can play, eh?'

When spoken by a gentleman to a street boy, expressions such as 'Us lads can play,' took on a different meaning and once again Silas had to refrain for making a smutty remark, passing a flirt, or getting straight down to business.

'You are confused, Silas?' the man asked, catching him out.

'True enough, Sir,' Silas replied.

'Why? And be honest.'

'Well, for one, Fecks and me are a bit out of our depth.' He indicated the room by circling a finger, and the circle grew to encompass the whole house. 'Then, we don't know why we are here. But, when a gent invites the two of us somewhere private together, it's usually for something… Well, you can guess. And then… What are you wearing?' It was forward, but Silas felt relaxed enough not to worry.

'I have a lot to learn,' His Lordship said, crossing to the bell-pull and tugging it. 'Gentlemen, please sit. We are here for business, but not your kind. I have many more questions, we need to talk more on a certain subject, we will eat, and then I'd like us to go out.'

'We're not much dressed for the music hall, Sir,' Silas said, making himself at home in the depths of a plush armchair.

'And neither am I, I hope,' the viscount replied.

Silas wasn't sure what he was dressed for, but said nothing.

'Where you going?' Fecker grunted as he wiped his mouth following a comprehensive gulp of whisky.

The viscount finally found the concentration to stand still and explain himself. 'I need to go to Greychurch,' he said. 'I want to see the places where your unfortunate associates met their deaths.'

Silas body flushed with dread as understanding kicked him in the gut. The man had taken a shot at dressing to fit in, but had missed the target completely. He would be set upon first by the whores, then the renters, and, if there was anything left of his dignity, by anyone bold enough to strip him of his new clothes. Men would kill for a pair of boots like that, and his jacket could be sold to feed a family of ten for the whole winter.

'I can see your consternation, Silas,' the viscount said.

Silas checked his fly was buttoned.

'He means you look bothered,' Fecker said, and winked proudly.

'Oh. Yes, of course I'm bothered, Sir. It ain't safe.'

'I'm not going alone. You're coming with me.'

'I know Fecker's a big fecker, Sir, but you don't know what it's like in there.'

'Which is why I want to go.'

'It's getting dark.'

'The darker, the better.'

'You been drinking that opium stuff, Sir? Or has life got too much for you?'

'Don't be insolent.'

'Then don't you be stupid.' Silas struggled from the armchair.

'I beg your pardon?' The viscount squared his shoulders.

'You heard.' Silas was suddenly too annoyed to worry what he said but aware enough of his surroundings to care how he said it. 'I'll happily tell you what you want to know, but I won't let you go down Greychurch, not at night.'

'You won't let me?' His Lordship was outraged.

'Not if I have a say in it.'

'You'll do what the damn I pay you to do.'

'I won't take no money for getting you hurt.'

The viscount took a step forward, his features twisted in anger. 'What kind of hypocrite are you?' he seethed, narrowing his eyes. 'You'll take money for being screwed as a whore, but assisting a gentleman is beneath you?'

'Getting you hurt is beneath me,' Silas shot back. The man didn't understand, and his blindness was maddening.

Powerful hands gripped Silas' lapels and tugged him closer.

'You will do as I ask.' Each word was articulated through gritted teeth. The viscount's eyes burned into Silas, defying his insolence while somehow seeming to enjoy it.

'I won't let you go. Sir.' Silas stood his ground, but his heart was banging against his ribcage.

Their faces were so close he could have touched the viscount's scar with his tongue.

'You couldn't stop me if you tried,' the older man sneered.

'You'd be surprised what I can do.'

Silas matched his anger but not his strength. The viscount lifted him to his toes. They were eye to eye and groin to groin, a whisper away from a kiss.

'Want to beat me do you?' Silas jeered. 'You ain't the first.'

His words caught the man off guard and Silas' won a point. His dick pressed against the man's crotch. It was hardening, and he was unable to control it. The smell of perfume and alcohol was as intoxicating as the possibilities their closeness allowed.

'Go on,' he taunted. 'It'd be good practice for you.'

'What?' Apparently, the viscount's anger was running out of steam.

'For when you get set upon,' Silas said, his throat dry. 'I ain't letting you go.' He leant forward, making the viscount take his weight, but the man didn't push him away as expected.

Instead, he swallowed.

'Why?'

'You'll get injured.'

'It's happened before. Try again.'

'I don't want you to get hurt.'

'Why?'

'Shame to mess up a pretty face.'

'Why, Hawkins? Why should you care?' the viscount pressed back, and Silas had no desire to push him away.

''Cos I do.' Silas was running out of excuses and had only the truth to fall back on.

'Why?'

It was yelled that time, but Silas could shout just as loudly. 'Because I fancy you, alright?' He laid it down as a challenge, but his eyes were pricking.

The viscount was caught by confusion. The tension in his face fell away like an avalanche of stubbled flesh, allowing a brief twitch of delighted surprise to shine through before annoyance took over. He let Silas go, stepped back and knocked into Fecker who had closed in, ready to protect his friend.

The viscount fumbled for words before settling on, 'Your fears are unfounded.' He edged away from Fecker. 'Yours too.'

There was a knock at the door. The viscount straightened his shirt and remembered himself. 'We will not be going alone,' he said, the matter decided as he addressed the door. 'Come!'

Thomas entered in his evening livery backed by the glow of the drawing room lamps.

If this was His Lordship's knight in shining armour, Silas thought, they were in trouble, but by Christ, he was sexy.

Anyone would have been sexy to Silas right then. The thought of the viscount putting himself in danger wound him up so intensely, he'd been furious and turned-on at the same time. He still was, but the anger began to seep away as he remembered the man's moment of happy shock. His state of sexual arousal took longer to soften.

'Thomas is coming with us,' His Lordship decreed.

'Oh,' Fecker grunted, unimpressed. 'Then we're all fucked.'

# *Fourteen*

Archer leant on the mantlepiece and studied Silas with admiration as he ate. It was a way of distracting himself from what was going on inside his head — a tangle of puzzles which he could only unpick by not thinking about them. He found that if he left questions alone, they answered themselves, usually by chance, as they had done at lunch when Quill, without realising it, suggested he employ Silas and not worry about what his household thought.

He was still recovering from his intimate moment with the Irishman, but, as it had taken place three hours before, recovering wasn't quite the right word. Relishing was closer.

Silas was eating one of Mrs Flintwich's sugary desserts, rolling his eyes in pleasure on every taste and throwing looks of approval the viscount's way. It was not only a delight to share the young man's enjoyment of the treat — they were one of Archer's favourites — Silas' expression personified the rush of joy Archer felt when the man admitted his feelings. His fancy, to be more precise. Apparently, Silas felt the same about Archer as he did about the renter, and he hoped it wasn't an act.

'Do you think our plan will work?' he asked the incongruous young men at his breakfast table. His mother would have screamed, but he enjoyed the spectacle.

'You're mad,' Fecker said. 'But I look after you.'

'Andrej,' Archer said, leaving the fireplace and taking his seat. 'You were listening when I told you about my time in the military, weren't you?'

Fecker nodded. 'Da. But ships have rules. None in Greychurch.'

'Like I told you, Sir,' Silas said. 'We can take a walk, stay on the main streets and be ready to call for a bobby, but we can't stay long. Not after dark. And it ain't just for fear of the Ripper.'

'I understand.' Archer was growing warm beneath his change of clothing even though the breakfast room, not usually in use at that time of night, was unheated.

After Thomas' appearance in the study and a discussion about disguise, Archer had sent the footman on an errand to the West City Mission to collect more suitable, working men's clothing for them both. He gave Thomas a letter of explanation, a donation and money for a cab, and he had returned with garments Silas considered suitable. Since then, the youth had taken over the arrangements. By the time they came to take supper, he had changed Archer's plan and forced him to agree on a few terms.

Archer knew the game Silas was playing, and he knew when he was being manipulated. Aware of it, he deployed his own subtle pressures until he achieved what he wanted. He had. Silas had taken on the role of leader, and who better? He knew the area, he had the required mix of intelligence and wariness, and as his earlier outburst had proved, was protective of Archer.

Immediately following Silas' admission of attraction, the viscount had been rattled, but now he was pleased with himself. He had chosen well in Silas and found a shrewd soldier, loyal to his commander and willing to show that loyalty, it would seem, in an East End street or Archer's bed. There was nothing stopping Archer taking him upstairs right now, except the unspoken rules of society and the fact that, if that were to happen, Archer wanted it to be because of desire and affection, not supply and demand. Could Silas stop being a renter and become a lover? Would there be any difference in the sex? What if…?

'This is intolerable.' He thumped the table.

Whatever he tried to think of, thoughts of Silas put themselves in the way. Where they had started as sympathetic and respectful, they had become lewd. Deliciously lewd, and they drew him even closer to falling in love with the man. A man, he reminded himself, he had not chosen, but who by chance happened to look similar to a drawing.

He had to concentrate on the matter in hand.

'Everything alright, My Lord?' Thomas had sailed in from somewhere with Lucy in tow and was waiting to clear the table.

'I do apologise,' Archer said, flapping his jacket. 'This wool is all very well, but the material doesn't breathe.'

He rose from the table scrutinised by the black-haired youth who stirred his groin as much as his heart every time his cobalt eyes twinkled his way. 'I need some air.'

Turning at his chair, he found Thomas standing behind him. At least, the face and its concern belonged to Thomas, as for the rest...

'Good heavens!' he said in alarm.

His footman wore shabby boots, filthy trousers, a leather jerkin over a grey shirt that had once owned a collar, while his glorious copper hair was barely visible beneath a Newsboy cap.

'Apparently I am a tosher, My Lord,' Thomas said with the faintest hint of a smile.

'You told him he was a tosser?' Fecker asked, grinning at Silas.

'No, mate. A tosher.'

'I have no idea what one is,' Thomas said. 'But I'm glad it's not my vocation.'

Archer didn't know whether he should slap Silas on the back gently for his prank, or hard for his rudeness. 'A tosher, Thomas,' he explained, trying to glare sternly at Silas but failing, 'is someone who sifts the sewers in search of lost valuables.'

Silas winked and said, 'Very dangerous work, mate. Only real men do shit-shifting.'

Thomas shot Silas a furious look. It wasn't exactly daggers, more like a canteen of cutlery and Archer wondered if he wasn't being over-ambitious. Did they need Thomas? He had thought there was safety in numbers, but was it right to put his man in danger?

Seeing his concern, Thomas said, 'I have a knife in the pocket of the jacket, but I didn't want to bring that into the breakfast room.'

'Would you know how to use it?'

He fixed Silas with a threatening stare. 'I slaughter cattle for my fader when I'm home for holidays, Mr Hawkins,' he said. 'Perhaps I will go and fetch it.'

'No need, Thomas.' Archer smiled, for which Thomas seemed grateful, and addressed the others. 'Gentlemen, I think we are nearly ready. Silas, the money I gave you last night. Have you spent it?'

'No, Sir,' Silas replied, trying to fold his used napkin back into its ring without success. 'No need. We spent the day waiting in your coach house. Bit of an imposition, but no-one noticed, and it were a lot safer than carting around five quid.'

Archer was about to ask why he had not taken the money home when the obvious answer prevented him. They didn't have a home, and he concluded Silas had acted sensibly rather than rudely. He would let them live in his coach house permanently if he could.

Now there was an idea.

'Sorry. Didn't ask.'

'No, Andrej, don't worry,' Archer reassured the man who was, somehow, still eating. 'I suggest you leave your money here.'

'Why?' Fecker grunted. 'You change your mind?'

'No, not at all. It will be here when you return.'

'We're coming back?' Silas had that look again, a practised blend of boyish enthusiasm and mischievousness.

'Yes, why not?' Archer was aware that Lucy was in the room. 'You may have another night in the stables for your troubles. Lucy, clear the table would you? Gentlemen, follow me to the study.'

He turned to the doors and waited, but no-one moved.

'Andrej, you may bring whatever you've not yet eaten.'

Chairs immediately brushed the carpet. Silas and Fecker accompanied him to the door, but Thomas remained static.

'I include you as a gentleman, Thomas,' Archer said. 'Later, I will treat you as a tosher. For now, we are all on the same crew. If Lucy needs help, I shall ring for Tripp.'

Thomas leapt into action and joined the others, leaving Lucy to insist there was no need to bother Mr Tripp. Archer was relieved. The old man was already snooping about his business, and he didn't want to further inflame the butler's curiosity.

Archer paused in the hall and removed his jacket, allowing the others to go ahead. It gave him time to cool down and temper a sudden rush of nerves.

He had fought in battle and commanded men aboard ship and on land, but he had always had prior knowledge of the waters and fields. He had no experience of the East End and had only read about what to expect, but he was not to be dissuaded. His greater cause demanded he go; there were things he needed to see for himself before he decided on his next course of action.

Besides, he had the strapping Ukrainian on his side, his growing affection for Silas to warm him, and Thomas knew how to disembowel a heifer.

What could possibly go wrong?

He thought of a hundred things that could go wrong the moment the cab dropped them at a junction just after ten that night. On one side of the road, where they grouped wrapping coats and pulling on fingerless gloves, they were backed by the sturdy offices of banks and merchants. Opposite, the entrance to the East End was marked by the deceptive beginning of City Street. Deceptive, because after a hundred yards, the semi-respectable establishments of hat shops and tailors, began to crumble into slaughterhouses and tanners. Within a quarter of a mile, what was a two-lane road became a single fleet of the city's worst leading to a labyrinth of slit-throat alleys and iniquity. Despite the late hour, the road teamed with life, denser the further in one walked, and, although Archer strained to see, there was no end to it. Mist hung wearily overhead, diffusing the light until moving figures became one with dark buildings and there was nothing but a black vanishing point.

'Remember,' Silas said, unbuttoning Archer's jacket and doing it up on the wrong holes. 'You ain't no lord and master, 'ere, Guv? Alright?'

'No excuse for rudeness, Mr Hawkins.'

'I ain't being rude, Guv. I'm breaking you in. First thing someone's going a-call you is a fart-sniffing nancy, or a shit-poking Jew, no offence to you, Sir, nor us queers, nor the Jews I suppose, but you ain't going a-be called My Lord. And people are going whistle and stuff, 'cos you might be dressed like an out of work coffin-knocker, but you hold yourself like the fucking Queen. Can't you limp or something?'

Silas' approach was more brutal than public school, but once Archer accepted the reasons behind it, he found it amusing. Anything to take his mind off what lay ahead.

'I'll do my best,' he promised.

'You and all, Tommy.' Silas turned his attention to the footman. 'You still got a bit of ginger showing, mate, watch out for that. Some of the fancy men go mad for ginger. Red hair means a big cock, so be ready. I'd pull your scarf up. You got just the lips men want around their dick, and whether you fancy that or not, 'ere and now ain't the place a-go looking for it.'

'I can take care of myself, renter,' Thomas scowled. He covered his mouth and bit on the scarf, presumably to stop himself saying something he would regret.

'Silas,' Archer stepped in. 'Where's the nearest murder site to here?'

'Nearest? Britannia Street,' Silas replied. 'After that, Lucky Row then Simon's Yard. From where we are, they kind of spiral out.' He tapped dots in the air. 'Four, three, two and one's further over there. It's a fair walk even using cut-throughs.'

'Not many people,' Fecker said, tipping his head towards City Street. 'Something's wrong.'

Silas watched the street a moment before turning to Archer. 'Right, Jack,' he said. 'If you get lost…'

'Hold on.' Archer stopped him. 'Jack?'

'Yeah, well, I ain't going a-shout out, "This way, My Lord", am I? More likely, "Jack? Where the fuck are you?" You've been a sailor, ain't you? So I reckoned Jack would do.'

'A good idea,' Archer winked. 'But I am likely to think you are calling someone else. Use Archie.'

'That your name? Archie?'

'No, it's Archer. My father lived and breathed the Battle of Agincourt, but my friends call me Archie.'

'Right, well, pleased to meet you, Archie.' Silas offered his hand, and Archer accepted.

'The pleasure is mine,' he said. 'I mean, right pleased to meet you… and all.' They were both smiling.

'Tommy?' Silas returned to him. 'You're Tommy, obviously, but same goes for you. You can't call him even Sir. So, Tommy? Meet your old mate from your shit-shovelling days, Archie.'

Thomas was embarrassed, and Archer felt for him. The other two were entirely at home, and if Archer was a fish out of water, Thomas was the entire shoal.

'Tom,' Archer said, putting out his hand and beaming because he hadn't been allowed to call him that for fifteen years. 'How've you been since we last got together in the pantry?' Thomas wasn't reacting, so Archer threw his arm around his shoulder and pulled

142

him close for a brief hug. 'Good to see you, mate.'

The scarf fell from Thomas' lips, and for a moment Archer thought he was going to run away, but the hug had knocked Thomas into shape.

''Ow be, Archie?' he said in his native accent. 'Aye, you be right an' all. I missed our meets 'mong the flour. Been keeping well?'

'Yeah, alright.' Silas shushed him. 'Stop pissing about and keep your mouths shut. Both of you.'

Suitably chastised, Archer let Thomas go and instantly missed the embrace.

It was at that moment that the reality of what he was about to do stabbed Archer in the chest. He was knowingly putting these men in danger without telling them the real reason. He hoped he would never have to, but, as they crossed the road, he had the uneasy feeling that the truth would come out sooner than he intended.

# Fifteen

Truth, Archer concluded, was easier to conceal than feelings, and covering up his true intentions a far simpler task than hiding what he felt for Silas. He watched him walk ahead, the plan being that Archer and Thomas walked behind with Fecker following. That way they appeared to be strolling into Greychurch as two individuals and one couple and aroused less suspicion. Not that Archer felt suspicious, but he was apprehensive. He had skirted the outsides of this area in carriages and daylight, walking through it on foot was a new experience, and his nervousness came from not knowing what to expect rather than any danger that might present itself.

At first, he saw a quiet street where a few respectable couples hurried from one side to the other returning home arm in arm. Within a few hundred yards, however, the lighting dimmed, and the mist thickened, as if there was something in Greychurch itself that caused the fog. It mixed with steam rising from below ground where ill-fitting and grated windows were set into basements and areas. Beneath his feet, children and women worked machines into the night, cutting, pressing, cleaning. They were badly lit by oil lamps whose soot blackened the glass preventing daylight when it came, thus lanterns burned during the day, the black thickened, and the cycle came around as relentlessly as the whirr and thump of the iron press.

The machines breathed and spat the smell of grease, straining leather and the hot-metal odour of moving parts. It mingled with the fug which hung at street level gathering the stench of rot and waste. The road narrowed to nothing more than rough cobbles either side of a stream of horse piss, plucked feathers and bones.

Thomas kept his scarf to his nose, a good idea, and Archer followed suit. Ahead, Silas seemed unbothered. In fact, from his ambling gait, one would have thought he was taking a Sunday stroll. The more Archer watched him, the more he wanted to know him, and the more he saw of where he lived, the stronger became the desire to help.

To help him, or to have him? He wondered.

To love him.

Archer cleared his throat and concentrated.

Fecker had been right; there were fewer people about than he expected. Understandable. The Ripper had not been caught, and his murders — and the potential for more — had been a spark that ignited tinder-dry unrest. The community of Greychurch was a desperate mass of immigrants, the sick, the lame and the hopeless. All they had here were sweatshops and dosshouses, hunger and funerals. They contended with an unchecked birth rate, poor housing, lack of sanitation and a hundred other disadvantages on a daily, never-ending basis. No wonder there had been talk of vigilante groups and reprisals.

Archer drew his wits about him as Silas crossed the street heading towards a tunnel. Thomas stepped closer.

'You alright there, Tom?' Archer said.

'Aye. Not as bad as I thought.'

Arched noted the name of the alley they entered. 'We're not far from the scene of the last murder,' he whispered.

Their footsteps echoed, and even Archer's whisper was amplified as the sound spiralled around the dripping walls. They passed through a short patch of complete darkness before emerging in a small square. In Archer's neighbourhood, a square meant a park, benches and railings. A square in Greychurch was little more than the meeting point of four narrow, covered lanes. Its centrepiece was a grate where four channels of muck gradually slid into a pit.

Silas waited for them to catch up.

'Things ain't right around here,' he said, his voice hushed even though they were alone. 'Feels wrong, eh, Fecks?'

Fecker nodded and glanced behind before saying, 'It's the vigils. Told everyone to stay inside while they guard against the Ripper.'

'Trouble is, that ain't all they're doing.'

'How d'you mean?' Archer kept his voice low.

'There's gangs of men about,' Silas said, stepping closer. 'Looking out for the Ripper maybe, but also sniffing for foreign blood. Too many Jews, see? Too many Russians and Poles and not enough work. The Ripper's given them an excuse.'

'We don't wait,' Fecker said and continued into the next alley.

The others followed, forced closer together now that the open streets had become a labyrinth of pools of weak light among stronger swathes of black. The mist turned to drizzle, damping their faces and footsteps.

Archer was thankful they were not drawing attention. They kept their heads down, but his eyes were raised to the prostitutes in the doorway swinging their legs, or the heap of cloth from which an arm protruded, tin mug in hand, and the men and women on doorsteps staring silently into the night. Were they waiting for work or sleep? Archer couldn't help but think they were waiting to die, although he convinced himself they were simply waiting for something to change.

Turning into an unlit alley and passing through in single file, Archer was aware of the rustles around him. Rats, but also clothing. The clank of a buckle, the scuff of a shoe, sounds of fornication mingled with hushed grunts and the slapping of bare flesh.

The bodies in the dark could be men or women. They could be strangers with no contract, married men and their lovers, or homosexuals meeting in consensual anonymity. They were more likely drunks with prostitutes, and his stomach churned at the thought; this is what Silas had been driven to.

There was no time to distress himself. Silas had stopped at the corner.

'Across there,' he said, pointing. 'Britannia Street. Don't hang about.'

The entrance stood a short distance to the right and across a lane, busier than the previous streets. People were gathering at one end, men mainly, carrying lanterns and tools.

Archer concentrated on his mission, and his eyes darted and danced as he crossed over. He tried to see every business name, every number, piece of graffiti, sign and poster. He noted the name of this lane, but it was irrelevant. Britannia, however, was not.

The location of the first murder, Harrington Street, could have been coincidence, the second too, perhaps, but when he had read

146

about the slashing and disembowelment of a renter in Lucky Row, the connection had been too hard to ignore. When the Ripper struck the fourth time, he chose Britannia Street, confirming Archer's incredulous suspicion. Out of all the squares and lanes, yards and alleys, the Ripper had selected places relevant to Archer's past. What he needed to do now was lay his incredulity to rest and find something that made his suspicion irrefutable.

He hoped to find a clue in Britannia Street, but there was nothing. It was an ordinary row of brick buildings, as dismal as the rest, quieter perhaps because it led only to a yard, but busier in recesses and deep alcoves, at least, until the unfortunate Alexander Chiltern was found slit from throat to groin, his genitalia removed and taken. His had been the worst abomination so far, and unless the police or vigilantes caught the man, there would undoubtedly be worse to come.

'Right here,' Silas said. He stepped back into the blackness of a deep doorway and vanished. 'His head was here, Archie, and you're standing where his feet were. I won't tell you what you're standing on Tommy.'

Thomas took a step back, and Archer crouched. He took a candle from his pocket and lit it. Holding it close to the ground, he swung it in wide arcs, his eyes squinting against the gloom.

'What you looking for?' Silas crouched opposite.

'Anything,' Archer said.

'Why?'

He stood and, without answering, examined the walls of the alcove as high as he could. There were no house names or numbers and no other clues, only posters calling for vigilante volunteers pasted on crumbling walls beside graffitied abuse of foreigners.

'And the murder before this one?' he said, stepping into the street for a broader view but seeing no clues.

'Not far.'

Silas led them back the way they had come, but veered off into a different alley, emerging where the backs of three tenement blocks met. Rats scurried from gutters to basements, but otherwise, they were alone. One more tunnel, mercifully short, and they came to Lucky Row.

'Down here in this yard.' Silas led them to the end of the short cul-de-sac and a wall with a gateless entrance. Beyond was a dark void. He indicated they should wait while he listened, but there was no sound other than a distant hum of voices from a clubhouse beyond. 'It's okay,' he said. 'We're alone.'

Archer stepped inside, but Silas held him back, insisting he go first. Archer gave him the candle. 'You two stay here,' he instructed Thomas and, alert and vigilant, he followed Silas.

His eyes adjusted beneath the faint glow of a porch lantern. It was barely enough to see by, but he made out the yard was square, empty and small. Buildings stood on two sides, and brick walls bordered the others. Plenty of windows looked down, closed and dark.

'This one was found here,' Silas said, crouching within the light. 'Cut from top to tail, worse than the one before, but nothing compared to the one after. The thing with this one...' he added, standing. 'Was that the night-watchman came out dead on the hour, as he always did, he said, to check the yard. And a bloke came in to have a piss ten minutes later, after having some kind of row with a woman over the wall, where Fecker's standing.'

Archer took in the information. He couldn't see Fecker or Thomas, but they were only a few feet away.

'When the pisser-bloke came in, he saw the body, and it was only ten minutes after the night-watchman, he was sure of that. Anyway, it was quick.'

Archer pictured it. A young man leading his punter through the gate, checking that they were alone, making sure of the time as if he knew the watchman's routine, and thinking of a few pennies in his pocket. Money for a bed, perhaps, or if not, for the rope-house. He imagined the lad, used for a man's pleasure as if a toy at best, thrown some coppers and, afterwards, left to clean away the traces from what remained of his dignity. Only, on the night Micky-Nick came here, there were no pennies, just the slash of the Ripper's knife and the tearing of his own flesh. Whether it had been quick for the boy or not, it was still death.

Sadness overwhelmed Archer, and he held the brickwork for support. Silas rested the candle on a ledge and came closer.

'You alright there, Archie?' he said. 'Shall we go?'

'No.' Archer grabbed his arm. His sadness became horror as

he looked into Silas' eyes and took in his face. 'I need to tell you something.'

Micky-Nick had walked into this yard bringing the chance of a loaf of bread, or a dry night's sleep, but he had also brought his killer. He had no idea his life was about to end. What dreams had he yet to fulfil? What woman or man had he yet to love? What ambitions to realise? It was too much to contemplate, but sad as it was, Archer could only think how easily it might have been Silas. Life was short enough, Micky-Nick and the others proved that.

Archer had waited long enough.

He took Silas by the shoulders. 'I'm not going to let you live like this,' he said. 'I can't.'

'I'm used to it, Archie.'

'No-one should be used to this kind of existence, but that's not what I'm saying.'

'We need to go.' Fecker's voice rang out in the mist-muffled night.

'Silas,' Archer said. 'I have this idea, this plan. I have so many things I need to tell you, but I can't get them out until I've told you...'

'Talk about it later.'

'No, it has to be now.' He had to know it as much as Archer needed to say it. 'What you said before,' he said. 'In the study. Did you mean it?'

'What did I say?'

'I was angry with you, wrongly as I see now. You said...' He lowered his voice. 'You said you had a fancy for me.'

Silas' eyes widened briefly, before narrowing again as he looked behind. Assured they were still alone, he nodded. 'Yeah,' he said. 'I meant that. Who wouldn't? I mean, look at you.'

'You are physically attracted?'

'Bit clinical, mate, but yeah.'

'So am I.' Archer's mind leapt madly, but there was more to say. 'Forgive me if I stumble,' he said. 'I have never expressed this aloud, and I don't know the words.'

'You fancy me, Archie, that's fine. It's my job, now let's go.'

'It's not your job!' Archer tightened his grip, pulling Silas to him. 'It's an evil necessity.'

'Luck of the Irish.'

'Stop being flippant.'

'Banyak?'

'In a minute, Fecks!'

Archer's heart raced, his body shook, and he strained to keep a level head. 'Silas,' he insisted, drawing the man's attention. 'You never have to live like this again. It's going to change. I want you to be at Clearwater.'

Some might have thought Silas' grin displayed triumph, as if he had seduced Archer into this decision, but to Archer himself, it was a heart-warming expression of joy. The moment passed, however, and Silas became thoughtful. The candlelight glinted from his eyes and sparkled on the water droplets on his cheeks. They gathered and trickled to his lips, so close and so soft.

'*Be* at Clearwater?' he questioned. 'What does that mean?'

'I haven't considered the details,' Archer enthused. 'But I want you there.'

'And Fecker?'

'We'll work something out.'

'Why are you holding me this close? Is that how you want me to be?'

'What?'

'You're stopping me from moving. You want to cage me in your cosy life and use me for sport?'

'How can you say that?'

'Because, I don't know what you're fucking talking about, Archer.'

The viscount was confused. He had offered the man a decent place to live, why was he fighting it?

'Hold me how you want me to be.' Silas said.

'I don't understand.'

'Look, Archie,' Silas sighed. 'I want to know what your game is. You're keeping something back, and until I know what it is, I don't know how to take you. That's all. So, you want me to be at your house as a renter, yeah?'

If that's all Silas understood, it would have to do. Archer pulled him chest to chest, folded his arms around him and gripped his buttocks one in each hand where they fitted perfectly. Layers of cloth separated them. Even in this dark and dismal place, they were kept apart.

150

'If you want to go that way,' Silas said, 'There's a fee involved.' He grabbed Archer in the same way and thrust his groin.

They were embracing, but Silas' words were inappropriate.

'That's not what I mean, Silas.'

He took the young man's face in his hand and held him at a short distance. Silas was a picture of concern distorted by lamplight. Everything about him was adorable, the jaunty angle of his cap, his straggly hair, his dark lashes and devilish twinkle. This sweet, lost man was everything Archer wanted to possess.

'Banyak!'

Fecker's bark focused Archer's mind. He was running out of time to say the one thing he couldn't leave without uttering.

He mustered his courage.

'I am trying to say, I am falling in love with you. I want you to be at my house. With me.'

The need to taste those soft lips was too powerful, and without word or permission, he kissed Silas. His heart overflowed, and his breath was taken away, leaving only the feel of the man's warm, soft flesh against his. He clutched his head, his fingers entwining his hair, his thumbs on his cheeks, savouring their feel. Passion rose instantly, the man's magic worked on every part of him, his longing free after years of secrecy. He opened his mouth, probing for the other man's tongue, but Silas' lips remained tightly closed.

Silas pushed him away. 'No,' he said.

He was half-shadowed, but lit enough for Archer to see the expression of pain as he turned.

'No?' Archer followed and took his arm.

'You can't.'

'Why?' What reason could he have? 'You won't have to live on the streets. You'll be safe. Andrej can come too. We'll find you respectable work if that's your worry. You won't be a kept man, but you will be my man.'

'Who has to stay hidden away, 'cos I'm from the gutter, and you're up there in the stars. It wouldn't work, Archer. It's not for me.'

'What?'

A commotion was taking place beyond Archer's concentration. He was hardly aware, not even of Thomas' voice now joining Fecker's in its urgency.

'You can't love me,' Silas said. He swallowed, fighting back some deeper emotion as angry words collected into one. 'No.'

He pulled away and made for the gate, but Archer was faster and held him against the wall. 'I must. I don't know where it came from, or why so fast, but it's happened. If you're telling me you can't feel the same way then... You still can't live like this. I can't bear to think of you hanging from a rope or begging for food.'

'I don't beg.' Silas struggled, but Archer's grip was firm. 'You don't want a boy what's used like me. You know what I am and where I've been. You can't love a rat like me, no-one can.'

'Archer, for God's sake!' Thomas was at the opening, a silhouette against an increasing glow of flames.

Archer heard nothing but Silas' words, and they cut his heart.

Silas wriggled free. 'Fecks, get them safe,' he shouted and was gone.

'Silas!'

'Archer!' Thomas was at his side, pulling his arm.

Free of the yard, Archer was instantly aware of the danger. He sniffed back the tears, breathed away emotion and took control. He had to. An army of men filled the street. They were closing on them, shouting, angrily waving fists and flares, batons and blades. They had no focus, they were there to frighten, and they were doing a damn fine job.

The Ukrainian stepped in front of Archer and pulled Thomas behind.

'Quick, with me,' he ordered, drawing a knife from his coat. 'And shut mouths.'

'It's another bloody Russian Jew,' a man yelled, and a cry went up loud enough to shake Archer's lungs.

'West.' Fecker ordered. 'Here.' He pushed them towards the advancing crowd.

Silas was gone, and as much as Archer wanted to run after him, Thomas was his responsibility too. He took his wrist, running beside Fecker diagonally across the street. They were heading for a narrow alleyway barely big enough for two and Archer saw Fecker's strategy. It was easy to defend.

He had no time for a battle plan, and Fecker had no intention to fight. He pushed Archer into the alley.

152

'Straight to end. Right, left, to the river. Safe there. Go west.'

Thomas stumbled, and Archer steadied him before spinning to face the foe.

'I will speak to them,' he said.

Fecker held him back. 'Then you die.'

The mob broke into a run.

'Go!'

'You can't hold them.'

Fecker's knife glinted in Archer's face. 'We both run.' He spoke through clenched teeth. 'Banyak needs you, and he wants you. I give you as long as I can.'

'Archer.' Thomas was tugging at his sleeve, and Archer heard his fear.

'Meet back at the house,' Archer said, squeezing Fecker's shoulder. 'Both of you.'

Fecker nodded before he turned back to the street, and shouting obscenities, ran towards the yard. The mob followed, and Archer hoped he knew what he was doing.

# Sixteen

They followed Fecker's instructions, but how His Lordship remembered them in the panic was a mystery to Thomas. He was doing his hardest not to show it, but he was sick to the stomach with fear. The only thing keeping him from screaming was the strength he gained from his master's firm grip. It loosened when they reached a wider, brighter road and slowed their pace.

'Where are we?' Thomas panted. The street was eerily quiet, and the sounds of their pursuers had long faded.

'Limedock,' His Lordship said, releasing his hand. Without pausing for breath, he turned right.

Thomas could no longer think of him as Archer, but all the time he had been allowed the privilege it had thrilled him to say the name. Walking in his master's company and being treated as an equal took Thomas back to his childhood when he had first come to the house as the junior hall boy. The young Honourable Archer Riddington had been permitted to mix with him as his mother's way of teaching him humility. He had just experienced a little of that warming, juvenile pleasure, but now it had to be shelved with any thoughts Thomas might have of friendship, let alone anything more.

'How are you feeling, Tom?'

'Calming, My Lord,' he replied, keeping a close eye on their surroundings. The street was better lit, but they were still among warehouses and factories.

'Hell, will we find a cab at this time of night?'

One of Thomas' duties was to order the Hansoms that brought and took away ladies in pearls and men in uniforms, and thinking of them helped normality to return.

'You are The Viscount Clearwater, Sir,' he said. 'You could knock at any coach house and demand a vehicle.'

'I could, Tom,' the viscount replied. 'But it would hardly seem fair.'

After an hour of walking, they found a cab on the embankment and rode homeward in silence. His Lordship was ill at ease. Thomas could see that from the way he rested his head on the window and stared into the damp night. His shoulders slumped, and his eyes were heavy. Thomas said nothing, it was not his place, but he longed to offer comfort and not to Viscount Clearwater, but to Archie.

He scolded himself and realised he had slouched. Tripp would have docked him pay for such slovenliness in his master's presence. Thomas had ambitions, and if he wanted to make something of himself, he had to remember his position. Yes, the adventure, though terrifying, had been a wonderful diversion from his station and status, but it would never be repeated. He must remain a servant, his fleeting time as a friend was over.

They arrived at the house a little after two in the morning, and as soon as the wheels had crunched to a halt, the viscount opened the door and jumped down. 'My study, please, Thomas,' he said, handing the footman the payment for the cabbie.

Two minutes later, Thomas found his master pouring a large measure of whisky. He had lit his desk lamp, but the rest of the room was in darkness. Thomas shrugged off his overcoat and set about the fire. He had lit the kindling when the viscount said, 'I am nothing but a beast, Thomas.'

Thomas, on his haunches, turned to look at him. The viscount was staring into his glass as forlornly as he had gazed into the sleeping city.

'My Lord?'

'Lord?' The viscount looked up from his lap, one eyebrow raised. 'Tonight, I am not worthy of the title. I made him feel like he was being bought. It was vile. Worse was to hear him say he could never be loved.'

Thinking it best to say nothing, Thomas attended to the fire. Once it had taken, he stood to find the viscount still watching him.

'It felt good calling you Tom,' he said, his voice distant. 'I was a boy again.' He put down his glass and huffed a breath. 'Did you hear the two of us speaking in that yard?'

Thomas had not heard the quieter parts of the conversation, but he had heard enough. He tensed. 'Partly, Sir.'

'I told Silas I was in love with him.'

Thomas remained silent.

'You know how I am, Thomas,' the viscount said. 'You won't be surprised.'

Thomas waited for the first signs of creeping embarrassment, but strangely, none came. 'Your private life is exactly that, Sir. And it shall remain so.'

He waited to be dismissed, but His Lordship didn't care to be alone. 'Will you sit and take a drink with me?' he asked.

'It is late, Sir, and…'

'Yes, I know. I'm sorry, but what is the point of this pile of a house if I don't have anyone to share it with?' He lifted his glass. 'I know people are constantly in and out for drinks here and dinners there, but eventually they all leave, and then all I have is me.'

Thomas wanted to tell him that self-pity didn't become him, that it was a weakness he wouldn't accept in others and did not need to accept in himself. It hurt him to see his master let himself down this way.

'Perhaps you will feel rested in the morning,' he suggested.

'My mind won't rest, Thomas,' the viscount moaned. 'I confused and angered Silas. I led him on, I used him for his knowledge. I drew him into my life.' He waved his hand towards the sketch resting on the desk. 'Literally.'

'I am sure they will be back for their money, Sir,' Thomas said. 'And you can clarify things with the gentleman then.'

The answer pleased Thomas' master, because he smiled for the first time since supper.

'Tom,' he said, 'I've known you longer than anyone else. Just about as long as I knew my father. We played together in the stables for years. There was that time… Do you remember? I was eleven, and you were nine, we were caught in the coach house. Wilson, wasn't it?' His face was suddenly animated. The fire had caught well, and His Lordship appeared to bask in its glow. 'Wilson found us turning his rooms into a farmyard and you were teaching me about calving down.' He laughed.

'But we only had use of Mrs Flintwich's chicken…'

'And Wilson found us pulling the giblets out of its arse and onto his best rug.' The viscount completed the memory, and the two men exchanged smiles.

The moment of joy turned to horror when His Lordship, without warning, clasped his face in his hands and threw his head back, howling with sorrow.

Thomas looked at the open doors. It was best to retreat and leave the viscount to his emotions. He would be thanked for his discretion. He should guard the fire and slip away discreetly. The Viscount Clearwater was the master of the house, a member of the Lords and many other things besides. What he wasn't was a man who cried in front of another, and Thomas wasn't confident with such a display. Creeping embarrassment welled up in him at last. It would be best if he left His Lordship to suffer in silence.

Best for whom? He questioned, knowing where his loyalty lay.

He added a log to the fire before putting the guard in place and hung his master's overcoat on the back of a chair where he stood a moment listening to the sobs. He even took hold of the doors and closed them, but from the inside. With his usual finesse, he placed an armchair opposite the viscount and brought the decanter with another glass. His actions slowly drew the man's attention, and he looked on with curious, red-rimmed eyes as Thomas poured himself a drink. He sipped and placed the glass carefully on the table before turning to the viscount, leaning in and taking his hand.

'Now then, Archer,' he said emulating the tone his mother used. 'You need to get everything off your chest.'

Yes, it would have been proper to follow etiquette and leave the man alone, but whatever the viscount was, at that moment he was a man who needed a friend.


Four miles away in Greychurch, a tall figure skulked silently through the twisting lanes and backstreets. Draped in black beneath a respectable bowler, he appeared to be just another businessman on his way to a pre-dawn rendezvous, or a semi-respectable gentleman returning home after a night's gambling and whoring. The streets had quietened after the near-riot whipped up by the vigilantes, and he laughed at their inadequacies.

They had missed him again, but only just. Interrupted in his work, he had left the boy dead, but his work was unfinished, and the interruption fuelled his anger. The need to feel the slitting, to peel back the flesh and examine the insides was still with him, and his fingernails itched at the prospect. The hour was late, but the opportunities were many.

A while ago he had been stalking a boy, following him until presented with the chance to engage him in conversation in a small yard that opened between the alleys and tunnels. The boy, apparently in some distress, had been amenable to his polite, well-spoken advances when he suggested they walk a short distance to somewhere more private. A place he had already picked out because of its relevance.

The whore-boy had been leading him there when the sound of the approaching mob forced a change in plan. He worked quickly and from behind. Hand over mouth, blade across the throat, pulling back, cutting deep to sever sound and arteries, the blood spurting forwards and away from his clothing. It was out of the pattern, but that was good. It would lead a false trail, cause more confusion and baffle the ridiculous authorities for the fifth time. It would drive them harder.

The boy was dead, but he was unsatisfied.

He needed another and in the right place. Something bloodier would show them he was set in his business, and tonight, he would again slice away part of his workings to demonstrate his skill. He might send it somewhere and include a note to whip the papers into more of a frenzy.

He wouldn't trouble the police. Inspector Adelaide and his incompetents had been given enough sport in the form of a letter written in his right hand, misspelt and intriguing. The words meant nothing and gave false clues, but they led Adelaide a merry dance which was amusing to read in the daily rags.

His chosen locations were the only clues, but no-one would be able to follow them. The boys meant nothing. They were random because he was down on all boy-whores. He had no intention to stop until the message hit home. The vigilantes with their flaming torches and hammer handles were nothing compared to the speed of his work.

He grinned at the thought through a scowl of frustration. He needed to sleep, to free his mind from the wrath and burning that bubbled within, but there was to be no stopping until his thirst was quenched.

He slipped easily unseen through the maze. It didn't matter where he met his victim, only that he was willing to follow him to Bishop's Square, but when he reached that location and found it perfectly quiet, he knew he had to search no more. A lone boy-whore waited beside a suitably dark opening to nowhere as if the meeting had been arranged. He was a tall and strong one, but it had to be now, and it had to be here. They were alone and with the mob scattering, there was no way of knowing how long he would remain undisturbed. Long enough for his indulgence, he hoped, as he crossed the small square, hailing the lad with a silent gesture of one hand.

The other held the knife within his cloak.

# Seventeen

The morning brought with it a sense of relief. Although his dreams had been troubled, they had the good grace to leave Archer as he woke. They faded into a mild headache which, along with the acidic taste in his mouth, brought back the excess of whisky and soul-baring he had indulged in the previous evening. He was left with only fond memories of Thomas' kindness, his open ear, his unjudgmental expression and his calming words.

Archer vividly remembered the events of the night up until his second glass. Then, as Thomas sat opposite exuding calm understanding, the memories blurred. They had talked about their pasts, how they were brought up together and yet apart, separated by convention in later years. His footman reminded him of incidents long forgotten. Mild misdemeanours long since blanketed beneath education, both intellectual and social, and it had been uplifting to be reminded of them. Their discussion had turned to talk of Silas, and Archer had gladly bared his soul. He needed to. The past few days had caused such uproar in his world he was at a crossroads with choices to make.

The path directly ahead was mapped and planned. It was his life, his title, and what was expected of him. That was the easy road, one where he would take a wife, have a society wedding, attend functions with her and leave the running of his house and life to women.

The crossroads, however, offered him an unexplored route, and one that was intriguing and magnetic, as if he had no choice but to walk it. Along it lay traps and pitfalls, because he could walk it with Silas.

At least, that was the dream. To have the man live with him, or, to be clearer, to be alive with the man. To be seen to live in such a way would set off the traps and cages, bring down the bars of authority and convention, and the road would end in disgrace for him and worse for Silas.

Thomas listened to his ramblings until late night became early morning and he said, 'Archer, Mr Tripp will be about soon. You should sleep.'

Archer wailed that he would never sleep again, not until Silas was with him, at which point Thomas had pointed out that he was spiralling into self-pity again and it was not becoming. The remark sobered him enough for him to agree, but he spoke with Thomas a few minutes more. Even when inebriated and emotional, Archer could still draw battle plans.

'Thomas,' he said as they helped each other to stand. 'Whether you like it or not, you are my friend.'

'I don't mind it, Sir,' Thomas said. He had only had two short measures, but was not accustomed to alcohol or late nights. 'I've always been your friend in ways you don't see.'

'What's that mean?'

'I'll just damp the fire.'

The footman lurched towards the grate and would have gone head first into it had Archer not caught him. He pulled the man back, Thomas turned, and their bodies became tangled. It wasn't quite a hug, they held each other for support more than anything, but it was a warm enough embrace.

'Feels odd,' Archer said, not letting go.

Odd, mainly because he felt no sexual attraction to Thomas. Until a few days ago, he could only dream of doing this, and when he did, sex always followed. Now, all he could think of was how it would be to embrace Silas.

'Imagine Tripp's face if he walked in,' Thomas whispered.

They sniggered.

'I understand you now, Tom,' Archer said, holding him tighter. 'The ways I don't see. You make me laugh. You let me get away with things like tonight. You're just… Well, you're just Thomas, and that's enough.'

'I meant things like…' Thomas giggled. 'Move your glass safely away from your first edition Dickens, or put your house key where you always find it, which is rarely where you left it, but thank you.'

'Don't thank me, Tom. Call me Archie.'

Thomas carefully separated himself from the viscount. 'The hour has passed,' he said trying to be Tripp, but slurring badly. 'You are now His Lordship, and the behaviour of your feetman has been most irreg'lar.'

'Stop it,' Archer chuckled. 'Feetmem?'

Thomas was correct, of course. Archer could play with the boundaries of his life, but his footman could not. He had to go to bed, but there was one thing more he needed to say.

'Tom?' He took Thomas' face in his hands as he had done with Silas. 'I ask a great deal of you, but I must test your discretion one more time.' He pulled Thomas to him and kissed his forehead. Still holding his face, now decorated with a docile smile, he said, 'I've always loved my boyhood friend as a friend, and that's what you will always be. But, sadly, you and your antique boss are correct.'

He let Thomas go, and their faces fell serious.

'The hour is late, Sir.'

What happened next came in brief snatches. Archer wrote a note at the desk and gave it to Thomas, telling him to leave it outside Mr Tripp's door. It instructed the butler not to wake either of them. The viscount would ring when he was needed, and Thomas was to have the day off. They supported each other to the main stairs where Thomas tried to veer to the left and the baize door. Archer wouldn't let him. They somehow made it to the top of the stairs where Thomas weaved along the passage, bumped into the servants' door and clawed his way through.

The next thing Archer remembered was undressing and falling into a cold bed.

Now he was awake and had caught up, knew where he was and what had happened, the events in the East End flooded back, bringing a pain far worse than his headache.

Silas could not love him.

He groaned and dragged himself upright. 'You've only known him two days,' he said and shook his head.

Tripp knocked on the door three minutes after Archer rang for him, and the moment the butler appeared in the room, his head jolted, and he sniffed.

'Good morning, My Lord,' he said, recovering with a small bow before placing a tray of coffee and a newspaper beside the bed. He

162

processed to the drapes and threw them apart with a flourish.

'Slowly, Tripp,' Archer complained. 'I have a touch of the Scotsman's revenge.'

'As the air would confirm, Sir,' Tripp sighed. 'I will open a window once Lucy has made up your fire.'

'Don't worry about that. I'm getting up. There's much to do.'

'As you wish.'

Waking up to Tripp was like coming round during a funeral and realising you were the one in the coffin.

'What time is it?'

'Beyond eleven o'clock, Sir.'

'Really? Is Thomas awake?'

'I doubt it.'

'You got my note then?'

'I was left a hieroglyph, My Lord, which I was able to decipher.'

'Sorry about that.' Archer needed no more wittily-wrapped sarcasm. 'Ask Thomas to come and find me when he wakes, would you? I'll be in my study.'

'You commanded he take a day off, Sir. At all costs.'

'Then he needn't wear his livery.'

Tripp was astounded. 'In the house, Sir?'

'He can come in his pyjamas as far as I'm concerned, Tripp. Just have him come.'

'As you wish, Sir. Breakfast?'

'Send something in on a tray.'

Archer swung his legs out of bed, and it was only when Tripp turned away that he remembered he was naked. He slipped back beneath the covers.

'I'll dress myself today, Tripp. That will be all.'

Tripp, facing the window, bowed and backed towards the door, only turning to face it when he thought safe to do so.

'Today's news may be of interest to Your Lordship,' he said before he slid from the room.

Archer needed to plan what to do about Silas. He would be back for his money, Thomas had been right, but what then?

He also needed to think carefully and deeply about the other matter, the street names, the coincidences or clues. His past, the Ripper, the drawing, Silas, they were connected through Archer.

They were also matters that would have to wait until his coffee was drunk and his headache had subsided. He turned to the newspaper intending to clear his mind with dull reading, the House business of the day, what the Commons was up to, what wrong the Prime Minister had done. He unfolded the recently ironed print across his legs and read the headline.

"Ripper Hacks Two More to Death."

It made no sense at first, because it was unexpected, but then it sank in. Two more? In one night? That was out of sequence. He speedread the columns searching for locations and found the first, Cornfield Yard. He repeated the name over and over, but it rang no bells. He read on and came to a mention of Bishop's Square. This time, when said the name aloud, it made perfect sense. Not only that, it also left him no room to manoeuvre.

He knew without a doubt who the Ripper was and felt sick at the thought of what it meant. He was sicker still when he reread the headline, and its full implications sank in.

'Two boys killed?'

Everything shut down as clammy realisation washed over him, and bile churned in his gut. He dived from the bed and vomited in the wash bowl. As he stood shivering, he forced his mind to think logically. He needed facts before he let his imagination free, but it was already chomping at the bit and ready to gallop to the worse possible finish line.

He dressed hurriedly, bent over the bed to read the report in full.

The first body was found at four… The second only twenty minutes later… The Ripper might have been disturbed…

Supposition. No-one could know. A paper's job was to sell papers. He searched for more details, dreading the names of the victims.

First youth… No name yet but known in the area for prostitution… Tall… Silas was shorter than Archer and he would not be classed as tall, more like medium. The body was slashed from… He didn't need to know those details. He read on.

Second youth… Bishop's Square… Seen waiting there as if to meet someone… No name but the worst mutilation so far and the clothes of a foreigner.

'Could be one of thousands,' Archer said, reassuring himself as he grabbed the newspaper and flew from the room.

164

He arrived at his study as Tripp was leaving it.

'I have placed a tray on the...'

'Thank you!' Archer called as he darted into the room and slammed the doors.

His mind worked fast. His panic pushed away the headache, but desperation roiled his stomach. He left the breakfast covered.

'Map,' he muttered, rifling through documents on the reading table.

He found what he was looking for and unrolled a detailed map of the East End. The print was small, and many alleys were unnamed, but, using a magnifying lens, he was able to peer close. He found Britannia Street where a tiny black square denoted the place he had last seen Silas, and from there, he spiralled out, checking the street names around it until he found Cornfield Yard. A short distance away was Bishop's Square. Silas had run to the east, and these murders had happened further west than where they parted. That didn't mean a thing. Silas could have doubled back.

His mind raced as he considered the timeline. Archer last saw Silas a good couple of hours before the estimated time of death. Deaths, he corrected. Anything could have happened in the meantime. Silas could have been...

Could and what if were not going to help him. One victim was described as tall. Fecker was tall. So were hundreds of other people. Dressed as a foreigner? There were thousands...

A knock at the door would have gone ignored had it not been followed by Lucy's voice.

'Your Lordship?' she called and knocked again.

'I don't need the fire,' Archer shouted, marching to the morning post Tripp had left on his desk. He flicked through the invites and envelopes, searching for the final piece of the puzzle. It had still not arrived, and he cursed.

Another knock and the doors opened without invitation. Archer spun on his heels, his frustration boiling over into anger. 'For God's sake, Lucy, what is...?'

Tripp stood in the doorway with Silas slumped in his arms.

An explosion of joy was immediately doused by a rush of cold realisation that Silas was dead. The heart-stopping thought was shunted away when the man groaned.

'What on earth…?' Archer had no clue what to say next, but Tripp always had a cool explanation for even the worst calamity.

'I think the gentleman should be put down,' he said, as if someone else was carrying Silas. 'He is not heavy, but he is awkward.'

'On the settee,' Archer clicked his fingers.

Tripp obeyed but hovered over the furniture. 'He is wet, My Lord,' he announced gravely. 'And bleeding.'

'Bleeding?'

'Both the result of an unfortunate accident. May I suggest…'

'No, Trip, you mayn't. Put him down for God's sake and never mind the state.' Tripp obeyed. 'Why is he bleeding? Where was he? Lucy?' Archer's training came into play, and he thought logically.

'Yes, Sir?'

'Please be kind and call on Lady Marshall's house. Ask Mr Saunders if he would dispatch someone to fetch Doctor Quill as a matter of urgency. He will be at his practice in Harvey Street. I shall pay the cab. Go quickly.'

Lucy curtseyed and left.

'Tell me the story, Tripp, and then fetch Thomas.'

Archer knelt beside the settee. Silas appeared unconscious or deeply asleep. Blood had oozed from the top of his head, matting his hair in a stream that led to his cheek and on beneath his chin. It had stopped flowing, indicating that it was not a deep cut, and Archer wiped it away with his handkerchief dipped in brandy.

'All most unusual, Sir,' Tripp began, towering over the viscount. 'Lucy went to empty the bucket in the yard having washed the vegetables for…'

'Just the important parts, Tripp.'

'The lad was curled up on the back step. She didn't see him until she was nearly on him and dropped the pail in surprise. Unfortunately, it struck the young man a blow and tipped, hence his brackish soaking and the graze.'

'What was he doing there?'

'One can only assume, sleeping, Sir.'

Archer couldn't see any other obvious injuries. He ordered Tripp to send Thomas 'Naked for all I care,' a command which raised one of Tripp's bushy, grey eyebrows.

'Silas,' Archer whispered. 'Silas, can you hear me?'

Silas' chest rose and fell in the steady rhythm of sleep. He moaned when Archer applied the alcohol to his wound, but his eyes remained shut. His delicate lashes flickered, and Archer hoped he was dreaming peacefully. He wiped a smear of blood with his thumb. Silas' cheek was lightly stubbled with downy hair, dark, like the rest of him and his lips, usually so pink and large, were sunken in and pale.

Archer's heart cried for the youth, and his body longed for him, but the only thing the viscount could offer was his care. Carefully, he undid Silas' jacket and slid his arms from the sleeves. Silas still didn't stir, not even when Archer lifted him and carried him through the drawing room to the hall. He was so light it was heart-breaking.

He met Tripp on the stairs. 'Thomas is on his way, My Lord,' the butler said. 'What shall I do?'

'Go ahead and open the green bedroom.'

'I fear the bed is unmade, Sir.'

'Then I will give him mine. After that, ask Mrs Baker to come up and have one of the maids bring hot water. Tell Thomas... tell them all, to knock first. Of course, show Doctor Quill up as soon as he arrives.'

They had reached Archer's rooms, and Tripp opened the door, stepping back to allow him to pass. To his credit, Tripp said and questioned nothing before he hurried away.

Archer lay Silas on his crumpled sheets, resting his head gently on the pillow. The man needed to be warm, but his clothes were soaked. He had suffered more than a pail of water. With no money, he must have walked, and the night had been heavy with drizzle. His flesh was cold as Archer removed his shirt revealing a well-worn, stained vest beneath. The string of his boots was knotted, and Archer was wrestling with one when Thomas knocked, and Archer called him in. He wore the same trousers as the night before, but his dress shirt was clean and pressed, though open at the collar. He wore slippers and a dazed expression.

'I came at once, My Lord,' he said, concentrating on standing without swaying. 'Apologies for my clothes.'

'Forget it, Thomas,' Archer said. 'Can you get these boots off?'

Whether Tripp had explained the situation or not, Thomas set about his duties with dubious dexterity, not once asking a question or passing judgement. Archer found night clothes and returned to the bed as Thomas pulled off the second boot.

'By Christ!' Archer said, pulling away from the smell. 'I suggest we burn everything.'

'It would seem the charitable thing to do, Sir.'

Another knock, another servant, this time Mrs Baker bustled into the room with towels. She glanced at the half-dressed man on the bed, but paid more attention to Thomas, her hawk-like eyes twitching from his feet to the boot he was holding at arm's length.

'The green room will be made ready, My Lord,' she said, depositing the towels on an armchair. 'I have asked Mrs Flintwich to make a broth.'

'Thank you, Mrs Baker,' Archer said, sitting beside Silas. 'So sorry to have interrupted your routine.'

'We are all Christians here, Sir,' she reminded him as she swished from the room.

'She wouldn't say that if she saw us take his trousers off,' Archer mumbled as he pulled Silas' vest free.

'Should I leave, Sir?'

'No, Thomas, please stay. Not that I want you to witness this, but for the sake of propriety...'

Thomas understood and planted himself on the other side of the bed from where he could stare at the fireplace while Archer worked under his gaze, but not in it.

The trousers practically fell to pieces, and Archer threw them into the pile of discarded clothes along with his socks.

Silas lay like a corpse in long johns, pale and thin. Archer gained no pleasure from the sight and wished he didn't have to do this. He would much rather have been undressing the man consensually and in the ecstasy of passion, but such thoughts had no place at that moment.

As he hooked his thumbs beneath the top of Silas' underwear, however, Silas groaned and rolled onto his stomach as if he knew what was taking place. Archer was relieved.

'That's for the better, I think,' he said.

The sight of Silas' small, round backside being gradually revealed was, if anything, more inappropriately erotic than seeing him from the front. A narrow line of dark hair ended at the base of his spine, but between it and a downy covering on his legs, there was nothing but smooth, white flesh. Archer remembered the feel of it through his clothes, and the desire to touch was overpowering.

He stood and covered Silas with his silk sheets.

'That wasn't so bad,' he said, trying to lighten his mood and failing.

'What do you suppose happened?'

'We will find out when he wakes.'

Another knock at the door.

'Hold!' Archer called before facing Thomas. 'There were two more murders last night,' he said in a whisper.

'Two?'

'One after the other, fast.'

Thomas shuddered.

'I know, Tom,' Archer said, reading his thoughts. 'He was lucky, and so were we. I am never sending you back there. Once more, thank you for putting up with me last night. I hate to think what I said.'

'I'm sure you remember as well as I do,' Thomas said. 'Which is just enough. Shall I let in the maid?'

Archer was closer and opened the door to Lucy.

The doctor had been sent for, she reported, but Lady Marshall's butler was concerned. Was there anything he should know, and could he help?

The message was relayed while another maid brought warm water, and, on the viscount's instruction, lit the water heater in the adjoining bathroom.

'What did you tell Saunders, Lucy?' Archer enquired.

'I told him there was nothing to be concerned about and there was nothing he needed to know,' she replied, as if answering the simplest question in the world.

'Good, thank you.'

The maids averted their eyes as they passed His Lordship's bed. Although it was their job to make it, to look at it when occupied was not. They left, closing the door quietly.

'Did you intend to bathe him?' Thomas asked, leaning to look into the bathroom.

'I had thought to,' Archer admitted. 'But not when he's out like this. I think we should dress him and leave him until Quill gets here. You could see to the grate.'

They worked together. Thomas made up the fire, breaking off to assist Archer in dressing Silas when needed. They managed to put him in a pair of pyjamas as he lay on his front and then gently rolled him onto his back to fasten the buttons. That done and the fire lit there was nothing more to do but await the arrival of the doctor.

'You can go back to bed if you want,' Archer said, sitting beside Silas.

'I am more than happy to stay with you, Sir, if you want me to.'

'You sound concerned about the lad,' Archer said, his wry smile demanding an honest reply.

'I admit I was uncertain of him at first,' Thomas replied. 'And I have the impression he is not that keen on me, but after what I saw last night…' His voice trailed off. 'Is it always like that, Sir?'

'Apparently so. I was as moved as you, Tom. It's another reason I am determined to help this man.' Thomas was well aware of the main reason for Archer wanting to help Silas, they had discussed it in their drunken state. 'Have you ever been in love, Tom?' he asked, as if it was the most natural thing in the world for a lord in love with a rent boy to question his footman on the subject.

'I admitted as much last night, I believe,' Thomas reminded him in a quiet voice.

The memory struck Archer between the eyes and shot him through with shame. 'You did. Quite right. Sorry.'

Thomas had admitted to being in love with Archer for a short while, but explained it as a crush. He agreed with the viscount that it was a deep friendship, the same as Archer felt for him. The conversation had been natural and meant in the early hours, now it brought crushing embarrassment for them both.

'And I said we would speak no more about it,' Archer said. 'Thank you for your help.'

'Very good, Sir,' Thomas said, resetting the boundaries. He bowed and left.

Archer stayed in his room, seated in the armchair and facing the bed as he waited for Quill. A little after two o'clock, a carriage drew

170

up outside and, looking from the window, he saw the familiar form of his old friend blundering with his medical bag. The sight was oddly reassuring, but he hoped Quill was sober.

He turned back to the bed.

'You're awake!' he exclaimed. Silas was sitting bolt upright staring ahead. 'It's alright.' Archer rushed to his side. 'You're at Clearwater.'

Silas' eyes remained wide and unfocused as his head turned slowly to face Archer. Only when they were an inch apart and lost in each other's bewilderment did he blink. His lips parted, and Archer imagined he was about to be drawn into a kiss of remorse.

Silas screamed and tried to thrash free of the bedclothes.

Archer held his arms. 'Calm, Silas. Be calm. You're safe.'

It was as if Silas came to and briefly understood where he was. He gripped Archer's shoulders in return. 'He got Fecker,' he wailed, tears pouring from his eyes. 'The Ripper. He got Fecker.'

# Eighteen

Most of the previous night was a blur for Silas, tumbling memories glimpsed through clouded thoughts and mist-soaked streets. He remembered Archer's kind face distorted in pain at what Silas showed him. He was standing in places where his kind died, thinking of them, opening himself up to accept the horror of what happened as he saw the last things they had seen; impenetrable walls, closed windows, no way out. The ghosts of dead friends were at his feet while Archer offered him an escape, protection, his love.

It had been wrong. Why should he single out Silas from the hundreds of others who needed safety? What could Silas have that the viscount found appealing? Why him?

Unable to cope with the weight of the man's kindness, and terrified by his own reaction to it, he ran. He couldn't be near Archer. He needed his own space to think, away from the stench of death and confines of the man's overwhelming friendship. The viscount had given him a way out, and much as Silas dreamt of such a thing, when it was offered it came with a condition; that he should make himself Archer's. It also came with a kiss that sealed the deal. Stay with him, and there would be many more. Give himself to the viscount, and he would want for nothing. He could leave the East End. He could have everything he wanted.

It was too much.

From then on, the images became more shattered. He scaled the yard wall, stumbled through the ginnel behind, lost himself and his direction in the twisting alleys strewn with fliers and posters calling for an end to the terror. Silas had his end in sight with a titled gentleman and a life of luxury, but he ran from it. Through the streets, avoiding the gangs spreading their own fear, under the railway bridges, past The Ten Bells where the nightly revelry rang out and the hurdy-gurdy played, its out of tune melody clanging from the barrel like death chimes.

He fled to Molly at the rope-house, somewhere familiar, somewhere to remind him of who he was. He found her slumped over her table, an empty gin bottle in her hand, out cold. Children had rifled her pockets and the money drawer, and the rope-room was a riot of angry voices and heavy men dragging screaming women away from the warmest bench. He ran from there, penniless and alone and kept running until he stood exhausted opposite the coffin shop in Cheap Street. A new sign in the window read, "Coffins 4/d a night." Even the undertakers had taken to renting to those more desperate.

This was not living. He had come to the city with ambitions to succeed and provide for his sisters, but how could he do that?

The answer was simple. Accept Archer's offer. Had it been purely a business transaction there would have been no debate, but Archer wasn't offering money for sex. He was offering love and all that came with it.

No-one could love Silas, and, as the bells of Christ's Church chimed the half hour — it could have been one o'clock or half-past two, he had lost track of time — the only thing he could think of was finding Fecker. Security, sensible advice and a warm body to hold. Fecks was all he needed.

They had two meeting places, the undertaker's shop and the corner of Bishop's Square where, in the early evening, the church sometimes gave out mugs of lukewarm soup. When they were alone, but looking for the other, they passed these places or waited at them and invariably they would meet. There was no time, no plan. You didn't make plans in this life, but Silas knew that Fecker would be waiting for him there.

When he emerged from one of the tunnelled alleys leading to the tiny square, however, he knew instantly he'd been wrong. There was no evidence, no-one was screaming Fecker's name, he didn't see the face, only a long body draped in a blood-soaked blanket, but that was enough. Through the police whistles and the baying crowd, he heard his worst fear confirmed. 'Looked Russian.' 'Bloody Jew, deserves it.' 'Just another molly-boy.'

After that, his memory faded until he was by the river, shivering and crying. Next, he was in the water, the mud sucking at his feet. He had nearly gone all the way and would have done, but for thoughts of his sisters.

He last saw them in the doorway of the tenement in Westerpool, one either side of the severe cousin who, under protest, agreed to house them until Silas returned with means to repay her. He had two pounds in his pocket, saved from weeks of labouring and hidden beneath floorboards until the day arrived. He remembered Ellie with the orange and pictured his sisters in her place. His last words to them were a promise he had yet to fulfil, and one he never would unless…

He shed his last tear of self-pity while huddled foetal beneath Iron Bridge, wet and freezing and watching the curtain of drizzle beyond the arch. He knew what he needed to do, and to do it should have been simple. 'No contest,' as Fecks would have put it. He cried for his friend and the memory of the body beneath the blanket exploded from him in uncontrollable tears that left him hollow. It was all he was. An empty shell of a boy who sold his body to feed his mouth.

It was worse. His soul gaped like a bottomless pit, and yet a man was standing over it, poised to fill it with the affection it craved. All he had to do was accept.

'You're so full of pride, Silas Hawkins,' he said, wiping his eyes. 'You'd let your sisters die because of it.'

He pulled himself to his feet, weak from hunger, his flesh burning from the cold. He needed help, and in the whole of the seething mass of humanity that fought for survival around him, there was only one place he would find it. He had an opportunity. Unlike Micky-Nick and Alex Chiltern, he had a way out if he could accept its conditions; to allow himself to be loved, not used; to break the bars of pride that caged him and to admit the truth.

He had fallen for Archer the second he had laid eyes on him, but was too stubborn to admit that it was possible to be loved in return.

Fecks had loved him.

Silas howled at his loss as he left the archway and stumbled crying through Limedock. Fecks would have told him to find help. 'Be you, Banyak,' he would have said. 'No proud, only happy.'

The rest of the night was an endless trudge of wet streets,

persistent drizzle and unfamiliar places. He knew the direction, but not the way, and when dawn broke somewhere above the low-hanging cloud, he was in the West End. At one point he was being chased. He'd stolen from a stall, an apple to stave off the pain in his stomach. It reminded him of Fecks, and he couldn't eat it. Daylight came, but brought no security. He was as vulnerable among the wealthy of the west as he was the poor of the east, dodging policemen, avoiding eye contact, passers-by and workers giving him a second glance, because he didn't fit in. He ignored them. He had nothing left as he searched the cleaner streets and mews desperate to recognise a building, a name, a tree until, half-starved, soaked and shaking, he staggered into the yard behind Clearwater House and collapsed.

Suddenly he was in a bed. There was light at a curtained window and a man silhouetted against it, strong and in command. Archer tried to speak gentle words, but Silas raved about Fecker and fought back until a second pair of hands held him.

He didn't know this other man, but he talked quietly and with authority until Silas gave in, exhausted. His vision was clear, but his mind cloudy as the doctor examined him, and Archer stood at the foot of the massive bed looking on in thought. He smiled when Silas caught his eye, but the kindness reminded him how he had treated the man, and he had to look away.

'Not much of a bump, but enough,' the doctor declared after examining Silas' head. He thought he heard him whisper, 'No lice,' and, a little later, 'No sign of disease,' but the words were spoken away from him. Chubby, gentle hands examined every inch of Silas' body, and he allowed it with dispassionate interest like an injured dog resigned to its fate. He felt no embarrassment, only gratitude that the bed was warm, the clothes he had been put in were dry, and the doctor knew what he was about.

'The lad's exhausted,' the doctor declared, having listened to Silas' chest for the third time. 'Can't detect any consumption. Heartbeat normal, no temperature, possibly hypothermia, but mild. Decent physical condition, considering.' He stood away from the bed and handed Archer a folded paper from his bag. 'Give him a little of this if he becomes agitated, but in my opinion, Clearwater, all he needs are decent meals and good sleep.'

Both sounded ideal to Silas, and he fought to keep his eyes open as the doctor laid him down and gently pulled up the covers. It was a simple gesture that took him back to his earliest memories of his mother, but in this case, he was alone in the bed, not sharing it with others.

Out of earshot, Archer spoke at length to the doctor by the window. Thomas appeared, and the doctor was shown out as the woman in black arrived bringing a bowl of thin soup and some bread. When she left, Silas was alone with Archer. There was much he wanted to say, and he began babbling as soon as the door was closed.

'Quietly.' Archer hushed him, sitting beside him and smiling with sympathetic eyes. 'Did you hear Doctor Quill? Eat, rest and sleep. We shall talk later.'

'Fecker...'

'There has been no definite news.'

'I saw him.' The horrific vision turned his stomach.

'What did you see, exactly?'

A stream of words poured from Silas' mouth as he related what had happened. He told Archer exactly what he remembered seeing, while interspersing his facts with apologies and remorse. Archer held the bowl and spooned him hot broth that warmed his insides, and made him drink a bitter liquid from a small glass, all the time calming him and promising to help. Tears that came unbidden were wiped away by the viscount's caring fingers, until Silas, empty of words, felt the irresistible pull of sleep.

'You need to rest,' the viscount repeated, and the last thing Silas saw, was Thomas entering the room and standing huddled with Archer deep in conversation.

'Find me something suitable, would you?' Archer asked, and Thomas followed him into his dressing room.

'It will be dark in a few hours, Sir.'

'I know, but I shan't hang around. Quill has given me a letter of introduction. I shall be no more than two hours at most.'

'I wish you would let me come with you.'

Thomas opened drawers and laid out what he thought his master would need while Archer stripped to his underclothes.

'I'm not taking you back there,' he said. 'I told you as much. You will be of assistance to me here. Stay with Silas even while he sleeps, but try and wake him around five.'

'If you're sure you will be safe?'

'Of course, I will,' Archer snapped back. He immediately pulled himself up. 'My apologies.'

'Not at all, Sir. We are having something of a stressful week.'

'Hell, Tom,' Archer said, grinning playfully. 'You sound more like Tripp every day.'

'Thank you.'

'Thank me?' Archer laughed as he pulled on a pair of breeches. 'You want to end up like that?'

'It is my ambition to become a butler, Sir, yes.'

'And you will, Tom.' Archie buttoned his fly. 'You will be my butler, I hope, but please, take the position as you, not as a relic from my father's day. We are a new generation. We have advancements, we have new technology. The phonograph, the telegraph and a device that allows one man to speak to another across distances, nothing my father would have understood or accepted. And that reminds me. As soon as I return I will need to know if there has been an afternoon post.'

'Very good.' Thomas handed him a sweater. 'Would this do for your journey?'

'My word, I'd forgotten about that. Will it still fit?'

It was a crew jumper Archer had kept from his navy days and, surprisingly, it fitted well.

'You are expecting important news, Sir?'

'I am, Tommy, and it concerns us all. I will tell you in good time, but for now, I need a jacket. Not too fancy, not too ostentatious, something down to earth.'

Thomas found a suitable garment and helped Archer into it. 'I'd suggest a warm coat and perhaps a bowler, rather than the top hat.'

'Do I possess one?'

'I can lend you mine. It's downstairs.'

Now dressed, Archer regarded himself in the full-length mirror. 'What do I look like?'

'To me? Like an unshaven Billingsgate fishmonger but without his apron,' Thomas replied.' 'Well, you did ask,'

'Thank you, but the question was rhetorical.'

'My apologies, Sir.'

'Thomas,' Archer said, turning to him. 'You never have to apologise for anything. But, you do have to do a few more things for me that are beyond the usual scope, but not beyond the pale.'

Thomas nodded gravely.

Archer rattled off a list of instructions, none of which fazed Thomas in the slightest. In fact, they polished his smooth features with pride.

'I will be back as soon as I can,' Archer said, striding back into the bedroom.

'You did say only two hours.'

'I don't know how long this will take, Tom.' He stopped to look on Silas, sleeping soundly on his side. 'I will aim to meet with you and Silas around seven. The draught wasn't too heavy, but if he sleeps on, so much the better. However, if you can wake him and he is able, have him ready. The sooner I get this matter off my chest the better it will be for everyone.' He paused at the door. 'One last thing. You're to treat him as any other guest.' With that, he was gone.

Silas woke to the sound of running water. He was drowsy, and it took a while for him to focus, but when he did, he slid up in the bed and remembered where he was.

'Hello?' he called. 'Archer?'

Thomas appeared at the bathroom door, his jacket off and his sleeves rolled.

'Mr Hawkins, you are awake,' he said, pointlessly.

'What are you doing?'

'Running you a bath, Sir.' Thomas glanced into the bathroom and back at Silas. 'Mrs Baker brought you some grapes,' he nodded to the table near the window, and then to the armchair. 'And, once bathed, you are to put on those.'

'Where's Archie?'

Thomas stiffened. 'His Lordship is out on business,' he said. 'But we have instructions.'

'We? When's he back?'

'I am unable to say. You are to take a bath, dress and be ready for His Lordship by seven. If you would like, Lucy could cut your hair. Rooms have been prepared for you, and I would suggest we move you there as soon as possible. Your presence in His Lordship's bed is perhaps acceptable in a time of crisis, but now you appear recovered… You understand, Sir?'

'I do, Tommy. Do you have to call me Sir?'

'Yes.' Thomas glanced again to the bath.

'And what should I call Archie?'

'Anything but that. Excuse me.' Thomas vanished into the bathroom, and the water stopped running. He returned a moment later trailing steam. 'Your bath is prepared.'

Had he not been so upset about Fecker, Silas would have laughed. A footman running a bath for him and announcing that it was ready as if was the throne before a coronation? Never in his wildest dreams.

Silas jerked in shock. 'Where's my clothes?'

'They were burned.'

'Burned?'

'I had to do it before they fled of their own accord.'

Silas was in no mood for jokes. 'And my coat?'

'That too.'

His face crumpled before the tears rained hot on his cheeks.

'What is it?' Thomas took a step closer.

'You burnt the only things I own,' Silas said, sniffing back the shock.

'Your money is safe,' Thomas assured him. 'But there was no saving even your coat. I am sorry if this upsets you.'

It wasn't Thomas' fault, Silas supposed. He wasn't to know.

'I did, however, keep this.' Thomas sat beside him and reached into his pocket. He pulled out a pebble. It was a perfectly round piece of rock, black and white in equal swirling measures.

Silas snatched it from his hand, coveting it.

'I sensed it might be of some sentimental value,' Thomas said.

Silas nodded, unable to speak until he had swallowed hard and taken a few deep breaths.

'This is the only thing I own,' he said. 'Not bothered about the clothes, but this and my hat… Fecker gave them to me. I suppose

I lost the hat last night sometime. Thought I'd lost this. I know it's only a stone.'

He looked up from it to Thomas whose eyes had moistened.

The footman stood. 'Can I be of any more assistance?' he asked.

'I'll be alright, Tommy,' Silas replied, swinging his legs from the bed. 'Thanks, yeah? For this.' Thomas said nothing. 'Tell you what, though. A haircut sounds like good…'

Silas crumpled to the floor as soon as he stepped on it.

Thomas was by his side in an instant, helping him to his feet and sitting him on the bed.

'Be careful, Mr Hawkins,' he said. 'You are not yet fully recovered.'

'Thanks, mate.' Silas' head thumped, and he thought he would bring up the broth, but the room slowly stopped spinning. 'Maybe you could help me to the bath. I'll be fine from there.' Despite it all, he winked at Thomas. 'Unless you want to join me.'

He didn't get the reaction he was hoping for. Instead of being embarrassed and blushing in his appealing way, Thomas' face flushed with fury.

'Don't speak like that here,' he spat. 'You have no idea of what a scandal would do to His Lordship. A maid only has to hear something like that for his entire house to come crashing down. You are here as his guest, not his whore.'

Silas was the one to blush. 'It's how I am,' he mumbled, and tried to stand.

'It must be how you *were*. Here.' Thomas took his arm. 'Silas,' he said, breaking etiquette. 'Archer is in love with you, and you know it. It's not my business to know yours, but it is to know his. If you have no feelings for him, dress and leave. But if you care about the man, you will take a bath and do as you're told. Either way, you're here because he cares about you and I'm here for the same reason.' He cleared his throat and spoke professionally. 'Now, Sir, if you are ready, shall I help you dress and show you out? Or will you accept His Lordship's hospitality?'

Silas fixed Thomas with an inquisitive stare before the wrinkles of his forehead flattened, and his lips crept into a smile.

'Assist me to the bath, if you would, my good man.' He put on what he considered an educated voice.

'As you wish.'

Thomas helped him across the room, but Silas stopped by the table. 'Oh, and, Thomas?' he said, his faux accent strengthening. 'Bring the grapes.'

Thomas tugged him onwards and adopted his home accent. 'Oi, nipper. Don't push your luck.'

# Nineteen

Night fell two hours before Archer returned to Clearwater. The west of the city settled into genteel peace as the lamplighters attended to the wicks and the messengers went about their deliveries. Drawing rooms glowed behind delicate lace curtains which twitched when a carriage passed, and footmen received callers at elegant front doors.

It was a far cry from where Archer had just been, and he had no thought for it. His mind was alive with news and plans as he stabled the horse, gave it a quick rub down and cursed himself for giving in to Mrs Baker and not hiring a new groom.

'I'll get you seen to properly,' he whispered in the animal's ear.

It shook its mane and snorted approval, not at its owner's words, but at the fast-paced trot it had enjoyed. Archer left it to nuzzle at whatever feed it had and crossed the yard to the back door. He glanced to the windows of the green bedroom and was pleased to see a light behind the curtains before he hurried through and into the passage. It wasn't his usual point of entry, but he was wet and his boots muddy. He shook off his overcoat as he walked through the kitchen and removed his hat when he entered the servant's hall.

The scrape of chairs and clatter of cutlery was followed by silence as the servants stood.

'No, please,' Archer said. 'Don't get up.'

They stayed as they were until Archer insisted they sit, and Mr Tripp told them it was acceptable to do so. He, however, remained standing.

'May I assist you, My Lord?' he asked.

'No, Tripp, thank you. I am sorry to disturb your dinner,' Archer said, 'but as you're paused, I would like a quick word.' He leant on the dresser and bent a leg to remove a boot. Tripp advanced, but was repelled by a shake of his master's head. 'Eat your dinner,' he said. 'All of you, carry on. I've disturbed you enough, but Mrs Baker if you could…' He wrestled with the boot. 'Can you send one of the girls to Saunders as soon as convenient and ask him to spare his stable lad? Emma needs a decent groom and feed, and I've not put the trap away in any kind of order.'

'Of course, My Lord,' Mrs Baker replied. 'Lucy?'

'When you've finished,' Archer told the girl as she leapt to her feet. 'It's not an emergency.' He turned his attention to Thomas as the boot came free. 'How is my guest?'

'The gentleman has been moved to the green bedroom,' Mrs Baker put in before Thomas could answer.

'Excellent.' Archer kept his eyes on Thomas. 'And?'

'As per your instructions, My Lord,' Thomas said. 'I am pleased to tell you that he is recovered and, although weak, is well enough to be waiting for you in the drawing room.'

Tripp curled his fingers into fists and relaxed them, a sure sign that he was about to complain. Arched didn't give him the chance.

'I expect you are wondering what's going on,' he said, starting work on the second boot. 'These past couple of days have not been what we are used to. Thank you all for putting up with my eccentricities, all will become clear in due course.' The boot came free unexpectedly, and he slipped on the flagstones. Tripp hovered nervously. 'In the meantime, Mr Hawkins is staying with us as my guest. He has fallen on difficult times, and it is our duty to look after him. Our Christian duty,' he emphasised directly to Mrs Baker to wipe the look of disapproval from her face. It was replaced by irritation thinly veiled behind a smile.

'I shall have one of the girls change your bed, Sir,' the housekeeper said. 'Sally? You can see to that.'

'What on earth for?' Archer said. 'It was only done yesterday.'

'You can't want to sleep in those sheets after today.'

'Mrs Baker,' Archer said patiently. 'My guest is a man, not a dog. Right, that's it. Carry on.'

He walked gingerly to the door trying his hardest not to slip.

'Oh, Thomas,' he said, holding the doorjamb for balance. 'Could you tell Mr Hawkins I will be with him shortly? I'm going to wash and change.'

'Allow me to assist you, Sir,' Tripp said gliding forwards.

'Honestly, Tripp, I am fine. I will be ten minutes.' Archer didn't want him asking questions, but he also didn't want to alienate him. 'On seconds thought, yes, please. That would be most helpful.' He knew it wouldn't. 'But finish your supper first.'

He suggested it to give himself enough time to change before Tripp arrived, but his butler put his master before his stomach and followed him to the baize door. There, Tripp turned left to continue up the servant's stairs and expected his master to enter the house, but Archer followed him, saying he didn't want to drag his muddy self over the carpets.

'You have been in the country, Sir?' Trip asked, as they took the first turn.

'No, Tripp. I had some business towards the east.'

'Not, I hope, to do with our unsavoury matter there the other night?'

'In a way,' he said. 'To do with the charity.'

It was partly true. The charity was to operate in the area, and it was to help young men like Silas. He had told Tripp enough and changed the subject to flatter the man about how well he had trained Thomas and to thank him personally for putting up with Archer's behaviour.

Tripp was grateful for both compliments and commented that Thomas would, in years to come, make a conscientious butler.

'But he will never replace you, Tripp,' Archer said, as they took the last bend and entered the first floor. Sometimes he sickened himself.

After that, their talk was of shirts and shaving foam, cufflinks and claret as Archer requested a couple of bottles from the cellar be brought at seven. It was nearing a quarter to, and he was keen to see Silas.

'I shall be in the study,' he told Tripp in the mirror as his man brushed the yoke of his jacket. 'Ask Thomas to bring supper for myself and Mr Hawkins. A tray, anything. After that, I shan't disturb you or the servants further tonight. I only need Thomas.'

Tripp stiffened as Archer suspected he might.

'Once again, Tripp, nothing can replace you. I ask for Thomas to save you the indignities I ask of him, all of which, I must add, is for the benefit of the likes of Mr Hawkins and the rest. Besides, I would rather eat into his time than yours, else who would run the house?'

Flattery always worked with Tripp. He was a shallow man.

'Whatever you say, Sir.' Tripp nodded once and stepped back.

Archer grimaced at his reflection. 'Is the high collar and cravat too much?' he asked

'Not at all, Sir.'

He tugged his waistcoat and raised his chin. He had shaved closely and trimmed his sideburns, a new style from Paris that Lady Marshall had suggested. His father insisted he wore a moustache, thus he had shaved it off the day after he died and was glad to be free of both. As soon as Tripp left him alone, he would take off the jacket he had so carefully groomed and go about in his shirtsleeves. Had he not already been dead, his father would have died at the outrage.

He dismissed Tripp and, a moment later, the jacket. He had returned from the East End with news, and it was to that which he turned his attention. Not all of what he had to tell Silas that night was pleasant, some of it, he might not believe, but whatever happened next, Archer was bound to the man, and there was much to be explained.

He left his room and looked at the opposite door as he closed his own. It had been his nursery and was still his favourite bedroom. Like the others on this floor, it had its own bathroom, dressing room and sitting room, and its only drawback was being at the back of the house. It was quieter, being away from the road, but there was less light in the mornings. For all its faults and memories, he hoped Silas liked it. The suite was to be his for as long as he wanted it, but how that was going to work, Archer wasn't sure.

He approached the stairs with trepidation, anxiety about what he had to say growing steadily within. His ancestors looked down on him from their oil-painted eternity as he descended beneath their thunderous glares. Forgetting that he had ordered Silas' clothes burned, he prepared himself to find a street-rat in his drawing room. An undernourished young man in ill-fitting, second-hand trousers and a jacket too big, wearing boots with string laces. He crossed the hall, relieved to see the drawing room doors closed. He paused there, gathering his thoughts and told himself not to overreact when he saw what state Silas was in, but to stay calm, keep his wits, offer support, yet not let his love for the man cloud his judgement. What he had to tell Silas was not going to make for a comfortable evening, and once he knew the truth, he may well be lost to Archer forever.

The glass doorknobs were cold in his hands as he turned them, taking a deep breath before entering.

'Oh!' he said, halting in his tracks. 'Can I help you?'

His train of thought was derailed by the sight of a man in a blue suit, facing the opposite wall. He had his back to Archer and was looking up at one of the landscapes. His hair was smoothed over to one side and its cut, along with the dark suit, suggested he was a messenger.

Archer's heart leapt. Had it arrived?

Any notion that this stranger had brought his long-awaited telegram evaporated when the gentleman turned. His head dropped and a long fringe, until then brushed back, slid gracefully like a curtain to shield part of his forehead. He adjusted his jacket which, Archer noticed, was slightly too long in the arms, and a pair of deep blue eyes looked up from beneath dark brows.

As if he needed further proof that he was hopelessly in love with this man, Silas' joy at seeing him brought Archer to the edge of tears. Short of breath, he swallowed an involuntarily sob and growled the emotion from his throat.

'Thomas and Lucy did it,' Silas said, as if blaming them. 'It's his old suit from about ten years ago,' he said. 'Bit long, but the woman in black stitched up the trousers. Lucy cut my hair.'

'I never knew she had such talents.' Archer had been right to thank his staff and made a mental note to do it again in a less hurried fashion.

They stared at each other in silence until Silas said, 'I don't know what to say.'

'Don't say anything. You are perfect.'

'Ain't so bad…' Silas checked himself. 'You look well, My Lord,' he said.

Hearing his title spoken snapped Archer back to the task ahead, and he reminded himself not to let his admiration for Silas dominate his thoughts. It was a futile hope.

'Silas,' he said. 'I have news for you.' Archer walked further into the room and met Silas halfway. 'Andrej is safe,' he said. 'I have seen him.'

He thought Silas would crumple. He turned pale enough, and Archer was ready to help him to a chair. Instead, however, Silas threw his arms around Archer and buried his head in his chest. He hugged him and, not caring if anyone walked in, Archer hugged him back. Silas held him so tightly he had to beg him to let go, and when Silas did, he was crying tears of joy.

He wiped them away. 'I got to stop doing that,' he said. 'Sorry.'

'Come in here.'

'How do you know?'

Archer led him into the study where the fire roared and poured them both a glass of Scotch. His hangover was long forgotten, but he didn't need another one and added plenty of soda. Silas drank his neat, banging the glass on a table before downing it in one in a tribute to Fecker.

'How do you know?' he repeated when he had stopped coughing.

'Quite straightforward actually.' Archer sat on the couch where eight hours earlier he had laid Silas, and invited him to sit beside him. Once Silas was comfortable, and they faced each other, he continued his story.

'I asked Quill where a body would be taken in such circumstances, and he put me in touch with the medical examiner working with the Greychurch coroner. I took the trap…'

'Were you alright? Who went with you?'

'Calmly, Silas.' Archer patted his leg, but the gesture felt effeminate, and he rested his arm across the back of the couch instead. 'I went in daylight and semi-disguise. Actually, I was surprised to see how many gentry were in the area.'

'Yeah,' Silas complained. 'They come in for a gawp during the day. We call them tourists.'

'That's somewhat common,' Archer said. 'I mean them, not you. How hypocritical. Anyway… The coroner, on seeing my letter from Quill and recognising my title if not my person, allowed me to see photographs of the unfortunate victims. Neither was Andrej. The first body had been claimed by the family and the second had been identified as an Arab.' He tried to think. 'I don't remember the name, but it certainly wasn't Andrej Borysko Yakiv Kolisnychenko.'

'You remembered all that?' Silas' mouth was agape. 'Bugger me.'

'Of course,' Archer said. 'I know how important he is to you.' He moved on, fearful of becoming oversentimental. 'Distressing though it was to be in the presence of two lives so brutally and pointlessly lost, I was relieved at the news. The coroner had no idea where I might find Andrej, of course, there was no reason he should, so I asked Quill's friend. He had been working like a dog all morning, he told me. There was quite some disturbance last night, and several men were injured. I described Andrej and where I had last seen him, and this chap sent out a couple of messages. When they finally returned, one boy arrived with news that a man fitting Andrej's description had been found outside the church abutting Bishop's Square...'

He held up his palm to prevent Silas from interrupting.

'He is alive,' he said. 'But he did suffer an attack and needs medical care for a few days.'

Silas became animated. 'How's he going to get that? I could take that five pounds! Where is he?'

'Calmly, Silas.' Archer had to laugh, the man's affection was not only worn on his sleeve but on his face where it displayed as juvenile concern. 'I took the trap to Lane End and the hospital for the poor where, after some outrage from the administrator and some name dropping from me, we negotiated his release. Not into my care, that is not possible yet, but I had him taken to the hospital of Saint Mary. My mother, Lady Clearwater, is a trustee.

'I stopped by the medical examiner on my way home to thank him with a bottle of malt and engaged him to tend Andrej. He assured me he would go directly he was free of his practice. So, Andrej is being cared for and will be brought here in time.'

'I still don't know what to say.'

'And I don't know what else to tell you.' Archer let his arm drop to rest half on the cushion and half on Silas' shoulder. 'Except to apologise for my outburst last night. I didn't mean to frighten you, or make you hate me, or whatever it was that set you running like a hound.'

'It was a lot of things,' Silas admitted and turned further towards Archer. He reached over his shoulder and took Archer's extended arm, pulling it closer and holding his hand. 'Lots to think of, See?

But... Am I allowed to do this in a posh room?'

'Only if you want to.'

Silas nodded. 'I'm the one who needs to say sorry,' he said. 'What was I thinking? You could have ended up in a lot worse state than Fecks.'

'Apparently, he fought off seven out of ten men before the police broke it up. They were so impressed, they didn't run him in. At least, that was the doctor's view.'

'He's a tough fecker is Fecker.'

'Agreed.'

'Wish I was.' Silas pouted. 'If I was, I'd have been able to tell you last night what I have to tell you now.'

The warmth suddenly left the room leaving rejection waiting icily in the wings.

'Go on.' Archer savoured the clutch of Silas' hand while he could.

'I was… It was like being slogged in the teeth by an Irish navvy,' Silas said. 'And that hurts, believe me. What you said didn't hurt, I don't mean that, but it was a shock.' Silas rested his free hand on Archer's thigh causing the blood to rush to his ears as his pulse quickened. 'Can I do this?' Silas asked.

'You may.'

'The thing is, Archie… Oh, can I…?

'Silas, just say it and worry about the etiquette later.'

'Sorry. It's all new to me.' He took a breath. 'Thing is, no-one's ever said what you said. I've never heard it before, and, 'cos I have to be honest, I don't see how you can. So, I don't know what to do about it.'

'You mean, you are unable to return my affection?'

'I only know one way.'

Silas' hand slid towards Archer's crotch, but the viscount prevented its journey.

'That's not why you are here.'

'Why am I here?' Silas whispered. He looked up at Archer with hopeful eyes.

'You know,' Archer said. 'I told you last night.'

'And I showed you how I lived, and you know what I've done. I'm not some gentleman, educated and untouched. I don't know about the world you live in, but you've seen mine. How…?'

'I don't know how it happened.' Archer's voice was hoarse. 'But it did. I don't care what's gone before except when it causes you pain. I don't give a damn about where you come from except to understand you more. What I do care about is you, and if you aren't comfortable here in any way, if this is not for you, then you say so, and you leave. I won't have you playact and suffer on my account. You know how I feel, and if it's not for you, then I would rather see you leave free than stay here trapped.'

'You think enough of me to let me go?'

'You are your own man, Silas Hawkins, but for my part, I would like us to be together, as much as that is possible in this world, and I have said why. I am in love…'

His words were smothered by Silas' lips. Soft but driven, they met Archer's with a passion he had never experienced, and he responded in a way he never thought possible.

He pulled Silas to him, freeing his hand which, instead of moving to his crotch, flew to Archer's face. Silas held him, pulled away beaming, searching Archer in amazement for a second before their lips locked again. Archer slid back, dragging the youth on top of him and their legs battled as their arms fumbled until they were wrapped together as closely as breathing would allow, Silas bearing down with unstoppable, wonderful kisses.

Their cocks rubbed together, but were left untouched, their hands were too busily employed in each other's hair, gripping shoulders, exploring.

Gradually, their tongues slowed, their breathing calmed, and their fingers released. Silas, resting weightlessly on Archer's chest, bit his bottom lip as if he had been caught doing something naughty.

'Yes, you are allowed to do that too,' Archer smiled. 'If you really mean it.'

Silas nodded silently.

'You can't say it, can you?' Archer teased.

It was as if in that brief moment of passion, he had come to understand Silas completely.

Silas shook his head.

As much as Archer longed to hear the words, he was not going to force Silas to say them.

'But you would if you could?'

Silas nodded. 'I will when I can, but for now, will you just believe me?'

'I will.'

They were so engrossed in each other's arms and kisses, Thomas had to cough loudly three times before they realised he was waiting at the door.

# Twenty

Silas rolled from Archer, and his joy became fear when he realised there were two maids in the other room on their way to deliver their supper. It was then that he remembered Thomas' harsh warning and understood how careful he and Archer had to be. Had anyone else seen what they were doing, he dreaded to think what backtalk they would cause. Gossip would become scandal that could lead to any manner of problems for the man he had fallen for.

Archer leapt from the couch and stood to face the fire, presumably so no-one saw the incredible bulge at the front of his breeches. Silas was in a similar state, and it struck him that he had never been so excited in a man's presence as he was with Archer. Up until now, sex had been sex, but just now, so close and intimate with the man, he had not been fuelled by lust. He knew exactly what it was that pumped his heart and fed his longing, and it wasn't so much that he couldn't say the words, 'I love you,' it was more that he was too surprised and confused by the uncharted feelings coursing through him.

He sat on the couch, legs crossed and pulled his ill-fitting jacket over his lap. Thomas, seeing the coast was clear, entered the room and instructed the maids to lay their trays on the reading table beneath the front window. There, he placed two bottles of fancy red wine.

'Thank you, Thomas,' Archer said, apparently examining the mantle clock in great detail as it struck seven.

'My Lord,' Thomas replied. If he was unnerved by what he had just seen, he didn't show it. In fact, as he backed away and turned, Silas caught his eye, and Thomas gave him a brief smile. It was reassuring, but Silas detected some sadness behind it.

'Lucy has a question,' Thomas said. 'If she may, Sir.'

It took a moment for Silas to realise he was being spoken to. It was going to take some time to adjust to being called Mr Hawkins, let alone Sir, and by a man he had groped. Thomas and Silas were bonded by more than their shared affection for the viscount, and perhaps it was time for Silas to stop his teasing.

'Er, yes,' he said. 'Of course.'

He looked to Archer for approval, uncertain if this was the correct form, but the viscount was now rearranging the clutter on the mantlepiece, his back to the room, his excitement still too obvious to show.

'Thank you, Sir,' Lucy said and curtseyed. Something else Silas would have to get used to. 'I wondered if there was any news of the Russian gentleman?'

Archer looked at him over his shoulder and nodded. Spying his smoking jacket hanging from the chair, he reached for it and put it on. It was long enough to cover him well below the waist.

It was probably best not to use his nickname, so Silas informed Lucy that, 'Andrej got into a fight and is in hospital,' news at which she blanched. 'But, His Lordship says he is going to be alright.'

'That's good to hear, Sir,' Lucy said, her smile of relief suggesting that this was not just casual interest. 'I'm glad for you.'

'Thank you, Lucy. Sally.' Archer dismissed them. 'I shan't need you again tonight, but Thomas, you are able to stay?'

'Certainly, Sir.'

The maids left, and Archer closed the door behind them while Thomas set out their supper.

'Sorry about that, Thomas,' Archer said. 'Thank you for being cautious.'

'Not at all, Sir.'

Archer invited Silas to the table, and they sat opposite each other, a spread of cold meat, pies, cheese and bread before them; a feast Silas was more than ready for. Thomas began placing an assortment of cutlery before him, arranging it neatly at precise distances until Archer said, 'We don't need to be formal, Tom. Pull up a chair.'

Thomas was uncertain.

'It's one of those times,' Archer said. 'I need to talk to both of you about this whole matter, and it's not going to be possible for me to do it if you are standing there like Tripp looking down his nose.'

'I didn't realise I was.'

'You weren't, but you were going to. Sit, Tom, but get yourself a glass first.'

Thomas hesitated, and Archer sighed.

'We are not going to be disturbed,' he said. 'Unless a messenger arrives in which case, I *need* to be disturbed. And if we are, it doesn't matter. It's my bloody house.'

'Are you sure you would not rather dine alone?'

Archer rose slowly, and Silas watched, a slice of pork pie hovering before his lips. The viscount brought another chair to the table, placed a wine glass in front of it and then held the chair out for Thomas. 'Take off your jacket,' he said. 'Roll up your sleeves too. We have work to do.'

Thomas did as instructed.

'How be, Tommy?' Silas winked, hoping it would put the redhead at his ease.

'Happy for you both,' the footman replied, but it was hard to tell if he meant it.

'Gentlemen…' Archer sat and began eating. 'It's high time I explained to you what I am up to. I have a story to tell you while we eat… Help yourself, Tom.'

'I have eaten, Sir.'

'Archer. Or Archie, if you can't manage that.'

Thomas poured the viscount and Silas wine before serving himself a token amount.

Archer leapt straight to business.

'You know I have an interest in the East End,' he said, forking thick slices of ham onto his plate. 'The charitable work which I am compelled to undertake, feeling as I do, that it is the business of those who lack for nothing to assist those who have nothing. Naturally, of late, my determination to act has been reinforced by the murders, but my interest in them is not morbid, as it appears to be among some of my class whom I saw in the area today. The society tourists.' He shuddered. 'I have a personal interest in these deaths which I shall explain.'

He paused for a sip of wine, and Silas followed suit. It was the smoothest tasting alcohol that had ever passed his lips.

'Long way from a tupp'ny gin,' he said, replacing his drink

carefully. The glass was probably worth more than he would earn in a lifetime.

'We are indeed,' Archer said. 'And we must work fast.'

'We?' Thomas queried.

'If you are willing,' Archer said. 'Let me tell you my story and explain what I have been doing, and then you can tell me if you are willing to work with me. I shan't be offended if you are not. I shall understand, but I think you can both help. Silas because he knows the area and you, Tom, because you have a far more practical mind than me, and that's what I need. That and your detached opinion.'

Silas loved the way he spoke. His words were always so carefully placed as if he had spent hours practising his speeches before delivering them. Silas spoke whatever came out of his head, a trait that had landed him in hot water on many occasions.

'As you know, Tom, I spent some time in the navy before I had to retire a couple of years ago.'

Thomas nodded, but Silas must have looked inquisitive because Archer explained that he had been injured and, although he could have served in some other capacity, the failing health of his father coincided with his honourable discharge, and affairs at Clearwater and the country estate needed his management.

'What injury?' Silas asked. 'That?' He pointed to the scar on Archer's cheek.

'That was part of it,' he said. 'But not all. I'll show…' He considered Thomas for a moment. 'Sorry, Tom,' he said. 'I'll show you later, Silas.'

'Sir,' Thomas said, laying his hands on the table. 'Archer. You're dodging around me as though I'm likely to be offended. Let me say, I am not. Nor am I upset at what I just witnessed, far from it. Whatever is taking place between you and Mr Hawkins is making you happy, and that's all I need to concern myself with.' He turned to Silas. 'He was nearly killed in hand-to-hand combat. He won't say it, but he has many medals.'

'Yes, thanks, Tom. Silas doesn't need to know all that. I'm just me.'

'That's a clagmire a-be speaking from,' Thomas muttered with a wry smile at Archer.

'Which, when translated means…?'

'You're being too modest,' Thomas said. 'And you stopped talking just then, because you didn't want me to be upset that Silas is going to see exactly where your scar is, and get a lot closer to it than anyone else, to my knowledge, ever has.' He turned to Silas again. 'It's across his side,' he said. 'From here…' He indicated below his ribcage. 'To here,' below his navel.

'Thanks, Tom,' Archer said. 'I appreciate your directness, but to be accurate, it wasn't hand-to-hand, but sword-to-sword. But what matters now are the murders in Greychurch.'

Silas settled to eating as he listened while Thomas turned his wine glass between his fingers, eying the viscount with interest.

'While I was a naval officer,' Archer began, 'I served with a most disagreeable man two years and one rank my senior. He was a man I knew well, but not one I cared for. At all.' He glanced at Thomas as if the footman knew who he was talking about. 'There was, however, another lieutenant, my rank, about whom I cared a great deal. So much so, that I was nearly driven mad by my love for him, and here, Silas…' he added, reaching across and taking his hand, 'you are not to become jealous.'

'Jealous, me?' Silas laughed. 'I'm sure whatever you're about to tell me ain't any worse than things I could tell you. I don't get jealous.'

'That's good to hear.' He released Silas and threw a knowing look at Thomas. 'Nor you,' he said before continuing with his meal. 'There was an attraction between the lieutenant and myself which was both mutual and undeniable. It was, sadly, also irrepressible and one night he and I were caught in a compromising condition similar to that just witnessed by Thomas.'

Although Silas liked the sound of Archer's voice, he wished he would use less complicated sentences. By the time he worked out that Archer and the officer were caught 'doing it', the viscount had moved on.

'More unfortunate was that we were discovered by our senior officer, the ship's commander. Of course, we both expected dismissal if not imprisonment, and from a state of exhilaration and love, I crashed into abject fear.' He looked at the curtains as if their pattern told the story of the past. 'In retrospect, it would have been better had we been discharged and shamed. You see…' He returned

196

his attention to Silas. 'The commander was so enraged by what he had seen, he took a very unusual step and said nothing.'

'He let you get away with it?' Silas clarified.

'Yes.'

'Suspicious,' Thomas said.

'And that's why you are here, Tom.' Archer squeezed his hand, but Silas didn't mind. 'You know some of this story, but not all, and your objectivity will be invaluable.' He continued to eat. 'Suspicion was also on my mind, and my fears were confirmed when my commander began his punishment. It started as if what we had done was a mild misdemeanour; having to swab decks with the midshipmen not officers, that kind of thing. It progressed over time and became more severe. Eating with the crew, backs turned to us in the mess, extra watches and so on. Eventually — and this lasted months — his retribution took the form of beatings, by him and unwitnessed. The worst kind of bullying was administered, but I was still grateful that we had not been shamed, and so I put up with it.

'My friend, however, was not made of the same stuff. The commander's anger turned to hatred, and its focus turned to the other lieutenant. I was free if you like, and yet my punishment continued because every day I saw the ruined state of a man I loved and the terror he was made to suffer.'

Archer's hands trembled, and he put down his fork to hold his fingers steady. He looked through Silas, unblinking, his pupils large in the candlelight.

'I was at the point of going to my Captain and admitting the entire story. It would have meant the end for all three of us, but it would at least stop the torment. Before I found the courage, though, it struck me that the situation was worse than I thought. The commander, I realised, was himself in love with my friend, but it was not reciprocated. He hated this man for not giving in and hated himself for loving him. He had tormented himself into something approaching a murderous rage. It was the only possibility, and it was...'

He suddenly became aware of Silas and sat back, taking a deep breath.

'It was a terrible time,' he said. 'Played out behind the uniform, under the normalities of daily life aboard ship, unseen by others and unspoken about by ourselves.'

Reliving the story was causing Archer great pain, and Silas wished he knew how to comfort him.

'The upshot,' Archer said, 'was that my friend took his own life. He ran himself through on his cutlass, so we were told. It was the night before we went ashore at Odessa and fell into the skirmish that earned me my injury. It was while we were en route that it hit me. My lover's death had not been suicide.' He paused for a sip of wine, leaving his meaning hanging in the silence until his glass was replaced on the table. He stood and unbuttoned his waistcoat.

'I carried that certainty into battle with me, and it showed itself in my ferocity towards the foe. On the edge of the skirmish, I finally confronted my commander in the manner I confronted the enemy, and the matter was ended.'

He lifted his shirt free of his trousers revealing his stomach and the scar. Silas was fascinated. The thick red ridge ran exactly as Thomas had suggested in one crescent sweep from his side and across towards his groin. The toned flesh around it was made more desirable because of it, and the heroic blemish somehow enhanced his virility.

Archer tucked in his shirt and sat. That appeared to be the end of the story, but Silas waited, just in case.

'I never knew the full details,' Thomas said, his voice far away. 'Only that you were injured.'

'You don't know how much easier it would have been had I been able to talk to you, Tom,' Archer said. 'But… The dreaded green baize door.'

He spoke as though talking about a demon, lifting his mood with a theatrically horrified expression. Thomas chuckled.

'What's that?' Silas asked. 'The door thing?'

'The door that marks the line between the house and below stairs,' Thomas explained.

'And a lot more besides,' Archer said.

'Oh, right.' Silas addressed him. 'And was that it? You got treated bad because you're queer?' Silas ignored Thomas' coughed outrage. 'Your boss went a bit mad, your mate topped himself, and you got cut up in a fight? Sounds like an average night in the East End.'

Luckily, the gloomy atmosphere that had accompanied his story was soaked up by Archer's laughter.

'It is a very distressing story,' Thomas said. 'But I've yet to get the connection with the Ripper unless you are suggesting that your commander is involved?'

'That's it exactly,' Archer said and calmly continued eating.

'Hang on…' This was too much for Silas to take in. 'You're saying you know who it is?'

'I have a suspicion,' Archer admitted.

'So why ain't you gone to the mutton shunters? The police, sorry.' Silas didn't understand. 'The way things are now, they'd take any help they can get and especially from someone like you. Tell them what you know, and it's done.' What had started out as confusion quickly became anger. 'Hang on. How long have you known this? Why ain't you done nothing about it?' Anger became rage. He stood, knocking back his chair. 'My mates have been dying while you've been sitting on your arse.'

'Sit down, Silas,' Thomas chided.

'I thought you was decent. Now look at you.'

'Silas!' Thomas shouted with such force that Silas was thrown off the rails. He controlled himself immediately. 'Sit down, please,' he said, lightly touching Silas' sleeve.

Archer looked so lost, and Thomas sounded so protective, Silas' anger calmed to mild confusion. He brushed his fringe from his eyes. 'I don't understand why you ain't done nothing.'

Archer and Thomas exchanged glances.

'Oh hell. You don't mean…?' Thomas' jaw dropped, and Archer held up a finger for silence.

'Silas,' he said. 'I am convinced that the Ripper and my old commander are one in the same person.'

'Go to Inspector Adelaide and tell him,' Silas insisted. 'It's what they're supposed to be good at.'

'I can't go to the police,' Archer replied. 'Even though I believe my old commander is the Ripper, and…' He looked once more at Thomas who appeared to know what was coming next. 'Even though he gave me my scar as he tried to kill me. He is my brother.'

# Twenty-One

At first, Silas didn't understand the complication, but as he sat in stunned silence, the implications began to sink in. He lost his appetite and pushed away his plate. Archer stood over Thomas who shook his head slowly, as shocked as Silas.

'Did you know about all that?' Silas asked.

'Not all,' Thomas replied. 'I mean, I was aware His… Archer had a brother, but I've never met him. He was always away at school or naval college, holidaying in the country where I wasn't needed. The last I heard, he was serving abroad.'

'And he slashed you?'

'It was intended to be more than a cut.' Archer said. He left Thomas and paced the room, his waistcoat hanging open. His hair was still messed up from earlier, and he straightened it by dragging his fingers backwards over his head. 'I have never seen so much anger in a man. His eyes were red with it, his reason distorted, and yet, he was my brother. That made no difference to him. As he drew his sword, I imagined it was because the enemy was on us, but I was the enemy, and before I could retaliate, he was hacking at me. Had the victory bugle not sounded at that moment and brought him to his senses, I would not be here today.'

'Your brother?' Silas couldn't imagine attacking his sisters, no matter what they did.

Archer turned at the fireplace. 'My brother, you may have gathered Silas, is not of his right mind.'

'I'll fucking say.'

'He never has been, not really.' He paced to his desk. 'And he wasn't away in the country, Tom. When he was not at school — or I should say schools, because he was constantly being moved from one to the next — my parents sent him to something akin to a correctional institution in the north. When that proved fruitless, it was military academy, and as soon as my father could arrange it, to sea.'

Archer leant on the desk with his arms folded staring at a silhouette on the opposite wall. No more than five inches high, a jet-black profile stood out from the white background. The likeness, not dissimilar to Archer's, was framed in dark wood.

'Poor Crispin,' Archer said and looked away. 'From an early age, he had a propensity for violence. He was sent from prep school at the age of nine for performing unspeakable acts on a boy in his dormitory.'

'You mean queer sex?' Silas asked.

'No. He used the boy as a cadaver wanting, as he put it, "To see how it all worked". Luckily, the boy's screams alerted a master, and all he suffered was an incision.'

'Where?' Thomas asked, rising and taking Archer's glass to him.

'From his neck to his groin.'

'That was your first clue, I take it?' Thomas said, handing over the wine.

Archer took it. 'Why don't you sit down?' He waved the glass toward one of the wingback chairs. 'Don't worry about Tripp.'

Thomas sat, and Silas turned his chair to face the room, resting his forearms on his thighs, his hands clasped.

'It didn't strike me at first,' Archer said, answering Thomas' question once he was seated. 'There was no reason why it should. "A murder in the East End", was the first unremarkable headline and no-one took much notice. But, when the second killing took place, and more details of the first were released, the similarity reminded me of the incident. Both victims were cut in a similar pattern as inflicted on the schoolboy.'

'I'm taking the sceptical view,' Thomas said, 'but even that similarity is not enough to make a definite connection.'

'You are correct, and I appreciate your cynicism.'

'It could be coincidence,' Thomas reasoned further. 'Or even, if you stretch your imagination, the boy himself, scarred internally by his torture as well as on the outside. Mrs Flintwich said her husband's sister went mad, because of the way she was treated as a child.'

'I don't doubt there's a lot of all that behind Crispin's actions,'

Archer said. 'Though I can't think why. We shared the same childhood and parents, and I have only harmed a man when necessary. But no, the madman at work in Greychurch is not the boy from Crispin's youth.'

'It's possible,' Silas agreed. 'How do you know?'

'I can assure you, Silas, there are many boys who are now men who have suffered similar abuse behind the closed doors of public schools and military academies, let alone in Greychurch itself. So why not any of them? I did not immediately leap to the conclusion that this was my brother's work, and although these consistent injuries wrenched the horrific reminder from my memory, I didn't entertain the idea that the Ripper was my brother's childhood victim.'

'Because, there was no other connection but coincidence.'

'Quite, Tom, but also, because I knew the Ripper could not be the boy my brother carved when he was nine. That boy became the man with whom I had my affair aboard The Britannia.'

'Bugger me,' Silas said. 'So he got him in the end?'

'That's a bit callous, Mr Hawkins.'

'Me apologies, Mr...?

'I am a Payne.'

'Don't doubt it, but I'll stick with Tommy.' Silas winked. 'But, Archie? Is that right? Your brother did all that?'

'If I am correct, he has done much worse.'

'Yeah, but if you went to the police, they'd understand, wouldn't they? I mean, you're a gent and you ain't to blame for what he's done.'

'I'm afraid it doesn't work like that,' Archer sighed. 'I may not be my brother's keeper, but I am the holder of his title. Being older than me by two years, he is or should be, The Viscount Clearwater. Because of his... condition, my father stripped him of the title, and it passed to me. But even that is not the point, although it is possibly connected. The point is, that a scandal surrounding a son or brother has repercussions for everyone. Firstly, the title, and then me, my mother and her side of the family, even down to the hall boy at the country house. Who would employ my staff if it was suspected they had served a murderer? And from pointing at us, the fingers of suspicion would slither like snakes to close friends,

202

business associates, people like Doctor Quill who helped you today, Her Ladyship next door, the peers with whom I associate in the House, and on and on. The newspapers would lap it up, as would those in society who have held a grudge against us for whatever reason, and my whole house would collapse.'

'Which is why you can't go to the authorities.'

'Exactly, Tom.' Archer pushed himself from the desk and approached Silas. Standing before him, he said, 'Along with the investigation would come a study of my private life. How long had I known? Why had I been to the East End? Who had I been with? "Where did you meet this young man, My Lord?" And the rest you can make up for yourself.' He ran a hand over Silas' cheek. 'I would tell them the truth, because I am not ashamed of who I am or who you are, or that I am in love with you, but you know what happens to people like us.'

Silas nodded. He would be sent down, and Archer would probably have to leave the country.

'I get it,' he said. 'Bloody unfair if you ask me. Right, I get why you haven't gone to the bobbies, but like Tommy says, you've still only got coincidences. A few dead renters all happened to be cut in the same way. That doesn't tell me why you think it's your brother.'

'Do you have a map of the area, Archer?' Thomas stood and, lost in his own thoughts, approached the desk, scanning it.

'I do, Tom, and I think you have just realised the same thing as I did.'

'Britannia?'

'There's a new map in that cabinet.' Archer pointed. 'I have others but have defaced most with my attempts at finding a pattern. Silas, help me clear the table.'

Just when Silas thought the matter was done, he found himself clearing the supper to make room for Thomas to unroll a map. Archer held the corners flat with some of his curios, one of which was a figure of a naked man reclining that Silas thought daring to have on display, and the three stood leaning over the table.

'Britannia?' Silas said. 'That was the name of your ship?'

'Yes,' Archer confirmed, following a road on the map and reaching a point where he stopped and tapped the paper. 'Here. Where we were last night.'

'Britannia Street,' Silas leant in close to read. He knew Greychurch was thick with alleys and side streets, but until he saw them laid out, he had no idea how many. He wondered how he'd ever found his way around.

'You could still argue coincidence,' Thomas said.

'You could if there was only the one.'

Archer put his arm around Silas sending a warm rush of pleasure through his bloodstream. With the viscount beside him, he was wanted and safe. It was hard to imagine what was going on at that very moment in the hash of black and white lines, smudged print and symbols that was the East End.

'What are the others?' Thomas prompted.

'I need to take you through this in order,' Archer said. 'Silas, can you find the places where the murders happened, starting with Harrington Street?'

Silas pointed to it and then found roughly the place the first body had been discovered.

'Remember,' Archer said. 'At this point, I knew nothing of this murder except that it had happened.' Using a fountain pen, he drew a circle in red where Silas' finger had been and underlined the street name. 'When the second was reported...' Silas found Simon's Yard. 'Thank you. More details of the first were also released, and the similar injury caught my attention, as did the location. That was when I first had the notion that this had something to do with Crispin.'

'Location?' Thomas spoke to himself as he looked between the two murder scenes.

'There had been a fair gap of time between the two events,' Archer said. 'And there was a decent length between two and three. Enough time for me to think little of it other than coincidence. But when the third murder took place...'

Silas had already found Lucky Row, and he took the pen from Archer to circle the location and underline the name.

'The unfortunately named Lucky Row,' Archer said. 'Micky-Nick.'

'May I take some paper?' Thomas asked moving to the desk. Archer told him to do whatever he needed, and he came back with several sheets of plain notepaper and a pencil.

'It was murder number three that made me take a more studied approach,' the viscount continued. 'A third body cut open and, in this case, partially disembowelled. Another coincidence? There was still a chance I was wrong. Another reason not to go to the police. Whether I was correct or mistaken, I would still be attaching the family name to the crimes and the outcome would be the same.'

'Would have saved another three deaths,' Silas said and immediately changed his tone. 'I'm sorry, Archie. I didn't mean it to sound bad on you. I wasn't criticising.'

'You would be right to,' Archer replied. 'I knew that I needed to do something, but I couldn't discuss this even with Quill or Lady Marshall. Again, a little time passed, but less than before, and then Master Chiltern was discovered in Britannia Street. It was then that I knew I had no choice but to act.'

'But you still didn't report your findings?' Thomas questioned. Silas thought he would have made a good police inspector. He wasn't afraid to challenge the boss.

'No.' Archer watched Silas highlight the locations of the fourth murder before he continued. 'It was then that I drew up my plan.'

'Which was to find someone who knew the area?' Thomas asked. 'Why?'

'Because, there was no order,' Archer explained. 'Four deaths, all linked by the way they were butchered. Otherwise, seemingly random. The dates of the events mean nothing, and to the police, the locations also mean nothing, except that they are areas where renters operate. But, so are they areas where female prostitutes work. Why was he choosing boys? These are questions Inspector Adelaide is addressing, I should hope, but he will find only randomness.'

'They've already attributed that to madness,' Thomas said. He studied the names he had written on the paper. 'He takes them by chance in the most private places he can find.'

Silas shivered at the thought of those places, the number of strangers he had gone to them with and how lucky he had been to come away unscathed.

'It's anything but madness.' Archer sat at the table, and the others followed, pulling their chairs to sit either side of him facing the sprawling depiction of the East End. 'Each location chosen so far has a paticular relevance to my brother.'

'Does he live in the Greychurch?' Silas asked. 'Or Limedock?' The horrible thought occurred that he may have encountered Archer's brother in the past.

'No. He is incarcerated overseas. Has been for years.'

'Really?' Thomas was surprised. 'I was led to believe…'

'That green baize door blocks many truths from infecting below-stairs,' Archer said. 'Crispin's condition has always been one of them.'

'So, if he's abroad,' Silas reasoned, 'he can't have done these killings. So why do these places make you think he did?'

'Ah.' Thomas blew a breath of realisation across the paper he held. 'Simon Harrington?'

'Was the boy victim from prep school and my late lover.' Archer smiled weakly.

'Britannia was the name of your ship.'

Archer nodded.

'Lucky?'

'Simon's nickname.'

Silas swore under his breath. 'Looks like you've got it sewn up there, detective,' he said and nudged Archer.

'I appreciate you trying to jolly me up,' Archer said. He held Silas' knee beneath the table, and the warm flush of happiness flowed again.

'But the two last night?' Thomas asked. 'Do they confirm your suspicions beyond a doubt?'

'Sadly not.' Archer returned his attention to the map. 'The police are quite correct that the murders are random,' he said. 'Even if they knew the significance of the locations, they are not in any logical order and thus do not help. Surname, Christian name, nickname and name of the ship in any sequence do not point onwards to the next potential crime scene where the man might be caught and brought in.'

'Cornfield, wasn't it?' Thomas asked. 'I haven't had much time to read today's news.'

'Cornfield, yes,' Archer agreed. 'I went there today while waiting for information about Andrej and looked for clues as I did last night. I thought that by being there, I might notice some other connection, another street name, a house number, anything that might suggest where next. I did the same thing last night, but then I also wanted to understand what it was like out there under those conditions.'

He stroked Silas' leg absentmindedly as he spoke.

Silas relinquished the pen to Thomas who marked the location on the map.

'I found no clues at any place,' Archer continued, watching Thomas draw. 'Nor at Bishop's Square which I think was the intended location. He came across a victim in Cornfield and intended to lure him to Bishop's, but was disturbed. The boy had seen his face, and so he had to do away with him there and then. Not part of his plan, but a necessity. A short while later, while attention was elsewhere, he found what he was looking for and in the right place.'

'I can swallow that,' Thomas said, sitting back.

'It isn't a clue as such,' Archer continued. 'But last night led me to understand these random time differences. He is waiting for the right moment. These places are popular, in your previous line of work? Yes?'

Silas nodded. The word "Previous" suggested that the viscount expected an end to his current way of life, but he needn't have been worried. Even if he was thrown out of Clearwater House tomorrow, he would not return to the East End except to find Fecker.

'That's what I suspected, Archer said. 'It meant to me that he was prepared to wait until conditions were right, as you would if contemplating a battle at sea. I imagine he waited in the darkest places until a lone youth happened by an appropriately named place, and that suggests stealth and planning, not madness.'

'He knows what he's doing.' Silas agreed.

'But he slipped up last night,' Thomas said. He rested back in his chair, his hands behind his head, deep in thought. 'He let his... Is lust the right word? He let his lust for killing get the better of him, and if your theory is right, killed in the wrong place. Then again, he is leaving clues and maybe he wanted to throw you off the scent.'

'Assuming he knows he has my attention.'

'Pretty obvious to me,' Thomas said, lurching forward and picking up his pencil.

'How so?'

'For a start, who else's attention is he trying to attract by giving the name of the man you suspect he killed…'

'Ah, no,' Archer cut him off. 'Sorry, I didn't make it clear. I did, at the time, suspect Crispin had killed Harrington, but now I suspect my brother's rage comes from the fact that Harrington took his own life before Crispin could exact his final revenge. Therefore, robbing him of the opportunity and exacerbating his madness. Now, he is exacting vengeance on other homosexual men, or those he considers somehow responsible for his own condition. I'm no student of the mind, so that is conjecture. But, I interrupted. Go on, Tom.'

'Your reasoning makes more sense each time you speak,' Thomas said. 'Try this and tell me if this means anything to you.' He drew a line from the scene of the first murder, diagonally left to the third. 'Numbers one, three…' Returning to the first point, he drew a second line diagonally right to Britannia Street and the scene of the forth. 'Four,' he said. 'Two and five either side.' He wrote the digits on his paper. 'One, three, two five.'

Silas ran through possible combinations in his head, as he assumed Archer was doing. His eyes were alive and darting across the map, his lips, moving.

'No,' he said. 'Numbers mean nothing. 'Why should they?'

'Because, if I do this,' Thomas said, leaning over with the pencil. 'And draw a line from murders two to five, it cuts straight through the other two lines…'

'And makes the letter A?' Silas was incredulous. 'Bloody hell, that was lucky.'

Thomas looked across Archer to Silas. 'What do you mean? It backs up the theory that the man is planning. He is committing the murders to spell out his initial. He wants your attention alright.'

'It's just a happy coincidence in a very unhappy matter,' Archer said. He let go of Silas' leg. 'I think you're looking for clues just to fit my theory, but I appreciate the thought, Tom.'

'Yes, alright,' Thomas said. 'Maybe it was a prod in the dark. Where does it leave us? What has Bishop's Square to do with anything?'

'I like the way you say "us", Tom,' Archer said. 'When we were at prep school, Simon Harrington and I were in Bishop's House.'

Silas' head was beginning to hurt. 'But there's no clue there telling us where he might go next?'

'Nothing.'

'Do any of the street names nearby mean anything?' Thomas asked. He glanced at the map. 'Lightfleet Lane, City Street, Downers End?'

Archer shook his head. 'I've studied the map these past few nights and no, I cannot see anything else that's relevant.'

'Perhaps that's the end of the matter then?'

'I doubt it, Tommy,' Silas said.

He too had been studying the map and Thomas' drawn letter A in particular and had come up with a theory of his own.

'What have you seen?'

Archer's arm was around him again, an encouraging hand cupping his shoulder.

'Tommy's given us a letter,' he said. 'Kind of. The line through the middle goes outside of the upside down V. If you connect one, three and four...' He drew a line. 'You get a triangle.'

'I can see that,' Thomas said. 'The letter A. So?'

'You ain't lived in the East End, Tommy,' Silas said, his confidence boosted by his experience. 'So you ain't seen as many of these as me.' He placed the pencil at murder site two and drew downwards on an angle to the right, stopping opposite the apex of the A. He drew another line from site six to the left to reach the same point, creating another triangle, inverted over the first. 'If you forget murder number five 'cos the street name doesn't fit,' he said, 'You can make a Jewish star.' He threw down the pencil and sat back, pleased with himself.

'You think this is antisemitic?' Archer asked.

Silas shrugged. 'I don't know what to think, Archie,' he said. 'But if that's right, then the bottom point of that star is going to point to the place of the next murder.'

# Twenty-Two

The three men discussed their individual theories into the evening. Silas' idea that the murder locations made a pattern of the Star of David and that it was somehow relevant, was soon dismissed and he saw why. How likely was it, Thomas reasoned, that a madman had found five locations — not counting Cornfield Yard — which not only fitted his purpose in name but also in such a precise pattern? When he found the same places on a larger and more detailed map of the area, it was clear that the lines of the star were not parallel and the symbol drawn was out of shape. Similarly, Thomas' theory that the Ripper was trying to spell out Archer's initial was also debunked.

'Which leaves us back where we started,' Archer said as he poured the last of the claret and handed the glass to Thomas.

The footman had his sleeves rolled again, and Archer had given him a cigar which he enjoyed as he stood, head down over the maps and his notes. With the lamp and candles reflecting light up at him from the paper, his face was lit through smoke which hung breathless about him as if not wanting to disturb his concentration. To Silas, he looked like a young businessman in his white shirt and black trousers pinching him at the waist, a fine figure of confidence who used his enquiring mind to challenge and create. He had to admit, that his initial impression of Thomas, that he was a stuck-up servant uncomfortable around, but fascinated by men like Silas, had changed over the last twenty-four hours, and he now harboured growing respect for the man.

The events of the previous night began to take their toll, and Silas found himself fighting back yawns as the room became stuffy. He took up a position on the couch, comfortable enough to take off his shoes, which were too big for him, and rested back on the arm, his legs up.

Where Thomas was static in concentration, Archer paced, and the more the clock struck the passing hours, the more his agitation increased.

'I know you said that the murders are coming faster,' Silas said. 'But maybe we should knock this on the head and come back to it in the morning. There's nothing you can do tonight, Archie.'

'I am compelled, Silas,' Archer said. He had discarded his jacket and waistcoat some time ago and like Thomas wore only his shirt. He had even removed the cravat and high collar, so that where his footman appeared to be a well-to-do man of business, Archer was the workman waiting for his employer to issue an order.

'I think Silas may be right,' Thomas said. 'Unless you can think of any other relevant names from the past which might direct us, I don't see what we can do to stay one step ahead.'

'Unless this is all purely coincidence,' Archer reasoned. 'In which case, we are barking up the wrong tree.'

'What are the chances this ain't your brother?' The thought had been with Silas for a while, but Archer had been so fired up and certain of his theory, he hadn't wanted to burst his bubble. Now, though, it was late, his headache had grown worse, and he was keen to get to bed. Preferably with Archer. He could easily put aside the horror and frustration if he was alone in the man's company.

'It's possible,' Archer said. 'It could all be happenstance. I might be reading too much into it. Perhaps Cornfield Yard wasn't a mistake, and the name does mean something, but not to me. Perhaps this is a Jewish tanner as some of the papers suggest, or a medical man with a grudge as others are saying, who just happened to find his victims in streets that only I would find relevant. I won't know until I catch him.'

His words brought a shift in mood. Thomas, from being statuesque and regal, spun on his heels to stare at Archer who was moving to the fireplace.

'Catch him?' he exclaimed. 'What on earth do you mean?'

'You can't do that.' Silas was also shocked by the idea. 'You can't just go charging into the East End brandishing a sword and...' It was preposterous. 'You can't mean it.'

'As I see it, I have no other choice. I can't inform the police. To be honest, I trust them as little as you do, Silas. They seem to be more clueless than me, but by the same token, I can't sit here and do nothing.'

'Do you think,' Thomas said, following Archer to the fire. 'That if this is your brother, he may come here for you?'

'The thought had occurred to me,' Archer admitted. 'But, as with the punishment aboard ship, that would be too direct. Not evil enough. He wants me to agonise as I did then, looking on helpless while those I care about suffer. I don't think he will come after me here.'

'I'd bloody slice his head off,' Silas said.

'If I hadn't got there first,' Thomas added.

'Yes, thank you, gentlemen.' Archer rested an elbow on the mantlepiece. 'But, I must be the one to restrain him. I don't want to see the man dead, no matter how much he might deserve it, that is a matter for the courts. What I intend to do is capture him and deliver him to the authorities.'

'Capture him?'

'It wouldn't be impossible, Tom.'

'Without getting your name in the paper?' Silas raised an eyebrow.

'Good point,' Thomas agreed. 'If this is your brother, the news will come out in the end.'

'Yes, well…' Archer sighed. 'We will have to face that if it happens, but at least by then, I would have done something to end this bloody matter, and that might possibly count in my favour.'

'And how did you plan on catching him?' Silas asked. 'Even if you could work out where he might strike next?'

Archer crossed the room to the silhouette and took it from the wall. 'This is the only image I have of him,' he said, examining it as he returned to the mantlepiece. 'Apart from the nightmarish visions in my head. I haven't spoken to him since I was discharged. He doesn't even know our father is dead and that I have his title. He is lost to me and me to him, but he is calling out to me using the locations as if he wants me to find him.'

'And you thought that if you turned up one night and there you both were, he'd stop?'

'No, Silas, but if I knew where he was to be, I could surprise him. Talk to him. Prevent him from committing another crime, upset

212

his pattern, if he has one, and persuade him to turn himself in.'

The naivety of the suggestion hung in the air with the cigar smoke as Silas and Thomas exchanged knowing looks. That would not happen, but neither was able to tell Archer. It was his only plan, and it gave him hope.

'So, what do we do?' Thomas asked. He took away the fireguard and threw his cigar stub into the flames.

'I'm damned if I know.' Archer said, and dropped the silhouette into the grate. The profile blackened and curled as it was consumed. 'I am waiting for news.'

'News?' Thomas said nothing about what Archer had just done, and Silas thought it best not to comment either. 'What kind of news?'

Archer looked at the time. 'It won't come tonight,' he said. 'After the third murder, I wrote to the sanitorium where Crispin is held. A few days ago, after the fourth murder, I dispatched a telegram. I have, as yet, had no response to either.'

'You think he has escaped?' Thomas asked, and Archer nodded.

'If they can confirm that he has,' he explained. 'Then I know who we are dealing with.'

'And if he hasn't?' Silas shifted uncomfortably on the couch. Something Archer had said previously came back to him and whispered a warning in his ear in words that had not yet formed into meaning.

'If he is still there, then I have to accept that I have been wrong all along and this is, perhaps, a crazed leather worker, or an arsenic-addled clerk, an immigrant with a zealously religious hatred of street boys, or whatever else the journals are proposing.'

'And if you do figure the next likely place for him to strike and lie in wait?' Thomas questioned as he replaced the fireguard. 'Apart from the possibility of waiting there night after night and being wrong, you could find yourself face to face with a madman you don't know, and in as much danger as those he is bent on killing. Apart from that, you're not exactly the kind of man he's after. You'd stand out a mile and scare him off, wouldn't you?'

'Hell, Tom,' Silas said through a wry smile. 'You have a way of saying things plain.'

Thomas shrugged.

The whisper in Silas' mind spoke again, and although its meaning was still unclear, something did come into focus, and his pulse quickened. Archer was looking at him deep in thought.

'As I see it,' Thomas said. 'There's not much we can do tonight.' He returned to the table and began tidying, the astute man of business becoming the conscientious footman once more.

'There's a great deal we can do tonight.' Archer spoke to Silas, quietly, as if not wanting Thomas to hear his double meaning. 'But you are right, Tom.' He broke the stare and stretched. 'It's late, and I've kept you long enough.'

'I don't mind one bit, Sir,' Thomas said. 'I just wish there was more I could do.'

'There's nothing any of us can do for now, except sleep on it and hope he doesn't strike until we are ready. Perhaps a message will arrive in the morning, and we will know more.'

Silas straightened his legs and put on his shoes. There was something Archer was not telling him, but his head was too full of streets, names and stories to think of it any longer. He was glad of the sight of Archer adjusting his shirt. His hand reached beneath his waistline to tuck it in and drew Silas' attention lower. The unease in his heart became a flutter of desire. Could he think of such things after a day like today?

When Archer faced him and asked if he was ready for bed, Silas knew that he could.

'I will clear these and leave you in peace, Sir, if you have finished with me?' Thomas rolled down his sleeves and reached for his jacket, transforming himself once more into the role of a dutiful servant.

'Tom, you have been most useful,' Archer said, his gaze remaining on Silas. 'I will find a way to repay you.'

'No need, My Lord. Shall I tidy away the maps?'

'Leave the room as it is,' Archer said. 'I will return to it in the morning when I am...' He winked at Silas. 'Refreshed.'

'Very good, Sir.' Thomas straightened his jacket. 'I'll just take the leftovers and Lucy can clear when she does the grate.'

'Whatever you want.' Archer held Silas' with impish eyes. 'And will you ask Tripp not to disturb either myself or our guest? I think we may sleep late if we can sleep at all.'

Every word held a double meaning now, and Silas felt a stirring in his underwear. He grinned back. He could think of no better way to rid his aching mind of everything they had discussed.

Only when Thomas opened the doors and let in the light from the next room did they break the stare. Silas stood as Archer began to blow out candles and extinguish the lamps.

'Sir,' Thomas said, collecting a tray. 'Can I just say that I am more than willing to assist you in this matter further, if you wish it, and...' He put down the tray and straightened his back. 'May I say thank you for your trust?'

'No, you can't,' Archer replied, taking him by surprise. 'Because there is no need to thank me.' He approached Thomas, taking a quick look into the drawing room as he passed the open doors. 'Excuse the inappropriateness,' he said standing before the man. 'But, I would do this to any friend.' He hugged him.

Thomas' eyes widened in shock and then softened. He returned the embrace briefly and blushed, meeting Silas' eyes with concern.

He had no need to worry. Silas was getting used to Archer's softness, and he liked it. Anyone who could have a sword fight with his commanding officer, tell horrific stories from his life so honestly, and put the lives of others before his own, was allowed to be sentimental with his friends. It was odd, though, how Archer craved so much affection, but when Silas thought about it, he could understand why. His talk was of boarding school and the military, a father he had hated, and his only brother absent and in a sanitorium. Archer had the world, his wealth, his house and time to indulge his passions, but no-one to share any of it with.

Well, he thought as he followed the others from the room, now he had Thomas as a friend and hopefully, within a few more minutes would have Silas as his lover.

The last to leave the study, he turned at the doors to close them, glancing in at the desk where the light from the drawing room fell like a shaft of moonlight. It lit Archer's sketch that rested there spotlighting similar features to his own. The dark hair, the helpless expression, the face of a boy from the gutter.

Silas knew exactly what the viscount had planned for him.

# Twenty-Three

Having said goodnight to Thomas in the hall, Archer and Silas mounted the staircase side by side. When he reached the landing, however, and had checked that all was silent and they were alone, Archer put his arm around Silas' shoulder and drew him close to kiss the top of his head.

Lucy had made good work of his hair. It was soft beneath his lips and had the faint trace of cigar smoke veiling the perfume of soap beneath. Silas wrapped an arm around Archer's back, a movement that caused his already swelling cock to fatten further. It occurred to him, in a chest-stabbing moment of anticipation, that this was the first time he had led another man to his bedroom.

'How are you feeling?' he asked, not entirely sure what he meant.

'Like my balls are going to burst,' Silas replied.

It was not the answer Archer had been expecting, but it confirmed that, like him, Silas had put the evening's discussion aside and was in the same state of arousal.

'I know the feeling,' he whispered.

They stopped at Archer's bedroom door, and Silas said, 'You know my history, Archie.'

'I do,' Archer said, turning him face to face. 'And you know mine.'

He put his hand on the door handle, but Silas stopped him. 'No,' he said, causing Archer's stomach to turn over. 'Come here.'

Silas took his hand and led him across the corridor to his room. He stood with his back to it and tugged Archer close.

'It's at this point,' Silas said, 'that I'd put on an act, but I don't want you to think I'm acting now.'

'I don't.'

'This is me, Archie.'

'That's all I want.'

Silas' smile broadened further, stretching out the dimple at the centre of his lips. He kept his gaze on Archer as he turned the door handle and backed into the room, gently pulling Archer with him.

As soon as the door was closed, their lips locked, and their arms wrapped around each other's backs. Archer intended to lift Silas and carry him to the bed, but Silas had other ideas. Even though he was slighter and shorter than the viscount, he pinned him to the door, holding his head in his hands and exploring every part of his face with his lips. He moved swiftly down to his neck, causing Archer to cry out in pleasure. He tried to reciprocate, but Silas was taking charge, kissing below his chin, licking his stubble, nibbling and kissing across and finally back to his mouth where their tongues collided.

Suddenly Silas pulled away, leaving Archer breathless, his cock straining painfully in his breeches.

'Can I really be me?' Silas whispered. He caressed Archer's face, looking up at him with dewy eyes that danced in the dull lamplight. 'Can I do what I want for you?'

Archer swallowed and nodded. He was grateful that Silas was leading the way. Although he had loved other men, he had less experience with them than Silas might suppose, and his skin tingled with nervousness as much as it did desire.

Silas became serious and put his finger to his lips. Archer understood and asked no more. The younger man took his hand and led him to the bed where he sat him down before kneeling before him and removing Archer's shoes and socks. He lightly kissed the top of each foot before standing and helping the viscount out of his waistcoat. Archer's cock was screaming to be touched by more than the heavy cotton of his trousers now rubbing tantalisingly against the sensitive tip.

Silas stood back from the bed, his eyes on the older man as he slipped off his jacket and kicked off his shoes. He slowly unbuttoned his shirt. His ill-fitting trousers bulged at the front, but Archer wasn't sure if that was the material, not until Silas undid them, discarded them with the rest of his clothes and stood naked by the bed. The firelight played on his smooth, pale flesh, causing shadows in hollows, highlighting his chest which showed only the faintest dusting of dark hair in the centre and two small nipples either side.

He took a step forward, his semi-hard cock swaying its length beneath a small bush of black. His balls were darker-skinned, and not the two far-hanging orbs that Archer sported. They were smaller, smoother and compact, drawing up in anticipation. His foreskin rolled back over a dark pink head as he stood between Archer's legs, but when Archer reached for it, Silas knocked his hand away. He raised an eyebrow and winked. It was cheeky, a flirt, a promise of wonderful things to come, but also a warning for the viscount to behave. It sent another thrill through his body, and his cock twitched.

It drew Silas' attention, and he looked down to see Archer's manly length outlined beneath the material of his trousers. Silas raised an eyebrow, another cheeky gesture that aroused Archer further, and nudged his legs apart, forcing the viscount backwards on the bed. Silas climbed between his legs and pushed Archer onto his back. With his mischievous eyes on his one moment and on his body the next, he undid his shirt, his firm balls resting directly over Archer's raging cock, warming it with their weight.

The shirt discarded, Silas rested over Archer, and his kissing began again. His forehead, his eyelids, cheeks, mouth, throat, chest and nipples were softly touched and tested by his lips and tongue. Archer was allowed to hold Silas' head. He adored the softness of his hair and the way it trickled through his fingers.

As the youth kissed lower, Archer tried to prevent him from kissing his scar. It was an embarrassment, but Silas worshipped it too, and his mouth travelled over every inch. He slid down until there was nowhere else for him to go but the buckle of Archer's belt.

The viscount watched, spellbound as the last of his clothing was removed. Silas gasped when Archer's cock finally came into view. His own was fully erect now, and as much as Archer wanted to feel it, his hand was again brushed aside. Silas was intent on what he could do for the viscount, and when he wrapped his fingers around the thick shaft, Archer thought he would spill himself right there. It was even harder to hold back when Silas licked the tip, glancing up impishly and teasing him with tiny nibbles, his tongue pressing into the eye and beneath the ridge. Before he let it into his mouth, he explored its entire length to the base and beneath, lifting

218

Archer's balls in the palm of a hand. He nuzzled his head between them and his legs and forced his tongue against the sensitive hip bone. The charge that streamed through Archer caused his back to arch, and he laughed involuntarily to release the tension. Silas kissed and licked his way to the other side and did the same until Archer had to beg him to stop.

Without replying, Silas returned to his cock and kissed his way up, clutching the shaft in one hand and pulling back Archer's meaty skin until the air cooled its burning tip. Silas' lips pushed gently against it, looking up at Archer as if he was afraid of being denied, while at the same time making it clear he was not going to stop. When his lips slid over the whole of Archer's cock-head, and his tongue worked in circles around it, the viscount's back arched again. Within a moment, Silas' face was buried in his mass of hair, his throat constricting around solid flesh.

Within minutes Archer was holding the youth's head and driving himself harder and deeper, causing Silas to choke. Each gag was followed by a moan of pleasure and his fingers worked Archer's balls faster. Archer felt his juice welling as his cock fattened, but Silas knew what he was doing. Before it was too late, he let go and held Archer's stare of amazement. Resting on his hands and knees, he crawled his way up his body until their rigid cocks touched. They kissed hard and passionately, and Archer drew Silas onto him so their naked bodies rubbed. He explored Silas' back. It narrowed to the dip at the base of his spine and his hands cupped his cheeks. They were smooth and firm, and Silas was light enough for the viscount to draw him further up his body, so his fingers could play beneath his legs. They stroked between his cheeks, over his warm, wrinkled hole and lower until they touched his smooth balls.

Again, Silas broke away, this time grinning, his hair flopping over his face. He knelt, swept it away and straddled Archer as he brought himself closer to his face. Archer held his thighs, stroking them while he licked his lips at the sight of the younger man's straight, dark cock approaching his mouth. He opened it and took Silas' inches in one swallow. Balancing, Silas held Archer's head, and keeping it still, drove his cock slowly in and out. He occasionally paused to hold it and stroke himself while he let Archer lick and kiss his swollen balls. He groaned softly when Archer rubbed them with his stubbled chin and took them into his mouth.

Archer's building orgasm had subsided, and he kept it at bay while he offered Silas the heat of his mouth for as long as the man could endure. It was some time, and Archer's jaw ached by the time Silas pulled back. He took Archer's hand from his thighs and kissed each of his fingers before shuffling backwards where he let Archer go and reached behind.

Archer felt a gentle hand wrap his shaft as he wallowed in the sight of the slim, handsome youth straddling him. Silas moved his hips. Now, instead of fingers around Archer's shaft, there was warmth and soft pressure on the head. Silas' grin widened and his eyes half closed. He gasped as did Archer when he lowered himself in one graceful movement until Archer was buried deep inside, and they were joined.

Silas raised his hips, so that Archer's cock once more felt cold air, but he was held tight at the tip and made to wait until the youth sank, throwing back his head and groaning.

It was hard not to roll the man over and thrust him hard, but Silas was only allowing him to go slowly, increasing the blissful agony of the build-up.

Silas used his entire body to give pleasure to the man beneath him, making himself tight around Archer's cock while his own rose, fell and swelled. Silas let him hold it and stroke it in the same rhythm before leading the hand to his compact sack, where Archer's fingertips teased and tickled. This made Silas' arse even tighter, and Archer's thrusts stronger until Silas' mouth opened, and his moans of pleasure became urgent.

Archer's grew in intensity, and he had no choice but to give up the fight against the explosion to come. He was desperate to hold Silas, to feel every inch of his body when he emptied himself inside, but Silas slowed his pace, lengthening the glorious torture. He took Archer's hands in his and held him down. His cock lay constrained between them as he drew upwards on Archer's cock until its head was the only thing trapped.

Silas fell on him, forcing Archer's lips apart and invading his mouth with uncontrolled kisses. At the same time, he sank back, impaling himself on Archer's mighty length, and a hot burst of juice forced its way between them as he came, each gush matching another thrust on Archer's dick until the man could hold back no longer.

He fought his hands away from Silas now whimpering and spilling his load, and held the youth, his hands gripping the cheeks of his arse as he slammed his cock and filled him with pump after pump of jism. Silas moaned in his ear, kissed it, sweat dripping from his forehead onto Archer's face as Archer filled him, and their bodies slid together, bound now by more happiness than Archer thought possible.

His body shook when Silas lifted himself and set Archer free. He sat on the top of his legs, his cock still rigid but now dripping beads of cum that glistened as they fell to mix with Archer's as the last of his own seeped from his cock. They were panting, both serious and bewildered until Silas climbed free and came to lie beside him. Archer took him under one arm, and Silas rested his head on his chest where one finger played with Archer's nipple as his other arm wrapped around his neck. He lifted one leg over, clinging on, and kissed the man's cheek. 'I do, you know,' he said. 'And I'll say it aloud one day.'

Archer had no doubt and didn't reply, except to plant a kiss on the top of the man's head and tighten his embrace.

The night was an ecstatic blur for Silas, and yet he remembered every detail over again until, at some time in the early morning, he sank into a heavy sleep wrapped in the viscount's protection.

When he awoke it was to the sound of the man's breathing. They were spooned together with Archer behind, and their fingers entwined.

Silas had never woken with another man apart from Fecks, and at first, it was hard to tell if he was still dreaming. The smell of sweat and sex hung in the cool air and Archer's stubble dug into his shoulder. He couldn't have felt happier, more content or safer.

They hadn't had sex last night, they had made love, and where a few days ago he would have shied from the notion, now he embraced it as tightly as Archer embraced him. It had to be love, or else Silas wouldn't be so prepared to do what he had to do.

He turned into the man beneath the weighty eiderdown and soft sheets, and Archer rolled onto his back. A door slammed somewhere in the house and outside, a horse neighed. The sounds woke the viscount, and he emerged from whatever dreams he had been having, blinking, concerned, until he remembered where he was.

Silas rested on one elbow and played with his chest hair as he watched him wake. Archer looked at him with mild confusion until his stern gaze softened into a dreamy smile.

'Hello,' he whispered, and yawned.

Silas kissed him. He wanted to tell him that he knew his plan and that he was, after last night, prepared to do anything for the viscount, but, as he gathered the right words in his head, the slam of another door, closer, sent Archer into a panic.

'What time is it?' he gasped, sitting up.

Silas fell from him. 'I don't know, why?'

'I shouldn't be here!'

'No-one's going to disturb us.'

'What if Thomas didn't tell Tripp? Or one of the maids comes to make your bed...' He fought his way from the covers.

Silas had seen him on his back beneath him as he rode his cock. He had seen him from underneath when Archer fucked him a second time, face to face. He had seen every inch of the man up close, but naked with his cock flaccid and flopping as he danced around the room, balls swinging, picking up clothes, was just as wonderful, if a little comic.

'Charming that is,' he said as if he was hurt. 'Seduce a boy and bugger off.'

Archer didn't realise he was having him on and dropped his bundle of clothes as if they'd bitten him.

'I'm sorry,' he gulped, leaping back onto the bed. He kissed him. 'It's not like that, but it's how...'

'I know, mate,' Silas grinned. 'I was joking.'

'All those things I said yesterday.' Archer's panic increased at the thought of losing Silas. 'I meant all of them. I still do. I am falling... No. I have fallen in love with you. You are just... so... You're everything. I feel it here...' He thumped his heart. 'I know it here.' His head. 'I want you to see it everywhere. It's all different. You are never going to want for a thing, and I am going to find a way that we can be together, here, without me having to skulk back to my room of fear of being caught by a bloody butler.'

Silas was laughing, but Archer read it as mockery and insisted on kissing him between each sentence to prove he was sincere.

'It's going to come right for both of us,' he said. 'Somehow. And it doesn't matter that you don't love me… Well, it does, but I understand this isn't your life and one day I might find you gone, but that's not going to stop how I feel about you. Infatuation, passion, fascination, all of those things, but something more. Something I can't describe that tells me this was meant to be and…'

Silas put his hand over his mouth.

'Archie,' he said, rolling his eyes. 'I feel exactly the same way, so stop worrying. Bloody hell, you talk a lot first thing in the morning.'

He felt Archer's smile beneath his palm and released him.

'I'm in love with you and wouldn't do anything to hurt you,' the viscount said.

'Except use me as bait to catch the Ripper.'

Silas had never seen a man turn as white as death, and it was alarming. Not only did Archer blanch, his face also fell, and he suddenly looked ten years older.

'What?' he stammered.

'Your drawing.' Silas explained in even tones, resigned and prepared for what Archer had intended. 'You got Tommy to find me based on that drawing. I'm the kind of boy your brother goes for, aren't I? You're going to work out where and when, and I'm going to be the bait.'

Archer fought for words, but whatever he was about to say remained unsaid as someone knocked at the door and walked in.

# Twenty-Four

Luckily, it was Thomas. He made a quick sweep of the room as, tailcoat spinning, he turned to close the door before heading directly to the windows. His expression gave nothing away except that he was intent on some vital purpose. If he saw Archer tumbling naked from the bed and trying to hide behind it, he didn't let on.

Petrified one second and relieved the next, Silas laughed.

'My apologies for bursting in like this, Mr Hawkins,' Thomas said, sweeping open the curtains. 'I have an urgent message for His Lordship, and I am under instructions not to wake him. Mr Tripp, however, had other ideas and will be on his way in five minutes.' He peered through the window. 'His Lordship has a guest in the drawing room who requires his immediate attention.'

Archer poked his head over the edge of the bed. 'Who is it?'

Thomas ignored him. He tied back the curtains saying, 'The weather is somewhat overcast today, Sir, I would suggest you dress, and perhaps you would like to take a late breakfast in the breakfast room. I am sure His Lordship will join you when he has seen Lady Marshall.'

Still without glancing at Silas, or the now standing, naked Lord Clearwater, Thomas turned back to the door. As he hurried to it, he scooped up Archer's discarded clothes.

'I trust you slept well, Mr Hawkins. And, if you would, please pass the message to His Lordship.' He opened the door and looked into the corridor. 'Actually, Sir, I find the weather surprisingly clear across the way. Now might be the best opportunity for a brisk walk.'

Archer dashed across the room, grabbed his clothes and scooted past Thomas, his bedroom door opening and closing a moment later.

Thomas finally looked at Silas. 'Whatever you do, Mr Hawkins, do not go outside,' he said before leaving.

Silas had no idea what might be going on, but he admired the way Thomas handled himself. He washed, dressed and was in the corridor five minutes later just as Tripp approached from the servant's door.

'Morning, Mr Tripp.' Silas greeted him loudly in case Archer could hear.

Apparently, he could, because he appeared from his room before Tripp had a chance to return the greeting, not that he looked much inclined to do so.

'Mr Hawkins!' Archer exclaimed as if he had forgotten he had a guest. 'Morning, Tripp. Silas, why don't you come and take tea with me downstairs. Tripp, we will breakfast later.'

'I fear breakfast later would be luncheon, My Lord.'

'Really?' Archer took a pocket watch from his waistcoat, tapped it, and said, 'Well, well. Come, Silas.' He walked towards the staircase.

'My Lord,' Tripp called after them. 'Lady Marshall is waiting in the drawing room.'

'Is she? Thank you,' Archer replied as if it was news.

Archer cut a stunning figure in his black suit and waistcoat, and Silas wondered how he had found time to shave. Although he had washed, Silas felt only half dressed. Thomas' old suit didn't fit him, the underwear was bunched at his armpits and waist, and he could still feel the night's sweat on him. He wished he looked more presentable, especially as he was about to meet a Lady.

He glanced at the front door as they crossed the hall, wondering what Thomas had meant about not going outside, but there was no time to dwell on the matter. Archer swept into the drawing room, and Silas had trouble keeping up. The viscount had incredible energy considering he had been asleep not fifteen minutes ago.

'Lady Marshall!' He beamed as he greeted a woman seated on the sofa.

'Archer,' she replied, 'what the hell is going on?'

He took her hand and kissed it. Awkward, Silas hung back by the door hoping to go unnoticed.

'I had what they call a lie in,' Archer said, and flopped down beside her.

He was still holding her hand, but she wrenched it away. 'I wasn't talking about that,' she snapped. 'And I am not in a good mood.' She picked up a folded newspaper from the table beside her and slapped it on Archer's chest. 'It's open at the right page. Read it,' she ordered.

Archer was concerned. His brow knitted, and he unfolded the newspaper, studying her questioningly.

'Read it,' she repeated and turned her attention to Silas. 'And who are you?'

Archer looked up. 'Sit down, Silas,' he said, waving vaguely to the opposite sofa. 'Dolly, this is Mr Hawkins.'

'And what school do you attend?' her Ladyship asked, rising from the pile of green velvet she had been sitting in. When it cascaded from her waist to hang elegantly at the front and stick out at the back, Silas realised it was a dress.

'I don't go to school anymore…' He wasn't sure what to call her. He couldn't remember if this was Archer's mother, they seemed very casual together, but he knew he mustn't call her Mrs anything. Archer was already engrossed in the newspaper, leaving Silas to fend for himself.

'I'm nearly twenty, Madam.'

'Congratulations,' she said, advancing on him with a small pair of glasses on a stick. 'From your appearance, I would say you are a clerk whose mother knows nothing about stitching. Having said that, I've always admired what my niece calls *rustic chic*. Perhaps you will tell me your occupation, but before you do, let me assure you, I am not a madam.'

'Oh, I didn't mean it like that…'

She offered her gloved hand to be kissed, and Silas took it, bowed as Archer had done, and touched his lips on the soft material. Her hand was light in his, and the glove soft against his fingers, giving the impression she was a gentle being. Her commanding presence, however, indicated the opposite.

She withdrew the hand and examined his face, standing too close for Silas' liking.

'Oh, my God!' Archer mumbled from the depths of the news report.

'Well?' her Ladyship asked, demanding an answer to a question Silas hadn't heard.

226

'Yes, I am, thank you,' he said.

'What is your explanation?' she tutted.

'For what, Miss?'

'Bloody hell.'

'Yes, Clearwater,' Lady Marshall barked. 'Bloody hell indeed. An explanation for your appearance, Mr Hawkins,' she said. 'Here, at Clearwater.'

'I'm with him,' Silas stammered.

'I can see. In what capacity?'

'His helper.' It was the first thing that came to mind, and was partially true.

'Assisting with what?'

Silas was decidedly uncomfortable now and looked to Archer for help, but he sat with a hand on his forehead and his mouth open, reading intently.

'How are you assisting my godson?'

At least that told Silas Lady Marshall was not Archer's mother. The question also gave him the chance to answer honestly.

'With his charity,' Silas said. 'In the East End.'

Her manner changed instantly. Her long, drawn face grew longer as she dropped her jaw in delighted surprise.

'Oh, how delicious.' She clapped her hands and put a finger to her lips in thought, keenly interested. 'Do you actually live there? Have you seen what's going on?' She took his arm and led him to the sofa, sitting beside him side-saddle. 'You must tell me all about it.'

Archer slammed the newspaper on the table, drawing their attention.

'How the bloody hell did they get hold of that?'

Caught off guard by her ladyship's switch from annoyance to enthusiasm, and Archer's change from enthusiasm to outrage, Silas could only think that the news report had something to do with his brother.

'Is it true?' Her ladyship demanded.

'Yes,' Archer admitted. He passed Silas a worried look and must have caught his confusion because he seemed to come to. 'Sorry. Dolly, this is Mr Hawkins. Did I say that? Silas, this is Lady Marshall. We found Silas in the East End the other evening. He and a friend were of immeasurable help to me, and Mr Hawkins is staying here. His friend, Andrej, a charming Russian you will adore, was injured and I went to see what I could do for him.' His anger rose as he did, swiping up the paper on his way. 'I certainly didn't go there to… "*Entertain himself with the business of the ghoulish pastime, so prevalent among the middle class, of gawping at the unfortunate poor, even going so far as to demand to see the bodies of their dead.*"' He gasped for air. 'It's inaccurate. Middle class? These hacks can't even write. It's far too long a sentence.'

'But you were there?'

'Yes, but not as a tourist.'

Archer leant against the mantelpiece, his head hanging and his back to them. Lady Marshall let out a sigh, and peace reigned for a few seconds before she tapped Silas on the arm.

'How is your friend?' she asked, smiling.

'Fecker? Oh, he's going to be alright, thanks to Ar… His Lordship.'

'Fecker? What an interesting name. Is it Russian? Fecker?'

Silas was mortified, but found it hard to cover a nervous laugh. 'It's a nickname, Miss,' he said and winked. 'Best leave it there.'

'Dear boy,' Her Ladyship said. 'But I am neither a madam nor a schoolmistress. I can see you're new at this.' He patted his hand. 'I am Lady Marshall, so you call me Your Ladyship when first we meet. After that, Ma'am will do. As you are gainfully employed as my godson's secretary, I should really call you Mr Hawkins, or even just Hawkins, but you have such an impish look about you, I want to call you Pixie. I shan't of course. You'd sound like a poodle. Now then…'

She paused for breath, threw a sideways look at Archer, still in despair at the fireplace, and then turned back to Silas.

'All that formality aside, I think I have given Archer enough time to formulate his reply to my next question.' Her ladyship caught Silas off guard again, this time by returning the wink. 'Archer?' She might not have been a school teacher, but she sounded like one. 'What do you intend to do about this mess, you…' A cheeky glance at Silas. 'You fecker?'

Silas' laughter was cut short as Archer rounded on them.

'This is not the time for flippancy, Dolly,' he growled and crossed the room to peek through the curtains. 'There's a bloody hack out there right now. Soon be more of them.'

'What's the problem?' Silas asked.

'It's ridiculous.' Archer threw himself on the sofa. 'Someone I met yesterday, probably a worker at the morgue, has gone to the papers and sold them an invented story about my presence in Greychurch. Now the press wants to know what young Lord Clearwater was doing gawping at Ripper victims.' He waved the paper angrily. 'Is he involved? Does he know the killer? Why is he interested in dead street boys?'

'At least they referred to you as young,' Her Ladyship quipped.

'It has implications for you too.'

'How so?'

'The charity, Dolly.' Archer sounded pained.

'Well that's easy to settle,' the woman decreed. 'You were on a mission to find facts, doing good works, assisting an unfortunate fucker… I mean, of course, assisting the unfortunate Mr Fecker…' She made it up as she went along. 'A man employed by us in the consultation process concerning His Lordship's philanthropic endeavours. The board, that's me, sanctioned the visit, not that there was anything wrong with it as I now see, and you have reported back. Bravo. The Times will carry the true story tomorrow and the…' She peered down her narrow nose at the newspaper. 'The Screamer, or whatever it is, will publish a retraction.'

'They won't. The Times will be baying for blood like the rest of them.'

'They certainly will not.' Her Ladyship stood, surprised to have been contradicted. 'My cousin John owns it.'

She collected the newspaper and threw it on the fire just as Thomas arrived with a tray, watched over by Tripp.

'Oh, tea at last,' Lady Marshall enthused. 'Over there please, Thomas.'

She directed him to leave the tray on the low table between the two facing sofas, and Silas smiled up at him as Thomas bent to place it. He was ignored, and it was the first time he understood the great divide between above and below stairs. Thomas was working, he was in the presence of a great lady, not to mention a lord, and no matter who Silas was, he was a guest. Thomas couldn't acknowledge him, or speak to him, unless Silas moved first. It was a weird feeling. After all, if there were class divisions in the room, Silas was the lowest of the low and Thomas was way above him in respectability.

Having set out the tray to Her Ladyship's satisfaction, Thomas left, but Tripp stood upright and didn't move. Apparently, this was a sign that he had something to say, because Archer told him to 'Go on. What is it?' From his tone, Silas could see he was still wound like a spring.

'There have been members of the press calling at the door all morning, My Lord,' Tripp said. 'I wondered if you had any specific instructions for them?'

'I certainly do, Tripp,' Archer grumbled. 'But none that you could repeat. Tell them I am not available and if they carry on, let me know and I'll... I'll see to it.'

'Very good, Sir.' Tripp nodded his head to Archer, but bowed low to Her Ladyship.

'Anyone would think he was taking applause for his Hamlet,' Lady Marshall whispered.

Silas didn't understand what she meant, but assumed it was funny.

'Close the doors on your way out, Tripp.' Archer instructed, and the butler left.

The viscount poured tea, his hand shaking and his mind clearly not on the task. Silas took the pot from him, and their fingers touched momentarily. A glance between them reassured Silas that Archer was grateful and calming down. Silas poured as steadily as he could. A silver teapot was a far cry from the saucepans he was used to, but he had seen it done and placed one finger over the lid to prevent it from dropping off. It burnt him, but he didn't want to add to Archer's troubles by tipping hot liquid over her Ladyship.

She regarded Archer closely, and Silas guessed it was her way; to study people while she thought of what to say.

'Now we are alone,' she said at length. 'Maybe you can tell me exactly what you have been up to.'

Archer began to repeat the story of his visit, but she cut him off.

'Perhaps I should ask your secretary,' she suggested. 'He might speak more honestly.'

Her eyes drilled into Silas, but he sensed she was trying to be helpful. He more or less repeated what Archer had said.

Lady Marshall considered Silas' words as she sipped her tea.

'You have trained him very well,' she said with distrust in her voice.

'Dolly,' Archer sighed. 'Silas is not my secretary, he's my lover.'

Silas choked on his tea, and Her Ladyship perked up. Her head turned so quickly that it took a second for her pearls to catch up. She clutched them as she looked him up and down, wide-eyed in amazement.

'Despite the fact I am old enough to be your grandmother,' she said. 'I should say my godson has good taste.'

There was no end to the surprises Lady Marshall could serve. Silas, still trying to remove a tickle from the back of his throat, coughed into his fist. Once his eyes had stopped watering, he looked to Archer for advice. He sat opposite, his eyebrows arched behind his cup. When he moved it away from his mouth, he was smiling.

'Surprisingly for a woman of her age,' he said. 'My godmother is something of a supporter of men such as us.'

'Yes,' Her Ladyship said, slapping Silas' knee. 'I suppose I am a fairy's-godmother.'

'By which she means no offence, Silas.' Archer put down his cup. 'Dolly, he said, 'as always, you see through me as easily as a knife cuts butter.'

'I clearly do not,' she said. 'Otherwise, I would know what the other matter is that you are concealing from me.'

'I'm not concealing… What other matter?'

'If I knew, I wouldn't be asking. What's going on?'

Archer pretended he didn't understand, insisted there was no other matter, and eventually, Lady Marshall gave up trying and made Archer promise to tell her when he could. He promised, and she laughed in triumph saying that he had just proved her suspicion was founded. She then changed the subject and asked for more details about Silas and what Archer's plans were for him, as if discovering that they were lovers — the word thrilled him more than he ever thought a word could — was the most natural thing to talk about over tea. More surprising was the way Archer answered her, honestly and proudly.

Silas had been out of place the moment he stepped foot inside Clearwater House, but to be sitting on an upholstered settee, drinking tea from bone china, beside a Lady, in the presence of a Lord, and discussing their homosexual relationship as if it was normal, was undoubtedly the most unimagined thing in the world. Except it wasn't. Being involved in their conversation as if he was acceptable and equal took the prize.

Archer didn't go into too many details, but described how he had fallen for Silas as soon as he saw him and how they had become instant friends. He praised Silas' knowledge of the East End, his survival, his loyalty towards Fecker and his plain speaking. His praise grew to such an unbearable level that Silas was forced to interrupt and repay the compliments.

'Well, that is all very lovely,' Her Ladyship said, putting down her cup. 'But we can't have you in second-hand clothing, Hawkins. People will gossip, and Archer does not need more of that at this moment.' She swung to Archer as an idea sprung to mind. 'Shall I take him shopping? A treat for his approaching twentieth birthday. We could go to the Row or... No! Better, to one of those shops in the suburbs. I could go in disguise and pretend he is my grandson.'

'Dolly, please,' Archer complained.

'Great nephew, then,' she said. 'A little more distance gives a lot more camouflage. Easier story to invent.'

'He is not a toy.' Archer snapped. He brought himself up short. 'I'm sorry. There's too much going on, Dolly, but, yes, please.' He looked at Silas and smiled pathetically. 'Only if you would like. It would get you out of the house while I get rid of the journalists and give me time to think. Would you mind?'

Mind? The offer was better than Christmas, but Silas didn't want to be a burden and said so. What he actually meant was that he didn't want to feel like a kept man, but as he could see no other choice, he kept that thought to himself.

The day was planned as they finished their tea, and Lady Marshall left to speak with her cousin at the Times.

Tripp oversaw a quiet, but tiresomely late breakfast, during which Silas and Archer only spoke when he was out of the room and then in whispers. Silas wanted to talk about last night and what it meant, how the viscount felt and what happened next, but

Archer deflected the talk and told him that they would meet again to discuss all that and the Ripper. Silas looked for an opportunity to tell Archer he knew his plan and understood the significance of the drawing, but there was never the opportunity. Before he knew it, he was being taken to Lady Archer's house by Lucy, who pumped him full of questions about Fecker in the short distance it took to walk from one back door to the next.

He waited in a servants' hall not dissimilar to Clearwater, where it gradually dawned on him that Lady Marshall's staff were mainly men. Even the cook was a man, and very few girls worked there. Not only that, but most of the men, in whatever capacity, were built like dockers, incredibly fit and spoke hardly any English.

Silas liked Her Ladyship even more by the time they returned from an afternoon excursion to shops so fancy Silas wouldn't dare sleep in their doorways, and a succession of smouldering footmen carried boxes from the carriage to Archer's back door.

Having checked that there were no journalists in the street, Lady Marshall delivered Silas to the front of the house.

As he was leaving the carriage, she wrapped her spider-leg fingers around his wrists in a fierce grip and said, 'Remember, dear boy, whatever you feel for my godson must not be shown, not even to the servants. You understand his position?'

'I do, Your Ladyship,' Silas replied. 'To hurt him is the last thing I want to do.'

She was satisfied and ordered the carriage home. Silas watched it travel a few yards to her door and then climbed the steps to Clearwater.

Her Ladyship had ordered suits, shirts and shoes to be delivered, enjoying the shopping spree as much as his company — and he hers — but also bought outfits 'off the middle-class peg,' as she put it. He was now, according to Her Ladyship, looking, "acceptable in the style of the New Wave", whatever that meant. He wore fashionable clothes, but nothing too classy — he'd never get away with that. He had a place to live, though would have to live there as an employee. He had a lover, but they couldn't show their love. He had even admitted to himself that he was able to love and be loved, though it was going to take him time to accept.

He rang the bell, and as he waited, looked down on the street.

Carriages rolled past. The men and women behind the glass nodded politely, and Silas copied. He attracted the attention of a passing messenger boy no older than himself. The boy wished him good evening with a Sir attached and touched his cap.

Life was so unexpectedly wonderful, he wished that he could tell Fecker about it. His friend had been on his mind all afternoon along with the business of the Ripper and the part he was unwittingly playing in the events.

The front door opened to reveal Tripp, dour as usual, but also showing signs of strain.

'Good evening, Mr Tripp,' Silas said, stepping in and passing him his hat.

'Mr Hawkins.' Tripp replied with dutiful politeness as he closed the door.

Archer came skidding out of the drawing room in his socks. He slid sideways, coming to an ungainly stop at the round table where he drummed his hands and turned to Silas.

'I have had the most incredible brainwave,' he said. His hair was a mess, his eyes wild. 'Tripp. What time is it? Never mind. Silas… Oh my word, you look spectacular. Come in here. Tripp!' His attention was all over the place. 'Please would you, without an inquisition, send Thomas to the study as soon as he is able. Send Lucy up with a tray for three. Make sure we are not disturbed and… And…' He bit his knuckle. 'That's it. No. A couple of bottles of the seventy-six.'

Tripp took such an elongated in-breath, Silas thought the air would be sucked from the hall.

'And the gentleman's boxes, Sir?' he droned. 'Newly arrived from south of the river.' Disdain tainted every word.

'Oh, leave them for tomorrow. You don't need them right now, do you, Silas? Good.' He was gone, slipping back across the tiles and into the drawing room.

'What's your brainwave?' Silas asked, trotting to catch up.

Archer threw up his arms and spun. 'Patterns,' he cried. 'I thought it wasn't, but it is. You were both right, but wrong. The Ripper is fixated with dates, places, times and patterns. What's more. I know when he intends to kill again.'

# Twenty-Five

Silas was practically dragged into the study where Archer closed the doors, took hold of him and kissed him passionately. Silas backed against the wall and, with their bodies pressed firmly together, wrapped Archer in his arms as their tongues clashed. The intensity of the moment left him breathless.

'I've wanted to do that all day,' Archer panted. 'You were gone for hours. I didn't have time to talk this morning. Servants listen. God, you're so bloody desirable.'

Silas was still trapped, but he adored the feeling of the man's body against his and revelled in his delight.

'Slow down,' he said. 'Blimey!' Archer released him, but Silas didn't let him escape. 'Not so fast.' He grinned. 'We've got a few hours to catch up on, but I can see you've got something more important going on.'

'There's nothing more important than you,' Archer replied and kissed him again. 'When this bloody mess is done with, I'll take you away. We can go to the country or abroad. Wherever you want, and I'll show you the true depth of my feelings. I promise.'

'You don't have to promise me nothing, Archie. Only that you'll tell me what's got you so fired up.'

'You, mainly.' Archer touched Silas' face, ran his fingers through his hair and kissed his forehead. His movements were quick, his eyes flickering and, when his hands began to travel downwards to clutch Silas' hips and join them there even more closely, Silas had to push him away.

'I got the message,' he laughed. 'But that's for later. What's happened?'

'I have to wait for Thomas.' Archer adjusted the front of his trousers, as Silas was doing. 'Where did Lady Marshall take you? She likes you, that's a good thing. And those clothes!' Archer stood back to admire him, and Silas allowed it. He had never felt so special and cared for and was pleased to show himself off. 'I love the way those trousers hug your cock. I can even make out your sack.' Archer was pressed against him in a second, his hands cupping Silas' backside.

'Oi!' Silas laughed. 'You keep doing that you're going to give Thomas a right eyeful of your massive dick.' It was again throbbing insistently against his.

'I can't control it when you're around. And it's not massive.'

'Off!' Silas wriggled free. Archer was overexcited, wild even, and there were more important matters. 'Sit down. Get a drink. What's got you so dizzy?'

'You.'

'Come on, Archie. We've got to think about your brother.' Silas stood at the desk and picked up the drawing. 'I know what this is about,' he said.

'Oh, that.' Archer snatched it from him and put it in a drawer. 'Don't worry about that. Where's Thomas?' He took three strides to the bell-pull and rang.

'It's me, isn't it?' Silas said. 'In the picture?'

'No.'

'I know why you were looking for a renter like me.'

His tone was challenging, and it caught Archer unawares. The manic smile faded from his lips as he approached. 'What do you mean?'

Silas opened the drawer to remove the sketch and held it facing Archer.

'That's him, isn't it?' he said.

'Who?'

'Your man from before. The one you and your brother fought over.'

'Harrington? No.'

'It's alright, Archie.' Silas put the paper down and took his hands. Archer didn't understand. 'I get it. You wanted to find someone to catch your brother's eye. Someone who looked like the boy he took from you. You sent Thomas to find a street boy you could use as bait to catch him.'

Whatever reaction Silas expected, it wasn't the one Archer gave.

His expression remained one of confusion and didn't change as he dropped Silas' hands and stepped back. Gradually, like lamplight brightening through a receding mist, his confusion cleared to reveal horror. His head moved from side to side, and his eyes glistened. He brought a hand to his mouth to cover the shock and used a knuckle to wipe away a tear.

Trembling, he took the sketch, looked at it once, and tore it into pieces.

'No,' he said, his words barely audible. 'You can't think that of me.'

'I don't mind. I'll do it.'

'How could you think that...?'

'It's alright, Archie.' Silas took his hands again. 'I'd do anything for you. Even that.'

'Oh, Silas.' Archer sniffed and swallowed. 'You've taken me so wrong, and it's all my fault.' A tentative smile breached his lips. 'That was never my intention. That drawing looks nothing like Simon Harrington. It was a fantasy, that's all.' His strong fingers pushed away Silas' fringe. 'I needed someone to tell me about life in the East End, so why not a man who was my idea of perfection? What I got was beyond my dreams, because he came with courage and heart, innocence and intelligence. I would never put you in harm's way.'

Silas fell on his lips. Even if he had been the greatest artist in the world, he would never have been able to draw the perfection he found in Archer.

They were still kissing and in a heightened state of arousal when there was a knock on the door.

'Hell,' Archer said as they broke apart. 'We can't keep doing this.' He looked frantically for some way to hide his prominent erection, and Silas did the same. 'You do believe me, don't you?'

'I ain't going to stop doing this.'

'About the picture,' Archer was laughing, his excitable state reinstated by panic.

'Yeah.' Silas shushed him. 'Sit at the desk.'

As Archer slid into the captain's chair and faced the desk while Silas grabbed a book and sat in an armchair with it open in his lap.

'Come!' Archer called busying himself with some letters.

Thomas entered. 'Your supper, My Lord.'

'Thank you, Thomas. On the reading table if you would.'

He thought about some trivial matter, pen raised, and scribbled notes while Silas read an Old Moore's Almanack upside down. The supper was delivered, the maids dismissed, and Thomas asked to stay behind. Once the drawing room doors were closed, Thomas shut the study to the outside world. No sooner had he heard the click of the latch than Archer slid his chair from under the desk and spun on it.

'Men,' he said. 'I have had a brainwave. We have a lot of thinking to do and a lot of planning, and we have no time. Tom, relax, sit and think. Silas, you've given me an idea. By the by, Tom,' he added as he searched the desk. 'Thank you again for your intervention this morning. Well played.'

'You're welcome.' Thomas removed his tailcoat and sat, giving Silas a tip of the head.

Silas winked a reply.

Archer found what he was looking for, and when the three were seated, opened a notebook to a marked page. 'Gentlemen,' he said. 'I have made progress, and just in time. But I must steady myself. This is the most serious of matters.' He took a deep breath and released it slowly. 'Let me take you through the morning. To do so will help sharpen my mind.'

Archer was grateful that Lady Marshall had not only taken an instant liking to Silas and accepted the difference in status, but had also taken him away for a few hours. It wasn't that Archer didn't want to be with Silas, his body ached for him, but Dolly had been right. For Silas to pass as his secretary — a stroke of accidental genius on Her Ladyship's part — he needed to look like a middle-class man of ability. Archer would give him a suite of rooms in the city house and a cottage on the estate, employing him on paper as an administrator. There would be no questions asked.

That problem solved, and with the house to himself, he was able to pull the strands of his life together and sift through them to find the most important thread. Regrettably, the journalists on his doorstep was it. As Silas made what Lady Marshall termed his *clandestine escape* from the back of the house, Archer addressed the gathering hacks on his front step, thereby creating a diversion. He sent them off with polite words confirming his presence with the medical examiner and explaining his interest from the charitable trust's point of view. Whether they believed him or not, he no longer cared. There would undoubtedly be more lucrative headlines waiting for them around the corner, and tomorrow he would be yesterday's news.

With Silas out of the house, his mind was free to concentrate on the Ripper. He dispatched Thomas to the telegraph office for any news from Holland, and to convey His Lordship's displeasure at the length of time it was taking to receive a reply. While there, Thomas was to send another telegram which blatantly demanded an answer.

"Urgent. Confirm Hon Crispin Riddington still with you. Matter of life and death. Immediate reply expected else legal action ensues."

It was when he was counting the days since his first message and the hours since the second, that a strange thought struck him. He was, at the time, idly staring at the map of Greychurch and Thomas' letter A, the lines blurring as he looked through them in thought.

He had written to the sanitorium following the death of his father a few months ago. He didn't remember the exact date because of everything else that was going on, but he knew the week. A letter of condolence had arrived six weeks later, so he took that as the accepted, though incredibly slow time it took the organisation to grind into action. He had written to thank them and assure them Crispin's bills would continue to be paid and had asked for news on his progress. He had not yet received a reply, but that was still within the six weeks to be expected. His telegram had followed after the fourth murder, seven days ago.

It wasn't the delays that sparked the notion, but the fact they made him think about time. He had first thought the dates of the murders were random. He had searched his Almanack for phases of the moon and the details of tides, even looked at the alignment of the planets, but he found no clues. The actual dates, the numbers, bore no pattern or relevance, and the only thing timewise that the murders had in common was that they happened at night, usually in the early hours. As there were no witnesses, he couldn't be sure of exact times, but he doubted they would be pertinent. The Ripper didn't book appointments, he took chances as and when they appeared.

For all his logical and clear thinking, something remained lodged at the back of his mind. An idea or a piece of knowledge fluttered like a caged bird desperate to fly, and the more he studied the names of streets that might mean something to Crispin, the more panicked the bird became. It wasn't until mid-afternoon that the annoying, flapping 'what is it?' in his head dropped from its perch and landed on the floor of his mind like a dead thing.

It happened when he read the name of an inconsequential street in Limedock, Lessening Lane.

It was a narrow alley that, as its name suggested, began wider than it finished. It appeared to have no purpose except to take a person from a street to a wharf. The location was appropriate, being not far from the scene of the first murder, but even that was not what fuelled his excitement.

It was the word *lessening* which caused the trapped thought to flutter and squawk.

Back at his desk, he noted the murder dates on a chart. This time, he wasn't looking at the numbers, but their relation to each other in a broader time spectrum. One month had elapsed between the first murder and the second, two weeks between the second and third. Between the third and fourth, one week had passed, and between the fourth and the double event, four days. The conclusion was obvious.

Silas and Thomas had been right. There was a pattern, but it was in the timing, not the locations.

'So,' Thomas asked when the viscount had finished talking. 'By your logic, there will be two days between the last and the next.' He closed his eyes in thought, opening them a second later in shock. 'Really?'

'Exactly!' Archer leapt from his chair. 'Tonight.'

Thomas thought about it calmly. 'And then what?'

'I don't understand.'

'One day? Then twelve hours? Six?'

'Until he disappears up his own arse.' Silas' attempt to lighten the mood was not appreciated. 'Sorry.'

'No, it's a good point.' Archer wheeled his chair closer to him. 'I hadn't thought further than tonight and my chance to catch him.'

'Our chance,' Silas corrected.

'Very well...' Thomas was still thinking, and Archer was regarding him keenly. 'But what if that wasn't the first murder and your timing is off?'

'The pattern is still there.'

'True.' Thomas conceded. 'But if there were any earlier ones, then by your logic, the Ripper is not your brother, because he was definitely locked up when the late viscount passed, and that would be within the two months before... I see.'

Silas had to picture a calendar to see the pattern, but he too understood. 'So that still leaves us not knowing for sure if it is him, and not knowing where he's going to be tonight,' he said. 'Unless "Lessening" is a name that rings a bell?'

'If it does it's a wren in an aviary,' Archer said, causing the others to glance at each other for a meaning. 'It just caught my eye. But...' He held up the map with the murder sites marked. 'I thought it might complete a circle. It's not a spiral, it's not an A or a Star of David, if there is any pattern to the locations, it's a dubious one. With that in mind...' He rose to find a second map which he held for them to see. 'I drew one but it's more of a six-sided thing, and there's no discernible centre. The pattern, if there is one, was not to be found on the ground but in time.'

'And that time's tonight?' Silas was dubious, it sounded too contrived, and he couldn't equate the logic of timed murders with the mind of a madman. He wished Fecker was with him. He'd have seen through the smoke and pointed out the fire, the clue they were undoubtedly missing.

'Yes, tonight,' Archer said. 'Which is why I came up with a plan. Or, I should say, three.' He brought his chair back to them, and they sat in a triangle. 'I was going to take some of Lady Marshall's household, the ones built like Coldstream Guards, enter Greychurch tonight and search for Crispin, so sure am I of his presence there. But then I saw that would mean having to explain to Her Ladyship what I am about. Besides, we would be little more than vigilantes, and there are enough of them. My second plan was to go alone...'

Silas gasped, and Thomas protested.

'Thank you, gentlemen,' Archer said, reassuring them with a gesture. 'I will not go unarmed.'

'And you won't go alone,' Thomas insisted.

'Of course he won't.' Silas wasn't having that. 'I'll go. The Ripper ain't going to come after you, you're the wrong sort. You need to lure him out.'

'Silas, say no more. I will employ a local youth to assist me, no questions asked.'

'And then what?' Silas was on his feet. His blood was beginning to boil at the thought of Archer's stupidity. 'You and him walk around arm in arm? No-one's going to fall for that. It's not how it works.'

'I will follow him closely.'

'No, you won't.' Silas had trouble fighting back his anger. ''Cos that ain't how it works neither. You don't pick up a rat and take him for a stroll. There's a… ritual, a code. You pass him under a lamppost, give him the eye, up, down, see how he replies. Looks away? Out of luck. Back-tip of the head? Off you go. Then you follow him 'cos he knows the places, what yard or alley is being used, who's doing business where.' He glared at Archer and his anger melted into fear. 'Even if you found a lad who knows what you're doing, doesn't think you are the Ripper and doesn't just take your money and scarper, you can't be anywhere near him else the Ripper will know what's going on and get scared off.'

He sat, trembling. He had imagined the whole scene in his mind except it ended in attack and bloodshed, the flash of a knife and death.

'I'll go with you,' Thomas said.

Archer made no reply. He was staring at Silas, pale and upset. Their eyes locked and Silas knew the plan would only work if it was him walking the streets. Archer couldn't trust anyone else.

'No, you won't, Tom,' Silas said.

He tore his eyes away from the viscount and put a hand on Thomas' knee. When he'd first met the man, he'd taken him for an idiot, the same as anyone else who spent their life working in the service of others, but Thomas was anything but stupid.

'Sorry, mate, but you'd stand out too much.'

'The decision should be Archer's,' Thomas said, moving his leg.

'He hasn't got a choice.' Silas smiled at the viscount. 'I believe you when you say this wasn't planned. It's obvious none of this has been planned much.' It was said in fake reproach with a supportive smile. 'But it's what we've got, so we have to use it.'

'I won't put you in danger, either of you.' Archer was adamant.

'But you'll put yourself in danger,' Silas countered. 'As if you don't mean anything to us.'

'I have my pistols.'

'Don't do you any good in the dark.'

'I have training.'

'Yeah?' Silas' annoyance was rising again. 'Did they train you what to do in the half a second you get when you work out that the cold scratch on your throat is the deep slash of a knife and it's too late?'

Archer was wavering.

'I'll observe from a distance,' he said.

'And what good will that do?' Silas shouted, tears coming to his eyes. 'By the time you're across the street, a boy'll be dead and you next, most likely.'

'It's my brother. I'll call his name, distract him. He wants me to be there.'

'So he can fucking kill you!'

'Silas!' Thomas had him by the shoulders. 'Please, calm down.'

Silas was too upset. There were too many horrific images.

'Ah, get off me.'

Thomas wouldn't let him struggle free, and Silas didn't want him to. He needed someone to hold him back else he would have flown at Archer and beat on his chest until he understood how much he meant.

'It's alright.' Thomas guided his head to his chest and held it there. 'I couldn't do without him either,' he whispered privately in Silas' ear. 'But you have to let him do it his way.'

His words were intended to reassure, but somehow they went further than that and bonded the pair.

Silas returned the hug, holding it for a moment too long before stepping back and wiping his eyes. Sniffing, he pulled himself together.

'Sorry about that, Tom,' he said.

'I'm not,' Thomas replied, offering a helpless expression before retaking his seat.

'Archie...?' Silas crouched before the viscount, held his arms and spoke softly, comforted by Thomas' concern. 'If you go on your own and something happens to you, I don't care that it would leave me back on the streets 'cos it won't matter, not without you. But what about Tom and the others, eh? What happens to them if you get yourself killed?'

Archer sighed, leant forward and kissed him.

'I didn't mean to involve you in this,' he said. 'I only wanted your advice.'

'Ha! You want my advice, My Lord?' Silas stood. 'Then you listen to Tommy. He's got more sense than anyone.'

'I will, and I have,' Archer said. 'But, it wouldn't be fair on Tom to make him decide our course of action. No. I said that I had three plans and one must be enacted tonight. We have the time frame, and we have the rough location, I'm sure of it. Lessening Lane, or the area nearby. What I propose is...'

He suddenly stopped talking, shocked. His mouth remained open, and his stare fixed on Silas. It was as if someone had slapped him in the face.

'What is it?'

Archer stood slowly, his eyes widening and his brow furrowing. He moved to the fireplace as a man in a dream walks a straight line to a destination he can't see.

'What is it, Archer?' Thomas asked.

He and Silas exchanged uneasy glances, both confused. The intrigue deepened when Archer turned to them, his fingers waving about his head like grass in a breeze.

'Birds in a cage,' he said, explaining nothing. 'I've got a raven, and it won't land.'

Silas checked the wine bottles. Still unopened.

'Do you want to explain?' he prompted.

'I can't... It's not quite there...' Archer struggled, his fingers lacing on the top of his head, and he stamped his foot. 'What is it?'

'Perhaps a brandy?' Thomas was on his feet.

'No. Shush... It's...' He struck the mantlepiece with a fist and growled in his throat. 'Damn it!'

'Archie, what's up?' Silas hurried to his side and turned his head. 'What's wrong?'

The viscount stared as if he had no idea who he was, but gradually, the memory returned.

'Lessening,' he said. 'It's my brother's lessening.'

# Twenty-Six

They had named him the Ripper weeks ago, now they were taking bets on where and when he would rip next. Policemen were losing their jobs because of him, and he had even been discussed in the Commons. Apparently, the Queen was quite disturbed, and rightly so. He had not finished his work yet.

The diary lay open on his table beneath the soft glow of the bowl lamp, it's pages free of handwriting, but the printed dates as bold as his determination. The street map next to it also showed no sign of the time he had spent poring over it, making plans and jotting notes in his mind. He had evaded and confused, deflected suspicion and triumphed over the authorities so far, but he had to proceed with caution and not let his desire overcome what little logic he had remaining. There must be no clues other than those the viscount alone would recognise.

Significant locations had been hard to find, and of all the coincidences, this last one was a leap, even for him. He was, however, satisfied that Archer would find the obscure reference. He had seen him in the anonymous streets with his servants. Poorly disguised, he had been easy to spot, being one of the few men walking Greychurch at night with a straight back and haughty gait, watching the shadows as acutely aware of his surroundings as any military trained man.

He had seen him with his boy and heard him in the yard where unaware of the killer behind the darkened window, he had professed his love.

Love? For a street-rat? For a youth as distant in years as he was in class? An immigrant and a molly boy. A sickening beast of corruption that deserved a fitting admission to hell, his blood let, body gutted, and his workings displayed for the world to see.

He took a deep breath, and his vision tunnelled until he saw only the diary. The blank pages counted the days in rising anticipation. He saw his hand cross his line of sight as if someone else was directing it and he followed. His skin, yellow beneath the oil flame, glistened with nervous sweat, and his fingers twisted into his palm as if they didn't want to touch what they reached for; a stoppered bottle, the glass as green as envy. The liquid inside drew him to its numbing drowse and its bitter-tasting promise of forgiveness.

*Take me, and all will be well.*

It spoke in seductive tones, its voice as warm as a renter's entrails, its welcome as homely as a gutted ribcage. His fingers uncurled, attracted to the bottle like magnets, and the cork was pulled.

Archer was no better than a street-rat. He never had been. He was a man who took. That was all he did. Take. He took his time, took liberties, chances and people. He took Harrington. Stole him, in the same way he stole hearts, trust and titles. As street-rats thieve, aristocrats appropriate. It was the same thing. Archer was no better than the boys he took to bed. He deserved the same punishment.

The liquid was cold on his throat and sour, but its bitterness matched his own. He welcomed its flavour as much as he embraced its effects. It would focus his mind until his intent was as sharp as the knife his hand now longed for. A blade to make himself complete. A tool that took as easily as a viscount stole. A thing as everyday as a street-rat. But sharper.

It must be different tonight. If this was to be the last, it had to be right. He must keep his wits about him. He was enticing an equal to battle and had the advantage, but his lust for the feel of a man's death must not deflect his concentration.

The medicine was working, its voice as comforting as a nanny in a nursery, its anger as piercing as a needle.

His hand reached for the turn of the lamp, and the flame began to die until the room was as black as his soul.

Thomas watched them leave disguised, armed and refusing his offer to go with them. Archer had promised never to take him back to the East End, and Thomas was grateful for the thought, but he was young, he was able, and, like Silas, he would put his life on the line for his master. Archer's refusal had hurt.

He crunched his way across the gravelled yard to the back door, his mind tumbling. These last few days had brought back so many memories. They had been noted and stacked away like the books on Archer's shelves, in no particular order, but each one read and waiting to be taken down and opened at a moment's notice. Their childhood together yet apart was placed alongside the viscount's kind words to him over the last few days and the times recently when they had been able to talk as friends. They had been as difficult for Thomas to accept as the day he was told His Lordship was too old to visit below stairs.

Beside those, the memory of Silas' touch on his crotch, the man's seductive eyes, the look of him in a suit and collar, his perfection. On another shelf, the look on Archer's face when he first saw Silas, and Thomas knew he had lost both to each other. But then, below that, their conversations. The times Archer told him he was his only friend. The times he had listened to him weeping in bed, deep in his cups, despairing of being alone.

Thomas had attended him through all those memories, so why was he forbidden to serve now? Archer trusted him enough to share his feelings for Silas, to let Thomas see that he had taken the man to bed. He trusted him enough to know this illegal secret, but not enough to let him drive the trap.

It was either because Archer cared for him too much, or it was because he didn't trust him at all.

'Are you with us, Thomas?'

It was Tripp, blocking the entrance to the kitchen, his arms folded.

Thomas brought himself to attention. 'My apologies, Mr Tripp. I was far away.'

'You always are, boy. Get in here and answer some questions.'

Tripp clipped his way through to the servants' hall which was empty apart from the smell of boiled cabbage, and on into the passage.

Thomas followed, dreading what might come next, and trying to clear his mind of what Archer and Silas were now doing. They would still be in the neighbourhood, trotting calmly through the night fog, safe and warm in their coats.

Thomas, however, was chilled, and became more so when Tripp opened the door to his pantry and ordered him in. He could tell

248

from his mood that he was unhappy and that was never a good thing.

'Mrs Flintwich is missing a baking ring,' Tripp announced solemnly as Thomas closed the door.

'A what?'

'A baking ring. A cake tin without a base, she tells me.'

'Would you like me to help her look?'

'I would like you to tell me what you were doing with it. You were seen.'

Thomas denied all knowledge when in reality he knew precisely what had happened to the metal ring. He fought off the accusation so well that after several minutes of swordplay on the subject, Tripp dropped it, and Thomas assumed he was free to go.

'Stay where you are,' Tripp growled.

'Yes, Mr Tripp?'

The butler sat at his desk and made Thomas stand in front of it like a schoolboy.

'How long have you worked for me, Thomas?' Tripp asked, apparently calm.

'I have worked for Lord Clearwater for nineteen years, Mr Tripp, as you know.'

'And in all that time, have you worked hard, learned much and progressed to the enviable position of first footman?'

'I have.'

'You have.' Tripp agreed, nodding thoughtfully. He smiled, lulling Thomas into a false security, because a second later, he slammed his palms on the desk and shot to his feet. 'Then you owe me an explanation,' he bellowed. 'What the hell is going on?'

Thomas contained his fear and kept his composure. 'I don't understand, Mr Tripp.'

'Of course you do, boy. The shenanigans in His Lordship's study these past two nights. The urchin in the green suite, Lady Marshall's visit, the newspapers, all of it. I demand to know what's happening, and it's your job to tell me.'

Trembling inside, but sure that his loyalty to the viscount would be reciprocated, Thomas said, 'I'm afraid I can't tell you.' If Tripp was going to shout at him, he would dispense with the niceties and not call him sir.

'Can't tell me?' Tripp's grey face blossomed red. 'Don't be preposterous. It is your duty.'

'To betray His Lordship's confidence?'

'If I say so, yes.'

What Trip said was partially true. Thomas was obliged to report any unusual, disturbing or unsavoury matters to his senior, but the rule book applied to illness or mice, not rent boys and murders. Certainly not to secrets shared between friends, if that was how he was to consider Archer. The fact that he was thinking of him by his Christian name proved that he was.

'Once again,' he said. 'I apologise, but I have been asked to say nothing.'

'And once again, I remind you, Payne, it is your duty.'

Thomas shrugged and kept his eyes on the shelf behind Tripp's desk.

Tripp came around the table to stand over him. He was taller than Thomas, but older and not as strong. Not that Thomas was afraid the man would do him physical harm. Tripp was a coward.

'It is the word duty... No,' Tripp corrected himself. 'It is the sentence, it is your duty, to which I refer when I ask if you enjoy your position in this house?'

'I don't understand.'

'Clearly not, else you would not be risking your employment by keeping this from me.'

Thomas could be fired on the spot, it had happened to others. He could be out of his room, homeless, unemployed and with no reference by the time Archer reached the East End. It was not a pleasant thought, but again, he was sure that if that happened, Archer would take his side.

'Mr Tripp,' he said, rising without permission, so he could enjoy the expression on the old man's face. 'If you are threatening me with dismissal, because I will not betray my employer's trust, then I suggest you take the issue up with His Lordship.'

'Don't be impertinent, boy. Sit down.'

It was in Thomas' mind to be more impertinent than this. He remained standing.

'If you will excuse me,' he said. 'I have duties to attend to, as I believe do you. As you remind me constantly, my responsibility is

250

to The Viscount Clearwater. As is yours.'

That would have had him fired for sure had not the bell rung at the front door. Tripp glared at him, breathing heavily through his hooked nose, his face an alarming shade of puce. A vein throbbed on his forehead.

Thomas doubted he had ever encountered such insolence and let him fluster for a reply for a second before suggesting the door be answered.

'Get out,' Tripp spat. 'I will deal with you on your return.'

Thomas nodded acquiescence as if the butler had politely asked him to serve tea, and left the room.

The moment he stepped into the corridor, he was overcome by nausea and the only way to allay his fears for Archer, and to a lesser extent Silas, was to concentrate on his duties. He might only have his job for a few more minutes, but in the meantime, the mundane matter of answering the front door was enough to hold onto.

He took the back stairs at his usual efficient, but unhurried pace, checked his appearance in the hall mirror where he suffered a minor slip in concentration when he asked himself what the hell he was doing, and, as composed and detached as any footman, opened the front door.

A young man stood on the step. He wasn't excessively attractive and yet turned something in Thomas' chest on sight. Shorter than him, he sported neat blond hair beneath a peaked cap, a smooth, young face and a stocky figure that fit snuggly in a blue uniform. Around his waist, he wore a thick belt to which was attached a leather pouch, and in his hand, he held an envelope.

'Yes?' Thomas said, once the shock of seeing the man had passed.

The messenger appeared to be caught by similar surprise, because he looked at Thomas, but said nothing, his message apparently unimportant. The pause gave Thomas a little more time to study the features and decide that they were, after all attractive. He couldn't tell what the young man was thinking, but he found his stare strangely exciting.

He smiled, and the youth grinned back.

'Yes?' Thomas repeated.

'Oh, sorry. I have a telegram for Viscount Clearwater.' He offered the envelope.

Thomas took it between his thumb and forefinger, but the messenger wouldn't release it.

'What's your name?' he asked, as if the two were meeting socially.

It was none of his business, but Thomas said, 'Thomas. What's yours?'

'James.'

He released the envelope.

'Thank you.' Thomas pulled himself together and searched his pockets for coins.

'Not to worry,' James chirped. 'It's on account. You could give me a tip if you want.'

'I'll give you a tip,' Thomas replied. 'Don't be so bloody cheeky.'

The messenger laughed and touched his cap. 'Fair enough,' he said. 'Best go, but I hope I get dispatched here again. See you, Thomas.'

'My mates call me Tom.'

James winked. 'Then I'm Jimmy, Tom. Hope to see you again,' he said. 'I drink in the Crown and Anchor most nights. Remember, us messenger boys always deliver.' With that cryptic statement, he was off, turning once along the street to look back, just as Thomas did at the door.

'Who was that?' Tripp was waiting for him in the hall, distant enough not to have heard the inappropriate exchange.

'A message for His Lordship,' Thomas said. He was trembling for a reason he didn't understand and fought to pull himself together. 'I shall put it in his study.'

'Do that, and then return to my parlour,' Tripp growled. 'I have not finished with you.'

The study was how they had left it after taking their supper together, listening to Archer's outline of his final plan. The sight of the charts and notebook, the maps and scribbled dates, brought back the viscount's peril, and his list of murder dates and the name of his brother written beside them struck a chord.

Thomas looked at the envelope. It would either be an invite to a last-minute party, some business from the House of Lords or news from Holland. The viscount would not be in the mood for a party and had little time for the House, but he was desperate to know of his brother.

Thomas checked that Tripp was nowhere nearby before he opened the envelope. His concerns left him the moment he read the words, and his blood ran cold as quickly as he ran from the room.

# Twenty-Seven

They said little after leaving Clearwater House, and it wasn't until Archer had the river on his right that he found the silence uncomfortable. He glanced at Silas beside him, huddled in an old coat, a wool cap pulled back on his head. He was a silhouette against the passing streetlamps that drowned in the thickening mist. The air around them was yellow and visibility bad, but now and then the trap's lanterns threw a flicker his way, and Archer was able to see his face. He bit a nail, staring ahead, lost in thought.

'I didn't plan for it to get out of hand and happen this way,' Archer said.

Silas nodded, looked up at him sideways and sat back. 'I know,' he said. 'And I told you not to worry about it.'

'You'll be safe. I know what I'm doing.'

'So do I, Archie.'

'Let's hope Thomas does. How is it?'

Silas pulled at his collar. 'Bloody uncomfortable, to be honest. Digs in when I put my head down.'

'You're to keep it on, no matter what.'

'Feel like a fucking dog,' Silas complained. 'But as long as it stops a knife.'

Archer tapped Silas' neck with the crop. It was solid. 'If it can contain Mrs Flintwich's fruitcake…' he paused. 'But it won't be necessary. As soon as I see him approach, I'll distract him.'

'You really think he'll listen to you?'

They had debated this back at the house. Archer was confident that as soon as Crispin heard his voice and saw him, his brother would have won the game and there would be no point in playing further. Crispin wanted him, not a street-rat. He'd used those unfortunate boys as bait. Archer was the catch. Whether that was because Crispin intended to kill him, or because it was a madman's way to engineer a cry for help remained to be seen, but Archer was prepared for either eventuality.

'He'll listen,' he said. 'Even if it's for one second it will be enough for me to identify him and you to run. After that, if he comes at either of us, I'll shoot him in the leg. If he breaks down in remorse as I expect, I will have time to disarm him and hold him while you blow the whistle.'

'Yeah, I know all that,' Silas said. 'But what if, for some reason, it ain't him?'

'Then I'll shoot for the chest. I would be within my rights.'

'Well, I hope you're a good shot.'

They skirted the edge of the West End and passed City Bridge as the clock struck ten.

'Can you see the map?' Archer asked.

'Can't hardly see the road in this peasouper,' Silas complained and held the map towards the lanterns. 'Keep going straight.'

There was now more distance between the streetlamps and the road had narrowed. The later the hour became, the fewer carriages passed, until, as the half-hour tolled from some distant and fog-muffled bell, they were alone. The steady clip-clop of the horse's hooves became conspicuous, and he drew her to a halt at a coaching inn on the edge of Limedock.

'You want me to do this?' Silas asked.

'No,' Archer said as he studied the front of the tavern. 'We're on the cusp of respectability here, so I won't look out of place. 'Can you lead Emma into the yard?'

'Daft name for a horse,' Silas mumbled as he jumped down.

'You should hear what she calls you.'

Archer arranged for Emma and the trap to be lodged in the stables and paid more than was required, because he said he might return late. He was dressed as a respectable artisan, a filigree cutter or gentleman joiner perhaps, and neither his request nor presence raised eyebrows. Anyone there would assume he was heading into the seedier parts of the docklands for a brothel or opium den, it was all above board.

He found Silas on the street, blending with the few people around him but waiting in the safety of a streetlamp's glow. He was the last person in the world Archer wanted to put in harm's way, but he was the only one who could perform the task. That Silas trusted him and had stated several times that he would do anything for the viscount increased his guilt.

'It's a fair walk,' Silas said and put away the map. 'But I know where we're going.'

As they followed the river's edge, around bonded warehouses and through lanes clogged with machinery and crates, they decided to split half a mile before their destination so that Archer could follow at an inconspicuous distance. Crispin's clues led them to Lessening Lane, and Archer didn't know what to expect when they arrived. Silas would select what he thought was the best place to stand and play his part, leaving Archer to find a hideout within sight. Assuming the street lent itself to their purpose, there they would wait.

Lessening Lane was a veiled reference at best, at worst, a red herring. Either way, it was the only straw to be grasped and the only connection he could make with the myriad of place names in Greychurch. He may not have even remembered the word correctly but "lessoning" was what Harrington had called the punishment so cruelly issued. The reason it hadn't struck him immediately, was because Harrington had never said it to his face. He had told someone else about it, and that's how it was reported back to Archer. He remembered Benji had said that, in his worsening state of despair, Simon Harrington had referred to his punishment as his "lessoning", because he was being taught a lesson. The word made no sense, and at the time, Archer had preferred not to dwell the matter. Seeing his lover suffer at his brother's hands and being unable to do anything about it was bad enough, but to think that Harrington was being driven mad by it was too much to bear.

He realised, after Simon's death, that he meant his will to live was *lessening*.

The river continued ahead, but they turned left to follow a dock that cut inland. Here, the street became busier, and Silas took to walking a few steps ahead so that if he was recognised or approached, he could converse while Archer passed by unnoticed. The viscount walked with his head bowed, and a cloth cap pulled down to shade his face. His collar was turned up, and his hands played with a revolver in each pocket. Their weighty presence was reassuring, as was his training in how to use them, but nothing had prepared him for the anguish.

Ahead of him, cocky and confident, was a man who had captured his heart. A man he would do anything for, and a man he could not live without. Yes, they had known each other for less time than it took a telegram to arrive, but that only made him more confident of his love.

It had taken him many painful years to fall in love with Simon Harrington, and when he finally admitted that was what it was, he lost the man. The grief he felt for Simon was nothing for what he would feel if he lost Silas, and yet here he was, possibly orchestrating a similar fate.

At one point, as they entered Cheap Street, Archer stopped, determined to call Silas back and go home. He remembered Silas' words, however, and he had been right. If anything happened to Archer, everyone in his life would be affected and badly too. From his mother to her maids, his friends to his fellow members of the House, all would be tainted.

The only way this evening could end was in triumph, with Crispin caught and back where he belonged, with no-one knowing, and with no-one dead.

If he walked away, his brother would go on killing in ever-decreasing circles of time until he was captured and exposed. Archer had to see this through, and he had to trust Silas, a man he had found in a gutter and known less than seven days.

'Death,' as Benji Quill used to say aboard ship, 'favours the weak.'

Silas had stopped at an undertaker's shop as if he was waiting for someone, his shoulders slumped in disappointment. Archer hung back until he moved off again. He hovered at the corner of a narrow alley until the viscount was closer, and led him through it, turning left at the end and crossing a square Archer recognised from their previous visit.

It was all he did recall. The cramped cut-throughs and yards became ever-more similar, the calls from whores, and the sound of breaking bottles the same in every street. Fog bullied lamplight as pick-pockets discretely did harm, and children under blankets watched and learned.

Above them, a wooden arch spanned the road announcing they were about to enter Limedock, one of several small docks cut in from the river. Bustling and teaming by day, it was eerily quiet after dark, something that could work either in their favour or against it.

'Right,' Silas said, stopping Archer on a corner. 'I'm going once around the warehouse, yeah? You stay here.'

'I need to follow you.'

'It's you he's after, Archie. Besides…' He knocked the metal collar beneath his shirt. 'I'll be back in five minutes. Don't speak to any strange men.'

That was another thing ridiculously lovable about the man. His inappropriate humour.

Silas drifted into the gloom and five torturous minutes passed before he broke through it again, the fog swirling at his feet.

'Hardly no-one about,' he whispered, holding his lantern to his face. 'Lessening Lane ain't far, but there ain't much in it. One doorway that goes into a warehouse. Not a deep enough doorway for his purpose and too far from the street. So, I'm going to hang around on the corner, there's a shop opposite, but it's not got a lock on the door. Not now.' He winked. 'You can hide in there and watch from the window.'

'Or we could walk away.'

'You're like one of them parrots at the zoo, you are,' Silas said, ignoring Archer's words. 'I didn't see no-one else around, but there's a lot of dark windows. He could be there, watching. I reckon it's best I go first, you follow. A good trick is to stop for a piss. Looks legit, and you can stand there pretending 'til there's no-one around and then shift into the dark.' He tapped his nose. 'We could be in for a wait, but don't fall asleep.'

'No chance of that. Is the corner lit?'

'Not much, but further up the street is. You'll see anyone coming and recognise your brother. Er, you will, won't you?'

'Oh yes, for sure. Six feet tall and mainly skeleton. You've got the whistle?'

'Yeah, stay calm.'

'Damn it, Silas.' Archer had to say something before he sent him off to await his fate. 'You know I love you, don't you?'

'Yeah.'

'Will you say it to me? Now, before we go?'

Silas looked at him with compassionate eyes. 'You're a romantic old sod, ain't you?' He smiled. 'Come on.'

Thomas left his room dressed in his civilian clothes, the telegram in his pocket. He knew Archer's rough location, and at that time of night, he hoped it wouldn't be crowded, and he would be able to find him in time. Getting there was a different matter. The viscount had taken the trap, and the landau would be out of place. Besides, he had taken Emma, and that only left one horse. He would have to ride Shanks, the older, larger of the team.

His first obstacle was Tripp, and he encountered him in the servants' hall as he pulled a cloak from the hook adding a bowler hat to complete his disguise.

'Where do you think you're going?' Tripp demanded, looking up from a newspaper.

'I'll explain later,' Thomas replied, fixing the cloak at his neck.

'You will explain now.' Tripp rose to his full six feet, his expression a wall of outrage.

'I can't.' Thomas hurried into the kitchen, heading for Mrs Flintwich's knife collection.

'Come here!' Tripp barked, pushing in his chair with an angry scrape before following.

'Very sorry, Mr Tripp,' Thomas insisted. 'It is His Lordship's business.'

'I know His Lordship's business, Thomas, you do not. Come back.'

The sight of the cook's knives reinforced what Thomas was about to do and where he was going, and a flush of dread rushed through him. He took a deep breath before selecting a six-inch blade Mrs Flintwich used for cutting meat. He wrapped it in muslin before dropping it into his jacket pocket.

'Thomas!' Tripp, red in the face with outrage, yelled across the expanse of kitchen, the name echoing from the vaulted ceiling.

Thomas headed for the back door.

'Stay where you are and answer me.' Tripp's voice rose in pitch and outrage.

Thomas ignored him.

'This is the last straw.' Tripp followed him into the passage. 'If you leave these premises now, Mr Payne, you will never enter them again.'

Thomas had already thought about that, but the content of the telegram and Archer's safety were more important.

He had his hand on the door handle, his mind was already made up and his career already over, so anything he said now would make no difference. He let himself out, slammed the door on a fuming butler and ran across the yard to prepare Shanks.

The animal seemed to know he was on urgent business and offered no resistance at being saddled. Tripp, however, would not let the matter drop and screamed from the steps, hollering threats until Thomas had mounted and was leaving the yard. The last he heard from him was something about putting his bags on the street, but his voice was soon lost in the thickening fog and beneath the clatter of hooves.

He rode hard and fast. Shanks enjoyed the exercise and responded well to being ridden with no complaint, even when Thomas took him to a canter. They fell into a rhythm, only slowing when the lighting was too dim, or the fog too dense, or when they encountered traffic which they did from the West End to the Auldlane Courts. Beyond there, the streets were less cluttered until he reached the edge of Greychurch where City Street led him into its heart.

Now it was a case of avoiding people, the inebriated staggering from a pub or brothel, whores working the night, street-rats in groups watching out for each other, and the bobbies in pairs, alert and suspicious. He blended in well, as long as he contained his fears and calmed the horse to an agonisingly gentle trot, walking when there was no other choice until he was able to turn south towards Limedock.

The fog thickened as the streets cleared until there was only him and the claggy mist, Shank's breath adding to the miasma. There was no sign of Archer. Somewhere, a clock struck, and he prayed he was not already too late.

Archer was crouched uncomfortably inside the shop. It was a chandler's hung with ropes, hooks and harpoons, and with so much clutter on show, it was easy for him to disguise himself. He had a clear view of Silas opposite, and the main street in both directions. He reckoned he had been there under an hour, but it felt like six. No-one had come past.

Crispin had chosen his location well. The other murders had taken place not yards from where people were about, and he must have worked fast to approach, strangle, cut a throat and disembowel without being detected.

He had found good cover in the maze of alleyways and hiding places further into Greychurch, but here, he could work undisturbed.

The image of the two dead boys in the morgue came back to him, and he shuddered. He felt sick when he imagined that it could have easily been Silas and Fecker, and the image helped focus his mind on his lover across the street.

Silas leant against the wall, his arms folded, apparently posed in a manner known to men seeking renters. Occasionally, to keep the blood flowing in his legs, he crossed the opening of Lessening Lane and rested on the opposite wall. At no time did he look at where Archer hid, but he did glance up and down the broader street, and that action comforted the viscount. It reminded him, as if he needed any reminder, that they were working together.

The minutes passed and so did the hours until one o'clock came, and there was still no sign of Crispin.

Just after the hour, a couple of men appeared at the far end of the road, talking quietly. Their voices carried through the still night, but their figures were merely diffused watercolour strokes of black. One was short and fat, the other taller, but neither was Archer's brother. They were on the wrong side of the road, and as they passed the shop, they were talking about barge deliveries and an early start in the morning. Dock workers, presumably, clocking off for a few hours' sleep. They faded into the fog.

Silas was still waiting.

Although the shop afforded Archer a good view of Silas, he was unable to see into the lane itself and unable to see the buildings either side of him. For all he knew, his brother was waiting in one of them, also watching, and had already seen them arrive. Maybe they had scared him off. Perhaps he had seen that Archer was onto him and had given up on his cause.

Archer doubted it, but it was a warming consideration. Except, if their presence had put the Ripper off his kill, there was nothing to stop him from going elsewhere. Greychurch would be full of street-rats, despite the vigilantes, and another, random, boy might be taken and gutted while Archer attempted to put his crazy plan into action.

He shook the thoughts from his head and blew on his fingers. Silas had moved back to the other side of the lane and was looking into it. Had he heard something? Archer tensed, ready to run, but Silas slouched against the wall and undid his jacket. He seemed bored.

This was apparently not a place where men came to find street boys.

Archer had got it wrong.

Approaching footsteps brought him back to the height of alertness, and he scanned the street. A shape appeared at one end, draped in a cloak and wearing a hat, it appeared crouched and skulking, a lantern barely effectual against the night.

Archer gripped his revolver and looked at Silas. He must have heard the approach too because he was away from the wall, his shoulders back, listening intently.

The figure crept closer on the far side, keeping against the buildings, slipping from one doorway to the other where he paused, presumably to check he was alone. When he did his, he unbent and stood tall, and although Archer was unable to see his face, his height was about right.

His heart quickened its pace, adrenaline building, ready to be released when he needed to run and fight. He stood silently and checked his path to the door. Four paces there, another ten across the road at speed, he would be on the attacker from behind in seconds. He took hold of his second revolver by the barrel ready to use it as a cudgel while his fingers prepared themselves at the handle of the other.

The cloaked figure stepped from the doorway and headed towards Lessening Lane.

As it passed beneath a lamp, something glinted in its hand, and Archer saw the knife.

He was at the door in seconds, stealthy and low and he slipped into the night as hidden and purposeful as the man now approaching where Silas stood.

Where Silas *had* stood.

Silas was gone.

# Twenty-Eight

Archer's heart was in his throat, and his skin was cold with panic. He stumbled from the shop and onto the street, his eyes flashing to the man in the cloak. He was running too and towards the same place, his knife drawn.

Archer was heading him off. 'Hold!' he yelled and aimed a revolver.

'Archer!'

The cry did not come from Silas. It came from the man in the cloak and Archer recognised it immediately. He reached the corner at the same time as Thomas.

'What are you doing here?' Archer was furious. He'd allowed himself to be distracted, and by his footman of all people. He pushed Thomas away and, running into the alley, saw the flaps of a black coat flipping into a doorway.

'Archer, wait!'

Thomas was on his heels, his lantern throwing strips of light onto the walls as they closed in. The cobbles glistened in the damp air, slippery underfoot.

'It's not your brother.' Thomas had caught up with him.

He heard the clank of a metal door before his words sank in, and they were at the entrance before the full impactions hit him.

'The message came,' Thomas said, wrestling with the door. 'Your brother hasn't left the institution in months. This is not him.'

There was no time to think. Thomas wrenched open the door, and they piled into a machine room where winches and chains were lit by vague streetlight through high windows. The same swish of black in the corner of his eye, this time mounting an iron stairway to the floor above.

A yell. Silas. Archer was across the room and on the steps with Thomas right behind him. He tightened the grip on his revolver.

'Hold!' He yelled. 'Stay where you are.'

The stairs opened into a storeroom as high as it was long. It housed rows of black shapes, the smell of straw, and dust clouded the air. Through it, he saw a lamp, dancing madly as Silas struggled. He was still alive. Why hadn't the Ripper struck? Why was he dragging him upwards?

Another iron stairway, another floor and Archer closed the gap. As long as the Ripper was running, Silas was safe. His attacker hauled him to the next storey, a hand clasped over Silas' face, dragging the youth backwards by his head. Silas squirmed and tried to force the hand away, but he was off balance, helpless.

'I said hold!' Archer let off a shot, and the explosion shook the warehouse before the echo scurried from danger.

He dropped to his knees for a steadier aim, but Thomas ran into his line of sight. It didn't matter. He had no clear shot. He was up and running, catching Thomas on the stairs where he took his arm, halted him and put himself in front. Aiming his revolver ahead and up, he slowed his pace. The footsteps overhead had stopped.

'Whoever you are,' he called. 'I am armed, and I know how to shoot.'

He reached the top to discover a void edged by catwalks, with one arm bridging from the stairs to the outer wall across the floor thirty feet below. The Ripper had taken that path, and the bridge led nowhere except through an arch and over the river to a gantry.

The Ripper was trapped, but so was Silas. His attacker stood behind him, the tip of a long knife pressed not into the metal collar as Archer had imagined, but with the blade upwards, under his chin. The killer was obscured by his victim who, seeing there was nothing he could do, calmed his struggles and handed his fate to the viscount.

'Stay behind me,' Archer whispered to Thomas. He refocused on Silas. 'You're safe,' he said. His voice was unwavering despite his breathlessness, and he was in command. 'Let the man go.' More commanding still and clearer, he said, 'Take away the knife and let him go.'

Silas was dragged back further, far out over the void.

'Hold!'

Archer was ignored, and the killer ducked around a hanging

hook and chain. Footsteps sounded on the metalwork, but Archer ignored them and stepped onto the catwalk, following cautiously. He had a mad idea that if he ran at him, the Ripper would panic and stumble, but then the knife might miss Silas' armour and slice upwards, severing above his Adam's apple. If he could get the Ripper to stand still and reveal himself, he would risk taking a shot. He had been a marksman in the navy, but nowhere near the best. He saw no other option until another quick flick of a coat over to his right caught his attention.

His eyes darted, saw what Thomas was doing, and were back on Silas in a flash. The killer had also been distracted and seemed to realise that he had nowhere else to go except onto the crane.

'You're trapped,' the viscount said. 'Set the man free and turn yourself in.' It was a pointless suggestion he knew, but he persisted, taking tentative steps forward. 'I have money and authority. I will see you are well treated.' He would do nothing of the kind, but anything was worth trying.

Again, he was ignored. The Ripper was restless now, swinging Silas towards the railing and bending him over as he looked below, one side and then the other. Archer fought nausea each time he thought Silas was going to be thrown over, but still, there was no clear shot.

'Silas,' Archer called. 'Silas look at me.'

Archer tipped his head towards Thomas. Silas raised a thumb, but the Ripper dragged him towards the arch.

'Hold, man!' Archer shouted. 'The police are outside.'

It did the trick. The Ripper stopped, uncertain what to do but he didn't have to think for long.

Thomas, on the side catwalk, gave an almighty yell and swung an iron hook from its housing. It arced down and up, the swing giving it enough momentum for the chain to crash into the ironwork and the hook to rise and strike the other side before it fell back. The impact, directly beneath the killer's legs, caught him off balance and he swayed, instinctively reaching out for the rail and leaving Silas free to throw himself forward. His lantern fell from his hand and tumbled over the edge.

Archer took his shot. The crack was deafening, but through it, he heard a scream of pain.

266

The lantern hit the floor below and burst into streams of burning oil which caught the straw as the Ripper turned and staggered through the arch.

Archer ran to Silas.

'Are you alright?'

'Where the fuck did he come from?'

'Tom! Take Silas and get out.' Archer was aware of the flames licking the floor below, but he ran on.

The catwalk led to an open platform which became an unguarded bridge to the crane cabin. Beyond, a fixed and narrowing iron beam reached far over the swirl of black that was the river below.

'There's nowhere to go,' Archer said. The killer was on the catwalk, arms out for balance. 'Turn yourself in.'

The man clutched his shoulder, his back to Archer. He was bent in pain, staggering.

'Come back, or I'll shoot.'

A laugh rang out. One syllable, one short burst of derision, and the killer turned to face him.

'I'm not afraid of death,' he snarled and lifted his head.

'Quill?'

For the first time since they had entered the warehouse, the Ripper had the advantage. He had shocked Archer into immobility and knew it. Before the viscount could say or do anything else, Quill was coming at him, his knife raised, his face distorted and hate dancing in his manic eyes.

Archer fired, but Quill had already knocked his arm. The two landed on the platform, and the gun skidded over the edge into the river. They had been trained in the same places, they had served on the same ship, they knew each other's tactics, but Archer no longer knew his friend.

Then again, Quill didn't know that Archer had another revolver, and he frantically tried to reach his pocket with one hand while keeping the knife from his throat with the other.

'They're all whores,' Quill spat in his ear. 'Those boys who tease and tell. Those rats who steal your heart and gift it elsewhere. They're never ours for long. Your Harrington. Crispin's Harrington. Never mine. Your helpful boy-whore. Everyone else's Irish boy, not mine.'

The man's weight kept Archer from reaching his gun, and the

pressure on his arm was too great to press back. He felt the cold of steel on his throat and fire on his back.

'You're insane,' Quill,' he gasped.

He jabbed with his knees, and the blow released Quill for enough time for Archer to reach his pocket, but the blade pressed harder on his flesh.

'You don't know insane until you've felt the insides of a street whore slip through your fingers. Seen their hell-blood drain from them…'

It was sickening, and Archer fought against the image as hard as he fought against the Ripper.

'I waited in the fire,' Quill rambled. 'Watched you take him. Heard you together. Kept your secret.'

The knife burned Archer's skin. He tried to turn his head, but every part of his neck was exposed.

'Didn't think, did you?' Quill's face was an inch away, and his opium-fuelled breath stank as Archer breathed it. 'Didn't think of me? Only thought of your deceiving, denying little whore of a Harrington.'

'Benji…'

He forced his hand into his pocket, but Quill pressed harder, trapping it there.

'What does it fucking matter?' Quill gripped Archer's coat, pushed the knife and drew blood. 'They bleed you. They lure you. They leave you.' His deranged face twisted into an agonised grin of triumph. 'Got you, at last, Clearwater. There's only one way out for the likes of us.'

Quill rolled towards the drop, dragging Archer with him. One moment there was hard iron beneath them, and the next there was nothing.

The last thing Archer saw were flames roaring from exploding windows and through the roar, he heard his name called from above as if by a welcoming angel.

Thomas knew the workings of a hay barn. The swing of the bail-chain caused enough of a distraction and, once he had recovered from the shock of the gunshot, he thought they had won. He was wrong. Archer and the Ripper disappeared through the arch, and

268

Silas lay prone on the catwalk. Thomas edged around the drop with his back to the wall until he came to the central bridge. He ran to Silas who was crawling to his hands and knees, groaning. Thomas was with him in a flash and helped him to his feet.

'You're cut,' he said touching Silas' chin.

'Forget it.' Silas pushed him away, his first priority was Archer.

'We have to get out,' Thomas said, pulling him back.

Silas struggled and rounded on him, angry. 'Get off me.'

Thomas held him tighter. 'We have to get out.' It was easy to manoeuvre Silas. He was light, but Thomas kept a firm hold of him as he thrust him towards the edge, showing him the fire spreading quickly below.

Silas wriggled free, but didn't run. He looked at Thomas, unclipping the metal brace from his neck and throwing it. 'What's more important to you, Tom?' he asked.

Thomas took no time with a decision. 'Come on.'

They ran onto the platform to be met by a wet breeze and cooler air. Below, a window blew out, and thick smoke pumped through. Thomas' eyes streamed, and he squinted to see the scene. Archer and the killer were rolling on the metalwork dangerously near the edge. Silas choked and dropped to his knees. Together, they crawled into the smoke.

Thomas had his hand on the killer's cloak when the men rolled, and suddenly he was holding empty air.

Silas screamed Archer's name as he tumbled into the curling smoke to be swallowed by flames and water.

Thomas' blood froze, and his legs refused to move, but he had to get Silas to safety. Coughing and with no clue where to go, he pulled Silas by the shoulders back towards the building. Below, the fire sucked in the night air and blasted it out through the arch. Thomas' skin began to burn. Their only way out was barred.

Silas had seen it and yanked Thomas' arm, pointing. He followed the younger man across the platform where the smoke was thinner, and his breathing came more easily. That was until he saw that the arm they had to traverse was no more than three feet wide and had no handholds. The crane cabin seemed a long way out, but there was nothing behind them except a fiery death.

'Button your coat,' Thomas ordered.

'Why?'

'Just do it.'

Silas did as he was told and when it was safely fastened, Thomas took a firm grip of his collar. If Silas slipped, he might be able to stop him falling. There was no time to think further. The sound of shattering glass and roaring flame was joined by the grinding of metal as it buckled.

'Go!'

Silas inched onto the beam. He tried to look down to where Archer had fallen, but Thomas directed him with his collar as if he was leading a badly-behaved puppy. He needed to keep Silas calm and in command of his senses. He spoke words of encouragement, not daring to look at his feet. They shuffled to the cabin and a second platform that offered no more safety.

'Now what?'

The building behind them was engulfed, and far off he heard alarm bells. The air was clearer, and they breathed fog, not smoke. Black smudges ran from their noses, and their eyes streamed.

'Into the cabin and out the other side.' Thomas had an idea.

The cramped space only allowed one of them to pass through at a time, but the brief seconds that Thomas spent scooting over the seat and negotiating the levers gave him a moment of respite from the stench and rage of the fire. Once through, they were faced with an even greater challenge.

The only way forward was further out across the river to where the beam narrowed to its chain pully.

'I hope you know what you're doing, Tommy', Silas shouted. 'I don't fancy diving.'

'Can you climb a rope?' Thomas had to shout through the wind as it was sucked towards the wharf.

With his back to the cabin, Thomas inched to the edge of the platform and lowered himself to the floor. He had hoped to find a ladder of some kind, or other manufactured access for the crane driver, but there was only a rope. It was knotted but hung directly down to the brick pillar that supported the crane. They'd be safer jumping into the water, but if the fall didn't break their backs, or knock them unconscious, they would drown in the eddies and currents. At least a fall onto bricks would be a quicker death.

'You're fucking joking, mate,' Silas bellowed. He crouched beside Thomas and looked over the edge, his face white.

'One knot at a time,' Thomas said. 'Hand under fist, wrap your feet, and don't look down.'

# Twenty-Nine

The rope swung in the strengthening wind, smoke clouded his vision, and his lungs burned from it, but Silas forced fear from his mind and concentrated on reaching safety. Hand under fist, he clung to the rope above each knot while his feet found purchase on one below. He repeated the movement, not looking down, moving as quickly as he dared. He thought of nothing but Archer and the rope. It was a long fall, but his lover had landed in water. There was hope.

His feet touched the ground, and he immediately ran to the edge of the piling to vomit into the river. Shock, tension, whatever it was, he brought up bile and black gunk, his head pounding as he coughed and retched, his body shaking and his eyes pouring tears of shock and despair. He howled, letting out whatever other emotions needed to leave him, an exorcism of hopelessness and anger.

He tried to process what had happened. How he had been watching Archer and the approaching figure one moment and the next, there was a hand over his mouth, and he was being dragged. The sound of the man's breathing, strange words, how he was going to be gutted. Archer's voice. Gun shots…

Above him, the warehouse was now engulfed in thriving flame, the fire could probably be seen for miles.

Men ran into nearby wharves to watch or climb into tugs, everyone running back and forth, shouting. The river reflected the spectacle in pools of shimmering yellow and orange that shattered when chunks of masonry fell. It was a wild dance of brick and plaster, flame and foam and somewhere beneath it was Archer.

Thomas was suddenly pulling Silas away from the edge.

'We must look for him,' he said. 'Can you stand?'

'Yeah.'

Silas mustered his strength and wiped his mouth with the back of his hand.

'We have to act fast.'

Thomas was on his feet. He climbed around the crane's footing, back towards the warehouse as close to where Archer had fallen as he could be without burning and yelled his name. Silas did the same, searching across the water to the next wharf in case he had managed to reach the other side. There was no-one in the oily black and gold which swirled fast around them, the current sweeping burning wood and debris downstream, dragging pieces under in fast-spinning whirlpools.

Thomas was at his side.

'Over here.'

He pulled Silas by the arm and swung him towards the shore, showing him their escape. A barge moored to the quay, its bow five feet from the piling. The leap was the only way off the brick island, and the barge was already on fire but, where its stern touched the quay, Silas saw a clear path.

He had no time to think. Thomas ran and jumped the gap, landing on the barge clear of the water. It was easy for him, he was taller and fitter, but Silas had no other option but to swim. He had never learned how.

He ran, throwing himself from the island and through the smoke. He reached out as he felt hot air engulf him, not caring where he landed as long as he could find Archer. His shins smacked against metal as he tumbled over the gunwale head first, crashing into a heap at Thomas' feet.

He was helped up, and with no time to think, half dragged towards the stern and the quay where shouts and whistles joined the cacophony.

'This way.'

Thomas' instructions were clear, and he left no room for debate. He led Silas away from the warehouse, and Silas couldn't understand why they were not scouring the banks for Archer. He was in there somewhere. He needed their help, but Thomas pulled and encouraged him onwards, away from the crowds and the smoke until they reached the next wharf.

Here, Thomas stopped, still within the glow of the fire, but away from its heat. He was bent at the knees, breathing hard. Silas' chest stung with the exertion, his arms were weak and his palms sore.

'Where is he?' he gasped and spat black spittle.

Thomas looked at him, his face reflecting Silas' fear. Lines of soot ran from his eyes, and his nostrils were black rings.

Thomas shook his head. 'I don't know.'

'Archer!' Silas screamed, but his voice was drowned by the melee.

Thomas shook him by the arms, forcing him to look into his bloodshot eyes. 'Silas,' he said. 'He knows what he is doing. He's a strong swimmer.'

He said a myriad of things that Silas didn't hear until the shock left him and reason returned.

'Downriver,' he said. 'The current?'

Thomas nodded and, still panting, approached the outer reach of the harbour arm. From there, they could see upstream as far as the fog would allow. It was as if it had backed off from the scene of the fire, or had been driven back by the heat as the men now were, uselessly trying to douse the towering flames with jackets and pails. Across the river, the southern bank was barely visible and downstream, there was nothing but high cranes and tethered barges swaying uneasily in the swirling blackness.

Silas stood beside Thomas as they scoured the surface, and when Thomas put an arm around his shoulder and drew him to his side, he was no less fearful of Archer's fate, but reassured that he was not alone.

'Look.' Thomas pointed to a crate, bobbing in the water and coming their way.

'Where?' Silas thought he had spotted the viscount, and his heart leapt, but Thomas was only watching the debris.

'See where it goes,' he said.

'We ain't got time to stand and wait.'

'Just watch.'

As the crate spun and bobbed, it occurred to Silas that, somehow, Thomas still wore his cloak and was sheltering him with it. He was grateful for the warmth against the breeze which, now they were away from the flames, chilled the sweat on his body.

'See where it goes.' Thomas explained his logic. 'It's floating with the tide.'

So were hundreds of other pieces of wood and cloth, some still smouldering, but they kept their attention fixed on the crate as it swirled past and on downstream.

Thomas was running again, this time holding Silas by the hand. They followed the quayside, staying close to the water's edge, cutting in and around the dock until they were free of it and the shoreline opened below them.

There in the mud, with his legs in the lapping water, lay Archer.

Silas was prepared to jump the six feet from the wall to the water's edge, but Thomas stopped him and pointed out a set of steps. Silas was on them in a heartbeat and a moment later, the riverbank, little more than sand leading to cloying mud. He sank to his ankles, strangely grateful that he was unable to smell the effluent and rot through his clogged nose. Thomas waded after him, and they arrived at the body together.

Silas was crying as Thomas turned the viscount onto his back, calling his name, tears drenching his blackened face. With a strength Silas didn't know he possessed, Thomas ripped the body from the squelching mud and cradled it in his arms, his ear bent to Archer's mouth.

Silas was hollow. Nothing existed within him anymore. He was just a shell. A pathetic, useless thing that had caused his lover's death. Archer was more than a lover. They had been forged from different moulds, in different classes, but they were two halves of the same whole; two chapters of the same story where one couldn't exist without the other. Silas fell to his knees, his hopes and dreams swallowed by the blood-chilling certainty that Archer was dead.

The river was suddenly very inviting.

'Silas.' Thomas' urgent voice cut through his misery. 'Silas!'

He didn't want to listen. He wanted to take Archer in his arms and carry him into the water so the two of them could sink beneath it and be together, but Thomas was insistent. Silas looked into the man's eyes and saw his own affection reflected there. Thomas' love for the viscount was as deep as his own.

'Silas.' Thomas hand gripped his shoulder and dug in. The pain brought him to his senses. 'Can you ride?'

# Thirty

A hard mattress and a firm hand. The feel of a pillow and the sweet, tarry smell of carbolic. Aching bones and a dull thud in his head. An unfamiliar material against his skin and the distant sound of shoes clicking on stone. Gunshots, screams, images like pieces of a broken mirror cascading into the bottomless pit of memory, thoughts shattered by the pain in his shoulder where powerful fingers dug into his flesh.

He opened his eyes to see a face staring back at him. Ashen and drawn with a black eye and a cut lip, it was framed by a parted curtain of blond hair revealing an expression of intent bewilderment.

'You look shit.'

A thick accent that made no sense until the man spoke again.

'Drink this. It is also shit.'

A glass was pressed to his mouth, and the liquid burned his throat when he was made to sip. A hand stronger than his helped him, giving no room for refusal. Brandy trickled its heat to his chest and made him cough. The cough became a retch which in turn became a stream of vomit that poured from him into a bowl held steady until there was nothing left to eject but pain.

He gasped for air and fell back against the pillow.

The bed sank as the man sat beside him. 'Tastes as shit as you look,' he said.

Archer wiped his eyes, and the face was clearer.

'Andrej?'

He tried to sit up, but Fecker held him down. 'You stay still.' He spoke gently but left no room for debate.

'Silas?' He was all Archer could think of.

'He is good,' Fecker said. 'Always in trouble without me.'

'Where is he?'

The Ukrainian shrugged. 'Riding horses,' he said.

Archer had no strength to inquire further. The deep well of sleep was calling, and he fell into it gratefully.

When he next awoke, it was to the sound of clattering plates and the murmuring of voices. Andrej was gone, and Archer thought he had dreamt him. He pulled himself to sit up, his body complaining against the movement, and tasted the acid tang of bile in his mouth. He was in a long room with a vaulted ceiling. Both sides of the room were lined with beds where men and women lay moaning or sleeping as women in white and black fussed over them. People clustered at the door, peering in and behind them, a man was wheeled past on a trolley, screaming, his face burnt beyond recognition.

The last thing Archer remembered was falling with Benji Quill beneath him, laughing, his knife maniacally slashing the smoke. He had a vivid picture of Quill's body hitting the water first and then there was nothing until the half-remembered face of Andrej and the man's firm grip.

A woman appeared at his side. Diminutive and clad in black, she wore a white apron, and her head was wrapped in a wimple. Her non-committal expression was at his eye level, and she had the faintest tuft of a moustache on her top lip.

'Name?' she demanded.

'What?'

'What's your name?'

'Where am I?'

'Name?' She prodded him with a pencil.

'What time is it?'

'Name?'

'Oh, for God's sake. Lord Clearwater.'

She looked at him in surprise before laughing and walking away.

'Oi!' The man in the next bed called to no-one in particular. 'Got one here says 'e's Lord fucking Clearwater.'

'Put 'im the bedlam and shut the fuck up,' someone complained.

A scream halted the exchange as, further along, the ward, a man in a black tailcoat ripped the bandages off a woman's face revealing torn flesh.

'Maybe he is Clearwater, maybe he ain't, but his suffering's as good as anyone's.' A familiar voice and a reassuring, powerful figure pushed through the bustle at the door. 'Move aside. Let me through.'

Complaints of 'La-di-da,' 'Who's he think he is?' and worse added to the mix of unfamiliar sounds as Thomas forced his way to the bedside. His copper hair was neatly combed, and he wore his Sunday suit, looking every inch a country gentleman.

'Thomas?'

'Good afternoon,' Thomas said. He leant in to whisper, 'Sir.'

'Where am I?'

'Saint Mary's. We haven't told anyone who you are. We thought it safest not to while you were unconscious.'

'We? Silas?'

'He's upstairs with his Russian friend.'

'Is he harmed?'

'No, My...' Thomas looked nervously around the ward.

'It's fine, Tom,' Archer said, his spirits buoyed by his footman's presence. 'This is definitely one of those times. What happened?'

'Silas is well,' Thomas said. 'I'll find him for you shortly.'

He appeared to be looking for somewhere to sit, and Archer patted the bed, an offer Thomas accepted.

'He was more shocked than physically harmed, but he's recovering. You, on the other hand...'

'I'm alright.' Thoughts of Silas and the knowledge that he was safe were the only medicine Archer needed. 'Are you?'

'Apparently so.' Thomas smiled. 'But don't ask me how.'

Archer had a barrage of questions, but as he started on them, Thomas insisted that he rest. He explained that the physician would be visiting before long, he had paid for his special attention and, all being well, he would release the viscount into the care of his staff. The talk of doctors brought back the image of Quill and with it, another onslaught of nausea.

'Archer, go slowly.' Thomas' voice was reassuring and tinted with the slightest hint of his country accent. 'Let's have you out of here and home. You have been here long enough.'

'How long?'

'Two days.'

Archer was shocked. There was nothing between the fall and seeing Andrej's face, and nothing between then and now except

278

the scrambled fragments of memory which he fought to arrange in order.

'Tripp will be demented,' Archer said.

'I have told the household that you were called away on unexpected business and left it at that.'

'What did Tripp say?'

Thomas took a breath and, it seemed, persuaded a smile to soften his worried face. 'Don't concern yourself with Mr Tripp,' he said.

'And Quill? Has he been caught?'

'In time, Archie,' Thomas insisted. 'Please, for your sake, calm yourself and appear well and in your right mind. The man who runs this hell hole won't let you leave otherwise.'

'He will when he knows who I am.'

'Leave the talking to me,' Thomas advised. 'This may be an uncomfortable experience for you, but bear in mind that many people are here because they have no choice, and most of them have nowhere to return to when they are thrown out, yet these are the lucky ones.'

Thomas' words were levelling, and Archer was suitably admonished. 'I'm sorry,' he said. 'And I am so grateful.' He took Thomas' hand. 'To you. I will think of a way to repay you when we get home.'

'There is no need for that.'

'You look worried, Tom. Is everything alright?'

Thomas sighed. 'Many things need explaining,' he said. 'But first, we need to convince that doctor that you can leave.' A young man with a bushy moustache was approaching the bed, flustered and ill at ease. 'Allow me,' Thomas said. 'I have the measure of this man.'

He stood and waited by his master's side as the doctor arrived.

'This is the one who thinks he's a lord, isn't it?' the doctor asked. He spoke as if he'd heard a hundred similar claims that day.

'He is The Viscount Clearwater,' Thomas replied.

'And you are?'

'He's my friend,' Archer said before Thomas had the chance to speak. 'Who are you?'

'Markland.' He took Archer's wrist and held it, sitting side-saddle on the bed and examining his face. 'Nothing wrong with you,' he declared. 'Nothing that rest and a good bath won't cure. I can't say for certain that you won't have caught something from the river, but you're not showing a fever. Any pains?'

'All over. I've had worse.'

'Slight scratch under the chin… I see you've had similar before. Any burns?' the doctor enquired, more interested in his fob watch than his patient.

'You tell me.'

'Good. You can leave. There are more important cases, and I don't appreciate men passing themselves off as nobility just to get my attention.'

He stood, and Thomas squared up to him.

'You are addressing a Lord of the House,' he threatened. 'I suggest you show more respect.'

'Thomas…'

'Maybe you are unaware of your own patron?' Thomas' indignation was not to be quelled. 'Or perhaps you, like me, are honoured to know The Lady Clearwater?' He spoke pointedly, but not rudely. 'I should hope you are, for without His Lordship's family…'

'Yes, alright Tom.' Archer patted his arm. 'Doctor.' He addressed the man politely and even offered a smile. 'I don't expect you to recognise me, and I am rather glad you don't, but if you say I may leave, I won't be in your way any longer. Thank you for your attention. I will see you receive recompense both personally and for your hospital.'

Markland shuffled his feet nervously. He eyed Thomas with suspicion, but Thomas turned his attention to Archer.

'He has been paid. I have the trap outside My Lord,' he said. 'We should have you home before dusk.'

'Do I have clothes?'

'I brought you some of mine. I thought it best to maintain the disguise for your own safety.' Thomas glanced at the doctor who was still hovering and listening. 'I wondered if you wanted me to call on Lady Marshall, Sir. She was asking after you.'

Now convinced, Markland stepped back to the bed. 'My Lord,' he said. 'You would be better cared for in my rooms. I can have you moved there.' He attracted the attention of the diminutive nurse.

'That won't be necessary, Markland.' Archer extracted himself from the rough blanket that covered him. 'The Lady Clearwater, as you will know, patronises St Mary's on the understanding that it treats the patient no matter their position. If your public beds are good enough for these poor wretches, then they are good enough for her son. However, in light of your...' he took in the crowded ward once more, 'popularity, and given the fact I appear to be in one piece, my own bed would benefit us both.'

'I meant no disrespect, Sir,' the doctor replied. 'But you can imagine what we have to contend with.'

The man was doing his best, Archer decided, and he did have many cases on his hands. He wouldn't like to be doing his job.

'I imagine you have to put up with disease, injuries and death,' he said, sitting on the edge of the bed. 'And who suffers from them makes no difference. I hope. Wasn't that your oath?'

'Your Lordship is correct, of course.' Markland, put in his place, turned to Thomas. 'I suggest His Lordship...'

'Please!' Archer hissed. 'Don't cause any more fuss. In a place such as this, call me Mr Riddington. I am a patient like any other.'

'But not for much longer,' Thomas said, helping Archer to his feet before addressing Markland. 'I assume you have somewhere private for Mr Riddington to dress? Or are all your patients subjected to the humiliation of nudity as well as distrust?'

'Thomas,' Archer admonished with a grin. 'You're sounding like Tripp again.'

'My office,' the doctor replied. 'If you would follow me?'

Archer's legs were weak, which he put down to lack of food, and every muscle in his body ached, but nothing pained him more than the thought that his friend, Benji Quill had been the Ripper and that he had drawn Silas and Thomas into danger. He shuffled on Thomas' arm, dressed in an itchy cotton shift and exposed to the glare and derision of those around him as they followed Markland from the ward.

'Are you usually this busy?' he asked as they entered a corridor lined with more unfortunates wailing and bleeding.

'More or less,' Markland said, adding, 'Sir,' as an afterthought. 'The fire at Limedock has brought a swell in numbers, and we are hard-pressed to attend everyone.'

'You need more staff?'

'We need more of everything. Medicines, linen, sanitation… Many who come to us have nowhere to return to and bring nothing with them. We provide what we can, but…'

'I will speak with Lady Clearwater at the earliest opportunity,' Archer said. 'But believe me, doctor, you already provide what very few in this stinking city can. You provide hope.'

The words affected the doctor, Archer could see it in his face. He was thankful for the comment, and the viscount assumed he didn't hear it often enough.

'You must come for dinner,' Archer said. 'When I am recovered and if you have time. I would be interested to know more. I am myself involved in a charity. One to assist a certain section of the society in the East End and your medical knowledge would be invaluable.'

'I am flattered, Sir,' Markland replied. He stopped at a glass panelled door and opened it. 'And I should be very honoured, not to mention interested. Here are my rooms. Please, make them yours.'

Archer entered on Thomas' arm and thanked him. It was a small, cramped office with one high window and a stone floor. More of a monk's cell than a doctor's surgery.

'May I ask who your charity supports?' the doctor inquired.

'What you'd probably call street-rats,' Archer replied, falling into a chair. 'Renters. You know, young men who have no recourse to funds other than offering their bodies. Does that shock you, Doctor?'

'Not at all, Sir.' Apparently, it didn't, because Markland said, 'It's about time someone did something.' He changed his tone immediately. 'Shall I bring you anything?'

'No, thank you.' Archer liked the man, and his offer of dinner had been genuine. He understood his initial scepticism, he had seen his working conditions and now, he thought, saw that he possessed more dedication to his calling than time to answer it. 'You have more important needs to attend to, please, I have all the care I need in Thomas.'

'Then I will leave you,' Markland said. 'Take your time.' He raised his dark eyebrows to Thomas and, in lifting them, revealed eyes the colour of chestnuts. 'Mr…?'

'Payne, appropriately enough,' Thomas quipped.

Markland gave a brief laugh. 'Indeed. Mr Payne, see that His Lordship drinks plenty of water, It helps to stay hydrated. If he shows any signs of illness, call a physician. I am sure you know how filthy the river is. Watch out for looseness of the bowls, vomiting, fever...'

'Cholera,' Archer said.

'Quite.'

Thomas promised that Archer would be well taken care of, they thanked Markland again, and he left.

'I like him,' Archer said as soon as the door was closed. 'But, Tom, I've got so many questions. Is Silas really safe? Are you...?'

'In time, Archer,' Thomas replied. He handed him a battered suitcase. 'Sorry, this is all I have, but change and I will find Silas.'

'See if you can bring Andrej too,' Archer said, catching his arm as Thomas left. 'I won't see him on the street.'

Thomas nodded and left the room.

# Thirty-One

Even dressed in Thomas' clothes, Archer felt better off than those around him as he waited for Silas. The sights he had seen reinforced his belief that he was right to do something for the East End. His mother had the hospital as her pet project, and Archer would advance his work with the street boys, though they were no pets. The entrance hall echoed with voices, foreign accents and languages, men shouting, women complaining, babies screaming, it was a hell on earth, but it was a hell that at least offered something. The city was a mess, with the privileged on one side of a gaping chasm, their backs to the destitute on the other. There was not much in the middle apart from hard-working people who had no choice but to struggle.

He had been fortunate, and when he saw three young men approaching him along the dimly lit green corridor lined with the sick and dying, he understood how far his fortune extended beyond wealth and privilege. A tall Russian with a flapping greatcoat strode purposefully, daring anyone to cross his path. Beside him, Thomas, his hair the colour of sunrise and his face as serious as a storm, and Silas, hands in pockets, head down, eyes up, his grin broadening with every step. Archer would find a way to repay their loyalty and friendship.

Silas ran to him and, not caring who saw, embraced him hard and long, muttering through sniffles. 'You're a bloody eejit, you know that? A fecking eejit.'

Archer nuzzled into his ear and kissed his neck. 'I am so sorry I got you involved in this.'

It had never felt so good to hold someone. He had never been so relieved or wanted, and he was determined to show Silas how much he meant, how much he was needed.

He took Fecker's large hand in his and pumped it. 'Good to see you, Andrej,' he said. 'I hope they treated you well.'

Fecker laughed. 'Da, they like me,' he said, but his meaning was clear. 'They didn't kill me.'

'And Tom.' Archer put his hand to Thomas' face. His freckled nose wrinkled, and he blushed with mild embarrassment. There was no need to say more.

'The trap is in the yard,' Thomas said. 'If you don't mind waiting, I'll bring it around.'

Silas stood beside Archer, with Fecker on his other side as if they were his bodyguards, and they waited for Thomas on the steps as dusk began to gather overhead. Boys wheeled barrows, singing as they went while respectable looking men in suits discussed the day's business as they passed. Across the road, a group of children sat in a line, hands out, heads down, women carried baskets of laundry from one door to another, and a lamplighter attended his duties. There was no sign of the nightly fog, but it would come. The days had warmed, and the cold snap of the previous week had passed. Autumn would become winter before long. Hopefully, it would bring no more senseless murders, but, with no news of Quill, only time would tell.

It was on the ride home, with Fecker driving and Thomas next to him that, in the back, Archer finally asked Silas to explain what had happened.

'We found you by the river,' he said, leaning in, the two of them holding hands beneath a rug. 'Tommy wanted me to go and fetch his horse, but I don't know how to handle one of those things, so I stayed with you while he ran for the trap. I thought you were dead, and I can't tell you how that felt, but you were breathing. You came round for a while... I reckon you'd hit your head when you fell...'

'I did. On Quill.' Archer had a lump on his forehead. 'I was lucky he broke water first.'

'Yeah, well, you came round, and I was able to get you up from the shore and onto the road, but you collapsed again...'

'You must have been terrified. He cut your chin.' Archer tried to touch the stitches, but Silas pulled away.

'Wasn't my neck, though. He wasn't after me.'

'I used you.' Archer mumbled, wretched at the thought.

'Yeah, well, you get used to that in my line of work.'

'Silas!'

'I'm making a joke of it, Archie, 'cos it's the only way I know how to stop myself going out of my head.'

'He was sane one day and mad the next…'

'Yeah, alright. Who's telling this?'

'Sorry.'

Silas nudged him gently in the ribs. 'I hope I have a scar like yours,' he said.

'What an eccentric ambition.'

'Whole bloody thing's mad, ask me. Anyhow… Thomas took his time 'cos the trap was a way off, and there was all kinds of hell going on. I've never burned down a storehouse before.'

'I think we'll keep that to ourselves.'

'Right. We got you to the hospital, such as it is, and no offence to your mam, and after that, I don't remember much. When I woke up, I was in bed with you… No, don't look like that. You were under the covers, and I was on top. Thomas said that I refused to leave and caused a scene, but, well, that's me ain't it? I don't remember that bit either, it was nearly dawn though. Next thing was last night, and I woke up in the same room as Fecks. They must have knocked me out to get me there.'

Thomas, who was listening, turned. 'Markland said they had to pull him off you. He was embarrassing the nurses.'

Archer imagined the scene and found it more than comforting. He squeezed Silas' hand.

'Alright, Tommy,' Silas complained. 'I was in no state…'

'Go on,' Archer said, and Thomas faced the road.

'That was it, really,' Silas said. 'I woke up this morning and was just like you see me now, except dirtier. I slipped into the yard and helped myself to their tap to wash my face. Tommy brought us some clothes and paid the doctor…'

'Thomas did?'

'Yeah. Had to. Otherwise, we'd get no attention.'

'That's not how it should work.' He tapped Thomas on the back. 'They shouldn't have charged you, Tom. I'll repay you. Was it reported?'

'That's a bit steep, they were only doing their job, and doctors have to be paid.'

'No, about Quill.'

'Not that I've seen,' Thomas said, speaking over his shoulder. 'The newspapers were full of the fire. There was nothing about the Ripper for a change.'

'How come it was your mate?' Silas asked. 'Or was it?'

'It was,' Archer confirmed. 'Took me right off my feet. Benji? It didn't add up at first, but if I think about it, it makes sense.'

'Sense?' Silas said. 'What sense?'

Although his head was thumping, Archer was able to put some of the broken images together to form a picture.

'Quill and I went through Dartmouth together,' he said. 'He was a midshipman with Harrington under the command of my brother. He said something in his madness up there on the gantry about him never being the one to have the... What was it?' The more he thought, the more nausea troubled him, and the harder it was to remember. 'Something about him... I had the impression that he was jealous. It's a blur.'

'You mean, you got the man he wanted.' Silas was more alert than the viscount. 'A jealous rage?' He said, incredulously. 'Is that a reason to gut six boys? Sick fucker.'

'Da?'

'Fucker, not Fecker, you fecker.' Silas shoved him in the back. He was his usual self, apparently unaffected by what he had been through. 'Begging Your Lordship's pardon,' he added with more than a hint of cheek.

Archer put his arm around his shoulder and drew him closer. They had left Greychurch and were following the river beneath the embankment lights.

'Why he did it is complete lunacy,' Archer said. 'But those clues, the street names? They meant the same to me as they would have to my brother and, of course, the third man, Quill, also enraptured by the boy. Harrington, Simon, Lucky... I should have seen it earlier. And then the "lessening" of time between each one...? Quill has far more rationality about him than my brother. I had lunch with the man.' The thought increased his queasiness. 'Almost told him my suspicions. I even let him treat you in my bedroom.'

'Oi.' Silas gripped Archer's knee hard, but his voice was soft. 'Shush, Archie. Don't think about it now. It's happened. You've

287

solved it, you did what you could. I doubt we'll be hearing more from him. People will be arguing for years over who he is. Was.'

'There's been no news at all?'

'No. But there ain't been no more deaths either.'

'Yet.'

'Stop it, Archie. You're upsetting yourself.'

'But, I need to rationalise.'

'No, you don't.' Silas was firm. 'Not now. You need to rest.'

'I need to take care of you.'

'With all due respect,' Silas said. 'Thirteen years in the navy ain't nothing compared to four years on the streets. I can look after both of us.'

'You don't understand.' Archer twisted on the seat, facing Silas as best as his aching back would allow. 'I need to take care of you, Silas. Otherwise, what else have I got in my life?'

It was a touching but sad statement. 'Is that your way of saying you love me?'

'One of them, I suppose.'

Silas rested his head on the viscount's arm, and they rode the rest of the way in silence. Archer longed to hear the words Silas seemed unable to say, but after all else he had asked of the man, he was prepared to wait.

They arrived at Clearwater House to find themselves in a procession of carriages, their lanterns barely needed in the spill of the lights blazing from Lady Marshall's house.

'Her Ladyship is throwing a party,' Archer observed. 'At least that will distract attention from our arrival.'

He climbed from the trap aware that he was dressed in a manner not at all suitable to enter his own house, but after everything he had experienced in the past few days, he didn't give a damn. Nor was he concerned that he might be seen entering with Silas. He was conscious, however, that should Lady Marshall see the costume her own pet project Silas now wore, she would want to know why his 'secretary' was not suitably attired. That would lead to more questions and, in a way, he was looking forward to relating the events to her, but that, along with many other things, was for a much later day. Right at that moment, he needed a bath to cleanse his body and time alone with Silas to wash away the pain.

'Tom?' he said. 'Would you stable Emma and show Mr Kolisnychencko to the coach house?'

'Just how do you remember his name?' Silas gawped.

Archer took no notice. It was a skill he had learned at prep school where most of his other manners had been whipped into him. 'And tell Mrs Flintwich we will dine at eight. Informally, but in the dining room. And...' he glanced sideways at Silas, ' Fecker will join us if he would like.'

'Of course, My Lord.' The master and servant roles were back in place.

'I would like you to join us, Tom, but... You understand.'

'I do.'

'Spasibo,' Fecker grunted, and the trap moved off.

Archer and Silas entered the hall to find Tripp bearing down on them from the turn of the stairs. He reminded Archer of an eagle on a church lectern. It was his expression and his nose rather than any regal bearing and, on seeing him, a cold shock of realisation ran through his veins. He was, once again, Lord Clearwater.

'We have been concerned, My Lord,' Tripp announced, descending. 'Good evening, Mr Hawkins.' The eagle screwed up its beak.

'Evening Tripp.' Archer headed directly for the staircase, and Silas followed. 'Most unexpected delay. Dinner at eight. We shall be three.'

'Perhaps I should lay out some suitable attire...'

'No, thank you, Tripp. I can manage. The house looks fine, by the way, well done.'

It never hurt to compliment the butler, even if the house looked exactly as it always did and that was thanks to the maids.

'There is a matter which requires Your Lordship's most urgent attention,' Tripp said, automatically following the viscount.

'There always is, Tripp,' Archer replied. 'But we are not to be disturbed.'

'But, if I may...'

'You mayn't.' Archer stopped on the turn, ensuring he was at least two steps higher than his servant, so he could look down on him for a change. 'Not yet, at least. Apologies, Tripp, but we have had a trying time, as you might see. Nothing for you to worry about.

Dinner at eight. Mr Hawkins' Ukrainian friend will be joining us. He is staying in the coach house. I will dress myself. Oh, and give Thomas the night off.'

'Sir, it is on that matter...'

'Later, Mr Tripp. Later.'

Archer only used the Mr to indicate when he was not interested, and the butler understood. He said no more as Archer and Silas headed towards their rooms. There, Archer waited for the sound of the servants' door to close before whispering to Silas.

'This is totally inappropriate,' he said. 'But I just want to get you in my bed and do everything we did the other night.'

'And as many times?'

'If I have the strength.'

He opened his door behind his back.

'I really need to wash properly,' Silas said, opening his arms and showing Archer the full extent of his second-hand, pauper clothes.

Archer did the same. 'Me and you both. I have an idea.'

With that, he pulled Silas into his room and slammed the door.

The bath was deep and long. Made of enamelled iron and standing on its own four feet, it had shells for soap rests and a large brass contraption that, when lifted, allowed the water to escape. The taps were connected to copper pipes which ran to the wall and disappeared into the ceiling above. The water was hot, and tingled Silas' skin as he sank as low as he dared. He was safe, though. Archer sat behind him with his arms around his waist, and Silas rested on the viscount's chest.

'Never done this before,' he said. 'It's a bigger bath than the one in my room.' He held Archer's legs and massaged his calf muscles. 'But then, everything about you is bigger.'

'Will you be happy living here?' Archer asked.

He splashed water onto Silas' chest and ran his palms across his skin.

'Are you touched?' Silas laughed. 'Of course I bloody will.'

'You won't feel like a kept man? A servant? Even though I will have to speak to you as one from time to time?'

'No. I get how it is, Archie. How it must be. And no. I won't feel kept. Even if I do, time to time, it won't take much to remind myself what I got and tell myself not to be so ungrateful. I mean, look! Taps have hot water and are inside. When I was growing up, we had nothing.' He laughed and put Archer's hands over his cock. 'Luckily, I was a boy, so I had something to play with.'

'You are incorrigible,' Archer snickered. 'But, seriously, if you change your mind. If something happens between us to turn you against me...'

'That ain't never going to happen.'

'But if it does, you will tell me? It's all I ask. Honesty.'

'Yeah, I will.'

Archer's hand held Silas' stiff cock. 'I love you for more than this,' he said. 'You do understand?'

Silas knew what Archer wanted to hear and he felt the same way, but the time was still not right to admit it aloud. He had fallen for the viscount the moment he saw him. He understood that and how he had no control over the passion he ignited. He had meant it when he said he would do anything for Archer, in the same way as he would do anything for Fecks, and now, probably Thomas. It wasn't because he didn't want to say, 'I love you,' it was because if he said it aloud, he would become someone else. He would belong to another man. He would have what he always wanted. So what was wrong?

He didn't understand his reticence until Archer left his cock alone.

'You're not a street-rat any longer,' he said. 'You are the respectable Silas Hawkins, secretary to The Viscount Clearwater and lover of Archer Riddington. Does that suit you?'

That was the problem, wasn't it? Everything he had desired and hoped for, those impossible dreams he had lived while hanging his body from a rope in Molly's dosshouse, or leading a trick to a back alley for a sixpence, they had come true. But what came next?

'It will,' he answered, and heeding Archer's insistence on honesty, explained himself. 'I just ain't sure if I can be what you want me to be. I'm used to different things, another way of life. I don't even have the training your maids have got. I called the Lady next door a whore's Madam and a schoolhouse Miss. I groped your footman and led him on. It's how I am, and you're going to think that's what I'm here for. I'm going to be taking money off you for being around your house doing… I don't even know what a secretary does. I only know what a renter does. I can't ride a horse, I can only ride a cock.'

He was gathering momentum as if the pain and trauma of the last couple of days was suddenly finding its release. 'I can't drive a carriage,' he babbled, and his eyes began to water. 'I don't know how to dress in anything other than what I find in the street, and I don't know how to behave in front of your fancy friends. Not even your staff. I speak my mind before I think, I've hardly been to school.' He was crying, and he let it happen. 'I'm going to let you down, or get you in trouble, say the wrong thing. They'll find out what I am, and it'll come down on your head…'

'Shush, it's alright.'

Archer's arms were strong, protecting him, and he knew they always would, but the bath water was turning cold, and they were surrounded by the scum of his life. His former life, if he could only accept that someone as kind and gentle, as passionate and intelligent as Archer could love him for what he was.

'But it ain't,' he sobbed. 'I ain't worthy of a man like you.'

Water splashed and he slipped on the enamel as Archer turned him until Silas was lying on him, their chests pressed together and their faces inches apart. Archer held his head, lifting it and looking at him with mahogany eyes as sweet as melted chocolate.

'I don't care about any of those things,' he whispered. 'I don't…' He stopped and thought for a moment. 'No,' he corrected himself. 'I do. I do care about where you come from, what you've done, what I am asking of you and everything you have said. I care about every part of you, everything you have endured and everything you say. How could I not? You know so much more of the world and our parts in it than I ever will. What I don't care about is what the world thinks about me. I'm strong enough to not let it matter, and so are you. But what I care about most is that you are happy, and if you being with me is not bringing you happiness, then I care enough about you to let you go.'

Silas was unable to stop the tears. He rested his head on Archer's chest, his own heaving, and forced his arms around the man's broad back. He wasn't crying because he felt trapped or used and could see no way out of it; Archer had given him that escape. He was crying because the happiness was overwhelming.

Archer kissed the top of his head and held it to his chest. Silas felt his heart beat a calm, steady rhythm as the viscount waited for the tears to subside, and when they had, he lifted Silas' head again and kissed him.

'I shan't ask you to say it,' the viscount said. 'I don't expect you to, and I cannot demand it as I can demand most other things in my life. I have no right to your love and if mine is not reciprocated, then I understand, but please, may I ask one thing?'

Silas nodded silently.

'That I will always have your friendship?'

Swallowing more tears, Silas struggled to his knees. Steadying himself on the edge of the bath, he got to his feet with water cascading over his body. He stood before Archer naked, a man too thin, a street boy too experienced in sex, but an innocent in love.

He stepped from the bath under Archer's concerned gaze, but didn't explain himself as he offered his hand. Archer took it, rose and, dripping, allowed himself to be led to the bedroom.

There, they made love. It was more than sex and, unlike the time before, Silas let Archer make the decisions and lead the way. He had nothing to offer but himself, and Archer was welcome to all of it.

When they finished, gasping and sweat-soaked, Silas on his back, and Archer kneeling between his legs, the viscount ran a finger over Silas' stomach, collecting a drop of the man's cum. He put it on his tongue, closed his lips around his finger and licked it clean. Silas, red-faced and panting, collecting the same from the tip of Archer's cock and copied his action.

'You see?' Archer whispered, breathless. 'It doesn't matter who we are, we taste the same.'

A gong rang out a floor below.

'What the…?'

'Dinner is served, Mr Hawkins,' Archer grinned.

'Don't know if I can,' Silas leered. 'I'm full up.'

'You better get used to it.' Archer pulled him to sit in his lap in one deft movement that wiped the cheeky smirk from Silas' face. 'That was just hors-d'oeuvres.'

# Thirty-Two

Archer and Silas met outside their rooms a few minutes later, Silas impeccably dressed courtesy of Lady Marshall's shopping spree.

The black tailcoat and red waistcoat he wore beneath were tailored to leave some room for growth. Her Ladyship intended Silas to fatten into it, a veiled signal that she hoped he would be a long-term visitor. He wore a ruffled cravat beneath a wing collar, and the only blemish were the stitches on his chin, a stark reminder of how he had come to be there.

Archer noticed that they were as neat as the tailor's and he wondered if Markland had seen to them. Now was not the time to ask. They could discuss recent events in the morning; tonight was about forgetting and looking forward.

He adjusted his dinner suit. 'You look resplendent, Mr Hawkins.'

'Ain't so bad yourself, My Lord.' Silas winked one of his cocky, knowing winks that suggested erotic things to come. Archer loved to see them.

They turned and, side by side trod the thick carpet to the staircase.

'Do you have any business on the morrow to which I should be aware of, Sir?' Silas asked in a faux upper-cut accent. It wasn't one of his most successful caricatures.

'Just be yourself, mate,' Archer replied in what he thought was a working-class accent.

'Maybe we should both just be ourselves,' Silas replied, unimpressed.

They descended the stairs beneath the watchful scowls of dead lords and ladies.

Archer ignored them. They were figures of the past, what mattered now was the future.

'How are you feeling?' he asked as they took the turn.

'Physically? Surprisingly alright. Mentally? Pushing stuff to the back of my mind. Regarding you? Same as the moment I first saw you. You?'

'The same, with a few older-man aches,' Archer said.

'Older man my arse.'

'Ten years?'

'Nine, and I don't give a tinker's cuss, mate.'

They stopped at the bottom step. 'Perhaps, when I said, be yourself...'

'I know, Archie.' Silas laughed. 'Don't worry about me. You've invited Fecks to eat with us and you ain't seen what a mess that can be.'

Fecker was waiting for them in the dining room dressed in what he had always worn, minus his impressive greatcoat. He sat rigidly at the table as if too scared to even look at anything in case he broke it.

'Mr Kolisny...'

'Fecker,' Fecker decreed leaping to his feet and knocking over his chair. 'Oh, fuck. Sorry.'

'Don't worry.' Archer helped him right it before shaking his hand. 'Please, sit.'

The table had been laid with the viscount's place at one end, but where Archer would have preferred his guests closer, Tripp had set a place at the far end and seated Fecker alone in the middle.

'Gentlemen,' he said, searching the room. 'It appears my footman is not yet in attendance. May I impose upon you the onerous task of moving your place settings to my end? I need to talk with Mr Fecker, and I'd rather not shout. I would also like to see Mr Hawkins, and that hideous centrepiece of my father's rather blocks the view.'

'Say that again?'

'Shift chairs, shift arse,' Fecker translated.

'Something like that.'

Actually, Archer thought, as this was a time of positive change at Clearwater House, he would dispense with the centrepiece once and for all. It was a military arrangement in silver and the ugliest thing in the house as far as he was concerned. He took it to a sideboard as the others moved their place settings.

They had just taken up seats, with his guests either side where he wanted them when Tripp processed into the room carrying a tourinne. He regarded the new seating plan with distress.

'My apologies for the tardiness, My Lord,' he said, placing it grandly before the viscount, sweating.

'That's alright Tripp. We're not exactly on time ourselves. Where's Thomas?'

It was most irregular to see Tripp doing such a thing and stranger still that he was assisted by Lucy.

The maid was distracted by Fecker and, it seemed, he by her. They exchanged what Archer could only describe as adolescent looks of admiration as she placed a dish of toasted bread on the table.

'It would be best if we spoke of that anon, Sir.' Tripp stood back.

'Is he unwell? He was perfectly fine before.' Archer was uneasy without understanding why.

'I don't believe so.'

'Then where is he?'

'It would be best to discuss this at another time....'

'Tripp!' Archer banged the table. 'I decide my subject of conversation and when and I am disinclined to wait. 'Where is my footman, man?'

Lucy curtsied and hurried from the room.

'Very well, Sir.' Tripp straightened his back. 'I dismissed him two nights ago.'

Silas had seen flashes of anger in Archer, but they were nothing compared to what happened next.

'Let him go?' Archer was dumbfounded. 'Explain.'

'His behaviour of late has not been becoming for a man in your employ, My Lord. I wished you no further embarrassment.'

'Further embarrassment?' Archer's face was white, as were his knuckles on the back of his chair as he twisted to face the butler. 'Explain that while you're about it.'

Tripp turned his head towards Silas, and his eyes towards Fecker, as if that was his explanation.

'Ah,' Archer seethed. 'I understand. You clearly disapprove of my guests.'

'It is not my place to disapprove.'

296

'Indeed it is not. I will remind you that it is not your place to dismiss staff without consulting Mrs Baker, and her, me.' Archer rose and faced Tripp head on.

'You were otherwise engaged, Sir. I thought...'

'You know what, Tripp?' Archer said. 'You do too much of that. Where is Thomas?'

'I have no idea. He stabled the horse, which, I will add, he took without permission and left.'

'On your orders?'

'Yes, Sir.'

'And went... Where?'

'He didn't say.'

'And you didn't ask?'

'Certainly not.'

Silas caught a twitch of concern in Tripp's eye and settled back to enjoy the spectacle. Fecks was ready to throw himself into a fight, but Silas signalled him to stay quiet.

'How long have you worked for my family, Tripp?' Archer asked, pacing the table behind Fecker.

'Since I was a hall boy under your grandfather.'

'And you were appointed footman by him?'

'I was. A great man, Sir.'

That could have been taken as a mild insult and Silas watched Archer intently for a reaction. His usually pouting lips were drawn thin, the only thing containing his anger.

'And under-butler too,' Tripp continued. 'Your father appointed me his butler in...'

'I know your history, Tripp,' Archer spat, his lips no longer able to do their job. 'It's as predictable as a penny dreadful, but not as much fun.'

Silas stifled a laugh.

'In fact, your career with my family has been long and your service impeccable.'

'Thank you, My Lord. I will leave you to your soup.'

'Yes, you will, Tripp.' Archer stood with his back to the sideboard. 'You will leave us to the soup, collect your coat and go and find Thomas.'

'My Lord?'

'I suggest you start at the Crown and Anchor. If he's not there, ask Lady Marshall's men, he is friendly with some of them. He must be staying somewhere.' He screamed a yell of frustration and even Fecker flinched. 'For God's sake! He paid for the hospital, he brought us home. And you fired him? Go, Tripp. Get out of my sight.'

'I have the dinner to…'

'You have your orders, man. And here are a few more.' Archer lowered his voice from a shout to a threat, his eyes narrowing. 'On your return *with* Thomas, you will sit down with Mrs Baker. Together, you will calculate your wages owing and, because of your long service, your wages for the next three months. While I arrange payment, you will pack your belongings and, in the morning, you will leave my employ.'

Tripp was too stunned to reply.

'I will give you a reference if you want another job, of course.' Archer was suddenly a reasonable man again. 'I know you have savings and you're getting on a bit. Now might be the time to retire.'

Silas had to laugh at the butler's expression, but covered it by shoving bread into his mouth. Tripp saw and looked as if he might pass out.

'I don't mean to be rude, Tripp.' Archer said. 'But you leave me no choice, but to be blunt. I, as you well know, am not my father. There are to be changes in the house, and I fear they will not sit well with you. Apart from that, I am sick to the back teeth of your attitude towards me, and sicker at the way you turn up your nose at my friends. If it lessens the blow…' He took Fecks by the shoulders. 'You will be outraged to know that, should he want it. Mr Kolisnychenko will, from tonight, run my stable and care for the horses. He will live in the coach house, and I will invite him to dine with us more often.'

Tripp gasped.

'Furthermore…' He released Fecks who shrugged, but grinned widely at Silas. 'Mr Hawkins will be living with me as my assistant.'

'I feel I must protest…' Tripp fumbled. 'Your reputation…'

'Is not your concern. I am the master of my house, not my father and certainly not you. But, in recognition of your loyalty, you can take this monstrosity as a gift.' He lifted the weighty, silver centrepiece and thrust it into Tripp's arms. To Silas, it looked like the recreation of an East End punch-up, but with spears and flags. 'It'll be enough to set you up in your own home or business if you wish it.'

Tripp was a loss for words, but his awe suggested he had always coveted the thing.

'You and my father were fond if it, and you've polished it enough over the past fifty years,' Archer mumbled as he resumed his seat. 'I am sorry it has come to this,' he said, his tone not exactly regretful, but a close approximation.

'But this is how it is. See me in the morning for your reference. You may send for your things later if you wish, they will be looked after. Before all of that, however, do two things. One, find my friend Thomas and bring him here, and two, don't utter another word, except to ask Mrs Baker and the maids to wait for me in the servants' hall. I shall announce your retirement, or that your ailing sister needs you, or something similarly honourable, and then I shall tell them that Thomas will buttle for me from now on. That will be all, Tripp.'

Tripp's chest filled and the sides of his waistcoat stretched at the seams. With the lump of silver in his arms, he made a fair attempt at a dignified bow before leaving the room.

Conversation left with him until Silas broke the silence.

'Bloody hell, Archie. Are you sure?'

'Of course I bloody am.' His anger was not yet spent, but Silas was not offended.

Archer took a deep breath himself and shook his head like a dog ridding its coat of mud.

'Sorry,' he said, taking Silas' hand. 'I've been looking for an excuse ever since my father died.' He also took hold of Fecker's hand, but the Ukrainian pulled away. 'Would you like to work here?' Archer asked. 'I meant it.'

'Just with horses, or you also want sex?'

'Er, just the horses,' Silas interrupted. 'You won't need to do sex anymore Feck's. Ain't that right, Archie?'

'Well, you can do what you want in your own time, Andrej,' Archer said.

'You mean job?'

'I do. And the coach house to live in. There are hall boy duties too, but not onerous. You may have to assist Lady Marshall's men from time to time, but I can see you are experienced with dumb animals.'

Fecker thought about it, ladling soup into his bowl, occasionally glancing at Archer thoughtfully. Once his bowl was full to overflowing, he dropped the ladle back in the tourinne and examined his meal.

He was still looking at it as he reached out, took Archer's hand and nearly crushed it. He let it go and began slurping.

'That was a thank you,' Silas whispered.

'Good,' Archer said. 'Now let us hope that bloody man can find Thomas.'

He continued to mumble, and Fecker continued to slurp as Silas settled into his first course.

Beneath the glittering chandelier, among the silver and fine china, the upholstered chairs and oil paintings, he suffered a pang of regret. It wasn't because he would miss his life on the streets, far from it. It was because for every one of him — lucky, charmed, loved — there were so many others out there scrambling for life who would never know such kindness.

'Oh, Archie?' he said. 'There's something I've been meaning to tell you.'

Archer regarded him with tired eyes. 'Yes?'

'I love you.'

Charles Tripp, fuming, humiliated and frustrated, left Clearwater House to carry out the last order for the man he had always considered the Dishonourable Archer Riddington. He was not worthy of the title Lord Clearwater. He was a man above his station. A youth with grand designs on change who failed to understand the way his world worked. What was worse, the man was a sodomite and, in society's eyes as in Tripp's, a criminal.

Fired by a criminal after fifty years with the household. Sacked by one sodomite and replaced by another.

What would the late viscount have done?

The answer came to him as he entered the humid fug of the Crown and Anchor where Thomas sat in a corner, deep in conversation with a messenger boy.

Revenge was not something Trip thought he would ever contemplate, but he found the idea of it suited him and, as he ordered an ale, he turned his mind to a variety of ways it might be exacted.

**Continued in part two**
**Twisted Tracks**

If you have enjoyed this story, here is a list of my other novels to date. With them, I've put my own heat rating according to how sexually graphic they are. They are all romances apart from the short stories.

References to sex (*) A little sex (**) A couple of times (***) Quite a bit, actually (****) Cold shower required (*****)

*Short erotic stories*
**In School & Out** *****
13 erotic short stories, winner of the European Gay Porn Awards (best erotic fiction). Boarding schools and sex on a Greek island.

*Older/younger MM romances*
**The Mentor of Wildhill Farm** ****
Older writer mentors four young gay guys in more than just verbs and adjectives. Isolated setting. Teens coming out. Sex parties. And a twist.

**The Mentor of Barrenmoor Ridge** ***
It takes a brave man to climb a mountain, but it takes a braver lad to show him the way. Mountain rescue. Coming to terms with love, loss and sexuality.

**The Mentor of Lonemarsh House** ***
I love you enough to let you run, but too much to see you fall
Folk music. Hidden secrets. Family acceptance.

**The Mentor of Lostwood Hall** ***
A man with a future he can't accept and a lad with a past he can't escape. A castle. A road accident. Youth and desire.

*MM romance thrillers*
**Other People's Dreams** ***
Screenwriter seeks four gay youths to crew his yacht in the Greek islands. Certain strings attached.
Dreams come true. Coming of age. Youth friendships and love.

**The Blake Inheritance** \*\*
Let us go then you and I to the place where the wild thyme grows
Family mystery. School crush. A treasure hunt romance.

**The Stoker Connection** \*\*\*
What if you could prove the greatest Gothic novel of all time was
a true story? Literary conspiracy. Teen boy romance. First love.
Mystery and adventure.

**Curious Moonlight** \*
He's back. He's angry and I am fleeing for my life.
A haunted house. A mystery to solve. A slow-burn romance.
Straight to gay.

*The Clearwater Mysteries*
**Deviant Desire** \*\*\*
A mashup of mystery, romance and adventure, Deviant Desire
is set in an imaginary London of 1888. The first in an on-going
series, it takes the theme of loyalty and friendship in a world
where homosexuality is a crime. Secrets must be kept, lovers must
be protected, and for Archer and Silas, it marks the start of their
biggest adventure - love.
(Book one in the series)

**Twisted Tracks** \*\* (May, 2019)
An intercepted telegram, a coded invitation and the threat of
exposure. Viscount Clearwater must put his life on the line to
protect his reputation. His life is complicated by the arrival of
new servants, a butler and a footman both experiencing the
confusions of first love.
Twisted Tracks follows on directly from Deviant Desire.

All these can all be found on my Amazon Author page.
Please leave a review if you can. Thanks again for reading. If you
keep reading, I'll keep writing.

Jackson

30347071R00180

Printed in Great
Britain
by Amazon